DARK AWAKENING

HIDDEN CURRENTS

THE CHILDREN OF THE GODS
BOOK EIGHTY-SEVEN

I. T. LUCAS

Copyright © 2024 by I. T. Lucas.

Published by Evening Star Press, LLC.

EveningStarPress.com

ISBN: 978-1-962067-50-8

JASMINE

The morning sun streamed through the floor-to-ceiling windows of the penthouse, bathing the dining room in a golden light and warming the side of Jasmine's face.

"It's a little stifling in here." Margo waved her hand in front of her face. "Are those windows tinted?"

Gabi turned to look at the glass. "I'm sure they are. It would be hotter in here if they weren't. You can turn the AC on."

Margo huffed. "Who turned it off?"

"I did," Frankie admitted. "It was blasting cold air this morning. I was freezing."

As the conversation around the table turned to the fascinating subject of immortals' supposed imperviousness to temperature swings and then shifted to a discussion about the importance of having a great view versus energy conservation, Jasmine sipped on her coffee while observing Ell-rom's interaction with her friends. Not that he was saying much.

He seemed distant this morning, contemplative, and he was avoiding her eyes. He also hadn't reached for her hand under the table like he usually did.

Had she overwhelmed him last night?

Had it been too much too soon for him?

Ell-rom had appeared to enjoy what they had been doing, and things had seemed to go well, but then Jasmine had freaked out, probably for no good reason, and had ruined what had been a wonderful experience that could have turned into a cherished memory.

It had been Ell-rom's first time, and Jasmine wanted him to remember it fondly, to have a positive memory that he could smile about centuries from now. She didn't want him to wince whenever he thought about it, the way she did every time she thought about her own first experience.

Instead, she had made him feel like his bite wasn't welcome, or worse, that she hadn't enjoyed what they had been doing.

Neither could be further from the truth.

Being his first had been exciting, even moving, and she considered introducing him to carnal pleasures a privilege. As for the venom bite, Jasmine knew what to expect and was looking forward to experiencing it with Ell-rom.

Just imagining it sent a tingle to her lady parts.

When he cast her a perplexed glance, she realized that he must have smelled her arousal.

Jasmine didn't mind him knowing what she was thinking, but she didn't want the other males in the room to know.

That keen sense of smell was the one thing she did not like about gods and immortals. Other than that, they were awesome.

Well, at least the ones she'd met so far.

Not all immortals were good people who strived to make life better for everyone on Earth. There was another faction of immortals whose goals were in direct opposition to the clan's.

She didn't know much about the conflict or who those other immortals were, only that the clan had enemies, one of the reasons the clan had to live in hiding.

Well, that and humans, of course.

After Jasmine smiled and shook her head at Ell-rom, he turned back to Aru, who was telling him about the wonders of the underground cities of Anumati.

The gods' planet was a fascinating subject, but Jasmine only listened to Aru with half an ear while replaying last night in her head.

Had her response been warranted?

Blacking out after a bite was a given, and it was dangerous when it happened inside a bathtub or a pool. Ell-rom was still weak, and once the lust haze had receded, there was a chance that he would have fainted. He would have survived a bath drowning because he was immortal and would enter stasis, but she wouldn't.

The fear of drowning had been overpowering, but now that she thought of it in the light of day, did it still make sense for her to freak out like that?

Was it even a valid concern?

Yeah, it was.

Her sense of self-preservation had kicked in, and after what had happened with Alberto, Jasmine had vowed never to ignore or belittle what that sense was telling her.

She could still fix things with Ell-rom, but if she were dead, there would be no fixing that.

Across the table, Margo pouted. "It's a shame that I will never get to see Anumati. It sounds wondrous."

Aru smiled. "Never say never. You are immortal now, and the future has not been written yet."

Margo let out a breath. "Tell me about it. When I was a girl, I thought everything would get better, and that progress, prosperity, and respect for human rights would continue spreading to every part of the globe, eradicating barbarism and savagery forever. Instead, we are seeing the opposite happening. I'm not as hopeful as

I was in my youth, and I'm praying to the universe to deliver a miracle."

Frankie snorted. "With what we know about the ruler of the known universe, you probably shouldn't pray for that. The Eternal King is not our savior."

Next to Jasmine, Ell-rom tensed. "Is there something bad happening on Earth that I should be aware of?"

It was curious that he was more worried about what humans were doing to each other than about the threat of the Eternal King. The truth was that Jasmine felt the same, but that was because one threat was imminent while the other was far into the future, and she was still human, thinking in human terms.

Ell-rom was immortal, though, and his perspective on time should have differed greatly from hers.

Gabi waved a dismissive hand. "Let's talk about more pleasant subjects."

Ell-rom shook his head. "If we are in danger, I need to know."

Gabi cast him a reassuring smile. "You don't need to worry about what humans are doing to each other. As an immortal living in the immortals' village, you will be well protected against the barbarians and savages of this world. If you can access your paranormal talents, you can protect yourself against them when you venture outside the village as well."

"I wish all of us could move in there." Margo sighed.

"The more I watch the news, the more I want to retreat from this world."

Frankie grimaced. "If we are ever permitted to live in the village, I will have to convince Kian to let my large family move in with us. I can't leave them behind."

Dagor's expression soured. "I wish that, too, but you know why that's not possible. We must continue pretending that we are doing our job on Earth so no one will be sent to replace us. To keep making out like we are searching for the missing pods, we need the trackers to keep broadcasting our location."

Jasmine had heard part of that argument before, and it had struck her as a challenge but not as an unsolvable problem. "Can't you put those trackers inside someone else? For the right amount of money, you will find no shortage of volunteers who will not ask too many questions."

Aru regarded her with a sad smile. "Regrettably, human volunteers wouldn't last long enough."

"Then you will have to move the trackers every so often." The wheels in Jasmine's mind kept spinning. "You could hire three guys and pay them to go to the destinations you are supposed to investigate and report to you. Just hire healthy, young people and move the trackers to a new trio every few years."

2

ELL-ROM

Ell-rom couldn't find fault with Jasmine's reasoning, and given Aru's contemplative expression, neither could he.

The god turned to one of his companions. "What do you think, Dagor?"

"It might work if the transfer is done quickly." Dagor rubbed a hand over his jaw. "Provided that our trackers only transmit locations, not biomarkers. We were not given details about what was implanted in our bodies. The old trackers the Kra-ell had in them were good only for pinpointing coordinates, but ours might be much more advanced."

It made sense that the technology had improved in the time between the deployment of the settler ship and the departure of the interstellar cruiser that had brought the three gods to Earth.

"We can test it," Negal said. "I volunteer to be the first one. We can remove it from me and put it in a human. If the commander contacts us and asks what's happening, we will know that the thing transmits biomarkers."

"How will we explain it?" Dagor asked.

Negal shrugged. "We can tell him that I got seriously injured, and the human doctor attending me removed the tracker, thinking it was a foreign object."

Aru arched a brow. "And the doctor immediately put the tracker in himself for some reason? That's not going to fly."

"What if you put the tracker into Dagor?" Jasmine suggested. "It'll still transmit godly biomarkers, just slightly different, and that can be blamed on the supposed injury."

Dagor shook his head. "That's not a good test for two reasons. If the tracker is not sensitive enough to pick up the differences between us and the commander doesn't inquire about it, we won't know if it just can't differentiate between two gods or between a god and a human. We have to put it in a human and develop a plausible story for the commander in case he asks us what happened."

"I volunteer," Jasmine said. "You can put the tracker in me."

To say that Ell-rom wasn't happy about her offer was putting it mildly.

Jasmine couldn't be their test subject because she was about to transition. It wasn't happening yet because of his accursed aversion to blood and his inability to bite her, but hopefully, he would find a way to get over that and start her induction.

Who knew what that foreign object could do to her transitioning body?

Besides, what if the thing was poisonous to her while she was still a human?

After all, the gods were impervious to diseases, so they didn't need to worry about foreign objects in their bodies.

And that triggered another question. How come their bodies hadn't rejected the trackers?

They should have expelled them.

Aru shook his head. "Thank you for your generous offer, Jasmine, but I'd rather not put the tracker in you. I like your idea about hiring volunteers, and I'd prefer to put it inside a human we can send to Tibet to continue the search. The biggest obstacle to your brilliant plan is coming up with a plausible explanation for our commander in case the trackers transmit biomarkers like Dagor suspects."

Jasmine chuckled. "Just feign ignorance. We can put it in me for a short while and then put it back in Negal. If your commander asks, you can say that you have no idea what happened because you were anesthetized throughout the procedure."

Aru rubbed the back of his head. "That could work, but I don't know if a short time is enough for the test. We can still feign ignorance and say that Negal underwent a procedure, but we don't know what happened to the tracker. We had no idea the medic had even touched it." He turned to Negal. "What do you think?"

The god snorted. "I'm not the mastermind here. If the commander confronts you about it, we will have to come up with one hell of a story about the supposed medic and her motives for implanting herself with the tracker she found."

"I have a question," Ell-rom said. "How is it possible that your self-healing bodies do not recognize the trackers as foreign objects and expel them?"

Aru shrugged. "They are most likely designed to fool our bodies into accepting them by mimicking our genetics. I'm pretty sure they used our genetic material to coat the trackers, or maybe the whole thing is a biological device. It's not like we've taken one of them out and examined it, and ours are obviously very different from what was inside the Kra-ell."

"Then how would a human's body accept this thing?" Ell-rom reached for Jasmine's hand under the table and squeezed it. "How can you be sure they won't harm Jasmine or the volunteers?"

She rolled her eyes. "What harm can a thing the size of a grain of rice do to me? There is only so much tech they can cram into it, and I'm sure there is no space left for explosives or poisons or whatever else you are imagining. Besides, it's morally wrong to expect a random human to volunteer for it without telling him or her about the danger and while suspecting that it could harm them. Since I'm the only human here, and I know what it is all about, I should be the one to test it. The medics are already in the keep and have surgical facilities in the clinic."

"Dear Fates!" Dagor suddenly exclaimed. "We could be in big trouble. I bet that when William checked Ell-rom and Morelle, he didn't consider the possibility that the trackers could be biological and match our genetics." He looked at Ell-rom. "You still might have it inside of you, which means the Eternal King could be aware of your survival."

3

KIAN

F ew things were more pleasing to Kian than a leisurely Saturday breakfast with his family. The aroma of freshly brewed coffee and warm pastries filled the air, and his beautiful girls were busy decorating Okidu's Belgian waffles with whipped cream, strawberries, banana slices, raisins, and chocolate syrup.

Allegra's small forehead was scrunched in concentration as she tried to make a face with the fruit pieces and syrup, and given that she wasn't even one year old yet, her efforts were admirable.

In the kitchen, Okidu was working on lunch for later today. The whole family was invited, including Toven and Mia. Kian planned to use the opportunity to update them about the ongoing investigation into the thefts and sabotages and Ell-rom's progress. However, he was pretty sure they were all well informed on that front.

Ell-rom and little Evander Tellesious were all his mother could talk about lately.

Annani was happy, which made him happy in turn.

It had been a long time since his mother had looked so upbeat and hopeful for the future.

Kian wasn't sure what had put her in a melancholic mood before, but he suspected that it was seeing all the new couples around her that had reawakened her grief for Khiann. When she'd realized that there was a slight chance that the witnesses who had reported her mate's demise might have lied to the council, it had given her renewed hope that he was still alive.

Syssi had promised to induce a vision on her behalf, and now that the twins had been found, it was time she made good on that promise, but Kian didn't want to remind her of it. No matter how often she reassured him that her visions didn't pose any danger to her, he had an instinctive aversion to her submitting to the universe's mercy when she opened herself for a vision.

The universe was not benevolent, and it didn't care that Syssi was one of the purest souls ever to grace the plane of the living. It wouldn't hesitate to use her for its purposes, even if it killed her.

"Are you concerned about lunch today?" Syssi asked.

"No, why?"

"You're frowning."

Allegra lifted her head and looked at him with her far too wise eyes as if repeating her mother's question, but then stuffed a piece of banana in her mouth and went back to decorating her waffle.

Their daughter must have been satisfied with what she had seen, but Syssi was still regarding him with a worried expression, suspecting that his frown had nothing to do with the lunch they were hosting.

"I'm concerned with the family's response to my update about the insurrection," he said.

"Insurrection? That's a strong word for petty thefts and sabotages."

"They are petty because the perpetrators are compelled to do no harm. If they could, they would have done worse."

Syssi shook her head. "Please don't blow this thing out of proportion."

"I'm not." Kian lifted a waffle off his plate and took a bite.

"If you want, I can summon a vision to see who is behind it and why they are doing it."

Right. As if he wanted her to risk herself for something so inconsequential.

Kian chuckled. "You've just proven that I was hyper-bolizing."

Syssi tilted her head. "How did I do that?"

"I realized that it wasn't important enough to me for you to risk a vision, which means that I don't really consider it an insurrection."

She let out a breath and reached for another waffle. "Good. You had me worried for a minute there. Back to the lunch issue today, I told Okidu to set it up buffet style. With the family growing so large, it's becoming impractical to serve things to the table."

"That's not a bad idea." Kian nodded, taking a sip of his coffee. "I've noticed how ridiculous it has become with passing the platters and people reaching over each other. A buffet solves that problem, but you need to instruct Okidu to fill a plate for my mother. I do not doubt that she would consider it beneath her to serve herself."

"Good point. I will do that."

"Nana," Allegra said resolutely.

"Yes, sweetie. Nana is coming over today."

The smile that spread over their daughter's face could illuminate a pit of doom.

"E.T.?" Allegra asked.

Syssi laughed. "Yes, your cousin Evander Tellesious, otherwise known as E.T., is also coming for lunch."

As Allegra kept asking about other family members, using the names she had invented for them, a sense of contentment washed over Kian.

These peaceful moments were precious.

When his phone buzzed in his pocket, he wasn't surprised. There was no way the universe would let him enjoy his morning without throwing a wrench or two in the works.

Checking the caller ID, Kian frowned. "It's Aru. I'll take it on the patio."

It couldn't be good if Aru was calling him on the weekend, and he didn't want to get stressed with Allegra watching him. She was like a barometer for emotions, immediately catching on and mirroring.

"Don't smoke!" Syssi called after him. "Allegra wants to play with you after breakfast."

He nodded. "I won't."

Opening the sliding doors, he stepped onto the terrace and accepted the call. "Hello, Aru."

"I apologize for calling on a Saturday, but something came up during breakfast that I thought I should share with you without delay. It's about William's detector possibly missing biologically based trackers in Ell-rom and Morelle."

Kian tensed. "Is that possible? Do you know of trackers that are biologically based?"

"No, but I'm not privy to the technology of the devices inside of me and my teammates. Ell-rom made a valid point when he asked why our bodies didn't reject the trackers. And when I said that they might be designed to match our DNA, it occurred to Dagor that Ell-rom and his sister might have been implanted with trackers featuring a similar technology. Their bodies would have rejected the type of devices the Kra-ell had."

If Aru was right, it could mean that the Eternal King knew of Ell-rom's survival, which was a monumental disaster. But how likely was it that the twins had been implanted with specially designed biologically based trackers seven thousand years ago?

Not very likely.

Kian felt the tension leave his shoulders. "I don't think we have anything to worry about. When the twins were smuggled onto the settler ship, they pretended to be Kra-ell. If they had any trackers in or on them, they would have to be the old style, the same as the Kra-ell. Their bodies would have rejected them immediately, and they would have been stuck somewhere on their clothing. William's wand would have detected them."

There was a pause on the other end of the line, and then Aru released a breath. "Yeah. That makes a lot of sense. We didn't think it through."

"No worries. But to be safe, I'll ask Bridget to put Ell-rom through a scanner."

"Thank you. There was another thing I wanted to talk to you about, but it's not urgent, so we can discuss it on Monday. Enjoy your Saturday."

Kian was curious, but with Allegra waiting for him to play with her, he could contain his curiosity for now.

Ending the call, he slipped the phone back into his pocket and went back inside, where Syssi and Allegra were already on the floor in the family room with an array of toys spread out before them.

"Is everything alright?" Syssi asked.

Kian joined her and Allegra on the floor. "Aru and the penthouse gang came up with a hypothesis that Ell-rom and Morelle might have biologically designed trackers inside of them that William's device had missed. I explained why that's highly unlikely and promised to ask Bridget to scan Ell-rom to make sure."

Syssi studied his face for a moment. "Dismissing a concern out-of-hand is unlike you. You always think of the worst possible scenario."

He snorted. "In this case, the worst possible scenario is so bad that I'd rather not entertain it."

4

ELL-ROM

"You should have seen the monasteries in Tibet," Margo said after Aru left to talk to Kian on the terrace. "The architecture was beautiful, but the sense of tranquility made the experience unique."

Ell-rom tried to recall details of the temple he and Morelle had lived in. He'd seen a few glimpses of it in his dreams, but he hadn't sensed tranquility. If anything, there had been a constant state of stress, of alert in the face of danger. But then those might have been the moments that had been etched onto his memory.

Perhaps the rest of the time, the temple had been peaceful.

Jasmine leaned forward to look at Margo. "It's funny how it feels like the trip was a lifetime ago. And the life I lived before going with freaking Alberto to Cabo seems like it belonged to someone else."

At the mention of the lowlife who had planned to harm Jasmine, Ell-rom's venom glands swelled, and his fangs started to elongate, which just served to irritate him.

These natural weapons he had been gifted with were useless because he couldn't stand the taste of blood, and the thought of biting anyone made him nauseous.

The depressing thought had his fangs receding and his glands deflating in no time, and he had a feeling that if he were erect, that would have deflated as well.

What kind of a male was he if he couldn't provide his mate with the pleasure of a venom bite or even use his Mother-given natural weapons to protect her?

Perhaps he should reconsider the priesthood. It seemed like he was much better suited for that than anything else.

Then another thought surfaced, more disturbing than the previous one. If he was indeed capable of killing with just a thought, it was possible that the unique ability had arisen in him to compensate for his inability to bite.

Whatever had made it manifest, though, he needed to control his emotions better or he might harm someone unintentionally.

"That's because a lot has happened during and after." Gabi patted Jasmine's shoulder. "You discovered immortals, learned that you might be one yourself, saved Ell-rom and his sister, and fell in love. No wonder you feel like years have passed. I felt the same way when

I met Aru. Within days, the life I had lived before seemed like ancient history."

Margo snorted. "Same here, but for me, it was the trip to Tibet that made everything else seem like it was ages ago."

"It wasn't falling in love with me?" Negal sounded genuinely upset.

"Of course it was, my love." She leaned to kiss his cheek. "Our bond deepened during the trip."

He didn't look convinced. "We barely saw each other. I spent more time with Aru, Dagor, and Jasmine than I did with you."

"That's true." Jasmine cast Margo an apologetic look. "And on top of that, Negal was the one who carried me after I'd twisted my ankle."

A growl started low in Ell-rom's throat, but he forced it down, stopping it from leaving his mouth. He had no right to feel jealous, but he would have appreciated it if Jasmine had told him that Negal had carried her on his back.

She cast him a wondering look. "Is everything alright?"

"Yes. It's just that hearing about you getting injured upsets me." It wasn't a lie, but it was a very small portion of the truth.

"Oh, Ell-rom." She leaned over and kissed his cheek like Gabi had Aru's. "That's so sweet of you."

"My favorite story from the trip is the army base," Dagor said. "That poor soldier is probably in some mental health clinic now."

Aru chuckled. "I feel bad about it, but I just couldn't help myself."

Ell-rom waited for someone to elaborate on the story, but when everyone just nodded and chuckled or snorted, he turned to Jasmine. "Do you know what they are talking about?"

She nodded. "We had to pass through a military base on the way to the mountain where your pod was. The gods took turns shrouding us so we were invisible to the soldiers and could pass unnoticed, but then one of the soldiers bumped into Aru, so Aru pretended to be an angry spirit. He told the poor guy that it was forbidden to bring weapons to a holy site and that it was bad luck."

Ell-rom frowned. "How is that done? The shrouding, I mean?"

Negal set his mug down and leaned forward. "Shrouding is manipulating perceptions. We can create illusions, mask our presence, or make ourselves look like someone or something else."

"I figured as much, but how is it done, and can I do it?"

Negal started nodding when the patio sliding door opened, and Aru walked in. "What did I miss?"

"Ell-rom was asking about shrouding," Negal said. "What did Kian say about the trackers?"

Aru took his place next to Gabi and reached for the coffee carafe. "He said we shouldn't worry about it, and I agree. Ell-rom and Morelle were smuggled into the settlers' ship pretending to be Kra-ell. If they were implanted with trackers, it would have been the same ones as the Kra-ell's, and their bodies would have rejected them. What's more likely is that they arrived at the last moment and did not get trackers at all." He turned to Ell-rom. "Just to be safe, Bridget will put you through a scanner. It wasn't possible when you arrived because you were so frail that they were afraid to move you. You were scanned with a handheld device, but now that you are better, you can be scanned by the big machine."

That sounded ominous. "What does it entail?"

Jasmine squeezed his hand under the table. "Nothing dangerous or overly unpleasant. You lie on a narrow platform, close your eyes, and try not to move a muscle until the machine finishes scanning your body. It doesn't take long."

That was a relief, but then he remembered the other thing that had bothered him about Aru's explanation. "How did my sister and I pretend to be Kra-ell? We don't look like them."

"You must have shrouded yourselves to look like the Kra-ell."

"I don't know how to do that. Is that innate or some-thing that can be learned and forgotten?"

"I'm not sure," Aru said. "Perhaps the technician in charge of your pod was cooperating with your mother and shrouding you both, but that's less likely. Although I still wonder how your mother pulled it off. She must have had more than one god helping her to smuggle you into the pod."

Regrettably, that knowledge had died with his mother, so it would remain a mystery.

"Can all gods shroud?" Jasmine asked.

Aru nodded. "Like any other talent, some are better at it than others, and from what I understand, the same is true for immortals." He looked at Ell-rom. "You were raised as a Kra-ell, and their abilities are a little different than ours and not as strong. I don't know how much you were taught."

"Can you teach me?" Ell-rom asked.

Aru rubbed a hand over his jaw. "Think of it as projecting your thoughts outward. You focus on the image or sensation you want others to perceive and then push it out. It's not just visual, though. Other senses can be affected as well, but it's not easy to maintain a shroud for long, especially when shrouding several senses. The immortals have a guy who is a master at this, and none of us come even close to his ability. Maybe he should be the one to instruct you."

It made no sense for a master to teach a novice.

Perhaps Aru was busy and did not want to teach him. The next time Ell-rom saw Annani, he could ask her about the gifted immortal, but he wouldn't even suggest wasting the immortal's time on teaching him to shroud.

Ell-rom smiled. "If I get very good at it, I might request a lesson or two with the master shrouder, but for now, some basic instruction will do. I understand if you have no time for me, though. Maybe Julian can show me while supervising my physical therapy."

"I have time," Aru said. "Not much, but I can teach you the basics, and then you can practice independently." The god seemed more resigned than enthusiastic about teaching him, but Ell-rom would take it.

"Thank you." Ell-rom dipped his head. "Does shrouding work on everyone? I mean, gods, immortals, Kra-ell, and humans?"

"It depends. Generally, gods can shroud themselves from immortals and humans, but immortals can only shroud themselves from humans. Within those parameters, there are varying degrees of ability. Also, some individuals are more susceptible than others. Those with strong mental abilities can often see through or resist a shroud. The Kra-ell are nearly impossible to thrall and are not susceptible to shrouding. Some humans are immune as well."

Jasmine wasn't one of those immunes; that was clear from what she had told him about her miraculous healing and her suspicion that one of the gods had thralled her and then bitten her to speed up her recovery.

Ell-rom was still angry with them for doing this without her consent, but it had been done to save her pain and discomfort, so he was willing to forgive them, but only this one time.

If any of them dared to deceive her in the future, for whatever reason, they would have to deal with him.

5

JASMINE

J asmine had gotten pretty good at discerning Ell-rom's emotions from subtle changes in expressions and body language. He had slightly different frowns for when he was worried, intrigued, or upset, and the one he was sporting now was clearly the latter.

What had caused it?

There could be several things, starting with her telling him about riding on Negal's back after twisting her ankle, to what she had told him before about her suspicion that one of the gods had bitten her to hasten her recovery.

Either way, it was time to change the subject, or rather take it in a different direction. "I've just remembered a concern that Ell-rom and I brought to Kian's attention. I don't know if he spoke with you about it or not, but do you think that your commander will ask for DNA samples to prove that Ell-rom and Morelle were indeed hybrids and to prove that they are dead?"

Aru leaned back in his chair. "That's a good question. My commander wouldn't ask that of his own volition but, given the Eternal King's agenda and his paranoid tendencies, it's likely that he will want proof of the twins' demise."

"Would a genetic sample collected from a live person differ from one collected from a dead person?" Ell-rom asked.

That was a good question for which Jasmine had no answer. She hadn't been interested in the subject before, and if they had taught it in her physiology and anatomy class in high school, she didn't remember it.

"Let's check." Margo pulled out her phone. "All the answers can be found on the internet if you know what to ask, especially with that newest chatbot version they've introduced."

Jasmine had happened to read about artificial intelligence in a magazine but had yet to try it herself. According to the article she'd read, artificial intelligence chatbots were easy to access, and some of them were free, but the answers couldn't be a hundred percent trusted because some AIs were known to hallucinate, which Jasmine found hilarious and a little worrisome.

Making up stuff was a human trait, so did it mean that the bots were becoming more human?

But that was less bothersome than the bias intentionally incorporated into those bots for whatever reasons and agendas.

Truth shouldn't be selectively modified or altered to better fit certain views and agendas of those controlling the bots, but that was the way of the world. Those with money and power decided what the plebs were allowed to know and needed to believe.

"Here is what I found," Margo said. "DNA itself doesn't change after death. However, the degradation process can make it harder to extract and analyze DNA from a dead body compared to a living one." She lifted her head. "But if we take tissue samples, like hair or finger-nail clippings, it wouldn't matter if they were taken from a live body or a dead one, right?"

"I don't know about that," Dagor said. "With how advanced Anumati's tech is, they might be able to detect subtle differences we're not even aware of."

There was a long silence as everyone mulled over the problem, and then Frankie lifted her finger. "What about a chemical solution? Something that would destroy DNA but look like it resulted from the crash? Could that work?"

Gabi nodded enthusiastically. "You could say the pod's fuel leaked and mixed with other chemicals, creating a corrosive substance."

Dagor chuckled. "The pod doesn't operate like one of your vehicles. It doesn't use fossil fuel."

"What does it use?" Ell-rom asked.

"The technology and substances used are not available on Earth, but its functionality is similar to nuclear fusion."

"Don't you mean fission?" Gabi said.

"No. I meant fusion. It's a different technology."

"Like what is used in nuclear submarines?" Frankie asked.

He laughed. "Not even close. I don't want to sound condescending, but in comparison, your nuclear submarines use Stone-Age technology. The nuclear fission generates heat that is used to boil water and create steam in a closed loop system that drives turbines, which are connected to generators and propel the submarine." He seemed to be barely able to contain his laughter. "It's not so different from the steam engines that powered your trains in the nineteenth century."

Jasmine sighed. "Okay, so that's out. What else can we do?"

"We can still use your idea of hair and nail clippings. Don't forget that the Kra-ell bodies had been kept in good condition despite them being brain dead. There shouldn't have been much DNA degradation, if any." Aru turned to Ell-rom. "Our greatest difficulty in faking your deaths is still staging a funeral pyre that will pass the scrutiny of Anumatian tech."

Ell-rom nodded and turned to Jasmine. "You are an actress, and you seem to have many great ideas. Any suggestions come to mind?"

She shrugged. "The best way is the simplest way that doesn't involve any trickery that can be discovered and put you and everyone on Earth in danger." She shifted her gaze to Aru. "Don't report that you found this pod and keep looking for the others. If and when you find one with everyone dead inside, report the find, and they might assume that everyone in the pods that are still missing is dead. After all, you wouldn't have found this pod without my help, right? So, it wasn't like you were on the right path to finding anything."

Aru closed his eyes and let out a breath. "The more I think about it, the more I'm inclined to do exactly that. The problem is that we will have to keep the dead Kra-ell of Ell-rom's pod in their stasis chambers in case we need the proof in the future. It doesn't seem morally right to keep them from entering their afterlife, and Jade won't stand for that."

"That's just religion," Margo said. "Even if there is an afterlife, which I sincerely doubt, the soul doesn't need any ceremony to find its way to wherever it is supposed to go. The body is just a vessel, and once it stops working, it doesn't really matter what happens to it. The soul makes us who we are, and without the body it's free of its material tether."

Frankie snorted. "That's awfully philosophical from someone who claims to be a non-believer."

Margo cast her a haughty look. "I didn't say that I was an atheist. I'm agnostic. Since we can't prove or disprove the existence of an afterlife or the existence of a divinity, I reserve judgment."

6

ELL-ROM

E ll-rom searched his mind for any inkling that he had an opinion on the matters of divinity and the afterlife. There was nothing in his memories, but he often found himself invoking the Mother of All Life, so the belief must have been planted so deep in his subconscious that it hadn't been erased along with the rest of his memories.

Not erased, he corrected himself, suppressed.

Since some of his memories had resurfaced, then the rest were still buried deep in his subconscious and would, at some point, emerge as well.

In a way, it was a blessing. He was free to reshape himself and become the person he strived to be. The problem was that he didn't know who that person was either.

Did he want to be like Annani? A powerful leader who was loved and admired by the people?

If he ever had to assume a leadership position, that was how Ell-rom would like to be perceived, but he wasn't sure he wanted to be the center of attention like Annani. She seemed to thrive in the spotlight, but he wouldn't. It would be a burden to have to put on a show at all times. Ell-rom preferred to work as a backroom advisor, but the problem was that he couldn't even be that because he didn't have any knowledge or wisdom to impart.

Perhaps Morelle was more like Annani, a born ruler, and he had always been meant to assist her and protect her. Deep inside, on a visceral level, that was the role he felt most comfortable with.

His mind and heart didn't rebel against it.

They embraced it.

Would Jasmine be satisfied with a mate whose ambitions were so modest?

He cast her a sidelong glance, admiring the beauty of her profile. She was such an amazing woman, and her physical beauty was just a small part of what made her so. She was intelligent, kind to a fault, friendly, outgoing, and upbeat. She was soft when softness was needed and resilient when resilience was called for.

He didn't deserve her, and not just because of his modest ambitions.

He couldn't even give her something as basic as a venom bite.

"So, Ell-rom," Frankie pulled him out of his thoughts. "Have you considered what you might like to do with your life once fully recovered? Any interests you want to explore?"

He hadn't been paying attention to what had been discussed since Margo's comment about divinity and the afterlife, and he had no idea how they had shifted from talking about the funeral rites of the Kra-ell to his life plans. Perhaps Frankie had read his mind?

"I don't know yet. There is so much I need to learn about this world, starting with the language." He patted his earpiece. "This is a wonderful invention, but I would like to learn all the intricacies and nuances I'm sure are lost in translation."

"Hmm." Frankie scrunched her nose. "Immortals are fast learners of languages, so maybe that's what you can pursue."

"Is there much need for a Kra-ell English translator?"

"Probably not," Aru said. "By the time you learn English, the Kra-ell in the village will be fluent in it as well."

Frankie pursed her lips and turned to Margo. "Maybe Ell-rom could join the Perfect Match testing team? Since he has no experiences whatsoever to compare to, he could be good at evaluating the different adventures. He's completely unbiased."

Jasmine had mentioned the service but in the context of exploring her world and all it had to offer, not as an option of working for the enterprise.

"There is plenty of time for choosing an occupation." Aru pushed to his feet. "If you want a quick lesson on shrouding, it will have to be now before I return to my tinkering, as Gabi calls it." He cast his mate a fond look.

She grimaced. "It's Saturday. Can't you take the weekend off?"

"Not today, but perhaps tomorrow."

"That's better than nothing," Margo said.

"Let's go to the other penthouse," Aru suggested. "You will need to concentrate, and having people watching you is a distraction."

Ell-rom stood up and looked at Jasmine. "Do you want to come? It might be a useful lesson for when you turn immortal."

As soon as the words left his mouth, he stifled a wince.

He still wasn't sure how they were going to overcome the hurdle of his aversion. Maybe he should swallow his pride and ask Julian if it was possible to harvest his venom and inject it into Jasmine without him having to bite her.

She shook her head. "I want you to be fully focused. I'll stay here and chat with my friends until you are done."

"Actually, we need you," Aru said. "Ell-rom's shrouding will probably not work on me. I won't know if he's managing to do it or not."

7

ELL-ROM

"Focus on the image you want to project," Aru instructed. "Visualize it clearly in your mind, then push that image outward."

Ell-rom closed his eyes, trying to picture himself fading from view. He imagined his form becoming translucent, then invisible. Concentrating, he willed the image to become a reality, but when he opened his eyes, nothing had changed.

Jasmine was still looking at him expectantly.

"I don't understand," Ell-rom said, frustration creeping into his voice. "I can feel it like it's right under my skin, but I can't make it happen."

Aru nodded sympathetically. "It's a subtle skill, and it takes practice and patience to master. It's easier to pick up as a kid, but since you must have done it before your amnesia, the ability should be there. You just need to reach for it."

After several more tries, Ell-rom's patience was starting to wear thin. His failure to access the ability he was supposed to possess made him feel even more inadequate than he already felt.

Maybe that was the problem. He doubted himself, and that was why he couldn't access the reservoir of his talents. He was also tempering his emotions out of fear of unintentionally killing Aru, putting another damper on his confidence.

"Do you want to take a break?" Jasmine asked.

Shaking his head, Ell-rom replied sharply, immediately regretting his tone. "I want to keep trying. I need to figure this out."

He needed a success, even a minor one, to shore up his confidence.

Aru eyed him with thinly veiled pity. "I know you're eager to learn, but you probably have a physical rehabilitation session later, and you shouldn't exhaust yourself."

Aru's words, though well-intentioned, sparked a flare of anger in Ell-rom. "I can handle a little mental exercise in addition to the physical."

As soon as the words left his mouth, fear replaced anger. He needed to control his emotions to keep people around him from dying.

"On second thought, you are right. I should rest."

"Small steps." Aru clapped him on his back. "Now that you know the technique, you can practice a little every day. Eventually, you will learn how to get in the zone."

When they returned to the other penthouse, Margo took one look at him and frowned. "No success?"

He shook his head. "I don't seem to be able to clear my mind and get in the zone."

Jasmine took his hand. "Let's go to our room. I want to show you something."

He was glad to leave the others and be alone with her. It was easier to keep his emotions in check when it was just the two of them, and he was less prone to bouts of anger.

No, that wasn't true.

He still got angry occasionally, but the peaks and troughs were not as extreme. If only he could also manage not to feel so inadequate around her, their relationship would be perfect, but that was on him, not her.

Jasmine led him to their bedroom and closed the door behind them.

The room, bathed in soft light filtering through the sheer curtains, felt like a sanctuary of tranquility to Ellrom, and his nerves settled down another notch.

"Sit over here," Jasmine instructed, gesturing to the plush carpet.

As he complied, she sat across from him.

"I'm going to teach you a meditation technique," she explained. "It's something I learned in one of my acting workshops. It might help you relax and center yourself."

Ell-rom nodded.

"Close your eyes." Jasmine demonstrated. "Focus on your breathing. In through your nose, out through your mouth. Slow and steady."

He did as she instructed, concentrating on the rhythm of his breath.

In and out.

In and out.

"Now, imagine a warm, golden light filling your body with each inhale," Jasmine continued soothingly. "Feel it spreading from your center to your limbs, all the way to your fingertips and toes."

Ell-rom followed her guidance with what seemed like practiced ease, and a sense of calm washed over him. He had done this before; he was sure of it. The tension in his muscles started to melt away.

Perhaps he had practiced meditation in the Mother's temple.

"With each exhale, imagine all your negative thoughts and emotions leaving your body." Jasmine gestured to the top of her head and moved her fingers. "Picture them as dark smoke, dissipating into the air and getting absorbed by the light."

Ell-rom visualized his frustration and fear as a murky cloud, watching it disperse with each breath out. He felt lighter, more at peace.

"Now, let your mind drift." Jasmine's soft voice was hypnotic. "Don't try to control your thoughts. Just observe them as they come and go, like clouds passing in the sky."

As Ell-rom sank deeper into the meditation, he felt a strange sensation. It was similar to what he had felt earlier when trying to shroud, but more natural and effortless.

He didn't fight it.

Ell-rom visualized himself becoming translucent and disappearing from Jasmine's view completely, but instead of pushing it out as Aru had told him, he simply let it wash over him.

Suddenly, Jasmine's gasp broke through his concentration, and his eyes snapped open. "What happened?"

"You turned invisible." Her hand was over her heart, and her eyes were wide. "You were shrouding!"

Ell-rom blinked in surprise, looking down at his hands. They appeared solid and visible to him. "I did? Am I still invisible?"

"No. I'm sorry for breaking your concentration. But you did it. You disappeared. If I hadn't experienced this before, I would have panicked."

Excitement bubbled up in Ell-rom's chest, tempered with a touch of disbelief. "I wasn't even trying to shroud," he said. "I was just letting go."

"Maybe that's the key." She leaned towards him and took his hand. "Maybe you were trying too hard before."

Ell-rom nodded. "When I practiced with Aru, I was stressed, and I had all these thoughts swirling in my head. I had a feeling that my overactive mind was an obstacle." He squeezed her hand. "I want to try again to see if I can hold on to the shroud longer this time."

"Of course. Let's start with the breathing again. In through your nose, out through your mouth. Slow and steady."

He managed to shroud himself in invisibility two more times and even to hold it for a minute or so, but when he tried to cast an illusion over himself, to appear as someone else, choosing Kian to model himself on, it didn't work.

Still, it was great progress, given that he had only just started.

"Thank you." He leaned toward Jasmine and wrapped his arms around her. "What would I do without you?"

She chuckled. "That's what mates are for, right? To help each other." She pulled away first and lifted her hand to look at her watch. "We should head down for your physical rehabilitation session."

"Yes, we should."

The truth was that Aru had been right, and Ell-rom was experiencing a severe energy drop. He would have loved a nap before heading to the pool, but Julian was waiting for him.

Besides, unlike the shrouding, pushing himself physically was precisely what he needed to do to get better sooner.

8

ELL-ROM

After Ell-rom had changed into his swimming shorts and put on his robe, he walked out of the large closet and knocked on the bathroom door. "Ready?"

"In a moment."

He was grateful for Jasmine's offer to change into her swimming suit in a different room.

Jasmine wasn't shy and had no qualms about undressing in front of him. She had done it so he wouldn't feel embarrassed while getting naked in front of her.

They had already seen everything there was of each other, but it was so new, so fresh, that he still felt awkward. Hopefully, that would pass once he filled out a bit and didn't look starved.

When he looked more like Julian.

Now, that was something to strive for.

When Jasmine opened the door, wearing similar attire to his, with her lush hair gathered in a knot on top of her head, she was so beautiful to him that she took his breath away.

"What?" She tucked a stray strand into the knot. "Do I have toothpaste on my nose?"

"You are just so unbelievably beautiful."

She rolled her eyes. "Given that I have seen what immortal females look like, I know that I'm nothing special in comparison. But thank you for the compliment." She leaned over and kissed his cheek. "It's always nice to hear."

"It's the truth. Every time I see you, the first moment is like a revelation. My heart feels like it's expanding. Is that what love feels like?"

"Maybe." She took his hand. "Probably."

Jasmine had told him that it was too early for them to fall in love and that they should take their time getting to know each other, but she was calling him her mate, and he was doing the same, and mates were supposed to love each other, so what was the point of waiting?

"What were you thinking when you were practicing with Aru?"

The question took him by surprise. "Why do you ask?"

"If you have a problem with intrusive thoughts, you should address them, or they will keep interfering with your training."

Ell-rom didn't want to tell Jasmine about killing the temple guard with a mere thought, but keeping it inside wasn't doing either of them any favors. Especially him. Perhaps if he shared his fears, they would loosen their grip on him.

"The dream I told you about, the one where the head priestess admonished Morelle and me, I left out something very troubling."

Jasmine didn't look surprised. "You didn't tell me the reason for the summons. What did you two do?"

"What I did, not Morelle. In the dream, I supposedly killed a guard with just a thought. I hope it was just a nightmare and not a memory, because if that's true, I'm a worse monster than everyone feared based on my parentage and the Eternal King's pursuit of me and my sister."

Jasmine shook her head. "Dreams are rarely literal, and even if this power is real, having the ability to do something doesn't mean you will. You are one of the kindest, gentlest souls I've ever met. I don't believe for a second that you would ever intentionally harm anyone."

Her words washed over him like a balm, easing some of the fear that had been gnawing at him. "But I did kill in the dream, so even if it wasn't real, it was something I was thinking about but felt guilty for feeling. That's why, in the dream, I didn't know I had that power. The priestess told the guard to taunt me and Morelle in order to provoke us to do something bad so she could find out what we were capable of. She sacrificed his life for the experiment."

"What did he do?" Jasmine asked.

"He threatened Morelle that he would yank off her veil to see what deformities she was hiding under there. I was scared that our secret would be revealed, so at night, when I was in my bed, I wished him dead, and then he was. I didn't know I could actually kill him with the thought."

"So, you didn't mean it, and you never did that again, right?"

"I don't know," he admitted. "I might have killed more people on Anumati and not remember it." He looked into her soft golden eyes. "What if my memory loss is not just the result of prolonged stasis but trauma?

"What if I did so many horrible things my mind decided to just erase them?

"What if I lose control? What if I get angry and accidentally take someone's life?"

Jasmine squeezed his hands. "I know you won't unless it is to defend the lives of people you care about. But so you won't be terrified of accidentally unleashing your power, we will continue working on your control through meditation. You will learn to manage your emotions better."

Having even the shadow of a solution, something he could do to gain control of his ability, was better than nothing, and he let out a breath. "Thank you. It's such a relief to get it off my chest."

She smiled and lifted on her toes to kiss him smack on the lips. "That's what mates do for each other, right? If I ever have a problem I can't deal with alone, you will also help me."

"Always." The words *I love you* were on the tip of his tongue, but he didn't want to say them in passing. He wanted to plan the where and when.

"Now, let's get you to that rehabilitation session." Jasmine tugged on his hand and headed for the door. "Afterward, if you have any energy left, we can practice your shrouding some more. I have a feeling you'll get very good at it very quickly."

9

ANNANI

The house was filled with the delicious aromas of the lunch Okidu had prepared, mingling with the scent of fresh flowers that adorned the centerpiece of the long dining table.

It was a perfect day for a family lunch, and Annani felt a swell of contentment as she looked around at her children and grandchildren, especially her newest grandson who was cradled in her arms.

She marveled at the perfection of his tiny features. The baby's warmth and weight stirred a mix of joy and longing that she had become accustomed to over the millennia. There was no other feeling like this, except perhaps for holding her own babies.

Annani glanced at Amanda, her youngest, and smiled. Her baby girl had always been such a joy and spirited, loving, and funny. But then, a disaster had stolen her joy, and for a while, it had seemed like her bright and cheerful daughter had allowed darkness to consume her. But somehow, she had pulled herself out of that abyss and had learned to love again.

Annani shifted her gaze back to the infant in her arms, the chatter and laughter of her family fading into a pleasant background hum. "Such a big name for such a sweet little boy," she murmured. "Evander Tellesious sounds like a general or a king."

"He might be someday," Dalhu said. "But I hope for his parents' sake that he chooses creative endeavors instead." He wrapped his arm around Amanda's shoulders. "After all, his Aunt Amanda is an artist."

"I'm not an artist." Amanda cast him an amused look. "I'm a scientist."

"You are, but you are also very visual, and you have an amazing eye for fashion. If you hadn't gone into neuroscience to search for Dormants, you would have probably pursued a career in fashion."

She laughed. "I don't think so. Being a compulsive shopper does not make me a designer. I just have a good eye for what's trending and looks good on me."

"What about the parties?" Syssi asked. "You are great at that too, especially the decorations."

Amanda waved a dismissive hand. "I'm good at everything I do. Let's leave it at that." She leaned over her nephew and pressed a soft kiss to his cheek. "And you, my sweet little nephew, can be good at anything you choose to do. Don't let anyone tell you what you can and cannot do."

"Well said." Alena leaned over Evander's other side and kissed the top of his head. "He is such a good baby. Look how calm he is with everyone talking around him."

Across the table, Syssi smiled. "That's because he's used to our voices. He participated in many family dinners throughout your pregnancy."

"Our family is growing," Annani said. "And my heart swells with gratitude to the Fates for making it happen." She smoothed a finger over Evander's soft cheek. "We have waited so long, and finally, our prayers have been answered. I even gained a new brother and sister."

"How are Ell-rom and Morelle?" Alena turned to Kian. "Any updates on their progress?"

"Morelle is still unconscious, but Bridget is confident she will wake up soon. I know it feels like we revived them a long time ago, but it has only been eleven days, so there is no reason to start panicking. As for Ell-rom, I'm happy to report that he has moved out of the clinic and is staying with Jasmine at the penthouse, which is also remarkable given the terrible state he was in when we found him."

"That's wonderful news," Alena said. "How is he adjusting?"

Kian took a sip of his water. "Surprisingly well, and we have Jasmine to thank for it. She is with him twenty-four seven, providing him with emotional support, encouragement, and I even dare say love."

"The healing power of love is tremendous." Annani handed Evander back to his mother. "I should do something nice for her to reward her for taking such good care of my brother."

"You already did," Kian said. "You welcomed her into the clan even before she attempted transition. In addition, I have promised her a job in Perfect Match once Ell-rom is restored to health."

Annani frowned. "Jasmine does not need to work for a living. We will provide for her and Ell-rom's every need."

"People like to feel useful, Mother." Alena cradled her son to her chest. "Both Ell-rom and Jasmine will need to be assigned tasks so they don't feel useless."

"Well, if you put it that way." Annani leaned back with a wine glass in hand. "But what can Ell-rom do? He does not remember his life on Anumati and his education there."

Amanda leaned forward. "When can we meet him? I'm dying to get to know our new uncle."

Alena nodded. "I would like to meet him as well and to visit Morelle. I want to welcome them both to the family." She looked at Syssi. "You've met him. What's your impression?"

Syssi smiled. "He is soft-spoken, eloquent, humble, kind —everything you would expect from an acolyte who had dedicated his life to service of the Mother of All Life. He seems as dangerous as a lamb."

Alena turned to look at her brother. "Did you get the same impression?"

"Yes, but with reservations," Kian said. "First, the Mother of All Life is not a benevolent deity who teaches love and compassion. She's ruthless and rewards bravery in battle. Also, we shouldn't forget that Ell-rom hasn't recovered his memories yet, and it's possible that the lamb is not as innocent as he seems, but on the other hand, he is not faking his mellow personality, that much I'm sure of."

"So, can we see him?" Alena asked again.

Kian nodded. "I'll see if I can arrange something for tomorrow. Since he is staying in the penthouse now, we can fit everyone in."

"If possible, I'd like to meet him as well," Toven said.

Annani leaned toward her cousin and smiled. "Of course, Toven. You and Mia are more than welcome." She shifted her gaze to Kian. "I can send my Odus ahead of time to prepare the meal and organize the space. I am sure Aru and his teammates and their partners have plans for tomorrow, and I do not wish to burden them."

The truth was that Annani hoped they had plans because she wanted to have this first family gathering just for the family.

"I can check with them." Kian glanced at her. "We have

two penthouses at our disposal, so I can arrange for the event to be just for our close circle."

Her son knew her so well. "That would be lovely. As much as I like and appreciate all of them, I would prefer it to be a family affair. Besides, they all got to meet Ell-rom already. I cannot wait to introduce him to all of you."

As the others began to discuss the timing for the gathering and whether it was better to make it a lunch or a dinner, Annani noticed a silent exchange between Syssi and Amanda. It was brief, just a glance really, but Annani had lived long enough to recognize a silent communication.

A feeling of unease settled in her stomach as she realized what it likely pertained to.

Syssi had promised to summon a vision about Khiann once the pod was found, which happened over two weeks ago. She could have summoned the vision on any of those days but was probably just as reluctant as Annani, and for the same reason.

Part of her desperately wanted to know whether Khiann had survived, and another part was terrified of having her hopes crushed.

Annani was pulled from her thoughts by a soft cooing sound. She looked down to see E.T. gazing up at her with wide, curious eyes from his mother's arms. She smiled, grateful for the distraction. "Well, hello there, little one," she reached for him.

Alena handed him over without a moment's hesitation. "He loves you. I wonder if it's your voice."

Annani gently bounced the baby in her arms. "It must be. It is certainly not my ample bosom." She was rather small-chested, proportionate to her petite frame, and she had no problem with that.

The only part of her body she disliked was her tiny child-like feet.

"It could be the power you are emanating," Orion said. "I wonder if babies get addicted to it."

"They do not." Annani kept smiling at Evander. "He feels my love for him. That is why he loves me in return. He knows that he is safe in my arms."

As she continued to coo at her grandson, Annani found her worry about Syssi's potential vision beginning to ebb. The baby's warmth in her arms, the laughter and chatter of her family around her—it all served to soothe her nerves.

From the ashes of her old life and the pit of despair over losing everyone she loved, Annani had created a wonderful family that continued to grow and flourish. It would have been so much better with Khiann by her side, but she should not be greedy. She had been denied the pleasure of spending her life with her beloved, but the Fates had blessed her in other ways, and it should be enough.

10

KIAN

As Okidu placed dish after dish on the buffet table, Kian braced himself for the topic he was about to raise, which he had no doubt would spark controversy.

When the last dish was served, and the Odu retreated to the kitchen, Kian cleared his throat, drawing his family's attention.

"Before you head over to the buffet, there's another issue I need to bring to your notice." He waited for the chatter to stop and for everyone to turn to him. "As you all know, we've been dealing with petty thefts and minor sabotages in the village recently, and it has become clear to me that we need to take more drastic action to resolve this situation."

Alena frowned. "What do you mean by drastic action?"

"I've decided to have Toven question all the Kra-ell and humans in the village using compulsion. It will save us weeks of investigation and surveillance efforts."

As a heavy silence fell over the table, Kian wasn't surprised by the concern he saw on the faces of his family members. No one liked using compulsion, and he had expected strong opposition to his idea.

Amanda was the first to speak. "Everyone? Even those we know couldn't possibly be involved?"

Kian nodded. "We need to be thorough, and we can't show favoritism. It's the only way to ensure we find the culprit and maintain trust within the community."

Amanda shook her head. "The Kra-ell and the humans are not everyone. If you are going to question all of them, you need to question all the clan members and Kalugal's people as well. You'll get enough resentment for that either way, but at least the investigation will appear impartial."

Orion turned to his father. "That's going to be a massive undertaking. Do you need help? I can handle the humans."

"Arwel is going to question them," Kian said. "There aren't that many, and his empathic ability should be enough."

Orion nodded. "If you need my help, don't hesitate to ask." He smiled. "I'm still considered an outsider, so perhaps less resentment would be directed toward me."

"I appreciate the offer," Toven said and then turned to Amanda. "The pureblooded Kra-ell are nearly impossible to compel or thrall. The only way I could do it before was with Mia's enhancing help, and I will need her help this time around as well. Taking on the clan members and Kalugal's men on top of that is too much, especially since it's unnecessary. Both coexisted with no problems or issues until the Kra-ell and the few humans arrived."

"There might be another way," Annani said. "While I understand the necessity of this unconventional inter- rogation, perhaps we can approach this in a less confrontational way."

Kian leaned forward. "What do you have in mind?"

His mother's eyes twinkled with that familiar mix of wisdom and mischief that Kian had come to associate with her brilliant and also the not-so-brilliant ideas that had caused him many sleepless nights. "What if we were to put something on the clan's bulletin board about the upcoming investigation? We could give the perpetrator a chance to confess with minimal repercussions."

As the table fell silent, with everyone considering her suggestion, Kian turned it over in his mind. If the culprit came forward voluntarily or semi-voluntarily because of fear of being found out and suffering greater repercussions, it would resolve the situation without the need for mass compulsion and without causing fric- tion in the community.

"That's a good idea," Toven said. "It could save us a lot of time and trouble if the perpetrator decides to come forward, and if not, at least it would give everyone a fair warning and make it clear that we are using compulsion as a last resort."

Annani acknowledged him with a nod. "If that does not work, I will question my clan members and Kalugal's people. There is no reason for you to shoulder the burden alone."

Toven looked relieved. "Thank you. I appreciate your offer and accept it with open arms."

Annani turned to Kian with a raised brow. "Any objections?"

"Not even one. There is no danger for you from the clan or even Kalugal's people, and it will give you a chance to reconnect with clan members that you haven't gotten to spend time with lately."

His mother rewarded him with a brilliant smile. "I love it when we agree."

"Shall we adjourn to the buffet?" Syssi asked. "The food is being kept warm, but we wouldn't want it to dry up." She rose to her feet and turned to Annani. "Would you like me to fill up a plate for you, Clan Mother?"

"I can serve myself." His mother surprised him by standing up and gliding toward the buffet. "The smells are fabulous. If everything tastes as good as it smells, we are in for a treat." She lifted a plate from the stack and started scooping brisket onto it.

Everyone waited politely until she was done before even approaching, and when her plate was full, Kian offered to carry it to the table.

His mother graciously accepted the offer.

Once everyone was seated with a full plate in front of them, Kian lifted his wine glass. "To family and our combined wisdom." He clinked his glass with those seated near him, took a sip, and put the glass down. "I'll ask Shai to post the announcement on the bulletin board first thing tomorrow morning, and we will give it until Monday evening. If no one comes forward, we will start the questioning Tuesday morning."

11

JASMINE

When Ell-rom was done with the pool therapy session, he was so exhausted that Jasmine didn't even offer to stop by the clinic to collect his vegan meals, and they headed straight for the penthouse.

His eyelids were drooping, and he was leaning heavily on his walker, but he tried to pretend he was fine and to keep up the conversation. Jasmine saved him the trouble by talking almost nonstop, so all he had to do was to listen.

"It's straight to bed with you," she said as he shuffled into their bedroom.

"I'm not going to argue with that." He discarded the robe, got in bed, and pulled the blanket over himself.

Ell-rom had used the pool shower just to wash the chlorine off his body, but even though it hadn't been a proper shower, it would have to suffice for now.

"Do you need anything?" Jasmine asked.

Ell-rom shook his head, his eyes already closing. "Just sleep," he mumbled.

He was out within seconds, but she couldn't force herself to leave just yet. It was difficult to tear her eyes away from his handsome face.

Ell-rom looked a little ragged with the five o'clock shadow growing darker, was still mostly bald, and his cheeks were too hollow, but he was breathtakingly beautiful as he was.

Jasmine could only imagine what he was going to look like when he was fully recovered.

Not that it mattered. He could have been much less good-looking than he was now, and she would have fallen in love with him anyway.

Ell-rom was a true prince. He was intelligent, kind, and had a pure soul despite what he had told her.

Was it even true?

Many kids dreamed about taking revenge on a bully that had been tormenting them, and in that regard, Ell-rom was no different. Even if his thoughts of revenge had indeed caused the guard's death, he couldn't have known that would happen.

And to think that the Head Priestess had set it up was so wrong on so many levels. She was supposed to be the spiritual leader of her people, the paragon of morality and goodness, but apparently, morality and spirituality meant different things to different people.

The Mother of All Life she revered was a benevolent deity, but the goddess Ell-rom and the Head Priestess believed in could be very different despite having the same name. Jasmine hoped that his Mother of All Life didn't demand that the Kra-ell kill in her name, but it was possible.

She'd heard extremist clerics preaching for the slaughter and rape of innocents, including children, demanding their blood and suffering as a sacrifice to their god. Even more unbelievably, some of their most vocal followers were women.

It proved how powerful brainwashing could be, or the presence of true evil.

Who would have thought that such barbarism and unimaginable cruelty could still exist in the twenty-first century?

But Jasmine didn't believe in the devil, right?

Her father had accused tarot of being the devil's play-things, forbidding her from touching them, and that had been total nonsense, so Jasmine resolved not to believe in the devil at all.

Sometimes, though, she wondered if she had been naive in dismissing it.

Sometimes, it seemed that the manifestation of evil was not only present, but it was thriving and gaining the upper hand in the war against good.

Shaking her head, she looked at Ell-rom's peaceful face and remembered all the good Annani was trying to do.

In the end, good always triumphed over evil, but if there was anything she'd remembered from history lessons in high school, it was that by the time things reached the tipping point where good people finally rose from their stupor to fight the forces of darkness, the loss of life was tremendous.

Hopefully, it wouldn't come to that.

Then again, given the threat of the Eternal King, the odds were not in Earth's favor, and Jasmine was finding it challenging to retain her optimism.

"I'd better stop this thought before it pulls me under." She walked over to the bed and kissed Ell-rom's cheek.

It was like getting a whiff of hope, even if it still smelled a little like pool water.

"I'm going down to the clinic to get your meals," she told him, even though he couldn't hear her.

Leaving him a note was also impossible because he couldn't read English and she didn't know Kra-ell.

The clinic was quiet when she arrived, with Julian sitting behind the desk. He lifted his head. "How is Ell-rom doing?"

"Exhausted. He fell asleep as soon as we got back."

"Good." Julian grinned. "The harder he works, the faster he recovers. There is no need to coddle a male of Ell-rom's pedigree. Being a half god and half Kra-ell, his genetics make him super resilient. Just ensure he eats enough to provide his body with the fuel it needs."

"That's why I'm here. I came to pick up his meals. Perhaps you should start sending them up to the penthouse."

"I should." Julian bent down and lifted an insulated bag off the floor. "Here you go. Two lunches and two dinners."

"Thank you, but you don't need to order for me anymore. I can make my own meals now."

With all the work she needed to do with Ell-rom, she might not have time to cook, but as long as there were ingredients for a sandwich in the fridge, she was good.

When her phone rang in her pocket, Jasmine thought it was Ell-rom looking for her, but then she remembered that he didn't have a phone, and even if he'd figured out how to use the landline in their bedroom, he didn't have her number.

Could it be her father?

He never called her unless it was an emergency.

Fishing it out, she was relieved and surprised to see Kian's name on the screen.

"Hello?"

"Good afternoon." Kian's voice came through, formal as always. "I hope I'm not interrupting anything."

"Not at all," she replied.

"I wanted to give you a heads-up. We're planning a family gathering tomorrow to introduce Ell-rom to the rest of the family. A couple of Odus will arrive around ten o'clock in the morning with groceries to prepare lunch, and the family will arrive around one in the afternoon."

Tension and excitement twisted Jasmine's gut. Normally, she had no trouble dealing with an audience of any size, but dining with a goddess and her children was like dining with the royal family.

"That's wonderful. Ell-rom would love to meet everyone."

She had no doubt that he would, but he would also be apprehensive about meeting the rest of the family, and he might get overwhelmed if there were too many new faces all at once.

"My mother is looking forward to introducing Ell-rom to my sisters, their mates, and their children. My uncle and his mate are coming as well."

That sounded like a much larger gathering than Jasmine had imagined. "How many people should we expect?"

"Let's see." Kian paused, and she could almost picture him ticking off names on his fingers. "Amanda and Dalhu, Alena and Orion, Toven and Mia, Syssi and myself, and of course, my mother. We'll be bringing the children along as well, but all three are still babies. Well, our Allegra is eleven months going on eleven years old, and she has a way of communicating her wishes with perfect clarity despite her young age and limited vocabulary."

Jasmine chuckled. "I can't wait to meet her."

She made a quick count in her head. Nine adults and three small children was not a small gathering, but it shouldn't overwhelm Ell-rom. After all, he'd done pretty well during meals with the gods and their mates.

12

JASMINE

B ack in the penthouse, Jasmine stored the vegan meals in the fridge, making a mental note to heat one up as soon as her prince woke up. She poured herself a glass of water and walked over to the floor-to-ceiling windows to gaze out at the sprawling cityscape below.

The sun was beginning to dip towards the horizon, painting the sky in vivid hues of orange and pink.

As her eyes swept over the rooftop pool and lush, artfully maintained greenery, she marveled at how much her life had changed in such a short time. Just weeks ago, she'd been a struggling actress, and now here she was living in a luxurious penthouse, caring for an alien prince, and about to be part of a gathering of immortals along with their mother—the goddess.

It occurred to her that Edgar had never mentioned the

Clan Mother to her when they had been together. Come to think of it, no one had.

Evidently her existence was a closely guarded secret, and the only reason she was privy to it was her relationship with Ell-rom.

Jasmine chuckled softly. If someone had told her this would be her life, she'd have thought they were pitching her a sci-fi script.

But her life wasn't a movie, and all the real-world problems still haunted her whenever she allowed them into her mind.

It was such a monumental waste of time and energy, though.

She could do nothing to change things, so why obsess over them?

Because things had changed for her. Before, she hadn't expected to live long enough to affect anything that would impact the world in a meaningful way. In fact, Jasmine lived with the fear of dying at the same age her mother had, and she had been driven by the desire to squeeze every bit of joy she could out of her limited time on Earth. But then she'd reached that age, and not only was she still around, but she was now entertaining the prospect of immortality.

There was a lot a person could do when they had unlimited time, but she hadn't figured out what that could be. She wasn't the leader type who could inspire people to follow her, but maybe she could become an influencer.

Naturally, she would have to change her appearance and her name and start anew from time to time, but that wasn't too difficult to pull off. She could sound inspirational and convincing, but the problem was that she had never articulated anything profound and didn't know how to do so.

Jasmine could only read what others wrote and sound good doing it.

Despite Ell-rom's assertions that she was smart, she was well aware of her limitations. Here and there she had good ideas, and she could think outside the box, but she wasn't a creator, and expressing herself in writing had never been her thing.

Perhaps Ell-rom could help her. He was eloquent, and he was a prince by birth. Maybe once he got a handle on what was going on around the world, he could write the scripts for her.

They could be a team.

Walking back into their bedroom, she stood at the foot of the bed and watched her prince. Even in sleep, his face appeared regal. His features were sharp and defined, hinting at the strength that lay beneath his current fragile state.

As if sensing her gaze, Ell-rom's eyes fluttered open. "Jasmine?" he murmured, his voice thick with sleep. "Is it time for me to get up?"

She sat down on the edge of the bed. "I have great news, but if you want to keep on sleeping, it can wait. It's nothing urgent."

"Now you've piqued my curiosity." Ell-rom stretched his long limbs. "How long was I asleep?"

"Not long. Maybe an hour. Are you hungry? I've got your meals in the fridge."

He nodded, pushing himself up to a sitting position. "I could eat. But first, I want to hear your great news."

"Kian called while you were asleep. Apparently, his sisters and their mates want to meet you." She closely watched his response. "They're coming over tomorrow for lunch, along with your sister, of course."

For a moment, Ell-rom looked stunned. Then, a slow smile spread across his face. "That's wonderful, especially since Julian doesn't expect me at the pool tomorrow. How many people are coming?"

"Twelve, including the three babies. Amanda, Dalhu, and their daughter. Alena, Orion, and their newborn son, Syssi, Kian, and their daughter Allegra, and Toven and Mia, and of course, Annani."

"It is somewhat stressful," he admitted. "Did you meet Kian's sisters?"

"I did, and they are all very nice. Sari is in Scotland, so she's not coming, but Amanda and Alena are both great, each in her own way."

"Tell me a little about them."

"I will, but you need to eat first. I will tell you about them over lunch." She glanced at her watch. "Actually, it's dinner time already."

"Are the others here?" Ell-rom asked.

"They are all gone. We are alone in the penthouse."

"That's good." He peeled off the blanket. "I like their company, but I like yours more. I'm looking forward to a quiet dinner with just the two of us."

He wrapped his arms around her, pulling her close, and for a long moment, they just held each other.

Finally, Jasmine pulled back. "Your belly is rumbling. We should get some food in you, and then we can practice shrouding before visiting Morelle."

13

ELL-ROM

E ll-rom walked down the long hallway toward the clinic with his back straight, and his head held high. His hands were resting lightly on the walker's handles, and he was proud of the fact that he was basically walking without its help.

It seemed like every time he woke up, he was markedly better than before rest. He would have considered taking more naps, but he was already resting too much for his liking. His body seemed to need it, though, and it was just shutting down on him after exertion without leaving room for negotiation.

"You are doing great," Jasmine said. "In a day or two, you might be able to discard the walker altogether."

"That would be a cause for celebration." He waited for her to open the door to the clinic. "Tomorrow, I'll try to do without when I meet the rest of the family." His chest expanded just from saying that.

He had a family. A nephew, three nieces, their mates, and many cousins, as all other more distant relations were called on Earth. Or was it only in English?

There was still so much to learn. If only there was a way to just pour it into his brain instead of having to learn everything over time.

"Hello," Julian called out from his office. "Had a nice nap?"

"The best." Ell-rom smiled at the medic. "I'm going to see my sister."

"Of course. I'm here if you need me."

Bridget was seen less and less in the clinic, and Julian had taken over most of the care for Ell-rom and Morelle.

Ell-rom didn't mind for himself, but Morelle was still fragile, and he would have preferred the more senior medic to supervise her recovery.

Today, though, he was happy that Julian was there and not Bridget. He needed to talk to him about his blood aversion and what could be done about it, but the problem was that he didn't want to have that conversation in front of Jasmine.

Jasmine hadn't realized what had happened last night, and he wanted to keep it that way, at least for now. Ell-rom preferred to find a solution before he had to confess his disability.

Jasmine pushed the door to Morelle's room open all the way, and as he stepped inside, she followed.

"Hello, sister," he said, moving to her bedside. "I'm sorry I couldn't visit earlier. The therapy sessions take a lot out of me."

He settled into the chair beside her bed, reaching for her hand. It was warm and somehow vibrant despite her unresponsive state. He studied her features, so similar to his own. The curve of her cheekbones, the shape of her eyes. It was like looking at a softer, more delicate version of himself.

When a buzzing sound disturbed the moment, he turned to look at Jasmine. "What was that?"

"My phone." She pulled it out and read what was on the screen. "It's Margo. She's back in the penthouse and asking if I want to have a coffee with her. Are you okay here on your own for a little bit?"

It was perfect. "Of course. Go and enjoy some time alone with your friend. I feel bad enough about taking up all of your time."

"I love being with you." She leaned and kissed his cheek. "Tell Morelle about the family lunch tomorrow."

"I will."

When Jasmine closed the door behind her, Ell-rom leaned over Morelle's hand and kissed the back of it. "I think I love this woman, and I can't wait for you to meet her."

Morelle's expression didn't change, but he imagined that her lips quirked up slightly in a ghost of a smile. It wasn't true, but it made him feel good to believe that it might be.

"I have news," he continued. "Annani's children and grandchildren are coming to meet me tomorrow, and I wish you could be there. So far, everyone has been so kind and welcoming to me that I don't expect anything different from those I haven't met yet."

The only response was the continued beeping of the machines, and Ell-rom sighed, running a hand over his face. "I'm struggling, Morelle," he admitted quietly. "There's so much I don't understand about myself, and there's something wrong with me." He leaned closer to share his shameful secret. "I can't stand the sight or smell of blood. The very thought of it makes me ill. And that's a problem because I can't bring myself to bite Jasmine, which is expected of me. Both Kra-ell and gods bite, but it's even more important in the culture of the gods and their hybrid descendants. No immortal female would accept me if I can't deliver a venom bite, but in Jasmine's case, it is even more crucial because it is necessary to activate her dormant godly genes. Unless I can bite her, she can't turn immortal, which means I can't keep her."

Ell-rom's grip on Morelle's hand tightened. "I need to find a solution and get over the aversion. I need to talk to Julian about it, but it's so embarrassing to admit that I'm incapable of something that every adult immortal male can do."

He was silent for a few moments, just watching Morelle's breathing. "I don't spend nearly enough time with you, and I feel bad about leaving you so soon, but I really need to talk to Julian."

Morelle was spending most of her days alone, without anyone talking or singing to her like Jasmine had done for him. Was it any wonder that she was still in a coma?

He was failing in his brotherly duty. He should make an effort to be with her more often and bring Jasmine with him to sing. Or perhaps he could sing her a song?

He didn't remember any, but he could improvise.

"I wouldn't know where to start. It would be better to just turn on the television for you. We could place the teardrop near the speaker so it can translate for you. Maybe hearing different voices and different stories would help. What do you think?"

As always, there was no response, but Ell-rom liked to imagine that somewhere deep inside, Morelle could hear him. "I'll talk to Julian about it," he promised. He stood up. "I have to go now, but I'll be back after I'm done talking to Julian." He leaned over her and kissed her forehead.

14

JASMINE

Jasmine stepped out of the elevator into the vestibule at the penthouse level, her mind racing with thoughts about Margo's message. Lynda had finally scheduled another lunch date with her ex, and it was time to implement the plan of showing Rob his fiancée's true colors.

As she opened the door and stepped into the living room, the floor-to-ceiling windows that offered a panoramic view of the city still took her breath away. She paused for a moment, marveling at how quickly this place had become home, and then made her way to the kitchen to brew fresh coffee and check the fridge for something to munch on.

She'd eaten lunch less than an hour ago, so she wasn't hungry, but she was nervous about what she and Margo were going to do next.

After getting the coffee machine going, she pulled out her phone and texted Margo. *I'm here. Where are you?*

The answer came a moment later. *I'm in my room. I'm coming out.*

Smiling, Jasmine put the phone back in her pocket.

By the time Margo walked into the kitchen, she had two steaming mugs of coffee and a plate of cheese slices ready. "Counter or living room?"

Margo thought for a moment. "Terrace. It's nice and cool by now, and there is barely any traffic on the weekend, so it's quiet."

"Lead the way." Jasmine handed her one of the mugs and carried the other and the cheese plate out onto the terrace.

They sat at a small bistro table facing the plexiglass railing, their backs to the sliding doors.

Margo smiled. "I can imagine Kian and Syssi sitting out here when they had just met. It used to be his place, you know."

"I know." Jasmine took a sip of the coffee, but it was still a bit too hot for her taste. "They are all coming here tomorrow; the whole family wants to meet Ell-rom. Are you going to be here?"

Margo shook her head. "Negal and I have planned a trip to the mall, and Frankie and Dagor are coming with us. Aru and Gabi are meeting her family in a restaurant in one of the clan's hotels."

Jasmine wondered if anyone had told them to find other things to do while the family was meeting Ell-rom. "I hope you were not told to make yourselves scarce."

Margo chuckled. "We were informed that Kian was commandeering the place for lunch and that we were welcome to congregate at the other penthouse."

"I'm sorry." Jasmine winced.

"Nothing to be sorry about. This is Kian's place, and he's letting us stay here rent-free. If he needs it back for one afternoon, it's not a big deal. Totally understandable."

They were both avoiding the real reason they were meeting for coffee, but even though it was an unpleasant task, it needed to be done, and Jasmine didn't have all day. Ell-rom was waiting for her at the clinic.

"So, what are Lynda's plans for tomorrow?"

"She's meeting her ex at Maria's Kitchen at twelve-thirty."

Jasmine's eyebrows shot up. "Maria's Kitchen? Isn't that the place you were gushing about yesterday? You wanted to take Negal there."

Margo nodded. "The very same. To be fair, I heard about it from Lynda, and it's really good. Anyway, she told Rob that she was meeting one of her girlfriends for lunch, and she even called her to make sure she would back up her story. Can you believe that?"

"At least she's thorough."

"That she is." Margo sighed. "She always thinks of everything down to the most minute detail. Maybe that's how
she manages to manipulate everyone around her with
such ease."

Jasmine chuckled. "She should go into politics. She
would find a lot of like-minded people there."

"Yeah, she would be the most poisonous viper in that
den of snakes."

"So, what's the plan?" Jasmine asked.

"That's why I need you here. I don't know what to do. I
mean, your advice about getting Rob to the same
restaurant was good, but if Lynda sees Rob, she'll just
come up with some cover story, and Rob, being the
pushover that he is when it comes to Lynda, will probably believe her."

"Well, you could always go in disguise," Jasmine joked.
"Or sit across the street with binoculars like in one of
those old detective movies."

"Right, because that wouldn't be suspicious at all."

"It doesn't have to be," Jasmine said. "You can pick a
place nearby, somewhere with outdoor seating, if possible, but get there at twelve. That way, you will be able to
spot Lynda and her ex arriving at Maria's Kitchen
without them seeing you. Once Rob sees that he will be
more open to what you have to tell him."

"That could work. There's a little café just down the
street from Maria's that has patio seating." Margo pulled

out her phone. "I don't remember the name, but it's easy enough to find on the Map app."

While Margo searched, Jasmine bit into a piece of cheese.

"Here it is. Bronx Café. I remembered the name had something to do with New York. I'm calling Rob."

Jasmine listened as Margo dialed her brother's number, her heart going out to the unsuspecting Rob. The phone rang twice before he picked up.

"Margo? What a nice surprise to hear from you. What's up?"

"Hi, Rob," Margo said, her voice carefully casual. "I was wondering if you'd like to grab lunch together tomorrow? It's been a while since we've had a chance to catch up, you know. Just you and me."

There was a pause on the other end of the line. "Tomorrow? Um, sure, that sounds great, actually. Lynda's meeting a friend, so I'm free. Where do you want to go?"

Margo shot Jasmine a triumphant look. "I was thinking we could try a café that a friend recommended. It's called Bronx Café, and it has patio seating."

"Sounds perfect," Rob said. "What time?"

"Does noon work for you?"

"Sure."

They talked for a few more minutes about their parents and how they were doing, and then Margo ended the call with a cheerful goodbye, but as soon as she hung up, her smile faded.

"Did you hear that?" Margo shook her head. "Lynda's meeting a *friend* for lunch, and he doesn't even question it anymore. Maybe he's just glad to get rid of her for a couple of hours so he can have some peace."

Jasmine felt a pang of sympathy for Rob. "I have no problem with him being a trusting fellow. What bothers me is that he shouldn't have to ask permission to see his sister. It sounded as if the only reason he could meet with you was because Lynda was busy doing something else."

"That's exactly like it is."

Poor Rob. The guy needed to be liberated.

"Hopefully, after tomorrow, he'll see the truth for himself. It'll be painful, but a little pain now will save him a lot more pain in the future."

Her words brought back memories of her own breakup with Edgar. He had been a decent guy, and for a while they'd had fun together, but he was not the right one for her. Ending things had been difficult, and she had hated hurting him, but in the end, it had been the right decision for both of them.

"By the way," Jasmine said, suddenly curious about Edgar's current love life, "how are things going with Edgar and Frankie's cousin Angelica? Have they seen each other again?"

Margo grinned. "Frankie says that they can't get enough of each other."

She felt a wave of relief and happiness wash over her. "That's wonderful! I'm so glad. I wish them the best, and I hope that Angelica is the one for him. Did he tell her already about who he is? I mean, she's a Dormant, so if they hit it off, he should give her the talk."

"I don't know," Margo said. "I'm not really following their love life, but speaking of Dormants and transitions, how are things going with you and Ell-rom? Any progress on the transition front?"

Jasmine felt a flutter of nervousness in her stomach. "We're taking things slow. He's still recovering, and there is also the issue of his inexperience. I don't want to overwhelm him."

Margo's eyes widened. "So, he's really a virgin?"

"Very much so, but not for long if I can help it."

15

ELL-ROM

E ll-rom walked over to Julian's office and rapped his knuckles on the door. "Do you have a moment?"

"I have more than a moment." The medic waved at the chair in front of his desk. "I have all the time you need and more."

Ell-rom left the walker near the door and took the three steps toward the chair without help.

"Nice," Julian said. "I'm thrilled to see your progress."

"Thank you." Ell-rom sat down. "I wanted to talk to you about the television in Morelle's room." That was certainly an easier topic to start with. "I'm concerned about her being all alone in there for most of the day and having no one talking to her like Jasmine did for me. If you can set it up for her so the teardrop is hung over the speaker, perhaps that could serve as a substitute for someone actually sitting in her room and talking to her."

Julian nodded, but he didn't look excited about the idea. "We could do that, but it's not quite the same as having a loved one talk to her. Research on the effectiveness of auditory stimulation for coma patients has shown mixed results. Those who had a loved one talk to them showed more significant brain responses compared to unfamiliar stimuli, but the truth is that not many studies have been done on the subject."

Ell-rom frowned. "I didn't know Jasmine, so hearing her talk and sing to me could have been the television as far as I was concerned, but it still helped pull me out of the coma."

Julian shrugged. "Something is always better than nothing, and I have no problem implementing your idea, but you need to know that your presence is more meaningful to Morelle. If you want, we can conduct an experiment. We can measure Morelle's brain activity when there are no sounds in her room, when the television is on with no Kra-ell translation, with translation, and lastly, when you talk to her. It would be fascinating to measure the differences."

"Is it difficult to do?"

"Not at all. I can get a more sophisticated piece of equipment to measure the electrical activity in her brain. Think of it as a way to listen to the brain's conversation." He chuckled. "It is fortunate that Morelle is nearly bald because I will need to place small sensors on her scalp, and having no hair will make it much easier. The electrodes are connected to a machine that records the brain's electrical signal."

"Is it painful?" Ell-rom asked.

"Not at all. It is completely painless and noninvasive, meaning it doesn't require any surgery or discomfort."

Sounded easy enough, and Julian seemed excited about conducting the experiment. "How soon can you get that equipment?"

"I have an EEG right here in the clinic, but it's pretty basic. I would like to get something better that can provide more information. Amanda, Kian's younger sister, has much better equipment in her lab, which is called Functional Magnetic Resonance Imaging, which measures brain activity by detecting changes in blood flow. It assesses brain function in response to stimuli and is much more accurate, but it's a big machine, and we can't transport it here or have Morelle transported to Amanda's lab." He tilted his head. "Well, it's not that we can't. We just can't do that easily, and Kian will not approve it just for the sake of an experiment."

"Hmm." Ell-rom rubbed a hand over his jaw. "I'm meeting the entire family tomorrow, so I'll mention it to Amanda. Perhaps if she is also interested in the results of this experiment, she will be willing to help us to either get a machine in here or transport Morelle to her laboratory."

"Transporting Morelle is out of the question," Julian

said. "But I wouldn't mind getting that lovely piece of equipment in here."

"I'll see what I can do." Ell-rom shifted in the chair, wondering how to broach the other subject he needed Julian's help with.

The medic narrowed his eyes at him. "I know that look. You want to ask me something and are embarrassed to do so. I think we have already established that you can ask me anything, and I will do my best to provide you with as much useful information as I can."

"That's true."

Julian had indeed helped him a lot, explaining intimate subjects in a nonjudgmental, matter-of-fact way.

"It's about overcoming aversions."

"Like your aversion to animal products?"

Ell-rom nodded. "Yes. Let's say I need to eat a piece of meat to hide who I am, and it's very important that I do so, but I can't bring myself to even put it in my mouth."

It was a good example that was close to his real problem and might even be connected to it. Perhaps he couldn't stomach animal products because of his aversion to blood.

Julian leaned back in his chair. "Overcoming aversions is a complex process. It might involve a combination of cognitive behavioral therapy, exposure therapy, and sometimes medication. The key is to gradually expose yourself to the source of the aversion in a controlled, safe environment while learning coping mechanisms to manage your anxiety or discomfort." He paused, studying Ell-rom's face. "But I have a feeling you're not asking about your aversion to meat. Being a vegetarian or a vegan is perfectly acceptable in human societies, and no one will force you to eat meat if you don't want to."

Ell-rom felt his heart rate quicken. This was the moment of truth. "I have a strong aversion to blood," he admitted. "The sight, the smell, even the thought of it makes me ill. I'm sure you understand why that's a huge problem. I must overcome it, and I don't know how."

Understanding dawned in Julian's eyes. "You can't bite Jasmine."

Ell-rom nodded miserably. "I can't bite anyone. I can't bite to bring my mate pleasure, and I can't use my fangs to protect her either. How can I be what I am and be repulsed by even a drop of blood?"

Julian leaned forward. "Aversions can develop for all sorts of reasons. Regrettably, you don't have your memories, so you don't know what caused it, but it must have been something traumatic."

"It was." Ell-rom winced. "That's one of the few memories that has resurfaced. There was some sort of function in the temple, and I had to pretend to drink blood from a goblet because I was supposed to be Kra-ell. The head priestess had told me and Morelle to only put our lips on the rim and not actually drink it because neither of us could tolerate it, but I accidentally took a small sip and had to run to my room to throw up. I got a serious scolding later because my slip-up endangered Morelle's and my life. Our survival depended on everyone believing we were normal Kra-ell kids or as normal as fraternal twins could be. I think we were the only such twins born in thousands of years."

Julian appeared thoughtful for a long moment. "That sounds like a pretty traumatic event to me, especially since you were still a kid when it happened. I think it might be helpful for you to speak with our clan's psychologist, Vanessa."

Ell-rom felt a surge of panic. "I don't want more people to know about this. It was difficult enough to come to you for advice."

"I understand," Julian said. "But you should know that Vanessa is bound by strict confidentiality. Nothing you discuss with her will ever be shared without your explicit permission. You don't even have to meet her in person. I can arrange a video call. But don't expect a quick fix. Psychological issues take time to resolve, and it would probably take a few sessions with her before you see any improvement."

Ell-rom nodded. "I'll speak with her, but I don't want Jasmine to know. Can you cover for me and invent some kind of testing that you need to perform from time to time?"

Julian regarded him for a long moment. "Honesty is always the best option, especially when it comes to your mate. You can tell Jasmine that you are talking to the therapist, but you don't need to tell her what you are talking about. You can say that you are not ready to share what is troubling you with her yet, and that will be the truth. She might get her feelings hurt a little because you are keeping things from her, but she will be hurt much worse if she discovers that you have deliberately deceived her."

Ell-rom winced. "When you put it like that, it sounds terrible. I'll follow your advice." He rose to his feet. "Thank you. I mean it. You are more than a medic to me. You are a good friend."

Julian smiled. "I'm honored to be your friend, Ell-rom."

16

JASMINE

As Jasmine stepped out of the elevator on the clinic level, her heart was heavy with what was about to happen to Rob the next day. While Ell-rom would be embracing his family, Rob would be facing his fiancée's betrayal.

He obviously loved Lynda, and they were to be married in less than a week. Seeing her with her ex would be like a stab to the heart.

Poor guy.

As she made her way down the corridor, her footsteps echoing in the quiet hallway, the heaviness gave way to anticipation. It was ridiculous how much her heart fluttered every time she was about to see Ell-rom, even after the shortest separation. It was like he was her sun, and when he wasn't near her, everything around her dimmed.

Was that love?

It must be, because she had never felt this way toward anyone else.

She paused outside Morelle's room, expecting to find Ell-rom there, but the room was empty save for the comatose princess and the equipment surrounding her.

Frowning, Jasmine turned and headed towards the doctor's office, but as she raised her hand to knock, the door opened, and Julian stepped out, quickly pulling the door closed behind him.

"Hi, Jasmine." He greeted her with a bright smile. "Ell-rom isn't ready yet."

Something in his manner set off alarm bells in Jasmine's mind. "What's going on? Are you running more tests on him?"

Julian hesitated for a moment before answering. "Ell-rom is on a video call with the clan therapist, Vanessa. It might take a while."

Jasmine felt a knot form in her stomach. "The therapist? What for?"

"I'm sorry, but I can't discuss that with you." Julian smiled apologetically. "I know that you are his mate, but I take patient confidentiality seriously. You can ask Ell-rom about it later, but I'd advise you to wait for him to volunteer what he talked about with Vanessa. I'm saying that not as a doctor but as a happily mated man. People need their space from time to time, even if it's only the space in their heads."

Julian was right, of course, but Jasmine's mind was racing, trying to piece together what could have prompted this sudden therapy session. Hopefully, it wasn't about Ell-rom's dream of killing someone with a thought.

Damn it. She was so stupid. She should have warned him to keep that to himself, but she assumed it was self-explanatory. What she hadn't taken into account was how naive Ell-rom was.

Still, it might be about something else, and she wasn't going to give Julian any hints by asking questions that would make him suspicious.

Plastering a smile on her face, she nodded. "Thanks for the advice. It's good. I need to remember not to overdo it and make Ell-rom feel like I'm mothering him."

Julian chuckled. "Some mothering is okay. Just not too much."

"Right," she agreed. "How long do you think it will take?"

"These sessions can sometimes run long. Why don't you go back to the penthouse? I'll make sure Ell-rom knows where to find you when he's done, and if he needs me to take him up there, I will gladly escort him."

It hadn't even occurred to her that Ell-rom could probably travel between the penthouse and the clinic without her help.

Talk about mothering.

Nevertheless, she wasn't comfortable leaving Ell-rom alone there, especially given what she suspected he had revealed to Julian.

If Kian thought that Ell-rom was dangerous, who knew what they would do to him? They were not bad people, but their sense of self-preservation might kick in, and they would not want someone who could kill with a thought anywhere near them.

"I think I'll wait for him in Morelle's room. I promised Ell-rom I'd talk to her."

"Sure thing," Julian said. "I'm going to take a break and get something to eat. But don't worry. I have my phone with me, and I will be notified immediately if Morelle needs me."

"I'm not worried. Is Gertrude around?"

He shook his head. "I'm the only one here for the weekend, but again, you have nothing to worry about. Morelle doesn't need constant supervision."

"I know."

17

ELL-ROM

E ll-rom drummed his fingers on the armrest of his chair as he waited for the video call to connect.

When Julian had called the therapist, the medic hadn't expected her to be immediately available to help, and neither had Ell-rom. She surprised them both when she told Julian that she was just finishing a meeting and would call Ell-rom right away.

It had been a few minutes, and Ell-rom was impatient, not because he was eager to talk to a stranger about his embarrassing problem but because he wanted it to be over, hopefully after being solved.

As the screen finally flickered to life, it revealed a beautiful blond woman with kind eyes and a warm smile.

"Hello, Ell-rom," she said, her voice carrying a soothing quality even through the speakers. "I'm Vanessa, the clan's psychologist, and I'm so excited to meet you, even if it's through a video call. It's an unexpected pleasure. I thought I would have to wait for you to arrive in the village for us to get to know each other, but here we are." She pushed her hair behind her ear. "Luckily, I had my earpieces upgraded with the new Kra-ell translation capability, or this would not have been possible. I only know a few Kra-ell words and definitely not enough to conduct a conversation."

"Hello." Ell-rom returned her warm smile to the best of his ability, given how nervous he was. "Thank you for speaking with me. Julian didn't expect you to be available right away, and neither did I, so I didn't prepare what I wanted to discuss."

"That's fine. Just let it flow, and we will piece it together. I actually prefer that to a rehearsed speech." She smiled. "This is about emotions, Ell-rom, not logic or eloquence, and emotions are messy."

It was comforting to hear her say that. "My problem is an aversion to blood." She'd said to just let it flow, and she was right. It made things easier. "The aversion is so strong that I can't bring myself to bite anyone, not for pleasure and not in defense, and as I am sure you can imagine, that's a serious problem for a male. God, immortal, or Kra-ell."

Vanessa nodded. "I certainly can see how this could be a problem. Before we begin, though, you should know that I'm mated to a Kra-ell pureblood, so I'm familiar with both sides of your heritage."

"That's good to know. Have you ever encountered anyone with this kind of aversion?"

She shook her head. "I have not, but all phobias share commonalities, and therefore can benefit from similar treatments. What is it about blood that you find offensive, and how does your aversion manifest?"

Ell-rom took a deep breath, steeling himself. "It's everything about it. The sight of it, the smell, and mostly the taste of it. All make me feel ill."

Vanessa nodded. "I see. And how long have you been aware of this aversion?"

Did she know that he had amnesia?

He probably should tell her just in case she didn't.

"I woke up from stasis not remembering anything about my former life, so naturally, I wasn't aware of having an aversion to anything. When Bridget asked me about my food preferences, it became obvious that I prefer a plant-based diet, but we assumed that it was because my sister and I couldn't get any cooked food in the temple while pretending to be Kra-ell. But then I dreamt about accidentally taking a sip from a goblet filled with blood that I was only supposed to hold and pretend to be drinking from. In the dream, I ran to my bedroom and emptied the contents of my stomach. After that, the head priestess admonished me for endangering my sister and myself."

"Was it some sort of a Kra-ell ceremony that you participated in? One that required drinking blood from a goblet?"

Ell-rom tried to remember more details from the dream, but there wasn't enough to determine what had been going on. "Everyone held a goblet, including my sister, but I don't know if it was a religious ceremony or a celebration or why we were there. I guess it had something to do with our mother, and that's why we had to attend. I wish I remembered more."

"That's okay," Vanessa said. "Let's focus on the present. Can you describe to me what happens when you encounter blood? What physical sensations do you experience?"

"I have not encountered blood since waking up from stasis. The closest I came was attending a meal with people who were eating cooked meat. The smell was not pleasant to me, but it was not revolting. It's the memory of how it tasted, how it smelled, and the viscosity of it that makes me nauseous." He swallowed. "Just talking about it now makes my stomach turn. I feel light-headed, and I just broke into a cold sweat."

"Those are all common reactions in phobias and aversions," Vanessa explained. "What we're going to do is work on desensitizing you to these triggers and teach you coping mechanisms to manage your reactions."

"Thank you. I would appreciate anything you could do to lessen those reactions."

18

JASMINE

As Julian headed out, Jasmine walked over to Morelle's room and stepped inside. She settled into the chair by the bed and took Morelle's hand the way Ell-rom did every time he visited his sister.

Now that Ell-rom had his own earpieces, the teardrop was no longer needed, and she didn't have it with her, but perhaps at this stage the sound of her voice would suffice.

"Hey there," she said softly. "I hope you don't mind me dropping in like this. Your brother is going through a therapy session." She sighed. "You should be glad that the clan has so many professionals dedicated to helping him and you when you finally wake up from your slumber. Ell-rom is doing great, and he is getting stronger by the hour, but some of the memories that surfaced are doing him more harm than good."

Jasmine glanced at the camera in the corner of the room. It was no doubt recording audio as well as video, so she should avoid mentioning the content of those disturbing dreams.

"I've got some gossip for you," Jasmine continued, adopting a conspiratorial tone. "I don't know if you are much of a gossiper, but since you lived in isolation your entire life, I assume that you will find tales of love lost and love gained interesting." She let go of Morelle's hand and leaned back. "Before I found your brother, I had a boyfriend named Edgar. Things fizzled out between us, not because there was anything wrong with him but because we were not meant for each other. I was meant for Ell-rom, and Edgar was meant for someone else. Still, I felt guilty about breaking things off with him. To my great joy, he found a new love interest, who is also a Dormant. Her mother is the aunt of my friend Frankie, who transitioned not too long ago."

She paused, a wistful smile playing on her lips. "It's funny how things work out sometimes, isn't it?"

Come to think of it, she should give Edgar a call. After all, he had checked in on her multiple times since their breakup. It was appropriate that she return the favor.

"What do you think, Morelle? Should I call Edgar and collect more juicy gossip straight from the source? That's what good friends do, right?"

Taking Morelle's silence as tacit agreement, Jasmine

pulled out her phone, found Edgar's name in her contacts, and hit the call button.

The phone rang several times before Edgar's familiar voice came through. "Jasmine? Is everything okay?"

"Everything's fine. I just had coffee with Margo and asked her about you. She told me that you and Angelica have become an item. I wanted to congratulate you and hear more about it."

There was no reason to beat around the bush. Edgar knew her too well not to guess what her call was all about.

His laugh came through the phone, warm and relaxed in a way Jasmine hadn't heard in a long time. "News travels fast, huh? Yeah, Angelica is amazing. She's feisty and funny, and she doesn't give me an inch."

"That's wonderful. I'm so happy for you," Jasmine said, and she meant it. The knot of guilt she'd been carrying since their breakup finally unraveled completely. "Did you tell her?"

"About who I am?"

"Yeah, and that little detail about her being a Dormant and your ability to turn her immortal."

"Not yet."

"What are you waiting for?"

"For the big declaration of everlasting love. As you told me so sagely, I shouldn't settle for anything less than everything."

Jasmine and Ell-rom still hadn't declared their ever-lasting love to each other, but it was kind of implied, and they thought of each other as mates.

What were they waiting for?

"Yeah, you are right. It's not like there is a rush. How old is Angelica?"

"Just the right age. She's twenty-five. But enough about me. How are you and your prince doing?"

Jasmine glanced at Morelle's still form, a mix of emotions washing over her. "Things are good. Complicated sometimes because that's life, and nothing is ever easy, but it's worth the effort. Ell-rom is recovering rapidly, but he has so much to learn. English, reading and writing, history, geography. I would feel over-whelmed, but he takes everything in his stride."

"I'm happy to hear that you are still enamored with your prince."

She chuckled. "And I'm happy that you found a new princess. So Morelle is out of the race?"

"Angelica is no princess, but it would appear that princesses don't do it for me. I like that she's feisty and sassy and doesn't mince words. She'll tell you what she thinks, whether you're ready for it or not, while waving her hands around to show off those pretty nails of hers. I just can't stop smiling when I'm with her. Not to mention that she has great investment instincts. In just a few days, I made a couple of thousand dollars following her advice."

Jasmine laughed. "I wish I had money to invest to check out Angelica's tips."

"The stock market is risky, Jasmine. It's like gambling, so never invest what you can't afford to lose."

"Good philosophy. I'll keep it in mind for when I actually have a job and money to spare."

19

ELL-ROM

"Let's start with something easy," Vanessa said. "Breathe in for four counts, hold for seven, and then exhale for eight. This helps activate your parasympathetic nervous system, which counteracts the fight-or-flight response."

Ell-rom followed her lead, feeling some of the tension leave his body as he focused on his breathing.

"That was good," Vanessa said after several repetitions of the exercise. "How do you feel?"

"Better. I'm not nauseous."

"Excellent. Now that your stomach is at ease, we can move on to the next technique. It's called cognitive restructuring. Often, our aversions are fueled by irrational thoughts. What thoughts go through your mind when you think about blood?"

Ell-rom hesitated. "I'm not sure."

"What is the first thing that comes to your mind?"

"Death. Suffering."

Vanessa nodded. "True, it could be both. But blood is also life. We can't live without it, and many people donate blood so it can be given to others when they need it, like in the case of an injury or during an operation. Think about the blood flowing in your veins and focus on how vital it is to your survival and the survival of your loved ones."

It was an excellent diversion of focus, and it was helping, but then another thought surfaced, one he hadn't been aware of until now.

"When I think about my blood, I also think about it being impure, contaminated."

"Those are powerful thoughts," Vanessa acknowledged. "But are they rational? Your blood is obviously not contaminated, but I get where these thoughts are coming from. The Kra-ell living among us divide themselves into purebloods and hybrids, and for the longest time, the purebloods felt superior to the hybrids. Some of them probably still do, but it's a fallacy. Here on Earth, the hybrids have had a big advantage over the purebloods. They can pass for humans, while the purebloods must put much more effort into camouflaging their alien looks. What I'm trying to say is that each has advantages and disadvantages, but neither determines the kind of people they are. The only thing that determines your worth as a person is what you do and how it affects others. Are you creative and productive? Are you kind? Do you protect the law-abiding and contributing members of your society from criminals and other evil-doers? What does society gain by having you as its member? Your deeds, or lack thereof, are what matters. All the rest are just prejudices and bigotry."

"Wow." Ell-rom leaned back. "That's such a clear definition of worth. I need to remember it for when I'm in the position to actually contribute. Right now, I'm only a burden."

She smiled. "We all need help from time to time, and some need more help than others, and that's okay. It's not going to be long before your health is restored, and even if you don't regain any more memories, you can learn everything you need to know anew and find your own way to contribute. Being immortal, time is irrelevant."

Vanessa's words eased a knot in his chest, and for the first time in days, he felt like he could take a full breath.

As they continued working through his thoughts, challenging and reframing them, Ell-rom's perspective was reshaped. He could see how negative thoughts had been feeding his anxiety.

"Now," Vanessa said, "I want to introduce you to a technique called systematic desensitization. We'll create a hierarchy of situations related to blood, starting with the least anxiety-provoking and working our way up. Then, we will pair each situation with relaxation techniques. Regrettably, we don't have any blood around to practice with, so it would have to be a thought experiment." She frowned. "Here is an idea. We can start with synthetic blood. It has the same properties as the real thing, but knowing it didn't come from a person or an animal might make it easier for you to tolerate the smell. I'll talk to Julian about getting some for you."

Ell-rom winced. "I hope you are not expecting me to drink it. No amount of talking could convince me to do that."

"Eventually, you'll have to taste it, or you won't be able to bite anyone. I'm talking about a lick, not a sip."

The revulsion surged up again, but he managed to push it back. "I'll think about it while doing the breathing exercises."

"Excellent," Vanessa said. "I also want you to do some positive visualization. Imagine yourself calmly and confidently handling situations involving blood. The mind is more powerful than you think, Ell-rom, and this can help prepare you for real-life exposures."

"I'll try. Thank you for spending so much time with me. It was more helpful than I ever expected."

Vanessa smiled. "I'm glad I could help. I'll talk to Julian later and schedule another video call, this time with a cup of synthetic blood at the ready." She lifted her hand. "It was a pleasure to get to know you, and I'm looking forward to our next session." She ended the call before he could tell her that the pleasure was all his.

20

JASMINE

As Jasmine waited for Ell-rom to be done with his session, she made the mistake of scrolling through social media. She'd wanted some mindless entertainment with a little bit of news, but that little news was enough to ruin her good mood after talking with Edgar and hearing how happy he was with Angelica.

The world was falling apart, and she doubted that the immortals with Annani at the helm would be able to save it. They had done it before, more than once, but the world used to be a much smaller place and not as interconnected as it was now. Everything was happening faster and, regrettably, not for the better.

That crazy idea of a colony on Mars suddenly seemed very appealing to her. The murderous primitive barbarians were only capable of slaughter and destruction.

They would never develop interplanetary travel capability.

The problem with that fantasy was that some idiots would no doubt decide it was a good idea to bring them along to Mars because even murderous primitive barbarians needed representation. It was ridiculous, but then so many things were these days.

The world no longer made sense to her.

Jasmine was so lost in thought that she barely registered the sound of the door opening.

Ell-rom entered, leaning on the walker, gave her a ghost of a smile, and settled into the chair next to her. His gaze fixed on Morelle; he didn't say a word, and the silence stretched between them, heavy with unspoken questions.

Julian had told her not to ask Ell-rom about his session with the therapist and to wait until he confided in her of his own volition, but she couldn't bear the silence.

"Is everything okay?"

He turned to her and nodded. "I spoke with Vanessa, the clan's therapist. She had a lot of good advice for me."

Jasmine desperately wanted to ask what the advice was about, but remembering Julian's words, she opted for a neutral response. "I'm glad you found the session helpful."

Ell-rom studied her face for a moment, his brow

furrowed. "Aren't you curious to hear what I needed help with?"

Jasmine took a deep breath. "Of course I'm curious, but I don't want to pry. I'm waiting for you to tell me when you're comfortable doing so."

Relief washed over Ell-rom's features as if he had been expecting a different reaction. Had he thought Julian had betrayed his trust and told her what the session was about?

Ell-rom should have known that Julian would never do that.

He let out a long breath, his shoulders sagging. "You are right. I didn't want to tell you about the problem I have, but now that Vanessa has given me tools to possibly overcome it, I feel more hopeful."

Jasmine frowned. "What problem? Did you tell her about the dream where you…" She looked up at the camera. "Where you did that thing with your mind that the head priestess confronted you about?"

His big blue eyes widened. "No, I wouldn't…" He looked at the camera. "It's about my aversion to blood. I didn't know how strong it was until last night when I couldn't bring myself to bite you."

It was Jasmine's turn to be taken aback. "I thought that it was just too much, too soon for you. That you weren't ready."

But then it suddenly made sense to her when she remembered the other dream Ell-rom had told her about, the one about drinking blood by mistake and puking his guts out.

No wonder that he had such a strong aversion to it. He'd experienced a traumatic event associated with blood.

"It's because of what happened with the goblet, right?"

Ell-rom nodded. "That was probably the trigger, and I didn't realize how bad the aversion was until last night."

Jasmine reached out, taking his hand in hers. "What advice did Vanessa give you?"

Ell-rom's shoulders slumped at her touch. "She suggested several techniques. Breathing exercises to help manage anxiety, cognitive restructuring to challenge negative thoughts, and something called systematic desensitization."

"Systematic desensitization?" Jasmine repeated the unfamiliar term.

"It's a method of gradually exposing myself to what I fear, paired with relaxation techniques," Ell-rom explained. "We're going to start small, maybe just looking at pictures of blood, and work our way up slowly."

Jasmine nodded. "That sounds like a solid plan. Did Vanessa give you any exercises to practice?"

"Yes," Ell-rom said, sounding a little more confident. "I'm supposed to practice the breathing exercises daily and try positive visualization—imagining myself calmly handling situations involving blood. Julian is going to get some synthetic blood for me to use in the exposure therapy. Vanessa thinks it might be easier for me to tolerate initially."

"I think it's a great idea."

Ell-rom smiled, the first genuine smile she'd seen from him since he entered the room. "I'm hopeful, which is a big improvement over how I felt before talking to Vanessa."

Jasmine tilted her head. "Why didn't you tell me? You should know by now that you can tell me anything."

He averted his eyes. "I've been so worried about letting you down. Biting should be such a basic function for a male of my kind, and being unable to do that felt emasculating."

"Oh, sweetheart." Jasmine squeezed Ell-rom's hand. "You could never let me down. For every problem, there is a solution as long as we are willing to put in the work, right? We are a good team."

A small smile lifted the corner of his lips. "What did I ever do to deserve you?"

"You don't need to do anything other than being your wonderful self."

He shook his head. "That doesn't seem like enough, especially in my current state."

"None of that." She cast him a stern look. "Remember what Vanessa said about challenging negative thoughts?

You are good enough to deserve happiness. Never doubt that."

It would take time, though.

The plan sounded solid, but Jasmine had a feeling that a venom bite wasn't in her immediate future. It was somewhat disappointing, but she had no problem waiting for it.

"Thank you for telling me." Jasmine leaned her head on Ell-rom's shoulder. "I know it must have been difficult to do."

He nodded. "It was. A Kra-ell afraid of blood seems so ridiculous."

"You are only part Kra-ell, and you can't tolerate it. That does not equate to being afraid of it." She lifted her head and offered him her lips.

21

MARINA

The Sunday morning sun filtered through the leaves of the trees surrounding the house, casting dappled shadows on the front porch. Marina stood at the window, watching a pair of birds flit between branches.

The house felt empty without Peter and Alfie, even depressing despite how nice it was. At first she had welcomed the solitude, using the time to clean and tidy up the place. But now, with every surface gleaming and not a speck of dust to be found, restlessness began to set in.

Usually Peter had Sundays off, but he was on duty today, attending a meeting with the Guardian chief and his team. They were planning a rescue operation for trafficking victims that had to be done tonight before the victims were shipped out to other destinations.

Marina's heart swelled with pride at the thought of Peter's work, but it also tightened with worry. Even though she knew he was incredibly capable, the dangers he faced never failed to concern her.

"I need to get out of here," she muttered to herself.

After putting her shoes on, she grabbed her bag and headed out the door.

The village walkways were quiet but not deserted. Marina nodded and smiled at the few people she passed by, and it felt nice to be smiled at in return. Thanks to her work at the café, everyone knew her by now, and other than Borga, she hadn't had problems with anyone.

For all the purebloods and many of the hybrids, visits to the café were rare because they mainly subsisted on blood. Only a few of them had a taste for coffee, and she was glad of it. Most of them still regarded her as a second-class citizen, and she was sick of being treated like that.

The café was closed on the weekend, but she could get something from the vending machines. She wasn't thirsty or hungry, but she would get something so she didn't look weird as she engaged in her favorite activity of people-watching.

It had always been a soothing activity for her, a way to quiet her mind when it became too noisy with worries and what-ifs.

Marina made her way to the vending machines and selected a cappuccino and an egg sandwich. With her purchases in hand, she chose a table at the back of the seating area, positioning herself for the best view of the comings and goings.

There wasn't much activity this early on a weekend morning, so when Bridget arrived and headed toward the vending machines, Marina raised her hand in a friendly wave, which was returned with a warm smile.

After getting a coffee and pastry, Bridget surprised Marina when she came over to her table. "Mind if I join you?" she asked.

"Please," Marina said, gesturing to the empty chair across from her.

Bridget settled into the seat, taking a sip of her coffee before speaking. "How are you acclimating to life in the village, Marina?"

"I love it here," she said earnestly. "Working at the café, the relaxed atmosphere, the sense of community—it's all wonderful. But do you know what the best part is?" She leaned in as if sharing a secret. "The feeling of safety. I know that nothing bad is going to happen to me here. It's incredible."

Bridget's eyebrows rose. "Were you worried about your safety in Safe Haven?"

Marina shrugged. "Safe Haven was pretty secure, but people are people, you know? As a woman, I always felt a certain level of vulnerability. But here..." She gestured around them. "Everyone knows I'm with Peter, so all the Guardians treat me like I'm under their protection. It's like having a hundred lethal soldiers for brothers. No one would dare to harm me."

Bridget nodded. "Feeling safe can make a world of difference. I'm glad you've acclimated and feel so at home here." She paused, taking a bite of her pastry before asking, "How are things going with Peter?"

A mix of emotions flitted across Marina's heart--joy and love, but also a touch of uncertainty. "Peter is amazing, and I'm thankful for every moment I spend with him. We are so well matched." She took a sip from her coffee before deciding to confide in Bridget. "He even proposed, and he wants me to start planning a wedding. But I'm hesitant."

"Why is that?" Bridget prompted.

Marina bit her lip, considering her words carefully. "It's mostly about our lifespans." She took a deep breath, steeling herself to ask the question that had been nagging at her. "Bridget, can I ask you something? As a physician?"

"Of course."

"Will being with an immortal who bites me nearly every night extend my lifespan? And if so, by how much?"

Bridget's eyes sparkled with interest. "That's actually a very interesting question, Marina. I haven't given it much thought before because none of our males had ever spent a significant time with a human female who was not a Dormant."

The clan's physician tapped her fingers on the table. "It's certainly worth investigating. The venom has healing properties, and regular exposure could potentially have cumulative effects..." She trailed off, lost in thought for a moment before refocusing on Marina. "Would you be willing to come to the clinic with me? I'd like to take some blood and tissue samples. If you are game, you can be the first subject in the study of the effects of venom on human longevity."

Marina nodded. "Of course. I'd be happy to help, and if you are interested in another subject, Lusha has started dating Alfie, and I can ask her to join your study."

"Lusha has mixed genetics with some Kra-ell in her, so her results might be different than yours, but I'll gladly investigate her case as well. After I take today's sample, I want you to stop by the clinic on Friday for another round, and if Lusha is game, she can come with you. I might not be there, but I'll leave instructions with the nurse."

22

SYSSI

S yssi stood in front of the full-length mirror, smoothing down the front of her dress. The soft, flowing fabric hugged her curves in all the right places, a far cry from the more practical outfits she usually wore to the university or around the house.

She wanted to dress up for the occasion of introducing Ell-rom to the rest of the family.

It felt like a significant step for the future of the clan, but she couldn't articulate what made her think that. Ell-rom didn't seem like the type of guy who reshaped futures. He was pleasant and intelligent, but he wasn't charismatic or possessed of any of the other qualities she'd come to associate with a leader.

Ell-rom wasn't Kian.

Not that anyone could be like her husband, but Ell-rom wasn't like Annani or Sari either. He just didn't have that extra something.

Then again, he was still basically a baby, finding out who he was, so it wasn't fair to judge him. After all, Kian had also been a sweet, naive boy before his mother had started training him to be a leader.

"You look beautiful," Kian said from behind her as he wrapped his arms around her waist, pressing a kiss to her neck.

Syssi leaned back into his embrace. "Thank you." She looked at his face in the mirror, her heart swelling with love. "You look as dashing as the first time I saw you."

It seemed like a lifetime ago that she had met Kian and moved into the penthouse with him, and yet the memories were as vivid as ever. The nervousness of their first encounters, the thrill of falling in love, and the passion of their early days together still burned with the same ferocity but also with a level of comfort and familiarity that could have only grown over time.

She could let go with Kian and feel perfectly safe, knowing that not only would he never hurt her, but that he would do everything for her.

"What's that faraway look about?" He nuzzled her neck.

"I was just thinking about the penthouse and our early days as a couple."

Kian's eyebrows rose. "Feeling nostalgic?"

She turned in his arms to face him, her hands resting on his chest. "A little. It's where our relationship started. The penthouse will always hold a special place in my heart."

Kian shrugged. "I don't miss it at all, to be honest. I love it here in the village."

Syssi playfully swatted his arm. "Where is your sense of romance?"

"Hey," Kian protested with a chuckle, "I never claimed to have one. You're the one who has been trying to convince me for the past five years that I am a romantic."

"That's because you are." Syssi rose on her tiptoes to plant a quick kiss on his lips. "You're romantic in all the ways that count. I love you more than life itself."

Kian's expression softened, his eyes filled with a warmth that never failed to make Syssi's heart skip a beat. He cupped her face in his hands, drawing her in for a deep, passionate kiss that left her breathless.

They were so blessed to have each other and Allegra.

It pained her that Annani had been robbed of her blessing when Khiann had been taken away from her only a few months into their relationship. They hadn't even had the chance to create a child together, and all of her children had been sired by human fathers.

If the prophecy Annani had been given was true, though, she would have two more children, and Syssi had a gut feeling that those children would be fathered by Khiann.

It could be just wishful thinking on her part. She wanted that for Annani as much as she wanted to have more children with Kian.

A wave of guilt washed over Syssi.

She had promised to summon a vision about Khiann's fate, and she'd been putting it off, fearing what she might see, but she couldn't delay any longer.

Leaning away, she looked into Kian's eyes. "Today, after we return from lunch, I will attempt to summon a vision about Khiann. It's not fair of me to drag my feet about it and leave your mother in suspense."

Kian's big body tensed. "You don't need to rush. You'll be tired after the get-together, and you shouldn't summon a vision when you are low on energy."

"I'll be fine. Allegra will probably fall asleep on the way home and keep sleeping when we get her to her crib." She put a hand over her chest. "Postponing the inevitable just weighs me down and stresses me. I don't want to wait any longer."

She could see the concern in Kian's eyes, the worry he always felt when she opened herself up to the visions. But there was understanding there, too. He knew how important this was.

"Alright," he agreed reluctantly. "I'll watch over you, making sure you're safe."

"Thank you. I wouldn't have it any other way."

A soft babble from the baby monitor interrupted their moment. Allegra was awake from her morning nap, right on schedule.

"I'll get her," Kian offered, pressing a quick kiss to Syssi's forehead before heading to the nursery.

Syssi followed, leaning against the doorframe as she watched Kian lift their daughter from her crib. At eleven months old, Allegra was a bundle of energy and curiosity. Her chubby hands reached for Kian's face, patting his cheeks as she leaned in and kissed the tip of his nose.

"Dada."

"Hello, sweetness," Kian cooed, bouncing her gently. "Are you ready for a little trip?"

"Nana?" Allegra's eyes lit up with excitement at the prospect of going out.

"Yes, sweetheart. We are going with Nana, Auntie Amanda, and Auntie Alena, Evie, and E.T. and their daddies. Uncle Toven and Aunt Mia are coming as well."

Syssi stepped forward, running a hand over Allegra's soft curls. "Let's get you dressed, sweetie. We're going to meet a new family member today. Uncle Ell-rom."

Allegra tried to repeat the name and got frustrated when nothing she said sounded even remotely close.

"Try saying Rom," Kian suggested.

"Om."

"Good enough." Kian handed her to Syssi.

Allegra seemed satisfied with the compromise and didn't even fuss about the dress Syssi chose for her.

"Wow, that must be a first," Syssi murmured under her breath. "Let's see if we get as lucky with the shoes."

Kian walked over to Allegra's closet and pulled out a pair of black patent leather Mary Janes with rhinestones on the buckles. "She never says no to these."

"Of course she doesn't." Syssi took the shoes from him and put them on their daughter's socked feet. "The shinier, the better."

23

ELL-ROM

The two Odus toiling in the kitchen and dining area fascinated Ell-rom. They had arrived unescorted, with bags full of groceries, and had gotten straight to preparing the meal for the upcoming family gathering. They worked efficiently and silently, never bumping into each other or getting in each other's way but still dividing the tasks between them in a coordinated dance.

Despite not exchanging a single word between them, Ell-rom had the distinct impression they were communicating on some subliminal level.

They didn't wear earpieces, and he wondered if they had been programmed to understand the Kra-ell language. Curiosity getting the better of him, he decided to conduct a little experiment and approached one of the Odus, who was arranging a dish on the counter.

"Excuse me," Ell-rom said, "Could you tell me what is in this dish?"

The Odu turned to him, bowing deeply before launching into an explanation. Obviously, he had understood the question that had been presented in Kra-ell, but Ell-rom couldn't be sure what language the Odu was responding in. The translation earpieces he wore were doing their job so flawlessly that the Odu could be speaking English, and he heard Kra-ell.

The interaction reinforced Ell-rom's growing awareness of how dependent he'd become on the translation technology. He wore the earpieces constantly, even to bed, because he didn't want to wake up in the middle of the night and not be able to understand Jasmine. She did the same, wearing her earpieces at all times. They were so comfortable that it was easy to forget that they were even there, but they were a crutch, not a solution.

"There you are," Jasmine said from behind him.

As he turned to look at her, his breath caught in his throat. She looked stunning in a dress that hugged her curves perfectly. She'd done something to her hair so that it cascaded down her shoulders in big, bouncy waves, and her lips were painted blood red.

He wondered if she had done that on purpose as part of his exposure therapy.

If that had been her intention, it was brilliant because there was nothing unappealing about those red-painted lips, and all he could think about was kissing them.

Jasmine laughed and did a little twirl in place. "You like?"

"You look absolutely stunning."

Jasmine's smile widened. "Thank you." She sauntered closer to him. "How are you doing? Nervous about meeting the family?"

"A little," he admitted. "But if Annani's daughters are as filled with light as her son, I'm sure I'll enjoy their company as much as I do Kian and his wife's."

Jasmine's eyebrows rose at his words. "Filled with light? That's an interesting way to put it." She glanced at the Odus, then back to Ell-rom. "Can you sense them? I mean, like you sensed light in Kian and darkness in Jade?"

He winced. "Those are just expressions. They don't mean that Kian is good and Jade is bad. Everyone has both light and darkness in them, and they take turns manifesting. Some have more of one than the other, but you are overestimating my ability to sense them. It's not a talent. It's just an instinctual sense."

Jasmine leaned closer to him. "As I said before, not everyone has that sense. Just try. I'm curious."

Ell-rom closed his eyes and turned his focus inward. "It's faint. They're machines, so there isn't much in there, but they are not entirely artificial. I can sense some emergent self-awareness in them, and they think of themselves as good, helpful, and needed, but I might be projecting my own feelings on them, so I wouldn't base any important decisions on what I've just said."

"Fascinating. What about Kian's bodyguards? What did you sense about them?"

"Like everyone else, they have both light and darkness in them. The blond guy lets his darkness manifest more, but I sense more light than darkness in both."

Jasmine frowned. "They're warriors, Ell-rom. I know for a fact they've killed people. Frankie saw them do that."

"They did what needed to be done to protect others. They're protectors, not killers. Kian is like that, too." Ell-rom shrugged. "All able-bodied males need to protect the vulnerable members of the community. If they are incapable of doing that, what are they good for?"

As soon as he asked the question, Ell-rom felt a wave of self-consciousness wash over him. He was acutely aware of his own lack of defensive or offensive capabilities. He was physically weak, and he couldn't even bite. "What am I good for?" he murmured.

"Oh, Ell-rom." Jasmine reached for his hand. "Not every male needs to be a warrior. That's why people live in a society and divide tasks between individuals based on their aptitude. Maybe you were meant to be a spiritual leader? Or a healer? Or a poet? And even if you were meant to be a warrior, you still have a long way to go till you are fully recovered. Once you're feeling stronger, you could start training with the Guardians. I could even arrange that for you if you'd like."

"I think every male should be able to defend his family, even if he is a poet or a healer. I don't know yet what the future holds for me, but I have to be able to do that, or I won't feel worthy."

Before Jasmine could respond, the doorbell rang, and one of the Odus rushed to open the door.

"Good afternoon, Clan Mother." He bowed nearly in half. "The luncheon is ready."

"Thank you, Ogidu." Annani glided into the living room with Kian and Syssi right behind her.

Kian had his little daughter in his arms, a beautiful child who looked like her mother but had her father's piercing gaze.

Kian's bodyguards entered next, which Ell-rom found curious. Shouldn't they have entered first and secured the place for their Clan Mother?

Evidently, he wasn't considered a threat.

Ell-rom bowed, and next to him, Jasmine did the same but with much more flourish.

"Ell-rom, my dear brother," Annani said warmly as she embraced him. "How are you feeling today?"

"I'm well, thank you. I'm excited to meet everyone." He shifted his gaze to the little girl. "I haven't been introduced to this little lady yet."

"This is our daughter, Allegra," Kian said.

"Lala," the baby said with a surprisingly resolute tone while still regarding Ell-rom with her piercing eyes.

"Remember me?" Jasmine walked over to her and kissed her cheek.

"Jaja." Allegra patted Jasmine's face before shifting her gaze back to Ell-rom.

"I can't believe she remembered my name," Jasmine said.

Syssi smiled proudly. "Allegra has a great memory for names. People fascinate her."

Ell-rom took the child's tiny hand between two fingers and bowed over it. "I'm Ell-rom. Your uncle," he said before he remembered that Allegra wasn't wearing earpieces and couldn't understand him.

"Om," she said with the same resolute tone she'd used for her own name.

Evidently, she'd understood at least some of what he'd said, probably from his tone of voice.

"You can call me Om. Can I call you Lala?"

She gave him a bright smile as if she understood every word. "Lala."

"She likes you." Annani threaded her arm through his. "She doesn't allow anyone other than close family to call her Lala."

24

JASMINE

J asmine stood back as Ell-rom was introduced to the rest of the family.

She knew Amanda, Dalhu, and little Evie, having met them before, but her eyes were drawn to the tiny bundle in Alena's arms. Alena's newborn son, barely a week old, was swaddled tightly in a soft blue blanket.

Sensing Jasmine's gaze, Alena turned towards her with a warm smile. "Would you like to hold him?"

Jasmine felt a flutter of panic in her chest. "Oh, I... I'm not sure..." she stammered, but Alena was already gently transferring the baby into her arms.

"His name is Evander, but Allegra calls him E.T."

"Little E.T.," Jasmine chuckled. "You are so sweet."

The weight of the newborn in her arms was both lighter and more substantial than she had expected. She held her breath, terrified of making any sudden movements.

The baby's face was so tiny, his features perfectly formed but miniature. She had never held a baby this small before, and the responsibility felt overwhelming but also curiously rewarding. She was holding a new life in her arms, a little boy who would one day be a man, and if she became part of this marvelous family, she would get to watch him grow and discover who he was along the way.

"Support his head like this." Alena adjusted Jasmine's arms.

"He's beautiful, perfect in every way." She shifted her gaze to Alena. "Is that okay to say, or is it considered bad luck to say good things about a newborn?"

"It's okay. I tell him the same things a hundred times a day. My little precious Evander."

Jasmine nodded and smiled, and after a few more moments, carefully handed the baby back to Alena.

The arrival of Toven and Mia drew Jasmine's attention. She watched as they were introduced to Ell-rom, struck once again by the stark difference between gods like Annani and Toven and the ones she had traveled with to Tibet—Aru, Negal, and Dagor.

They were all gods, yes, but Annani and Toven exuded a presence that was almost palpable. It wasn't just their physical appearance, though they were undeniably beautiful. There was something more, a sense of power and ancientness that seemed to radiate from them.

Was it a matter of genetics or heritage?

Were Annani and Toven simply born more powerful, or had their experiences shaped them into these awe-inspiring beings?

Ell-rom wouldn't know, but maybe Aru could answer that for her. He'd said something about royals being different from commoners, but even with her fascination with princes, Jasmine didn't hold monarchs in any special regard. They were people like everyone else, who had just happened to be born into a royal family.

As everyone settled around the large dining table, Jasmine took her seat next to Ell-rom. The Odus moved silently around them, serving dishes that looked and smelled divine, but despite the mouthwatering aromas and the distinguished gathered guests, Jasmine's thoughts drifted to Margo and her brother.

She pictured them sitting in a café across the street from where Lynda and her ex were meeting, and her heart ached for Rob even though she had never met him. He was about to have his world turned upside down and experience an avalanche of emotional pain.

"Jasmine?" Ell-rom's hand tightened around hers. "Are you okay?"

She blinked, realizing she must have been frowning. "Yes. I was just thinking about Margo and her brother," she whispered.

Ell-rom's eyes widened in understanding, a look of sympathy crossing his face as he nodded.

Amanda, who was seated across from them, leaned in, her eyes sparkling with interest. "What's that about Margo and her brother?"

Damn. She should have realized that with the immortals' incredible hearing, whispering was futile. It was impossible to communicate anything in secret.

Jasmine smiled apologetically. "It's a private matter, and I don't want to gossip."

"Well, that's a shame." Amanda pursed her lips. "I love juicy gossip, but I respect your reluctance to divulge Margo's secrets."

As the meal progressed, Jasmine relaxed, drawn into the warm atmosphere of family togetherness. She watched with growing pleasure as Kian's sisters engaged Ell-rom in conversation, their initial curiosity giving way to genuine interest and affection. It was incredible how quickly Ell-rom was being integrated into the family.

Annani, who was seated at the head of the table, turned to coo at Allegra, who was reaching out for her grandmother with chubby hands.

"Nana," she demanded.

Annani's face lit up with joy. "Come to Nana, sweetness."

Kian handed the baby over, and Annani sat Allegra on her lap so she faced Ell-rom and Jasmine.

"Om. Jaja."

Ell-rom waved his hand and smiled. "You are a remark-able young lady, Allegra."

"She is," Kian agreed. "Her memory for names is very uncommon for a child her age."

Annani looked at her granddaughter and then shifted her gaze to Ell-rom with the same love and approval in her eyes.

Jasmine's heart swelled. Surrounded by the warmth and love of this incredible family, she felt a sense of belonging she'd never experienced before.

As unbelievable and surreal as it felt, she knew this was where she was always meant to be.

Jasmine had never felt like she belonged in her father's house, and she couldn't remember if things had been different when her mother was alive.

What had happened to her mother?

Now that Jasmine had powerful friends, perhaps she could finally find out.

25

KIAN

Kian watched with quiet satisfaction as his sisters engaged Ell-rom in conversation. Amanda peppered him with questions about his experiences since waking and whether physical therapy had helped with his memories. Alena just listened, occasionally interjecting with her own inquiries, but Dalhu and Orion didn't say much and were content to let their mates talk and get to know their new uncle.

He was glad that his sisters seemed to like Ell-rom, mostly for his mother's sake. It was important to her that her family accepted her brother.

The penthouse was alive with the buzz of family. His mother's Odus moved unobtrusively among them, refilling glasses and clearing plates. The rich aroma of the gourmet meal lingered in the air, mingling with the scent of fresh flowers adorning the center of the table that he had no doubt the Odus brought along with all the ingredients for the meal they'd prepared.

He still remembered the days when this dining room was rarely used, mostly because he'd hated entertaining and also because his mother and Alena were in Alaska, and Amanda lived in her own condo near the university. None of them had mates, and the only time there had been gatherings of any kind in his penthouse apartment was when he had been hosting a council meeting.

A lot had changed during the last five years, and it had all started with Syssi. He reached for her hand under the table and gave it a little squeeze.

She turned to him. "Is everything okay?"

He nodded. "I went down memory lane when this dining room was never used, and I'm so grateful for all the blessings the Fates bestowed on us, but mostly I'm grateful for you." He lifted her hand and kissed her knuckles. "You made my life worth living."

As his sisters and mother all oohed and ahhed, Orion and Dalhu nodded in agreement while Toven and Mia exchanged knowing smiles, and Ell-rom and Jasmine had twin looks of surprise on their faces.

They didn't know him as well as the rest of those present did, and they had never seen him go all mushy over his love for his wife. He usually refrained from making such grand gestures in front of anyone other than his close family.

Across the table, Amanda grinned like a Cheshire cat. "And to think that I had to work so hard to convince you to meet Syssi. I knew you were meant for each other as soon as I finished running my tests on her."

"What kind of tests?" Ell-rom asked.

Amanda gave him a quick overview of her research on paranormal abilities and then waxed poetic about Syssi's incredible results.

"Regrettably, I didn't find any more strong talents among my test subjects." Amanda sighed. "But the Fates have kept sending us Dormants with powers I have never imagined. We have one lady who can tether her consciousness to that of another and spy on them; her sister can hear echoes of conversations embedded in walls, and Mia is an enhancer. She can make any other paranormal talent stronger."

As he glanced at Mia, a look of apprehension flitted over Ell-rom's face, but he schooled his expression so fast that Kian wasn't sure he had seen it.

Why would Ell-rom fear Mia's talent?

Was he hiding a talent of his own that he was afraid she might inadvertently enhance?

"How do you do that?" Ell-rom asked her. "Do you need to concentrate? Touch the person? How does the enhancing work?"

Mia shrugged. "I just need to be close to them. The closer, the better." She chuckled. "In Karelia, Toven carried me on his back in a special harness, so that was really close."

"I was carried in a harness as well," Jasmine said. "I twisted my ankle when we were searching for the pod, and Negal carried me on his back, but it didn't benefit him in any way. It was a pure act of charity on his part. I don't have any enhancing powers. I can hold a scrying stick, though, and point it in the right direction." She demonstrated with a pretend stick, getting several laughs.

As a conversation about tarot and other Wicca para-phernalia continued for a few moments, Kian observed Ell-rom. The guy tried to look amused or interested, but Kian had the impression that he was scared.

Perhaps it was time to have a one-on-one talk with his new uncle and see what he was so afraid of.

"By the way," Amanda said. "Has there been any response to the announcement on the bulletin board? Did anyone come forward?"

Kian shook his head. "The last time I checked, there was nothing. But I can check again if you'd like."

"Please do," their mother said.

Kian pulled out his phone, navigated to the village's digital bulletin board, and as he scrolled through the recent posts, he frowned. "There are no confessions, but there are a lot of negative comments. Many are pointing fingers at the Kra-ell."

As a palpable tension settled over the table, Syssi placed a comforting hand on his arm. "You can't make everyone happy all of the time. There will always be voices of dissent."

"The integration isn't going as smoothly as we'd hoped," Toven said.

Kian leaned back in his chair, taking Syssi's hand with him. "I'm not great at all this social stuff. I thought that providing everyone a nice place to live and supplying them with all they needed would do the trick, but apparently, that's not enough. If anyone has ideas for how to make it work better, I'm all ears." He cast a side-long glance at Amanda, who was supposed to have been organizing social activities that incorporated the Kra-ell.

"I must apologize," she said. "I haven't had time to arrange the get-togethers between clan members and Kra-ell as we discussed, and I have also encountered a couple of obstacles that I'm not sure what to do about."

"Such as?" Kian prompted.

"Well, for one, the age disparity. The Kra-ell have many young adults and older teenagers, while our clan has very few in that age range. Those we do have are all mated and... well, not as interested in the kinds of activities young people typically enjoy."

Kian nodded. "And the other one?"

"The food barrier. Humans and immortals often bond over shared meals, like barbecues, wine and cheese nights, etc., but half of the Kra-ell can't participate in any of that because they only drink blood." She snorted. "If they were to mingle while holding goblets filled with blood, it would further alienate the immortals instead of bringing them closer."

Ell-rom made a gagging sound and reached for a glass of water while Jasmine looked at him with worry in her eyes.

Kian tapped his fingers on the table. "Even the pure-bloods can process alcohol. What about arranging get-togethers at Atzil's pub? It's neutral ground, and everyone can partake in drinks."

Amanda's eyes lit up. "That's a great idea. I can work with that."

"I have a different perspective to offer," Toven inter-jected. "Perhaps it would have been better to segregate the groups from the start. Let the Kra-ell govern them-selves independently. They've lived under Igor's thumb for so long, chafing for freedom. Now, they have the clan imposing restrictions on them. It's not surprising there's friction."

Kian shook his head. "We considered that. I offered Jade and her people the option of returning to Karelia and living in their former compound. They declined."

Toven put his wine glass down. "Maybe it's time for Jade to call another assembly and have them vote again. Some might have changed their minds after experi-encing life in the village."

From the corner of his eye, Kian saw Ell-rom shaking his head. He no longer looked like he was about to gag, so Kian felt it was okay to engage him in the conversation.

"What's your opinion, Ell-rom?" he asked.

Ell-rom looked surprised at being addressed, but he composed himself quickly. "I'm not sure I can offer an opinion. I don't know either person well enough yet. But thinking about it logically, a tiny number of immortals and an even tinier number of Kra-ell stand a better chance of surviving together than apart. Jasmine tells me that there are eight billion humans on the planet, and if they ever discovered the aliens living among them, it would be very dangerous. It seems to me that it's in everyone's best interest to find a way to coexist peacefully. United, you're stronger. Divided, you're more vulnerable."

Despite his amnesia, the prince showed a keen mind for strategy, and Kian admired his confidence to voice his opinion. "Ell-rom's right. Safety is the overriding factor here. We need to remind everyone of that."

He leaned forward, a decision crystallizing in his mind. "I think it's time to call a grand assembly and address every resident of the village. I need to remind them why we're living in hiding."

"It's a good start," Toven said. "Combined with other initiatives, like the pub gatherings and more joint training sessions between the Guardians and the Kra-ell warriors, people might start seeing each other as individuals, not as 'us' and 'them.'"

26

ELL-ROM

When the last of the family members filed out of the penthouse, their voices fading as Jasmine closed the door behind them, Ell-rom felt a wave of exhaustion wash over him. The luncheon had been filled with warmth and acceptance, but it had also been draining. He leaned against the wall, trying to steady himself as a faint dizziness threatened to overtake him.

Jasmine approached him with concern etched on her face. "Everyone is heading down to see Morelle. Do you want to join them?"

Ell-rom shook his head, forcing a weak smile. "I think I need a few minutes to rest. Besides, there's not enough space in her room for everyone to gather around her. I'll go later after I've had a chance to recover a bit."

Jasmine nodded. "Do you want to lie down?"

"Actually," Ell-rom said, his gaze drifting to the floor-to-ceiling windows, "I'd like to go out onto the terrace and absorb some sun."

He needed the sunlight to chase away the darkness in his soul.

After the panic he had felt when Mia's talent had been explained to him, he had tried not to show how afraid he was of her enhancing his killing ability, which no one other than Jasmine knew about.

"Of course. Let's get you out there." Jasmine wrapped her arm around his middle, steadying him and helping him walk.

He'd wanted to meet his extended family without leaning on a walker, and he had managed it, but now that he was so exhausted he needed something or someone to lean on, and right now, that someone was Jasmine.

His rock, his everything.

It was time that he told her how much he loved her, and if she said that it was too early and they hadn't known each other long enough, he would tell her that he was willing to wait until she realized that she loved him too, but he already knew that with absolute certainty. He didn't need any more time.

As the glass doors slid open silently, and the warm afternoon air enveloped them, Ell-rom took a long breath.

The terrace was a beautiful space with a breathtaking view of the city. A row of comfortable loungers faced the narrow pool, and green planters added splashes of color to the tiled floor.

Jasmine guided him to one of the loungers, and as he sank into it, he felt some of the tension leave his body. The sun's warmth on his skin was soothing and grounding, and as he had expected, it chased away the specter of death, which he supposedly could wield with a thought.

"What's the matter?" Jasmine asked, settling into the lounger next to him. "You did so well during lunch, and then something changed. You look troubled."

Ell-rom closed his eyes for a moment, gathering his thoughts. When he opened them again, he turned to face Jasmine. "I was terrified to shake Mia's hand," he confessed.

Jasmine's brow furrowed. "Mia? Why?"

"Because of what her talent might do to mine. I don't need my ability enhanced." He put a hand over his forehead. "I don't know how to control it."

"You don't even know it's real. It could have been just a nightmare or a memory that got twisted in your dream."

"But the fear feels very real."

Jasmine was quiet for a moment, her thumb tracing soothing circles on the back of his hand. Then, to his surprise, a mischievous glint appeared in her eye. "You know, even if it's true that you can kill with a thought, it's not all bad. Consider the positive side. The clan could use you in combination with Mia to remotely eliminate their enemies. And who knows? Maybe you could even kill the Eternal King with a thought. Wouldn't that be extraordinary?"

Ell-rom recoiled. "Jasmine! How can you say such a thing?" He pulled his hand away, pushing himself up on the lounger. "I don't know how this so-called talent works, so I cannot be used like a precision weapon to kill just the evildoers. I have no way to test this ability, either, because I'm not willing to kill someone just to see if it works and, if it does, who it works on. Besides, I don't want to kill anyone."

Jasmine's smile faded, replaced by a more serious expression. "Says the man who just earlier today told me that he feels inadequate because he is not strong enough yet to protect people. Did you already forget?"

Ell-rom felt his cheeks warm in embarrassment. After Julian had explained how the venom bite could incapacitate an opponent and put a male in stasis, Ell-rom hadn't even considered having to kill anyone. As long as they posed no further threat to those he loved, the final kill blow was not needed.

"I didn't forget. But can't I protect my community without killing someone? Wouldn't putting them in stasis be enough?"

Her eyes softened. "I know the prospect of killing is not a pleasant thought, Ell-rom, but that's the reality of the world we live in. Fangs and venom might be effective one-on-one, but not if you are fighting multiple opponents or getting bombarded from the sky. Besides, some people are so evil that they not only deserve to be killed, but they need to be eliminated to save countless victims. Being idealistic and naive might feel good, but when you realize that you could have done something to save innocents from terrible cruelty and death and didn't do what was needed, I promise you that it won't feel so good anymore."

Her words hit Ell-rom like a physical blow. He felt a surge of anger, of hurt, but he pushed it down, not wanting to let Jasmine see how deeply she'd affected him. Instead, he swung his legs off the lounger, planting his feet on the terrace floor.

"I think I need to go to bed and rest," he said, his voice carefully neutral.

Jasmine's expression immediately softened. "Oh, Ell-rom, I'm sorry. I didn't mean to distress you. Do you want me to bring the walker?"

He nodded, not trusting himself to speak.

As Jasmine hurried inside to get the walker, Ell-rom remained on the terrace, his mind a whirlwind of conflicting emotions. The sun no longer felt warm and comforting. Instead, it seemed to beat down on him accusingly, as if disappointed in his weakness.

He thought back to the luncheon, to the way Kian and the others had spoken about protecting their community. He'd even voiced his opinion about them being stronger together than apart.

If he became part of their community, it would be his duty to protect them in any way he could.

The idea of using his ability in any fashion made him sick. It wasn't like fighting an opponent with his fists or his fangs or even with a sword or a staff. That seemed slightly more fair because the opponent could defend himself and attack in turn.

Killing from afar was the mark of an assassin.

It dawned on him then.

Dear Mother of All Life. That's precisely what I am.

An assassin.

JASMINE

As Jasmine helped Ell-rom settle into bed, she couldn't shake the feeling that something had shifted between them. His face, usually so open and warm, had closed off, a subtle tension lingering in the set of his jaw.

"Rest well." She tucked the blanket around him and kissed his forehead as if she could smooth away the discord with those simple, familiar acts of care.

Retreating from the room, she closed the door softly behind her and headed to the kitchen, where the Odus were putting the finishing touches on their cleanup in their silent, efficient manner.

The penthouse, which had been alive with laughter and conversation less than an hour ago, now felt oddly hollow.

"Thank you," she said as the Odus prepared to leave. "Everything was wonderful."

"You are most welcome, Mistress Jasmine," said the one on the left as they bowed in unison, their movements so synchronized it was almost eerie. "We shall see ourselves out."

The place was just as spotless as it had been before their arrival, and she had no doubt that the dining room was similarly immaculate.

It was nice to have robotic servants, and what was even more amazing was that human tech was catching up to science fiction, and a robot in every household was going to be the reality in the not-too-distant future.

Walking over to the bar, Jasmine surveyed the impressive collection of bottles and chose the one name she recognized. After pouring half a shot of Jack Daniels into a tall glass, she pulled out a can of ginger mixer from the small fridge, popped the lid, and poured it into the glass. When she added some ice cubes, the clink they made against the glass sounded unnaturally loud in the quiet space.

Jasmine leaned against the counter and took a long sip of the cocktail.

The look of horror on Ell-rom's face when she'd suggested using his ability as a weapon haunted her, and she winced, regretting mostly her bad timing, not the words themselves.

It was natural for him to abhor violence and to recoil at the idea of being used as a weapon for someone else's agenda. If she had his power, wouldn't she be just as horrified and scared?

Maybe, but to a much lesser extent.

She had life experience and was aware of all the horrible things happening to good people around the world. As much as the idea of killing repulsed her, she knew she'd be inclined to work on that aversion if her power could help save innocent lives. Ell-rom, though... well, he might look like an adult, but in many ways, he was like a child.

Jasmine set her glass down as a wave of guilt washed over her.

He had no memories, no real-world exposure, and he was naive, like a baby. Children weren't born killers. They didn't want to see anything die, not even a bug. It was the adults around them who had the power to eradicate that innate goodness and turn children into monsters.

Then again, she wasn't an expert.

She wasn't even a mother.

Maybe some kids were born with a predisposition towards violence. It was an interesting question, one she'd never really considered before. Maybe she could find a book about it, something with solid research backing it up, and not religious preaching or pseudo-science with an agenda to push, but real, empirical data.

Jasmine chuckled to herself, realizing how much she was starting to sound like her father. Maybe he hadn't been as extreme as she'd thought when she was a naive young girl herself. As an adult who had to earn a living and pay bills, she was seeing things through a different lens.

She lifted her hand and glanced at her watch. It was nearly four in the afternoon, and Margo's mission to expose Lynda's betrayal should have been over by now.

Was it too early to check?

Or was the fallout so bad that Margo couldn't contact her?

Curiosity getting the better of her, Jasmine pulled out her phone and typed out a simple message: *Updates?*

The response came a minute later, but to Jasmine it felt like forever. *Not yet.*

Jasmine let out a breath. Maybe Lynda hadn't shown up for lunch with her ex after all. Maybe she'd smartened up and told the guy that she was getting married in a few days, and it wasn't appropriate to keep seeing him like that.

On the one hand, it would save Rob a lot of heartache. But on the other, he'd miss out on his opportunity to become immortal. Jasmine didn't know what the clan's policy was, but she was quite sure they wouldn't allow him to bring his human wife to the village when they turned him immortal.

They would probably not allow Margo to even tell him that he was a Dormant.

A sharp knock on the door startled Jasmine from her thoughts.

For a moment, she thought it might be one of the lunch guests coming back for something they'd forgotten, but when she opened the door, she found herself face to face with Edgar.

"Edgar?" she said, surprise coloring her voice. "What are you doing here?"

He flashed her that familiar charming smile of his. "I came to see Frankie and Dagor. Angelica and I are going on a double date with them."

Jasmine blinked. The other three couples had all made plans for today.

"I don't think they are back from whatever they have planned. Where is Angelica?"

"We are picking her up from her nail salon." Edgar looked inside the room over her shoulder. "I came a little earlier because I wanted to see how you and Ell-rom were doing."

It felt odd to keep him standing in the vestibule, but given what was going on with Rob's fiancée and her ex-boyfriend, perhaps she shouldn't hang out with her ex, either. There was nothing going on between them, and they had both moved on, but Ell-rom might not see it that way.

Still, she couldn't tell Edgar to go away.

Stepping back, Jasmine gestured for him to come in. "Ell-rom's resting," she said, closing the door behind him. "We just had a big family lunch."

"Ah, yes. Frankie told me about it. How did it go?"

Jasmine led him to the living area, settling into one of the plush armchairs while Edgar took a seat on the couch across from her. "It was nice," she said. "Everyone was very welcoming to Ell-rom, but it has exhausted him."

"I bet." Edgar glanced at the glass she was still clutching in her hand.

"Oh, I'm sorry. I should have offered you a drink. What would you like?" She started to rise.

He motioned for her to remain seated. "I can pour a drink for myself." He got to his feet.

"So," she said. "How are things going with Angelica?"

Edgar's face lit up. "It's great. She's fierce, funny, and she doesn't put up with any of my nonsense."

Jasmine smiled. "I'm so happy for you."

"Thank you." He poured himself a glass of one of the whiskeys and returned to the couch.

"Have you told her yet?" Jasmine asked.

Edgar shook his head. "Not yet, and I'm dreading the day I have to do that. It's not exactly an easy conversation to have."

"No, I suppose it isn't." Jasmine imitated Edgar's posture and deepened her voice. "Hey, by the way, I'm immortal, and you're a Dormant, which means I can turn you immortal too. Want to live forever with me?'"

They both chuckled at her delivery.

"That was a good impersonation," Edgar admitted. "Do I really sound so cocky?"

"Yeah, you do, but don't change it. Somehow, it fits you. All that 'I'm a pilot' swagger seems to define you more than your immortality."

"Well, of course it does. Except for you, I can't tell the women I'm flirting with that I'm immortal, but I can tell them that I'm a pilot."

She arched a brow. "Women? Are you planning to flirt with anyone else now that you are in love with Angelica?"

ELL-ROM

Ell-rom stirred from his slumber, his consciousness slowly rising to the surface and registering voices and laughter that did not match what had been happening in his dream, which had been a lot of nothing.

He'd dreamt about silently meditating in front of the Mother's altar.

The bright and melodious laughter filtering through the slightly ajar bedroom door was as familiar to him as his own, and he wondered what Jasmine had found so funny.

Then he heard another voice, which he did not recognize and was decidedly male.

Ell-rom's eyes snapped open, the cobwebs of sleep vanishing in an instant. He sat up straight, ignoring the slight dizziness that accompanied the sudden movement. The male voice continued, its tone warm and friendly, and it elicited another peal of laughter from Jasmine.

A hot sensation suddenly bloomed in Ell-rom's chest. Jealousy. Intense and undeniable.

Was Jasmine entertaining another male while he was asleep?

Who was that male, and what was he doing in the penthouse?

Supposedly, the place belonged to Kian, and only people he approved were allowed to come in. Given that logic, the male must be a clan member, who Jasmine knew somehow and seemed to enjoy the company of a little too much for Ell-rom's liking.

Taking a deep, steadying breath, he swung his legs over the side of the bed and walked into the bathroom.

As Ell-rom splashed cold water on his face, he caught sight of his reflection in the mirror. His hair was growing back slowly, a dark fuzz covering his scalp, and his cheeks were no longer as hollow as they had been, but he still looked gaunt.

Dressing as quickly as he could, he decided to leave the walker behind and enter the living room unaided. If this male was a potential competitor for Jasmine's affections, Ell-rom did not want to show any weakness.

He wasn't sure where those convictions were coming from, especially since he had never vied for the attentions of a female before, but his response must have been instinctual, much like the jealousy he felt.

The short walk to the living room was not as difficult as Ell-rom had expected, and as he entered, Jasmine's eyes widened in surprise.

"Ell-rom!" She rose from her armchair and rushed to his side, wrapping a supportive arm around his waist. "Why didn't you call me to help you? I left the door open on purpose so I would hear when you woke up, but you snuck up on me anyway."

As Ell-rom allowed her to guide him to the couch, he noticed that the male hastily put a pair of earpieces in. Did everyone who visited the penthouse have a pair? Or was it standard for all clan members to carry them?

"It was not my intention to sneak up on anyone," he said in a level tone. "You seemed to be preoccupied with your friend." He hoped that hadn't sounded as petty and as jealous as it had in his mind.

Jasmine helped him sit, then gestured to the man occupying the other side of the couch. "Ell-rom, this is Edgar. He's the pilot I told you about, the one who flew us during the trip to Tibet."

Edgar leaned over, extending his hand with a friendly smile. "It's good to finally meet you in person, Ell-rom. I've heard so much about you."

He shook Edgar's hand, noting the firm grip. "Likewise," he said, even though it wasn't entirely true.

Jasmine had mentioned Edgar, but only in passing.

As they settled back into their seats, Ell-rom wondered if Edgar was just a friend from the Tibet expedition or more. The easy familiarity between him and Jasmine hinted at the latter.

"Edgar was just telling me about his upcoming double date with Frankie's cousin Angelica and Frankie and Dagor," Jasmine said.

Ell-rom remembered Jasmine telling him about Edgar and Frankie's cousin finding each other attractive, and he was relieved to learn that Edgar was still seeing her.

Jasmine had never mentioned that Edgar had any romantic interest in her, but then, if he wasn't inter-ested, why was he working so hard on making her laugh?

She'd never laughed like that at anything Ell-rom had said to her, and if the guy was so amusing, then he had an advantage in more than just his robust health and vitality.

Without knowing much about courtship or how males competed with each other over females, Ell-rom had no doubt that making a female laugh gave a male a leg up over his competition.

"What was so funny?" he asked, trying to keep the suspi-cion from his voice.

A moment of silence fell over the room, and Edgar and Jasmine exchanged a glance that spoke volumes.

"Well," Edgar said, a rueful smile playing on his lips, "Jas-mine and I used to date, and we were recounting some funny moments from those days. Did you know that

Jasmine loves period romances? Our first date started with us making up a story."

Ell-rom didn't even know what period romances were, and the fact that Jasmine hadn't told him that Edgar used to be her partner hurt. Why had she kept it a secret?

On top of that, Edgar appeared to know so much more about Jasmine than Ell-rom did, and it made the jealousy in his chest flare anew.

"What happened?" he asked. "Why did you end things?"

He hoped that they had ended it and that Jasmine was not entertaining the two of them at the same time. Did people do that on Earth? Did they do that on Anumati?

It was so frustrating not knowing the first thing about anything.

Edgar chuckled, though there was a hint of something else in his eyes that looked a lot like regret. "What happened? You did, mate. I can't really blame Jasmine for dumping me for a prince. How could a simple guy like me compete with royalty?"

Ell-rom felt as if the floor had dropped out from under him.

Was that all he was to Jasmine? A title? An upgrade from a pilot to a prince?

The insecurity that had been simmering beneath the surface bubbled up, threatening to overwhelm him.

Jasmine glared at Edgar. "That's not true, and you know it. You're just being contrary. We ended things because we both realized we weren't meant for each other, and it was a very wise decision for both of us." She turned back to Ell-rom. "Now, both Edgar and I have found our one and only. I found you, and Edgar found Angelica."

At the mention of Angelica's name, Edgar's face lit up in a way that eased some of Ell-rom's tension. Whatever Edgar had felt for Jasmine in the past was still there in some form, but it seemed that his heart now belonged to Frankie's cousin.

As Edgar and Jasmine reminisced about their trip to Tibet, sounding like two old friends and not lovers, Ell-rom relaxed further. He was still upset that Jasmine hadn't told him she used to be with Edgar, but at least he was no longer worried that she was still interested in the pilot or that he would have to compete for her.

"Flying the aircraft in the Himalayas was one of the biggest challenges of my career," Edgar said. "The thin air and the unpredictable weather are not for the faint of heart."

Jasmine frowned. "I wonder how the earpieces translated aircraft." She looked expectantly at Ell-rom.

Ell-rom's brow furrowed. "A vehicle capable of flying," he said.

"That's what I thought." She turned to Edgar. "The earpieces have a limited Kra-ell vocabulary, and they group things by their function. Carrots and potatoes are both just vegetables, and in the same way, they don't differentiate between types of aircraft."

Edgar's eyes widened. "Right, sorry. The type of aircraft I pilot has rotating blades on top that allow it to fly straight up and down and hover in place. It's incredibly useful for navigating difficult terrain like mountains."

As Edgar delved into more technical details about piloting the strange aircraft he'd described, Ell-rom couldn't shake the feeling that he was showing off. There was an undercurrent of insecurity in Edgar's demeanor, though Ell-rom couldn't fathom why.

After all, Edgar had an important skill, and he had a crucial role in the clan's operations. Ell-rom, on the other hand, felt the weight of his current uselessness keenly. He might be called a prince, but it was a meaningless title. He had no profession, no skills he could remember, and nothing to contribute to the clan that had taken him in.

Well, except for becoming an assassin on their behalf, but he had no intention of assuming that role.

"That sounds like incredibly challenging work," he said when Edgar finished his explanation.

Edgar nodded with a hint of pride in his expression. "It's not an easy job, but I love it. There's nothing quite like the feeling of being in control of such a powerful machine."

Jasmine, who had been listening quietly, suddenly stood

up. "I'm going to make coffee. Would you like some, Edgar?"

"That would be great, thanks," Edgar replied.

"Ell-rom?"

He nodded. "Thank you."

As Jasmine disappeared into the kitchen, a moment of awkward silence fell between them. Ell-rom searched for something to say, feeling the pressure to make conversation.

"How long have you been a pilot?" he asked.

Edgar leaned back against the couch cushions. "Oh, let's see. I'm a young immortal, so I'm much less experienced than the other clan pilots, well, with the exception of Eric, the latest addition to our fleet, who has a comparable number of flight hours to mine." Seeing Ell-rom's confused expression, he added, "It's been about eight years now."

"That doesn't sound like long." Ell-rom rubbed a hand over the back of his head. "Thank you for assisting Jasmine and the gods in their search for us. I owe you a debt of gratitude."

Edgar's expression softened. "You are welcome. I'm glad we found you in time."

"Are you?" Ell-rom lifted a brow. "You said that if not for me, Jasmine wouldn't have ended things between you two."

Edgar shrugged. "Even though it hurt like hell when she did that, it was for the best. She did the right thing."

29

JASMINE

J asmine regretted not telling Ell-rom about her fling with Edgar sooner, so this awkwardness could have been avoided.

It wasn't that she had deliberately hidden it.

Somehow, it had just never seemed like a good time to bring it up.

Well, that wasn't entirely true. She could have told Ell-rom about her relationship with Edgar when she first mentioned the pilot, but she had chosen not to because she didn't want to put any emotional strain on Ell-rom, who was struggling with enough as it was, or on their relationship, which was still in its budding stage and fragile.

Thankfully, Ell-rom's initial jealousy was gradually melting away, and the longer he talked with Edgar, the more the accusation in his eyes faded. He seemed to no longer feel threatened by the guy, probably because Edgar had found Angelica.

It was also a relief that he had lost interest in Morelle.

Jasmine could only imagine how Ell-rom would have reacted to that particular complication.

"So, Edgar," Ell-rom was saying, "do you have much family in the clan?"

Edgar shook his head. "It's just my mother and me, but the entire clan is my extended family."

"I'm excited about joining the clan," Ell-rom admitted. "I only have my sister, and I don't remember much about my life on Anumati. I have a couple of vague memories of our mother, but that's all. I don't think we interacted with anyone outside the head priestess and occasionally the temple guards and acolytes."

The hint of sadness in Ell-rom's voice sent a pang of sorrow through Jasmine's chest. She reached out, placing her hand over his. "I only have vague memories of my mother, and my father was not the warmest of guys, but at least I had friends in school. You and Morelle didn't even have that."

"Not that I remember," Ell-rom said. "How did your mother die, if I may ask?"

"I don't know. I was a little girl when it happened, and my father refused to tell me how she died. She was only twenty-seven when she passed."

In the back of her mind, Jasmine had always harbored the morbid thought that she wouldn't live longer than her mother and would die at twenty-seven, but now that she was facing the possibility of becoming immortal, it no longer made sense to cling to that belief.

Not that it ever had, but beliefs were not rational.

"Did you try to find out what happened?" Edgar asked.

Jasmine shook her head. "My father was adamant about me leaving it alone, and he instilled such fear in me that every time I thought about investigating her death, I would chicken out."

Ell-rom frowned. "I don't understand that expression."

"It means that I was scared. Chickens are scared of everything, so when you say that someone is a chicken, it means that they are gutless."

The furrow between Ell-rom's eyes deepened. "You are not gutless."

"Well, if the shoe fits…" She laughed. "I need to stop using idioms and confusing you."

"I actually got that one." Ell-rom took a sip of his coffee. "But I still disagree. I think that you are very brave."

"I second that opinion," Edgar said.

"Aren't the two of you sweet?" She cast them a charming smile. "But the fact is that I didn't have the guts to investigate what happened to my mother."

"She might be alive," Edgar said. "She might have left your father, and he claimed she was dead because she was dead to him or something like that."

The thought had occurred to Jasmine. She didn't even know where her mother was buried, and her father refused to tell her. Sometimes, she fantasized that her mother wasn't dead at all. Maybe she had found love in the arms of another man and had run off with him?

It was painful to think that her mother had left her behind to pursue her own happiness, but Jasmine preferred that to the finality of death. If her mother was still alive somewhere, there was still a chance that they would be reunited.

Then again, it was just a fantasy, and she was probably gone.

"I wish that was true, but I don't think it is."

"Did she look like you?" Ell-rom asked.

Jasmine nodded. "I got my coloring from her. My father is a typical Russian dude with pale skin, brown hair, and blue eyes. I have a few old pictures of my mother. They are with the rest of my things in storage."

"I think you should find out what really happened to her, just so you can put the issue to rest." Ell-rom gave her hand a gentle squeeze. "I would have loved to help you investigate, but I'm in no position to do that. I can't even thrall. Not well, anyway. If I could, a visit with your father could have solved the mystery."

It hadn't occurred to her that it was a possibility. Any one of the immortals could get into her father's head and retrieve the information from there or force him to reveal it.

Not Ell-rom, though. He had managed to shroud, but they hadn't even practiced thralling yet.

Edgar leaned forward, his eyes sparkling with interest. "I could do that," he offered.

Jasmine felt a jolt of anxiety at the suggestion. Part of her desperately wanted to know the truth about her mother, but another part was terrified of what she might discover. "That's not a priority right now."

She caught the glance that passed between Ell-rom and Edgar, a look of silent understanding that made her narrow her eyes. "Don't even think about doing anything without consulting me first," she warned. "And especially nothing that involves my father, my step-mother, or my stepbrothers. They are all mine to deal with."

Edgar held up his hands in mock surrender. "Of course not. But you know, I could ask Roni to do some digging. Nothing invasive, just a preliminary investigation."

Roni was the clan's hacker who had gotten them fake identities that could be verified and even included university credentials, so she knew how good he was. But something in the way Edgar had suggested it made Jasmine pause. A suspicion began to form in her mind.

"Roni has already looked into my past, hasn't he?"

Edgar had the grace to look sheepish. "Roni probably did some basic background checks when you became involved with the mission. It's standard procedure."

It made sense. After all, they had trusted her with monumental secrets, so it was only natural that they would want to ensure she wasn't a threat. "I get it," she said with a sigh. "So, what did he find out?"

Edgar shook his head. "I honestly don't know. That kind of information is strictly need-to-know. But I can talk to Roni and ask. He'll probably call you to get permission to share any details with me."

Jasmine snorted. "He didn't ask for my permission to dig into my past, but he'll ask for it now?"

Edgar shrugged. "He checked up on you for security reasons and reported his findings to Kian. My clearance is high, but I'd need a legitimate reason to access that information."

"If Roni calls, I'll give permission. But I want to know everything he finds out."

"Of course." Edgar nodded solemnly.

The possibility of uncovering the truth about her mother both thrilled and terrified Jasmine. For years she had pushed those questions to the back of her mind, but now, with the clan's resources potentially at her disposal, she had a real chance at finally getting answers.

30

PETER

The setting sun cast long shadows across the neatly manicured lawn as Peter headed home. He was looking forward to a couple of hours with Marina before leaving on tonight's mission.

It was not the usual personnel, and they were raiding a large cell that was supposed to receive a new delivery of trafficked people from south of the border. They had to get to the victims before the monsters had a chance to violate them and then distribute them down the chain.

Lately, it seemed like the number of victims had been steadily increasing, and they were also getting younger. In the last raid Peter had taken part in, there had been two girls under ten years old and three boys even younger than that.

It was a disturbing trend that made Peter sick to his stomach.

What kind of monsters did that to children? It was so revolting, so evil, that the only way he could deal with it was to keep the information locked in a small compartment in his head that was dedicated to all the atrocities he'd witnessed over the years.

It wasn't the kind of stuff he could share with Marina or anyone else who wasn't on the force and exposed to the same cesspool of the so-called humanity.

Having another Guardian as a roommate was helpful because he could at least unload some of that crap on Alfie and vice versa.

Not that talking about it did either of them any good—they just got themselves more worked up—but according to the clan's therapist, it wasn't healthy to keep things bottled up.

Her advice was to find someone who could deal with what they needed to unburden, and if they didn't have someone they felt comfortable doing that with, she encouraged them to talk to her.

Whatever. Talking or not talking about it didn't really make a difference to him.

The only light in the gloomy state of affairs was that more Kra-ell were joining the force each day, and they didn't need a lot of training to become mission-ready. They had trained in hand-to-hand combat for most of their lives and just needed to be taught the handling of guns and explosives.

The hardest part for them was learning English, and that was still a work in progress, probably because they kept to themselves and watched television with Russian subtitles.

But even that shouldn't keep them from missions.

With William's latest improvement to the translating earpieces, the language barrier was not a problem.

Stepping through the front door, Peter let the familiar scent of home wash over him, instantly soothing his irritation and pre-mission jitters.

"Marina?" he called out as he closed the door behind him.

"In the kitchen!" her voice rang out, warm and excited.

Coming home now that Marina was waiting for him was so much more pleasant than it had been when it was only him and Alfie.

He found Marina at the kitchen island chopping vegetables for dinner, and the sight of her, so domestic and contented, made his heart swell.

She looked up as he entered, her face lighting up with a smile that never failed to take his breath away. "Hey, you," she said, setting down her knife and wiping her hands on a dishtowel. "How was the prep?"

He crossed the room in a few quick strides, wrapped his arms around her, and planted a kiss on her forehead. "The usual. I'm glad it's done and that I have a couple of hours I can spend with you before heading out."

The smile slid off her face. "You look tense. Is the mission dangerous?"

It was hard to hide things from Marina. She was too attuned to him to miss the slightest change in mood.

"No more than the others. It's a bit of a larger operation than what we usually do, but we are also going in with a larger force, so it's going to be alright. You have nothing to worry about."

She shook her head. "That's what you always say, but I can't help it. I know that you are immortal and that your body expels bullets, but still. A well-aimed shot could be deadly even to an immortal."

"True, but it is highly unlikely any of these humans will prove to be trained snipers or that they will even think that accuracy is needed. All any of the scum will care about is hitting their target to slow us down so they can escape like the rats they are."

Marina frowned at the vehemence in his voice, but she didn't comment on it. She knew more than she let on, and he loved her even more for understanding and not pressing him for answers he preferred not to give.

"Just be careful, okay? Don't rely on your fast-healing body to withstand an assault. Wear your Kevlar vest and your helmet to protect your heart and your head."

"Yes, Ma'am." He saluted and then kissed the top of her nose. "I have the best reason in the world to want to come home in one piece." He let go of her. "When will dinner be ready?"

"When you sit down." She turned around and dropped the vegetables she'd been chopping into a bowl. "Is Alfie coming, too?"

"Not right away." Peter sat down. "I think he and Lusha are meeting for coffee at the café."

Marina poured dressing over the salad and put it on the table. "Enjoy." She sat across from him.

"You first." He pushed the bowl toward her.

She rolled her eyes but didn't argue. He never served himself first, and she knew it would be futile for her to insist that he did.

Peter wasn't a great fan of salads, but everything Marina made tasted great, even vegetables, and he was hungry.

"I ran into Bridget at the café this morning," Marina said. "We had a very interesting conversation about the possibility of your venom prolonging my life."

Peter's eyebrows shot up. "What did she say?"

"She thinks that's a valid hypothesis, and she wants to test it. Apparently, no one has ever really studied the long-term effects of immortal venom on humans who aren't Dormants. She thinks it could potentially have cumulative healing effects and prolong my life. I agreed to provide blood samples once a week to monitor my aging process and see if it slowed down over time."

"What is she going to check?"

"She wants to monitor my cellular aging and check for any changes in my telomeres."

"What are telomeres?" Peter asked, reaching for his phone to search for a definition.

"Let me see if I remember what Bridget said. Telomeres are kind of protective caps at the ends of our chromosomes, and supposedly, they get shorter as we age. I mean, as humans age. Bridget thinks the venom might slow down that shortening process or maybe even reverse it."

Peter let out a low whistle. "Wow. I mean, I knew my venom was good for you, but I never imagined it could be that good."

"Bridget seemed pretty excited about the possibilities, so I suggested that she test Lusha as well since she's dating Alfie now. Bridget said that Lusha is part Kra-ell, so her results might be different than mine, but she is excited about testing her, too."

"That's great. I don't know how serious Alfie is about Lusha, but I have no doubt that he will enjoy participating in the study." Peter chuckled. "It's not like it's a great hardship for him."

"It is not." Marina smiled suggestively. "For the study to have the best chance, you will have to bite me every night."

Peter got hard just thinking about the duty he was going to perform with utmost pleasure. "If my venom can really prolong your life, I will double up on the biting. Every morning and every night."

Marina laughed. "You can't produce that much venom every day, and if you could, I can't blackout in the morning when I need to go to work."

Peter waggled his brows. "It depends on what time we wake up."

Normally, even once a day was considered a lot. Immortals could climax many times without even pausing to rest, but their venom glands were a different story. They usually were good for only one bite a day.

Usually.

There were ways to make them produce enough for two.

Peter puffed out his chest. "I'll make it happen even if I have to double up on food intake. I will produce enough for two bites. And there's no better time to start than now." He wiped his mouth with a napkin and rose to his feet.

"Oh really?" Marina quirked an eyebrow, amusement dancing in her eyes. "What about dinner?"

"It can wait. This can't."

"And what about Alfie? He might come home any minute."

Peter waved a dismissive hand. "Alfie's not going to bother us." In one swift motion, he scooped Marina up and threw her over his shoulder, eliciting a squeal of surprised laughter from her. "To the bedroom! We have a mission to accomplish."

As Peter carried Marina through the house, her laughter echoing off the walls, he marveled at how light his heart suddenly felt.

The worry of the upcoming mission, the weight of all the evil he witnessed day in and day out, it all seemed to melt away in the face of hope.

A hope for a future with Marina that would last longer than her limited mortal lifespan.

He deposited her gently on their bed, taking a moment to drink in the sight of her.

Her cheeks were flushed from laughter, her eyes bright with love and mirth, and her blue hair fanned out over the pillow. Peter felt a wave of gratitude wash over him.

How had he gotten so lucky?

What if it didn't work, though?

What if they got their hopes up for nothing?

As if reading his mind, Marina reached out and took his hand. "Hey," she said softly. "I have high hopes for the study, but even if they get crushed, I'm still grateful for the time we have together."

31

MARINA

"So am I." Peter lay down next to her and pulled her into his arms.

Marina wasn't surprised that he'd chosen sex over food, but she was worried about him going on the mission without a proper meal. She was also worried about not smelling the freshest.

"Let's get in the tub together," she suggested.

Frowning, Peter lifted his arm. "Do I smell bad?" He sniffed his armpit.

"You never do, but we've both had a long day. We can celebrate the news with a bottle of wine."

He grinned. "That sounds like a plan. You get the water running, and I'll get the wine."

She shook her head. "I left a roast warming in the oven. I don't want it to dry out. I'll get the wine while you get the tub going."

"Deal." Peter jumped out of bed. "Just don't take long. We don't have a lot of time."

Her gut clenched at the reminder that he was going on a mission tonight. "I'll be quick."

With the roast taken care of, a bottle of wine in one hand and two glasses in the other, Marina made her way back to the bedroom and grinned when she found Peter already soaking in the tub.

It was only half full, which left his magnificent nude body on full display.

For a moment, she just gazed at him, getting her fill of his masculine beauty.

Peter tilted his head. "Do you like?"

"I like it a lot." She put the bottle and the glasses on the tub's deck and got undressed.

"Beautiful." His eyes roamed over her. "I never get tired of looking at you."

She knew better than to say she was nothing special compared to his gorgeous immortal relatives. It was true, but Peter didn't like it when she made self-depre-cating comments.

Marina got into the tub across from Peter and lowered herself carefully into the water.

"Too hot?" Peter asked.

"A little, but I'll get used to it in a moment."

"I know how to make it better." He leaned over, lifted her like she weighed nothing, and laid her down on his chest, just not the way she'd expected.

Nevertheless, it was nice to feel his hard length poking her butt, and as she rested her head on his hard muscles, he cupped her breasts and started to play with her nipples.

Closing her eyes, she let out a soft moan and rubbed her bottom over his erection. In response, it twitched against her backside.

"Umm, that's nice." She spread her legs a little and adjusted the angle to get more friction.

"Impatient?" He kissed her neck in the spot where it met her shoulder, then nipped a little, letting his fangs scrape against her skin.

As usual, the thought of him biting her sent a shiver of desire down her spine, and more moisture pooled between her legs. It had become an addiction, and although Peter claimed that it was the venom itself that was addictive, she just loved the whole thing and couldn't get enough of it.

Now that there was a valid reason to strive for two of those a day, she wasn't sure she would be able to function in the café with so much euphoria scrambling her brain.

"We don't have much time, remember?"

"Oh, right." He removed one of his hands from her

breast and slipped lower to cup her center, his middle
finger parting her folds.

The moan she let out sounded throaty and loud as it
echoed in the tiled bathroom.

"Feels good, love?"

She wiggled to get more of his finger. "You know it
does."

He slipped it into her and added one more while his
thumb pressed against her clit.

"That's good." She rubbed her bottom against his cock.

Peter hissed into her ear and caught her chin, twisting
her head around and taking her mouth in a hungry kiss
while he pumped his fingers in and out of her.

She wanted to tell him that she preferred to have his
shaft inside of her, but he was devouring her mouth
while tormenting her nipple and fingering her to
oblivion.

Was he going to bite her when she came?

The thought was enough to send her over the edge.
Peter kept kissing her through the tremors and rubbing
his erection against her ass, but he didn't enter her, and
he didn't bite her.

When the storm he'd unleashed inside of her subsided,
he gently slid out from under her, stepped out of the
tub, grabbed a towel, and spread it out for her to step
into.

When she did, he wrapped her in the bath sheet and lifted her into his arms.

PETER

Peter lowered Marina to the bed and waited for her to pull the blanket over her before taking her towel to dry himself.

When he was done, he dropped the towel on the floor and joined her on the bed. Pulling her close against his body, he rubbed his hands over her back and then cupped her lush bottom.

She felt so fragile, and it dawned on him that even if his venom kept her alive much longer than normal for a human, it wouldn't make her immortal, and she could get hurt.

He would never stop worrying about her.

The solution was simple. She should never leave the village. When surrounded by immortals, Marina was safe.

The distressing thoughts made him deflate, but as her hand closed around his cock, it inflated in no time to its former glory. A few more up and down strokes, and he would explode all over her hand.

Not that there was anything wrong with that, but he wanted to come inside of her.

Shifting on top of Marina, Peter took her mouth in a gentle kiss that soon turned into more and had her moaning softly and undulating under him. He let go of her mouth only to slide down and pay attention to her perky nipples.

Marina liked a little sting with her lovemaking, but Peter was in a mood for sweet and gentle, so he lapped at each turgid nub while palming her small breasts with his hands.

She arched her back, her moan sounding more like a demand than an expression of pleasure, and he knew that he needed to give her what she wanted, or she wouldn't be pleased.

He took one nipple between his lips and sucked it hard, then let go and moved to the other. She threaded her fingers in his hair, encouraging him to do more, but he had other plans. With a little nip to each nipple, he slid further down until his nose was right where he wanted it to be.

"My favorite nectar." He took in a long breath and then speared his tongue into her opening.

As Marina gasped and lifted her bottom, he slid his palms under it and cupped each cheek, holding her up and open for his delight.

When he pressed two fingers into her and lashed at her clit with his tongue, Marina let out a deep, throaty moan and tugged on his hair. "I need you inside of me."

Lifting his head, he chuckled. "Yes, ma'am."

She narrowed her eyes at him. "Now."

He liked it when she got bossy. It didn't happen often, but when it did, it was sexy as hell.

Surging up, he took her mouth and aligned his shaft with her entrance at the same time.

He pushed, and as the head glided effortlessly through her wetness, he lost it, growling into her mouth as he pushed all the way inside her with one powerful thrust.

Marina gasped, and he forced himself to hold still for a moment. She was human, and he needed to be in control, or he would hurt her.

She wrapped her arms around him. "Fuck me, Peter. Fuck me hard."

Fates, he loved when she talked dirty to him.

Nevertheless, he wasn't going to obey her command and hurt her. Moving slowly, he was careful not to surge all the way, keeping his thrusts slow and shallow.

"Peter, please." She dug her fingers into his shoulders.

Increasing the tempo gradually, he was struggling to remain in control, and soon he was pounding into her fast and hard.

When her sheath convulsed around him, and his seed rose in his shaft, he licked his favorite spot on her neck and hissed, biting her at the same time he erupted.

She cried out, and the small muscles in her sheath fluttered around his cock, again and again, as she climaxed once, twice, three times.

When he finally was spent and she lay motionless under him with a euphoric expression on her beautiful face, he wrapped his arms around her, rolled them both on their sides, and pulled the blanket over them.

He couldn't stay long, but he needed a few more minutes of bliss with the love of his life.

SYSSI

Kian pushed open the front door, letting Syssi walk ahead of him with the sleeping Allegra cradled against her chest.

Behind them, Annani and the two Odus stayed on the pathway, waiting for Kian to join them, not because the goddess needed his protection inside the village but because it was a measure of courtesy that a son should show his mother.

"I'll walk Mother home." He kissed her cheek and then gazed lovingly at Allegra before lifting his head. "Don't start anything without me," he whispered.

"I won't." She walked toward the nursery.

Laying Allegra carefully in her crib, Syssi pressed a soft kiss to the top of her head, covered her with the blanket, and turned on the nightlight.

Her little girl stirred slightly, her small fingers curling around the edge of her blanket, but she didn't wake up.

Watching her daughter's angelic face, Syssi marveled at how much she had grown.

Where had the time gone?

Allegra had been an easy child from the start, who ate well, slept through the night more often than not, and was hitting her developmental milestones much sooner than a child her age should. The only real challenges were her mile-wide stubborn streak and her surprisingly strong opinions regarding her outfits.

Syssi didn't mind accommodating her daughter's fashion choices, but she worried about what to expect as Allegra grew older. She anticipated more displays of Allegra's strong will, and she and Kian would need to set clear boundaries without stifling their daughter's spirit.

A soft chuckle escaped Syssi's lips. Being a parent was the most important and challenging job she had ever had. Yet, it came with no instructions and was expected to be intuitive. Was it a surprise that so many parents struggled with it?

Then again, love was the most important ingredient in parenting, and almost everyone knew how to do that. A child who grew up feeling loved would become a loving adult.

On the flip side, Allegra might become entitled and spoiled, but Syssi had a strong hunch that their daughter would not succumb to those first-world maladies that afflicted so many young humans these days. She had two hard-working, dedicated parents who never took anything for granted, so hopefully she would follow their example.

Besides, Allegra was exceptional. There was something undeniably special about her. It was the way her eyes seemed to hold wisdom far beyond her years or the uncanny way she sometimes seemed to anticipate events before they happened. Her memory for names, or rather the nicknames she coined for those around her, was unique to her.

As the sound of the front door opening drew Syssi from her reverie, she gave Allegra one last loving glance before quietly exiting the nursery.

Kian was at the living room bar, surveying his assortment of whiskeys. "How's our little princess?"

"Sound asleep." Syssi sank onto the couch. "She'll probably wake up in a couple of hours, play for a bit before bath time, and go back to sleep."

Children did well with a set schedule, but Allegra was flexible in that regard, which was one of the many blessings of raising such a unique child.

Kian poured himself a drink and started walking toward the couch but then paused. "I didn't offer you a drink because you usually don't like to consume alcohol before bedtime, but given what you are about to do, maybe a cocktail would help you relax?"

Syssi shook her head. "It can't be done artificially. I need to reach a state of calm on my own. Alcohol would be an impediment rather than a catalyst. A cappuccino, on the other hand, would do wonders to calm my nerves."

Kian laughed. "You're the only person I know who relaxes with coffee."

"Maybe I have ADHD. Stimulants are known to have a calming effect on people with attention deficit disorder."

"You don't have any problem with attention." Kian sat on the couch next to her and draped an arm over her shoulders.

"I was just joking." She leaned over and kissed his cheek. "Do you want a cup as well, or are you happy with your whiskey?"

"What kind of a husband would I be if I let you drink coffee alone?" He lifted his glass and estimated the amount left. "I'll be done with this by the time you are back with the cappuccinos."

"Indeed." She chuckled as she headed to her coffee station.

As she busied herself with measuring out coffee grounds and frothing two kinds of milk, regular for her and oat for Kian, Syssi felt some of the tension begin to ebb. The familiar routine and the aroma of exceptional coffee were soothing.

Making a great cappuccino was a precise and laborious process, and she never rushed it.

When she was done, she walked back to the couch with two red cups resting on two red saucers, the latest addition to her collection.

So yeah, she was a little obsessed, but then everyone needed a hobby, right?

As she settled back onto the couch, the aroma of the coffee and Kian's solid presence beside her helped to further ease her nerves.

For a long moment, they sipped on the exquisite brew, but then Kian set his cup down, pulled out his phone, and powered it off.

He never did that. He even slept with the device right next to him on the nightstand.

"What are you doing?" she asked.

"I don't want anything to interfere with your process of calming down, and I just know that if I leave it on, I'll get a call with some disturbing news that will ruin things for you."

Syssi frowned. "But what if someone urgently needs to reach you? I'll be worried about that, and it'll stress me out more. It's better if you leave it on."

Kian shook his head. "You are a strange woman, my love."

"I know." She leaned in to press a kiss to his cheek. "But you love me anyway."

"I love you because of that, not despite that. My mate is unlike anyone else in the world."

That was true of every single individual on the face of the planet. Even identical twins had two separate souls and their own unique personalities. But Syssi didn't say any of that.

This wasn't a good time for a philosophical discussion.

She had a job to do, and the sooner the better.

Setting her now-empty cup on the coffee table, Syssi stretched her arms above her head. "Are you going to stay here and watch the baby monitor while I summon the vision in Allegra's room?"

Kian nodded, reaching for the monitor. "I've been thinking about Allegra's presence enhancing your precognition abilities. Maybe Allegra has Mia's talent, and that's why your visions are stronger and clearer when you summon them next to her?"

Syssi considered this for a moment before shaking her head. "I don't think so. I'm sure Allegra is a seer like me but stronger, and she lends me her strength when I'm near her. She might also have other talents." A smile spread across her face as she looked at Kian. "Maybe she also has your unnatural knack for business."

"I hope she does. If she's to become the leader of this clan, she needs to be a savvy businesswoman."

The future that awaited their daughter was not easy, and Syssi felt a twinge of anxiety every time she thought about it. But that was a concern for another day. Right now, she needed a few more moments in her husband's arms before she braved the mysteries of the universe.

34

MARINA

"I have to go, love." Peter leaned over Marina and took her lips in a sweet kiss.

She was still woozy from the venom bite, but thankfully, she no longer blacked out for as long as she had at the beginning.

"It's been half an hour, more or less." Peter got up, giving her a wonderful view of his ass. "Your blackouts are getting shorter, which means that your euphoric trips have gotten shorter as well, and I'm sorry about that."

"It's okay." She turned on her side. "I think that the venom trips never took more than a few minutes. The rest was just sleeping off the effects."

He smiled and looked at her longingly. "I wish I could stay in bed with you."

"Yeah, I wish so, too, but you have places to go and people to save."

"True." He stepped into the bathroom but left the door open.

She couldn't see him from her side of the bed that was closer to the window, but every cell in her body was still infused with the warmth of their lovemaking.

It had been a good day, and Marina felt a surge of optimism. The earlier conversation with Bridget had opened possibilities beyond what she'd dared to imagine. If the test results proved their hypothesis, she might stay young and vibrant for much longer than she could have ever hoped for, and in that time, Kaia could find the secret key to turning ordinary humans immortal.

The prospect of an eternal life with Peter filled her with a giddy excitement.

She turned her gaze away from the window and swept it to the dresser, where she had arranged several framed photos of her and Peter. Some were from the cruise, others were from Safe Haven, and a couple were from the village. Each told a story, a moment in time, and now they might get to create so many more.

"I need a larger dresser," she murmured.

Peter emerged from the bathroom clad in his fatigues. "What for?"

Naturally, he'd heard her murmuring with his bat hearing.

"For all the framed photos of us that I'm going to put out."

"You know you can have a digital picture frame that automatically rotates your pictures. I'll get you one."

"I prefer real photos in nice frames, but when our mementos become too numerous, you can get it for us."

Understanding dawning in his eyes, he grinned and leaned over her. "We will make so many new memories that we're going to need an Anumati-made digital frame." He kissed her forehead. "I'll be back in about four hours."

"Call me when the mission is over. Otherwise, I will keep worrying until you get home."

"I will call you as soon as I can."

"I love you." Marina wrapped her arms around Peter's neck and kissed him. "Be safe."

"Always." He removed her hands. "I really have to run."

When the door closed behind him, Marina's fingers itched to grab her phone and call her friends to share the incredible news. Larissa would be thrilled and would resume her search for an immortal boyfriend, and when she told the others about it, every unattached human woman of the former Kra-ell compound would want to move into the village and look for immortal partners.

It was too soon.

She needed to wait for the results of the test before getting anyone's hopes up. Still, the doctor's excitement had been palpable, and that was encouraging. Bridget didn't strike her as the type who got easily excited, and for her to react with such enthusiasm, she must have believed that the results would be positive.

As Marina got up and returned to the kitchen, she realized that Peter hadn't eaten anything other than the salad and was probably hungry. Perhaps she could prepare a quick sandwich for him and rush to the training center to give it to him. She might make it in time before the Guardians left for their mission.

Assembling the ingredients, she started working on the sandwich when she heard the front door opening.

"Marina?" Peter called out.

"In the kitchen," she called back. "Is everything okay?"

He'd only left a short while ago.

Peter appeared in the doorway, still in his mission gear. His face was flushed, his eyes bright with an intensity that made Marina's heart skip a beat.

"What's wrong?" She set down the knife. "Did the mission get called off?"

Peter shook his head, crossed the room in a few quick strides, and before Marina could say another word, gathered her in his arms, pressing a deep, passionate kiss to her lips.

When they finally broke apart, Marina laughed. "Not that I'm complaining, but what was that?"

Peter's hands cupped her face gently, his thumbs

stroking her cheeks. "I love you so much. I want you to hurry up with those wedding plans."

Marina blinked in surprise. "Shouldn't we wait for the test results?"

Peter shook his head. "No, I want to do it before. I want to marry you regardless of what those tests say."

"But what's the urgency?" With her hands resting on his chest, she could feel his heart beating rapidly beneath her palms. "Why did you run back to tell me that?"

Peter's eyes, which usually were so confident and assured, held a hint of vulnerability. "I want to prompt the Fates to make you immortal," he admitted. "And proving my devotion to you might just do the trick."

For a moment, Marina was speechless. Then, a bubble of laughter escaped her. "Oh, Peter." She shook her head. "I don't think the Fates will be all that impressed by a wedding ceremony. If they exist, they probably expect grander gestures than that."

Nevertheless, Marina felt a warmth spreading through her chest. The fact that Peter would even think that proved how much he loved her. "I love you so much for thinking that, though," she murmured, standing on her tiptoes to press a soft kiss to his lips.

Peter's arms tightened around her waist, pulling her closer. "I mean it, Marina. Start planning today."

She felt tears prickling at the corners of her eyes. She blinked them back, not wanting to get overly emotional. "Okay," she said. "Aren't you late?"

The smile that broke across Peter's face was radiant. "It's okay. They'll wait for me." He lifted her off her feet and spun her around the kitchen as she laughed, clinging to his shoulders.

When he set her down, Marina couldn't stop smiling.

"I really do need to get going now."

"Hold on." She turned to the counter. "You didn't eat dinner, so I made you a sandwich." She finished stacking the cold cuts on top of one slice of bread and covered it with the other. "I wanted to run to the training center to give it to you, but you surprised me by coming back." She didn't have time to wrap it nicely and just handed it to him.

He took it and then lifted his head with a smile. "That's how it all started. With a sandwich."

She laughed. "Go. We can reminisce when you return. Be safe."

"Always."

35

PETER

The familiar scent of leather and gun oil filled the air as Peter strapped on his tactical gear.

He adjusted his Kevlar vest in front of the mirror on his locker door and smiled at his reflection. The possibility of prolonging Marina's life had injected him with a new sense of hope and excitement, burning off the vestiges of malaise that had been plaguing him as of late.

It was a win that he had desperately needed, a piece of good news, of hope, a light to push back the encroaching darkness. There wasn't much he could do to save the world from what was coming, but he could rejoice in this victory that promised a better future for Marina and him.

Well, it wasn't a promise, not yet. At this point it was just a hypothesis, but Peter would take whatever he was given and embrace it.

He couldn't wait to share the news with Alfie and Jay, but it was too soon. He didn't want to sell them a dream and then take it away because Bridget's test results didn't indicate any longevity benefit from frequent venom injections.

Jay would probably kick himself for dumping Larissa when he heard about this. Peter could already imagine the regret on his friend's face. And Alfie? Well, this might just be the push he needed to get serious about Lusha.

Peter made a mental note to arrange a guys' night out when Marina got the positive results. This was news best delivered in person, preferably over a few bottles of Snake Venom.

As he holstered his weapon, Peter's thoughts drifted to the wider implications of Bridget's research. This could be a game-changer for many of the clan males who had all but given up hope of finding Dormant mates. Amanda's research wasn't yielding any new results, and the Fates seemed in no hurry to bring more Dormants their way.

Theoretically, immortals had all the time in the world to find their fated truelove mates, but watching others find their happily-ever-after while they remained alone wasn't easy. People were impatient.

As someone who had been in the same boat only a few weeks ago, he had experienced that helpless longing first-hand. Hell, he had even convinced himself that he was in love with Kagra because he had been so desperate for a mate.

Not that he would have admitted it while he had been with her, but looking back, he couldn't lie to himself and claim that he had truly believed that Kagra was the one meant for him. She was a Kra-ell, and although attractive, she was alien in her looks, customs, and beliefs, which did not align with his.

What he couldn't understand, though, was why the clan females did not find mates among Kalugal's males. They were perfectly compatible, attractive, and shared similar values. So yeah, they used to be Doomers, but they hadn't wanted that life and had escaped. They had more in common with the clan than they ever had with the Brotherhood.

The only explanation Peter could come up with was that the Fates had other plans for them.

"You look deep in thought," Onegus said from behind him.

He turned to the chief. "Just thinking about the mission," Peter lied smoothly. "I wonder how many kids will be in this rescue."

Onegus grimaced. "More than the last one. You know what I fantasize about?"

Peter was surprised that the chief was sharing his musings with him. "What?" he asked.

Onegus leaned closer, his eyes blazing with inner light and his fangs elongating. "I fantasize about finding

those who want to buy those children and doing despi-
cable things to them. I want to tear them apart with my
fangs."

Peter felt his own fangs elongate in response. "I'm in.
Just tell me when and where."

Onegus nodded and kept on walking.

The chief's small briefing room was already packed
when Peter entered, and as Onegus began the final
briefing detailing entry points and contingency plans,
Peter's thoughts drifted once again to Marina, the afternoon delight they had shared and the future they might
have together.

Shaking his head, he forced himself to focus. They had
gone over the details this morning, but there was no
substitute for a refresher right before the mission.

When the briefing concluded, the team filed out
towards the vehicles. Peter fell into step beside Jay and
Alfie.

"What's up?" Jay asked, his keen eyes studying Peter's
face. "Everything okay?"

Peter nodded, a small smile lifting one corner of his lips.
"Everything's good and getting better."

36

JASMINE

"I'm worried about Margo's brother," Jasmine said after the door closed behind Edgar. "She didn't call or text me."

She pulled out her phone and typed—*Any news?*

Her phone rang a moment later. "There was a major blowout with Lynda, and Rob is devastated," Margo said in a hushed voice. "Lynda turned nasty when Rob confronted her about seeing her ex in secret, and she said very hurtful things very loudly and publicly. Rob was so devastated that I brought him to the other penthouse because he needed to be alone, and I didn't know what else to do. I wish I could tell him about his potential immortality to cheer him up, but I can't without asking permission first and taking the proper precautions."

Poor Rob. Jasmine's heart ached for him, but Margo shouldn't have brought him to the keep. "Did you ask

Kian's permission to bring your brother to the penthouse?"

"I didn't, but I should. I need to call him and ask him what to do. Someone needs to tell Rob about being a Dormant, and what it means, but before that can be done, someone also needs to compel him to keep it a secret."

"So call Kian. What are you waiting for?"

"I'm scared that he will be mad at me for bringing Rob up here, and because I'm a big chicken, I'll probably call Negal and have him do that. The problem is that I can't leave Rob alone for long enough to explain to either of them what's going on and why Rob is here."

In the time it had taken Margo to talk to Jasmine, she could have probably managed to tell either Negal or Kian what happened, but Jasmine had a feeling that Margo wouldn't have called Kian even if Rob wasn't there.

Kian was intimidating, and calling him on a weekend when he was spending time with his family wasn't a good idea. Even Jasmine would have hesitated, and she wasn't timid in the least.

Well, she knew that Kian owed her for saving the twins, so she felt emboldened to contact him directly if she needed to, but only in case of emergency, which this was in a way, because Margo had made it so. If she hadn't brought Rob to the penthouse, everything could have been done at a much slower pace.

"Where is Rob now?" Jasmine asked.

"In the bathroom. I think he's crying in there."

Jasmine winced. "That bad, huh?"

"Yeah."

"I'm coming over. I'll try to console him while you make the necessary call or calls."

Margo released an audible breath. "Thank you. You are a lifesaver."

"I helped cook up this disaster. The least I can do is put salve on the burn marks." Jasmine ended the call and looked at Ell-rom. "Are you going to be okay by yourself here?"

"Of course. Go help your friend."

"What are you going to do while I'm gone?"

He shrugged. "I can watch television and learn a little more about your world."

That wasn't the best way to learn about Earth and humans, especially when she wasn't there to guide what he chose to watch and explain what he was being shown, but there wasn't much else he could do to pass the time.

As she glanced at the lap pool on the terrace, it was on the tip of her tongue to suggest that he take advantage of it to exercise, but she changed her mind at the last moment. She didn't want him doing physical therapy exercises without her or someone else watching over him.

Was she being overcautious?

Probably.

Jasmine leaned in and pressed a soft kiss to his lips. "Take everything you see with a grain of salt." When he gave her a perplexed look, she laughed. "It means don't believe everything you see and hear on television. Everyone has an agenda and something to sell, and you are not familiar with the players."

He nodded. "I understand. I will reserve judgment."

"Excellent. I'll come get you when I'm done, and we will go visit your sister."

Smiling, he picked up the remote. "Sounds good. Just show me how to work this thing before you leave."

"Of course." She kept forgetting that he didn't know the most basic things and needed to learn everything.

After showing him how to operate the remote and bringing him a bottle of water so he would remember to stay hydrated, Jasmine headed across the vestibule to the other penthouse.

37

JASMINE

J asmine stood in front of the door of the other penthouse, took a deep breath, and rang the bell.

Margo answered a moment later, her mask of worry turning into relief when she saw her. "Thank goodness you're here." She ushered her inside.

The tension was palpable in the air, emanating from the siblings but mostly from the figure hunched on the plush living room sofa.

When Rob turned to look at her, Jasmine was struck by how much he resembled his sister. His hair was a darker shade of blonde than Margo's, but he shared the same Nordic features—high cheekbones, clear blue eyes, and fair skin. Those eyes were now red-rimmed.

"Hi, Rob." She approached him with a smile attached firmly to her face. "I'm Jasmine, Margo's friend."

He seemed puzzled by her appearance. "Do you live here?"

"No. I live across the hall in the other penthouse. The owners of Perfect Match were kind enough to provide lodging for several of us here."

That was the cover story Margo and Frankie were using with their families, and she could work with that.

She sat next to him. "I heard what happened. I'm so sorry you're going through this."

Rob cast an accusing glance at his sister. "Did you tell all of your friends about your duped brother?"

Margo winced. "I'm sorry. I've been suspicious of Lynda for a long time, and I've been pretty vocal about it. Jasmine was the one who prompted me to tell you my suspicions. She said that it's better to suffer a little pain now than much more of it in the future."

"Thanks," Jasmine said with a note of sarcasm in her tone. "Why don't you throw me under the bus?"

"Sorry." Margo winced again. "I'll leave you two alone for a few minutes. I need to talk to Negal."

Rob didn't say anything, but he watched his sister leave with an accusatory look in his eyes.

For a moment they sat in silence, the weight of Rob's pain pressing on Jasmine in an almost physical way. Finally, Jasmine spoke. "You know, I went through a breakup not too long ago. It wasn't as dramatic as what you're going through, but it still hurt."

Rob looked up, a flicker of interest in his eyes. "What happened?"

Jasmine sighed, thinking back to those days that now felt like a lifetime ago. "There wasn't any big betrayal or fight. We just realized we weren't right for each other. But even without a major reason, it was still hard. Letting go of someone you care about hurts even if you know that it's for the best. I knew that both of us needed to find the right person and that compromising would only make us miserable in the future. "

"But I love Lynda," Rob's voice cracked. "I can't believe she could be so deceitful, but even worse than that was how nasty she turned when I confronted her. The way she talked to me, it was as if she hated everything about me. Why was she marrying me, then? How do I move on from that?"

Jasmine's heart ached for him. The pain of betrayal was a unique kind of agony, one that couldn't be easily soothed with words.

"She probably didn't mean most of what she said. You caught her red-handed, and she got defensive. Not that I'm excusing her behavior. She is a nasty piece of work. What I'm trying to do is to take the sting out of her words. I don't know what insults she hurled at you, but you shouldn't take any of them to heart because none are true."

Rob let out a breath. "Thank you for saying that, but you don't know me. What if I deserve the insults?"

"I know you a little bit from what Margo has told me about you. You are smart, successful, and you are a nice guy who takes people at face value because you are an honest man who doesn't expect deceit from others."

He arched a brow. "You mean a patsy?"

She shrugged. "There could be worse things to be called."

He shook his head. "I can't believe how blind I was. We've been together for over five years. We lived together. How could I have not seen her for who she was?"

Jasmine smiled. "I'm the last person to ask. I was the patsy who went on a vacation to Mexico with a cartel thug, believing he was an honest businessman."

"Right." He grimaced. "And you dragged Margo into that mess. I don't want to think what would have happened if the FBI wasn't watching that yacht."

That was another cover story that Margo and Frankie had told their families, but Jasmine didn't have all the details of the story, so she needed to change the subject.

"It's not easy to realize that you've been duped," she admitted. "And it's okay to hurt and to be angry. But you need to realize that you were saved from a disastrous marriage in the nick of time and that you deserve better."

Letting out a breath, Rob slumped against the couch cushions. "I can't go back to the home I shared with her. I can't be near her right now."

"That's totally understandable." Jasmine placed a comforting hand on his shoulder. "You don't have to figure everything out immediately. Take it one step at a time."

"I need to find a place to live," he said.

"There is no rush. For now, you're safe here. Let yourself breathe. Let Margo take care of you for a little bit. That's what family is for."

Not her own family, but it was for most.

Rob nodded. The raw edge of his pain seemed to have dulled slightly, though the hurt was still evident in every line of his face.

Margo returned, her eyes shining with excitement. Or maybe tears? Had she talked with Kian after all, and he had yelled at her?

"What happened?" Jasmine asked.

"Mia and her fiancé are coming over."

Rob's brow furrowed in confusion. "What? Why would they come now? I barely know them, and I'm in no state to talk to anyone." He cast a sidelong glance at Jasmine. "Except for you. Talking to you was actually helpful."

"I'm glad."

Margo hesitated, clearly struggling with how much to reveal. "Tom, Mia's fiancé, has an interesting proposition for you. I can't say more about it right now."

That was a good call to bring Toven in. He would be able to compel Rob to keep the secrets he was about to learn.

Rob looked between them, confusion and a hint of frustration in his eyes. "What's going on? Why all the secrecy?"

Jasmine leaned forward, meeting his gaze. "I know this is confusing, but I promise you that what you're about to learn is going to turn your world upside down and in the best possible way."

He let out a bitter laugh. "My world's already been overturned."

"I know," Jasmine said softly. "But this time, it's going to put everything back to rights and make things better than you could possibly imagine."

ROB

J asmine was a beautiful woman, and she was also
kind.

Rob was sorry to see her leave.

Now that he was a free agent again, he could and should
look for a new partner.

Right.

As if that was a good strategy while his heart was in
shreds on the fancy rug under his feet.

He needed to let himself heal first and not look for ways
to get back at Lynda. Still, showing up at their house
with Jasmine on his arm could be so sweet, even if there
was nothing between them.

Would Jasmine agree to be his pretend girlfriend so he
could get back at Lynda for destroying him?

How had his life unraveled so completely in such a short time?

Pushing to his feet, he walked over to the glass doors and stared unseeing at the panoramic view of Los Angeles spread before him. It would have been beautiful if Rob could appreciate it, but all he could see was her face contorted with anger and disdain, hurling accusations and insults at him.

Lynda had always been strong-willed, opinionated, and, yes, a little selfish. But she had loved him... hadn't she?

Rob ran a hand through his hair, tugging at the roots in frustration. What had happened? How could she throw away all the years they had been together, the wedding that was less than a week away, the home they had built together?

And for what? A loser ex-boyfriend who had disappointed her before and was bound to do so again?

With a sigh, Rob returned to the couch and hung his head.

The pain in his chest intensified as he thought about all he had sacrificed to be with Lynda. All the times he had swallowed retorts to her complaints and pretended to commiserate with her, weathering her mood swings and going with everything she wanted just so she would be happy.

He had even distanced himself from his family, who had never quite warmed to Lynda and vice versa.

Margo had never liked Lynda, and his parents barely tolerated her. He had pretended not to notice their lack of disappointment when he and Lynda couldn't make it to family dinners or their thinly veiled joy when he showed up without her.

Nevertheless, he had loved Lynda and had believed in their relationship.

How could he have been so blind?

As a new urgent thought struck him, he felt a wave of nausea. "I need to call Mom," he said suddenly, breaking the heavy silence that had fallen over them. "Mom and Dad have to cancel the wedding and notify everyone that it's off."

Margo moved to sit beside him and took his hand. "There's nothing they can do on a Sunday, so there's no rush. Take some time to process."

Rob looked up, meeting his sister's big, sad eyes, and a question that had been nagging at him finally found its way to his lips. "How long did you know?"

Margo's expression softened with sympathy. "I didn't know about her ex, but I saw the way she acted in Cabo during her bachelorette party. It wasn't how a woman who was in love behaved."

Rob felt his eyes narrow, a surge of anger rising in his chest. "Did she fuck anyone there?"

The moment the words left his mouth, he saw Margo's eyes widen in shock. He had never used such crass language around his little sister before. But the pain of betrayal coursing through him had stripped away his usual filters.

Margo recovered quickly, though, "I don't know if she went that far, but she flirted with everything that had a dick."

Despite everything, Rob felt a surprised laugh bubble up in his chest. "I didn't know that my prim and proper little sister talked like that."

"And I didn't know that my brother ever used the word 'fuck' out loud."

Rob's amusement faded as quickly as it had come. "I was never as angry and as jaded as I am now. I feel stupid. How come I didn't see Lynda for who she was?"

Margo squeezed his hand. "You're a good man, Rob, so it never even crossed your mind that Lynda might be in it for anything other than love. I'm sure she loved you in her own selfish way, but mostly, she saw you as her ticket to a good life. You make good money, and you're a nice, solid, dependable guy. But she was not the one meant for you. And you were not the one meant for her, and when Tom and Mia get here, you'll understand why."

Puzzled by the cryptic words, Rob frowned. What did Margo's best friend and her fiancé have to do with any of this? And what could they possibly tell him that would make him understand why Lynda wasn't meant for him?

As if sensing his confusion, Margo stood up. "I'm going to make some tea. It might help calm your nerves."

Rob nodded absently as his mind drifted back to earlier that day when he confronted Lynda and discovered how she really felt about him.

Among other insults, she'd started with accusing him of spying on her and of being controlling and suffocating. The words had cut deep, each one a dagger to his heart. But it was what came next that had truly shattered him.

"You want to know the truth, Rob?" Lynda had sneered, her beautiful face twisted with contempt. "I never loved you. Not really. You were safe and dependable. A good provider. But God, being with you is more boring than watching paint dry. You are so predictable. Spying on me was the first unpredictable thing you have ever done. I need more than that. I need passion and excitement. And that's something you could never give me."

She wasn't wrong. If not for Margo, it would have never occurred to him to check who Lynda was meeting with for lunch. Come to think of it, how had Margo known where she would be?

Did it matter?

Not really.

What was done could not be undone.

Rob closed his eyes, trying to block out the memory of the cruel words, but they kept echoing in his mind, relentless and devastating.

39

JASMINE

I n the hallway, Jasmine leaned against the wall for a moment and let out a long breath. The emotional intensity of the last hour had left her drained, but there was also a spark of excitement. Rob's life was about to change dramatically, and she couldn't help but feel a twinge of envy.

It was an awakening.

She remembered her own introduction to the world of immortals and the wonder that had accompanied that revelation.

It had been so marvelous to discover that the reality she had been aware of hadn't been complete, to learn that there were many populated worlds out there and that an entire civilization of gods was colonizing planets and patrolling the galaxy.

Rob wasn't going to learn all of that today, but he was about to start a very exciting journey of discovery.

Perhaps it would soothe some of the poor guy's pain.

Taking a deep breath, Jasmine composed herself, put a smile on her face, and opened the door. She didn't want to bring any residual tension into Ell-rom's space. He had enough to deal with without her adding stress to it.

The moment she stepped into the penthouse, though, she felt the tension in the room. The television was blaring in the living room, and Ell-rom sat rigidly on the couch. His eyes were glued to the news broadcast, his jaw was set, and his hand was fisting the remote control with so much force that the plastic was creaking under the pressure of his grip.

Without hesitation, she crossed the room and gently pried the remote from his hand, clicking off the TV.

Ell-rom blinked as if coming out of a trance. "Why did you do that?" he asked.

Jasmine sat beside him, placing a comforting hand on his arm. "You are not ready to see all that ugliness. Remember what I told you? The news editors like to pick the worst of the worst to broadcast because that's how they get viewers, and viewers bring advertising money. Showing people spending happy afternoons with their families is not newsworthy."

"So that wasn't real?" He waved his hand at the television set.

"Oh, it was real, but it was an ugly slice of reality. Not everything is like that."

That was true, but those pockets of evil were popping up more frequently around the world, and things were getting worse for most people. Still, she could shield him from that for a little while longer.

Los Angeles was still relatively safe, although not as safe as it was only a few years ago. Other major cities were seeing a more rapid rise in violent crime, and part of the world was receding into darkness. The sad part was that women and children were always the first victims when things were starting to deteriorate. It seemed like lately, travesties committed against women and young girls had become a daily occurrence.

Darkness was on the rise. There was no doubt in her mind about that.

"Even that much is bad," Ell-rom said. "How are things like that allowed to happen in human societies? What is this savagery?"

Jasmine was asking herself the same questions, but Ell-rom couldn't allow himself to get so upset. "You need to calm down. We don't want you to accidentally..." She trailed off.

Ell-rom swallowed hard, his Adam's apple bobbing. "You're right," he said, his voice barely above a whisper. "I need to control my emotions. I can't allow them to boil over."

Guilt washed over Jasmine. She should have known better than to leave him alone with access to the news. "I'm sorry. I shouldn't have left you alone with the remote. It's my fault."

As soon as the words left her mouth, she saw something shift in Ell-rom's eyes. The anger and dismay over what he had seen in the news were replaced by a flash of hurt.

"What's the matter?" she asked, though she had a sinking feeling she already knew.

Ell-rom's jaw clenched, his eyes meeting hers with an intensity that took her aback. "I'm tired of being treated like a child. I appreciate your concern, but I can handle watching television without your supervision."

The words hit Jasmine like a physical blow. She opened her mouth to protest, but the truth of his statement stopped her short. She had been treating him like a child, hadn't she? In her desire to protect him, to shield him from potential triggers, she'd been stifling him.

"You're right," she said softly, the admission difficult but necessary. "I'm sorry for having been overprotective. You're not a child, and you are perfectly capable of making your own decisions. My job is to supply the information that you might be lacking, but I shouldn't decide for you."

Ell-rom's expression softened, but there was still a hint of hurt in his eyes. "I know you mean well, but I need to learn to navigate this world on my own terms. I'm not an impulsive person, and I know what I can handle and what I need help with."

"You're absolutely right. I'll do my best to keep in check my overprotective instincts."

A moment of silence stretched between them, not uncomfortable but charged with unspoken emotions. Finally, Ell-rom broke it. "How's Rob?"

Grateful for the change of subject, Jasmine launched into an explanation of Rob's situation, and as she spoke she watched Ell-rom's face, seeing the empathy and understanding dawning in his eyes.

When she finished, he shook his head. "Poor Rob. To have someone you love turn on you like that must be devastating."

Jasmine nodded. "It is, but I believe that it's for the best. Lynda clearly wasn't right for him, and now Rob's world is about to change dramatically for the better, but it will take him time to realize that."

"Does Rob know about the spying device Margo put on his mate?" Ell-rom asked.

"No. But I imagine it will come out soon. All the secrets are about to be revealed."

A soft chuckle escaped Ell-rom. "I was in Rob's situation not too long ago."

"You didn't have a cheating fiancée," she teased, trying to lighten the mood.

"No," Ell-rom agreed. "But I didn't know who and what I was. It was pretty profound to find out, and there is still a lot to learn."

The weight of his words hung in the air between them. Jasmine thought back to those first few days after Ell-rom had awakened, the confusion and fear in his eyes as he grappled with his new reality. She had been so focused on protecting him, on helping him adjust, that she hadn't fully appreciated the magnitude of what he was going through.

"I can't even imagine." She reached for his hand. "How are you really doing with all of this?"

Ell-rom was quiet for a long moment, his thumb tracing circles on the back of her hand. "It's overwhelming. There are moments when I feel like I'm drowning in all the new information, all the things I need to learn and remember, but then there are moments like this. Moments with you, where everything feels right. Where I feel anchored."

The honesty of his words brought tears to Jasmine's eyes. She leaned in, pressing a soft kiss to his lips. "I'm glad I can be your anchor," she whispered.

40

ROB

At the sound of the front door opening, Rob winced.

The last thing he wanted was to smile and be civil to Mia and her rich fiancé, but he was curious to learn about the earth-shattering news Tom was about to impart.

It would have been better if they had waited at least one day to visit so he could gather the broken pieces of his heart and pretend to be whole, but they were here, and he had to deal with them as best he could.

With a sigh, he looked up and was surprised to see Mia enter, walking on what he assumed were her prosthetic legs. She must have gotten a new and advanced model because her gait looked completely natural. He had known Mia for most of her life, and since losing her legs, she had never walked so well.

Still, that wasn't as jarring as the guy walking in next to her.

He'd heard Margo talk about Mia's fiancé being movie-star handsome and richer than the devil himself, but he'd thought that his sister had exaggerated. As it turned out, she'd downplayed the guy's god-like appearance.

Why had Tom chosen Mia when he could have any woman on earth?

The pair made no sense.

Mia was a lovely young woman, pretty, sweet, and talented, but she was not in the same league as her guy. According to Margo, Tom had taken her to Switzerland to see a world-renowned expert for her heart condition. The treatment she'd gotten there and the protocol they had prescribed had restored her health, and evidently, he'd also gotten her much better prosthetics.

Rob rose to his feet and approached the couple. "Mia, it is so good to see you." He leaned down and kissed her cheek. "You look amazing." He turned to the fiancé and offered him his hand. "I assume you are the man responsible for Mia's good health."

"You could say that." The man shook his hand. "I'm Tom, or Toven to my close friends."

After that introduction, Rob wasn't sure what he should call the guy. Margo had always referred to him as Tom, so maybe that was what he should use.

"I think I'll stick with Tom for now. I'm Rob. Thank you

for helping Mia and for coming here on such short notice."

"Margo is like a sister to Mia, and there is nothing I wouldn't do for Mia and her family." The god-like creature smiled, and Rob felt weak at the knees.

He had never been attracted to men, but there was something about Tom that transcended the normal and mundane.

It was unsettling, to say the least.

Perhaps Lynda's betrayal had shaken up his foundations so profoundly that even the basic pillars of who he was were showing cracks.

"Your sister calls me Toven, so you should call me Toven as well."

"Thank you," Rob said, because he couldn't come up with anything better. Right now, his brain was not firing on all cylinders.

"Where should we do this?" Margo asked.

Rob cast her a questioning look. "Do what?"

"Talk," Toven said. "We can sit down right here." He motioned at the couch and armchairs that flanked the massive coffee table in the center of the room.

As Rob sat back down in the same spot he had been sitting in for the past hour or so, Margo sat next to him, and Mia and Toven each sat in an armchair facing them.

"Perhaps a drink is in order." Margo rose back to her feet. "The bar is fully stocked, so you can take your pick."

Rob realized that he was thirsty despite finishing the bottle of water Margo had given him when they had entered the penthouse. Evidently, emotional turmoil burned through liquids faster than normal.

"Can I have another bottle of water and also a beer?"

Margo grimaced. "You won't like the kind of beer we have, but I can get you some very good whiskey."

"I'll take it." He wasn't a great fan of whiskey, but he needed some alcohol to dull the pain.

"I'd like some tea." Mia rose to her feet with a fluidity that should not have been possible with a prosthesis.

Toven looked at her with adoration in his eyes. "I would like some tea as well, my love."

She smiled back. "Of course."

When she and Margo ducked into the kitchen, Rob turned to Toven. "I've known Mia for many years, and I've seen her with all kinds of prostheses, but I've never seen her walk so naturally with them. You must have gotten state-of-the-art tech."

Toven smiled. "Indeed. There is nothing more state-of-the-art than what nature makes. Mia no longer needs prosthetics. She has regrown her legs."

For a long moment, Rob just gaped at Toven. "How is that possible?"

"Many things are possible when you have the right genes."

Rob frowned. "Gene therapy? Is that how it was done?"

Toven chuckled. "You could say so." He leaned forward, bracing his elbows on his knees and his chin on his fist. "Before I go into what made it possible for Mia to regrow her legs, I need to take care of security concerns first. What you are about to hear from me, Mia, and Margo is a big secret."

"I understand. I will not breathe a word of it to anyone."

Toven smiled. "I will make sure of it, but I need your permission first."

That was an odd request. "What do you want to do that you need my permission for?"

"It's a mind control trick that will prevent you from telling anyone who I don't approve as safe what you are about to learn."

Was he talking about some sort of hypnotic suggestion?

Rob wanted to laugh. He couldn't be hypnotized, but Toven didn't need to know that. "You have my permission."

41

ROB

"Very well." Toven leaned forward and looked into Rob's eyes. "You are not allowed to reveal any of it to anyone I don't specifically approve. For now, that covers everyone not present in this apartment, but once we are done, I will enlarge the number of people you can talk to about this."

Toven's words settled around him like bands of steel. The guy was using some sort of hypnosis on him, but even though Rob had never been successfully hypnotized before, he felt that this was very different from his other experiences.

He frowned. "What's going on? What did you just do to me?"

"I compelled you to keep this conversation a secret."

"Compel? You mean hypnotize?"

"In a way. Compulsion is a much stronger form of hypnosis."

Rob swallowed. "I didn't know I could even get hypnotized. I always thought that I was too analytical for that."

Toven nodded. "That's possible. My type of compulsion is very difficult to resist. But my ability is just the tip of the iceberg, so to speak. What I'm about to tell you is going to sound impossible, and I hope that my small demonstration of power will suffice to help you suspend your disbelief."

As Mia and Margo returned from the kitchen with tea, water, and a tray of cut fruit, Rob couldn't take his eyes off Mia's legs. She was wearing pants, so it wasn't immediately obvious that what was underneath was flesh and blood and not plastic and metal, but now that he looked more closely, he could see the contours of her shapely legs.

Toven looked up at his fiancée. "I've already started, but only with the compulsion. I'm about to delve into the history."

Was he going to explain about the miracle of Mia's legs?

"Good." Mia put the two teacups on the coffee table while Margo continued to the bar. "I want to hear you explain it," she said. "This story never fails to wow me."

"Me too." Margo looked at Toven. "Can I offer you some whiskey as well?"

Toven shook his head. "No, thank you."

"You knew about Mia regrowing her legs?" Rob asked Margo.

She nodded. "Why do you think I asked Toven to come over? I know much more than that, but I couldn't tell you any of it without someone first making sure that you can't tell anyone who is not supposed to know."

It made sense.

Toven could compel his silence.

Toven lifted his teacup, leaned back in his armchair, and crossed his legs at the knee. "How well do you know the Old Testament, Rob?"

He hadn't expected that question. "I'm not a churchgoer. I know what most people know."

Toven nodded. "How about Greek and Roman mythology?"

"I'm probably a little better acquainted with those." Rob smiled. "It was much more fun to read about the shenanigans of the Greek and Roman gods than the angry God of the Old Testament."

Toven laughed. "I agree. Those stories were much more relatable because they were based on real people, and they were not shortened and adapted to meet the biblical narrative. The gods were not mythical characters that humans invented to make sense of their existence. They were real, and they took human lovers, and a race of immortals was born from those unions."

Was he reciting some biblical story? Or was that a metaphor for something else?

Rob waited for Toven to get to the point of his story, but he just sat there and sipped on his tea.

He frowned. "That is it? That's your big secret?"

Toven shrugged. "In a nutshell, yes. But I guess you need more to internalize the meaning of what I'm trying to tell you. I guess the confusion about what the scriptures meant when they described the descendants of gods is the result of a faulty translation."

Rob remembered vaguely the passage about the sons of gods taking the daughters of men and the giants who were the product of those unions.

"You mean the giants?"

Toven smiled. "Very good. The word Anakim was translated to mean giants, but the correct translation is immortals. I'm sure you are familiar with the Ankh, which most of the Egyptian gods are depicted holding."

Rob nodded. "It looks like a cross with a loop at the top."

"The symbol is referred to as the key of life or the breath of life. The Ankh symbolized life, both in this world and the afterlife, and was associated with deities, who were depicted holding it as a symbol of their life-giving power. Single—Anakh, plural— Anakhim. Does that make sense to you now?"

Strangely, it did, but as a fascinating lesson in etymology. It still didn't mean that the mythological gods had been real.

"Let's assume that you are right and that the correct translation should have been immortals and not giants. That still doesn't prove that the gods were real people. Besides, what does it have to do with me?"

Toven regarded him with an amused smile. "I'm one of those gods, and you and your sister are descendants of gods. We call carriers of godly genes Dormants, and we know how to activate those genes. Margo has already turned immortal, and now it is your turn."

Toven was insane, or the leader of some strange cult, or this was a dream.

Rob leaned over, grabbed the glass of whiskey his sister had put in front of him, and emptied it down his throat.

The burn felt too real for this to be a dream, and as he put the empty glass down on the table, he felt faint.

"I need to get some fresh air." He rose to his feet. "You'll have to excuse me for a moment, your divine highness." He mock-bowed to Toven.

The guy, or the god, chuckled. "Toven will suffice. I don't require any special honorifics."

Mia leaned toward her fiancé and whispered loudly, "I think Rob needs some proof. Show him your glow."

"Good idea."

A mischievous grin playing on his lips, Toven snapped

his fingers, and as his skin started glowing, Rob's tenuous hold on reality disintegrated.

42

SYSSI

S yssi walked into Allegra's room and closed the door softly behind her. The nursery was peaceful, filled only with the soft sounds of Allegra's steady breathing.

Settling into the plush rocker in the corner, she closed her eyes and took several deep breaths.

Opening herself to a vision was always a delicate process. It was like trying to slip through the cracks in reality. Too much blunt force, and she would bounce back, the crack closing and refusing further attempts. Too little, and she wouldn't make it through.

Over the years, she'd learned to find the balance and let her mind drift with just the right amount of guidance on her part, not too much and not too little, and at the same time, trying to maintain a tether to the present. The last was the most difficult to pull off. To summon a vision and slip through the cracks in space-time, she needed to let go as much as possible, but if she lost her tether to reality, she wouldn't be able to find her way back.

Trust, clear conscience, and good intentions were required as well.

She needed to trust the universe to keep her from harm, or she wouldn't let go enough to make it through. The clear conscience and good intentions were just a hypothesis, though. Since Syssi had never had a guilty conscience or harbored bad intentions, she couldn't test whether negativity would impact her ability.

All these thoughts delayed the onset of the vision, but she knew better than to try to push them aside. She had to let them flow through her and run their course until her mind quieted down and entered the receptive state.

As her breathing evened out and she entered a relaxed state that was very similar to the one between wakefulness and sleep, she felt the familiar sensation of the world falling away. Colors swirled behind her closed eyelids, formless at first, then slowly coalescing into shapes and scenes.

A vast expanse of sand stretched out before Syssi's mind's eye—an endless sea of golden dunes undulating to the horizon. The desert landscape shimmered under the relentless sun, its heat almost palpable even though she was just a specter, viewing the scene but not a part of it.

Nevertheless, she felt the dry, scorching wind against her skin and the fine grains of sand that seemed to permeate everything. The air was thick with the scent of sunbaked earth and ancient stone, but she was probably just imagining it based on what she was seeing.

Smell was unusual in visions.

In the distance, jagged mountains rose from the desert floor, their rocky peaks jutting into the cloudless sky like the spine of some great slumbering dragon. Their shadows stretched long across the sand, offering some respite from the sun's glare.

As her vision swept across the landscape, Syssi noticed the ruins of an ancient settlement half-buried by the surrounding dunes. Crumbling stone walls and broken columns peeked out from beneath the wavy sand, a silent testament to a long-gone civilization.

A lone figure stood atop a dune, the form wavering in the heat haze. At first, Syssi thought it was a man, but as the vision coalesced, she realized that the shape under the loose desert garb was feminine. The turban was male, though, as was the clothing.

Was the woman pretending to be a man?

It made sense. A female alone in those parts of the world would not survive for long.

As if her thoughts got the woman to reconsider her position, her form started to waver, but before she disappeared, she turned, and suddenly, Syssi was right in front of her and could see her face, or rather her eyes, which were the only part of her face that was not covered with a frayed scarf. They were big, brown, and had golden flakes swirling inside of them.

They were familiar, but before Syssi could remember where she had seen them before, the female disappeared.

The sun began to set, painting the sky in breathtaking hues of orange, pink, and purple. The temperature dropped rapidly, and Syssi could almost feel the chill settling over the land. Stars began to appear in the darkening sky, more numerous and brilliant than she had ever seen in the city.

The vision began to fade, the desert landscape dissolving like a mirage, but the impression of that harsh, beautiful land and the mysterious woman lingered in Syssi's mind.

Suddenly, everything stilled, the kaleidoscope collapsing into a single point, and reality rushed back in.

ROB

Rob woke up with a wet washcloth draped over his forehead and Margo's face hovering a few inches above his.

"Are you okay?" she asked.

"Am I? I don't know. Is there a glowing god sitting across from me on the armchair?"

If that had been a dream, it was the most lucid one he had ever experienced.

"I'm still here," Toven said.

"Damn." Rob groaned. "I hoped it was a nightmare."

"Why a nightmare?" Margo frowned at him. "You were just told that you can become immortal, and you call it a nightmare? What's wrong with you?"

"What's wrong with me? Are you kidding? There is a

glowing man sitting across from me, claiming to be a god."

"Would alien be a less frightening word for you?" Toven asked.

Rob removed the washcloth and pushed up on the big couch pillow Margo had tucked behind him. "Is that what you are? An alien?"

Toven shrugged. "My ancestors came from elsewhere in the universe, and they created humans, so in a way, humans are, at least in part, aliens as well."

He went on to explain the origins of humanity and how a group of beings from another world created humans through genetic manipulation. These gods possessed extraordinary abilities, including immortality, rapid healing, and the power to control human minds.

"Over time," Toven continued, "the gods took human lovers, resulting in a new breed who retained some of the gifts of their godly progenitors, with the most important one being immortality. You, your sister, and Mia are the descendants of those immortals, carrying the genetic legacy of the gods."

"How do you know that?" Rob dropped his feet to the floor and sat up. "I mean, how do you know which humans carry godly genes and which ones do not? According to your story, every human should have at least traces of those genes. Our race was created in your image." Just not as perfect.

"The process was different because the goals were not the same. Only the descendants of actual unions carry the godly genes and not all of them. They are transferred through the mothers, which means that Margo's children will have them, but yours will not. You will have to find an immortal mate for your children to be immortal."

Margo leaned over and patted Rob's knee. "That's the main reason I wanted to tell you about it right away. There are many immortal hotties waiting to snatch up a male, Dormant or immortal."

That didn't make any sense to him, not that any of it did, but he had to admit that there was something to the story that rang true. "Why are they waiting? Is there a shortage of men among the immortals?"

Mia cleared her throat. "There is a shortage of males and females who are not related to each other. Almost all of the immortals in our community are the descendants of one goddess, and according to their rules, they are forbidden to each other. If they were the descendants of the same male god, there wouldn't have been any prohibition." She looked at her fiancé. "Toven did not know that any of the gods other than him had survived, and he roamed the Earth for thousands of years on his own, thinking that he was all alone."

Holy shit. Thousands of years?

Was he that old?

"What happened to the other gods?" Rob asked. "Are they all gone?"

"I'm here, and the Mother of the Clan is here as well, but now is not the time to go over what happened and why. It's a long and sad story," Toven said. "It will take a long time even to give you a summary, and you will have many questions, which will take even longer. Right now, though, I'm sure that the most pressing question you want an answer to is how you are going to turn immortal."

Rob was intensely curious and wanted to hear the rest of the story, but if Toven thought that he should hear that part first, he wasn't going to argue with the guy, especially since he didn't know what powers he had. What if that damn glow was radioactive?

Mia and Margo had supposedly turned immortal, so they were in no danger from it, but it could be deadly to humans.

"Can you turn off your skin?" Rob waved a hand at Toven's exposed arms. "Is it even safe to be around you?"

Toven laughed. "It's safe, but if it bothers you, I will turn it off." The glow disappeared.

"Thank you."

He was trapped in *The Twilight Zone*.

"You are welcome." Toven grinned, revealing what looked suspiciously like fangs.

Rob was positive that the god's canines weren't that long before. "Are those…?"

Toven nodded. "Yes. Those are fangs. All male gods and immortals have fangs that elongate on demand, and we also have venom glands. Female goddesses and female immortals have small fangs that do not elongate, and they do not have venom either. The venom is what activates the dormant godly genes."

Things were just getting weirder and weirder, and Rob wondered whether there was something in the water his sister had given him or the whiskey, but since that was unlikely, his next hypothesis was that he was suffering a mental meltdown because of the traumatic breakup with Lynda.

44

ROB

"I think I need another drink," Rob murmured. "Or maybe an appointment with a shrink."

"I can help you with the first one." Margo pushed to her feet.

Toven just regarded him with amusement dancing in his blue eyes. "I know that it's a lot to be exposed to and process, but I suggest that you suspend your disbelief until I'm done."

Rob swallowed.

So far, he had seen Toven's skin start and stop glowing on demand, and he also saw the guy's fangs. Unless this was the strangest dream he'd ever had or he was hallucinating, Toven was really an alien from a race of alien beings who called themselves gods.

Also, Margo was not disputing a word he'd said.

Maybe it was all true?

"My sister vouches for you, and Margo is not easily fooled. I'm listening."

"Good." Toven seemed relieved. "So here is how the induction process works for males. It requires a fight with an immortal. The goal isn't to win, as immortals are much stronger than humans. Still, the resistance you put up needs to be enough to trigger the production of venom in the immortal's glands. When he bites you, and the venom enters your system, it triggers the activation of your immortal genes. It doesn't always work with the first bite, and sometimes the process has to be repeated, but at least you don't need to worry about not having the genes. Since your sister turned immortal, there is no doubt that you will turn as well. You share the same mother, right?"

"We do." Rob frowned. "Can our mother be activated as well? Given what you have told me so far, she should also be a Dormant."

"It's risky at her age," Mia said. "And since for females, the bite is not enough and sex with an immortal is also required, it's problematic because I doubt your father would be okay with that."

Suspension of disbelief was getting more and more difficult, but Rob had promised Toven that he would try. "Why is sex required? Is it because females can't put up a decent enough fight to trigger an immortal's aggression?"

Toven laughed. "It's not about a female's inability to put up a fight. There was one case of a male who aggravated an immortal into producing venom by reciting vile poetry, so physical strength is not the issue. It's just that we are programmed not to respond that way to females, no matter what they do. We produce aggressive venom only in response to male aggression, and we produce erotic venom in response to desire, mostly toward females, but I assume that for some, the response is the same toward males they find desirable."

"That could get confusing," Mia murmured. "I mean between two males who are into each other. What if they get into a fight?"

"I wouldn't know," Toven admitted. "But I agree that this is an interesting question. My guess is that when desire and love are involved, the venom produced can only be the erotic kind."

"I'm exclusively into women," Rob said, to make sure they were all on the same page. "Who do I need to fight and when?"

Toven leaned back, his expression serious. "This is a lot to take in, and it's not a decision to be made lightly. Becoming immortal seems like a no-brainer, and it opens up a world of possibilities you've never imagined, but it has some downsides that you should be aware of, so take your time deciding."

The words hung in the air, heavy and impossible. Rob felt a hysterical laugh bubbling up in his throat. This had to be some kind of joke, right? Some elaborate prank to distract him from his heartbreak?

But as he looked at his sister's earnest face, he felt the laughter die in his chest. "What downsides?"

As Toven began to explain further, Rob felt a strange mix of emotions washing over him. Fear, excitement, disbelief, hope—they all swirled together in a dizzying emotional dance. But beneath it all, there was a spark of something he hadn't felt for a long time, much longer than the recent breakup. It was a possibility.

The world as he knew it had already been turned upside down by Lynda, but now the future didn't look as glum anymore.

By the time the god was done explaining the possible dangers of transitioning into immortality and the limitations of leading a life that had to be shrouded in secrets, Rob had made up his mind.

"I don't want to wait. I want to do it as soon as possible."

Toven looked at Margo before returning his gaze to Rob. "There is one slight complication. Your transition probably needs to happen in the immortals' hidden village, and Margo can't come with you. I didn't explain about her transition and why her situation is unique. I leave it up to her, but I need to call the leader of our community to ask how we should proceed."

"Who is your leader, the goddess?" Rob asked.

If it wasn't Toven, the only other one could be the other

surviving goddess. The Clan Mother, the one who had created this clan of immortals.

"Her son," Toven said. "The goddess is semi-retired. She is still the head of the clan, but her son runs the American part of the clan, and her daughter runs the European one."

"When can I go there?"

Toven sighed. "If I get approval from Kian, I can take you there right now, but I'm sure that you need a few days to organize things so you can take the time off. The transition process can take between several days to several weeks."

Rob felt a thrill at the idea of leaving everything behind right now and starting a new adventure.

"If the boss agrees, I would love to go with you. I don't want to go back to the house I shared with Lynda. The only thing I need is my laptop, and I have it with me. I can work from anywhere as long as there is internet access."

Margo snorted. "Don't be silly. You need to get some clothing from the house. You can't just go. Where will you even stay?"

"Rob can stay with us," Mia offered. "We have an extra bedroom. And as for clothing and other things, we can stop at a department store on the way and get him whatever he needs."

Margo shifted her gaze back to him. "Is that what you want to do?"

"Yes. More than anything. I don't want to see Lynda's face ever again if I can help it."

Toven pushed to his feet. "I'll call Kian from the terrace."

45

KIAN

K ian paced between the living room and the closed door of Allegra's room. The silence stretched on, broken only by the soft sounds of his daughter's steady breathing coming through the baby monitor. Syssi had been in there for what felt like an eternity, and with each passing minute, his worry grew.

Summoning a vision wasn't easy, and the intensity, duration, and effect on Syssi varied tremendously. Some left her just a little shaken or puzzled, while others made her lose consciousness, and those were the ones he feared the most.

She was immortal, he reminded himself. Nothing was going to happen to her.

It wasn't self-talk to make himself less worried. It was the absolute truth, and yet he couldn't help the churning in his stomach. Maybe Syssi was right, and it was his obsessive need to be in control of everything that made her visions seem so dangerous to him. He didn't understand them; he couldn't do anything about them, and they affected the person he loved most in this world.

Syssi would be appalled to hear him say that, which was why he never did, but as much as he loved their daughter, one day Allegra would fly the coop to find her own destiny, and then it would be back to just Syssi and him, and that was fine. She was his entire world.

It was taking her too long this time.

Perhaps he should check his emails as a distraction from the gnawing concern in his gut.

When his phone rang the moment he pulled it out of his pocket, he nearly dropped it. Cursing under his breath, Kian checked the caller and was surprised to see the name on the screen.

Frowning, he accepted the call even though it was the worst timing. "Toven. Is everything okay?"

"Everything is fine. Mia and I are visiting Margo at your penthouse, and I'm happy to announce that we have a new Dormant who wants to join our village as soon as possible." He continued explaining about Margo's brother's situation and why he wanted to move into the village right away.

"It's okay," Kian cut in at the first opportunity. "I'm dealing with something else right now, so I leave it to your discretion."

"Thank you. Mia and I will host him until his situation resolves."

As Toven ended the call, the baby monitor clipped on Kian's belt crackled, and then he heard Syssi say something almost too faintly for him to understand.

It sounded like she'd said, "What the heck was that?"

Her bewildered tone sent a jolt of adrenaline through him, and he sprinted toward Allegra's room. Yanking the door open, ready to rush to Syssi's side, he nearly collided with her.

He steadied her with his hands on her shoulders and searched her face. "What happened?"

Syssi's eyes were wide, but that was probably because of their near collision. She wasn't pale or shivering or exhibiting any other signs of trauma from the vision.

Had she seen a spider or a cockroach?

His brave mate was terrified of both, but then her response would have been much more vocal.

Syssi took a deep breath. "I had a vision, but it was very strange."

All of her visions were strange, but pointing that out wasn't constructive.

"How so?" Kian guided Syssi back to the living room, settling them both on the couch.

"It was a vast desert. I could feel the heat and smell the sand. It felt so real." She closed her eyes as if trying to recapture the image. "There were endless dunes, stretching as far as I could see, and mountains in the distance that looked like camels' backs." She opened her eyes. "I need to draw them, those distant mountains. Maybe there is something distinct about them that can point us to their location."

"Was there a clue about Khiann?"

"Maybe." Syssi leaned her head against his shoulder. "I didn't see him, but I saw someone else who seemed significant."

"Who?"

"It was a woman," Syssi said, her brow furrowing. "At least, I think it was a woman. She was dressed in men's clothing, with a turban and everything. Like she was trying to hide her femininity." She chuckled. "Not that it was working with all those curves."

Kian nodded. "I can understand the necessity for such a disguise. In certain parts of the world, women cannot move freely. Could you see her face?"

"Only her eyes, but they were striking, and her gaze looked familiar. They were dark brown on the outer ring of the iris and lighter near the pupil. It looked like they were reflecting the sun or swirling golden flakes."

Kian felt a jolt of recognition. "Golden flakes? Syssi, we both know a woman with such eyes. Jasmine."

Syssi didn't look surprised, which meant that it had occurred to her as well.

She smiled. "Those curves certainly looked familiar. Her eyes were different, though. Probably because she was squinting against the sun. Anyway, the implications are profound. Jasmine has the ability to scry for a location, and she helped locate the twins' pod. She might be able to locate Khiann."

Kian held up a hand, tempering her enthusiasm. "It's not the same. Jasmine had been seeing the prince in her tarot spreads for a long time before we approached her, and she came up with the idea to scry for his location. The Fates wanted her to find Ell-rom."

"Maybe the Fates want her to find Khiann now," Syssi countered.

Kian ran a hand through his hair. He hated to dampen her spirits, but he needed to be realistic. "The vision didn't show you whether Khiann was alive, right? And it didn't provide you with any specifics about the location either."

Syssi let out a breath. "I agree that this case is much weaker, but it was also pretty weak for the pod, and yet Jasmine still found it."

"We know from my mother's tale that Mortdh murdered Khiann when he was en route from Sumer to Egypt. The desert between those two locations is vast. It's a much bigger area than what Jasmine had to work with in Tibet. We could be just wandering aimlessly for decades in hopes of stumbling upon a clue as to where we should dig for him."

"I also saw ruins." Syssi perked up. "I forgot about them, but I saw remnants of ancient buildings protruding from the sand."

That was a thread they could actually follow. "Do you remember more details? Anything distinct about their architecture or layout?"

Syssi closed her eyes. "There were crumbling stone walls. Pieces of broken columns were strewn about, weathered by centuries of sand and wind." She paused, her brow furrowing. "I think I saw hieroglyphs carved into the stone. Some looked like depictions of birds and flowers, and others I didn't recognize."

Kian quickly pulled out his phone and opened his notes app. "This is good. Keep going. Any other details you can remember?"

She opened her eyes. "I'm afraid that's all. Maybe I should summon another vision."

He shook his head. "This is a good start. I don't want you to summon another vision so soon. I'll ask Shai to do an internet search for ancient ruins in the Arabian desert that match this description. It might not narrow things down a lot, but it might give us a place to start."

Syssi nodded. "Should we talk to Jasmine about the vision?"

"Not yet. Let's see what Shai comes up with."

"I'm sure that another vision is needed, but I'll wait a few days before I attempt it again. What are we going to tell your mother?"

He winced. "Nothing. Not until we have something concrete."

"Yeah, I guess you are right."

For a few minutes, they sat in silence, and then Syssi stirred in his arms. "What if we're interpreting the vision all wrong?"

Kian pulled back to look at her. "What do you mean?"

"Well, we're assuming the vision is about finding Khiann because that's what I asked for, but I also asked about Khiann when I was shown the twins' pod, so it might be trying to tell us something else." Syssi's eyes lit up with renewed energy. "Maybe this isn't about finding Khiann but something that Jasmine needs to do. Or maybe something that's going to happen to her? After all, the vision showed me her, not Khiann."

Syssi's intuition had proven invaluable time and time again, but he had a feeling that she was wrong this time. Jasmine had already found her happily ever after, so the Fates were not making her the star of the story this time. They had a job for her to do. She had a valuable gift that would only get stronger once she transitioned, and it might help them find what they were looking for.

46

ROB

After Toven left to call the goddess's son, Rob sat in stunned silence, struggling to process the idea that not only were immortals real but that he was about to become one.

It felt like something out of a science fiction movie, and yet, this wasn't fiction.

"I'm so glad that Toven is here to make that call," Margo said. "Kian is a great guy, but talking to him is not easy. He's always so gruff and impatient."

A small smile played on Mia's lips. "He's a little grouchy, that's all, and his bark is worse than his bite. Nevertheless, everyone knows not to bother him on the weekend and interrupt his family time, so I'm also glad Toven is making the call. He is one of the few people who Kian is not going to bark at."

"I think that's admirable," Rob said. "The guy has his priorities straight." The words caught in his throat as memories of Lynda flooded his mind. He sighed heavily. "Unlike some people I know and wish I didn't."

The room fell silent, the weight of his unspoken pain hanging in the air.

It was startling how much insight he had gained in a few hours—things he had been aware of but had suppressed. Lynda had convinced him that she was interested in the same things he was, but it had all been a big lie. She didn't want a big family with lots of kids like he did. She wanted to travel and see the world with her flake of an ex-boyfriend.

Well, he was her ex no more. Now, he was her current boyfriend.

A humorless chuckle escaped Rob as a new thought occurred to him. He was sure that if he did a little research about the guy, he'd find that he had recently come into money. Lynda wouldn't have dropped him for a poor dude who couldn't support her lifestyle.

The sound of the sliding door opening pulled Rob from his brooding, and when he shifted his gaze to look at Toven re-entering the room, he was glad to see that the god seemed in a good mood.

His talk with the boss must have gone well.

"Kian is okay with whatever I suggest," Toven announced. "If you still want to start the process right away, you can come with us to the village. Mia and I will gladly host you in our house while you attempt the transition, and we will watch over you." He gave him a sad smile. "It would have been nice if you had a mate to sit by your side while you are transitioning, but I have faith that you will find your one and only sooner rather than later."

That was such a nice thing to say.

Rob blinked, touched by the words and by the offer. Toven barely knew him, and yet he was willing to open his home to him during what promised to be a life-altering experience. "That's so very kind of you," he said. "But I can stay with Margo. I don't want to impose."

Margo winced. "You can't because I don't live in the village. I can't."

He'd already forgotten what Toven had said about Margo not being able to come with him to the village. "Why can't you live there?"

"Because of Negal."

"Your boyfriend?" Understanding suddenly dawned. He hadn't met the guy yet, but after Toven's story, he assumed that Negal was immortal. Evidently, he'd been wrong. "Because he is human?"

Margo laughed. "Negal is a god."

Rob blanched. "How is that possible? Toven said that only he and the Clan Mother survived whatever happened to the other gods."

"Negal and his friends are new on Earth. They arrived not too long ago." Margo launched into an explanation about Negal and his friends, their mission on Earth, the evil Eternal King they were trying to fool, and the trackers embedded in their bodies. With each word, Rob felt his grip on reality slipping further away.

Slapping a hand over his eyes, he shook his head. "Stop. I can't take more of this. My brain is going to explode."

Margo chuckled. "I know how you feel. I felt the same way when I learned about this alternative reality. It's like falling down the rabbit hole."

Rob nodded emphatically. "Totally."

In the span of a few hours, the world as he knew it had been turned upside down. Immortals, gods, secret villages, and the evil master-of-the-galaxy dictator who did not know about Earthly gods and immortals and would destroy Earth to eliminate them. It was too much to absorb.

Toven's voice cut through Rob's swirling thoughts. "Mia and I would love to host you. It would be our pleasure."

Rob looked between Toven and Mia, seeing nothing but sincerity in their expressions. Despite the surreal nature of the situation, he felt a spark of hope reignite in his chest. After Lynda's crushing betrayal, the idea of starting a completely new life was intoxicating.

"Thank you," he said finally. "I can work from home, so that should be fine. I'll just need to call my boss and let him know that I won't be coming into the office for a while."

"What do you do?" Toven asked.

"I'm a programmer," Rob replied.

A smile spread across Toven's face. "If you are not too attached to your current job, there is plenty of work for you in the village. Skilled tech people are in high demand, and you'll be working with cutting-edge technology."

"I bet." A thrill ran through him at the prospect of working on alien tech.

It was strange how quickly he was adapting to this new reality, but he supposed shock had a way of making even the most outlandish situations seem plausible.

"What about our parents?" Margo asked. "They need to know that the wedding is off."

Rob felt a wave of exhaustion wash over him at the thought of dealing with his mother. "I can't do that right now," he admitted. "It's still too raw."

"I'll handle it." Margo cast him a sympathetic look. "Are you sure that you don't want to go home to pack a bag? I can do it for you if you want. You can wait in the car while I collect your things."

For a moment, he considered her offer but then shook his head. "It's a fresh start, right? There is nothing in that house that I feel attached to. I'd rather buy everything new."

The furniture and everything else in there had been purchased by Lynda. She hadn't even consulted him about any of it.

She could keep it.

He didn't want to ever again set eyes on any of that stuff. Fortunately, the house was leased, not purchased, and the lease was expiring in four months. He would pay the monthly payments, and once the lease expired, Lynda's new boyfriend could foot the bill or get a new place for her and her stuff.

The reality of his situation hit him anew. He was about to leave everything behind—his home, his job, the life he had built with Lynda. It should have terrified him, but instead, he felt a tremendous sense of liberation.

"When do we leave?" he asked, the eagerness in his voice surprising him.

"We can go whenever you're ready," Mia said. "But there's no rush. We want you to be sure about this decision."

Rob appreciated the consideration, but he had made up his mind. "I'd like to go as soon as possible. The longer I stay, the more I'll overthink things. And right now, moving forward feels right."

Toven nodded approvingly. "That's a good instinct. Sometimes, when faced with life-changing decisions, it's best to trust your instincts."

Rob winced. "Please don't say that. My gut hasn't been doing its job too well. Just this morning, I was planning a wedding and looking forward to a future with Lynda. Now, here I am, preparing to leave that life behind and embark on a journey to become immortal."

The word still felt foreign in his mind, like something out of a fantasy novel.

Margo leaned over and put a hand on his arm. "Are you sure that you're okay? I know this is a lot to process."

Turning to his sister, he was struck by how much she had been carrying on her shoulders and keeping inside. Knowing about this secret world, going through her own transition, all while watching him plan a life with someone she knew wasn't right for him, must have been so difficult for her.

"I'm okay," he said, surprising himself with how true the words felt. "It's overwhelming, but it also feels right. I feel like everything that's happened today, as painful as it's been, led to this moment."

Margo's eyes welled with tears, and she pulled him into a tight hug. "I'm so proud of you, and I'm sorry I didn't have the guts to tell you sooner."

Rob hugged her back, feeling a sense of peace settle over him. "It's okay. I understand why you couldn't."

"I'm glad, and don't worry about Mom and Dad and all the mess with the wedding. I'll clean it up and deal with Lynda." She leaned away and smiled. "Now that I don't need to walk on eggshells around her for your sake, it's going to be fun."

He grinned. "Do your worst."

Her smirk was evil. "Oh, I will."

"Shall we get going?" Toven asked.

Rob nodded, standing up. "Yes."

Margo escorted them to the door and hugged him once more. "I will come to visit you in the village. I can't bring Negal with me, but I want to see the place."

"I will come to get you and Frankie," Mia said.

Mia and Margo hugged, and then they were off, riding the elevator to the parking level.

Rob felt a mix of emotions swirling within him—fear, excitement, sadness, hope. But underlying it all was a sense of rightness, a feeling that he was exactly where he was meant to be.

The future, which had seemed so bleak just hours ago, now stretched before him, filled with possibilities he had never dared to imagine.

He was leaving behind the world he had always known and heading toward a future that promised immortality, adventure, and perhaps, if he was lucky, a love that would stand the test of time.

47

ELL-ROM

E ll-rom's hand rested on the cool metal of the door handle to Morelle's room, hesitating for a moment before pushing it open. The familiar clean smell with some flowery undertones washed over him as he entered with Jasmine close behind.

The rest of the clinic smelled different, and he wondered why his sister's room had its unique scent.

Was it Gertrude's doing? Did she wish to provide Morelle with a touch of femininity in her surroundings? If so, he needed to thank the nurse for her thoughtfulness.

As usual, Morelle lay motionless in the elevated bed, her eyes closed, her face relaxed in a dreamless slumber, and her chest rising and falling in a slow, steady rhythm.

"Hello, Morelle," Ell-rom said softly, moving to her bedside.

He bent down to place a gentle kiss on her forehead, careful not to disturb any of the tubes or wires surrounding her.

Jasmine hung back, fiddling with the teardrop device hanging from a string looped around her neck.

"Compared to the earpieces, this seems so crude," she murmured as she sat down.

"True." Ell-rom pulled up a chair, settling himself next to her. "Still, I'm beyond grateful to the clan's tech guy for coming up with the idea and building the device just so you could communicate with us. I'm positive that understanding what you were saying to me sped up my recovery more than just listening to the sound of your voice would have done."

"Oh, I'm sure of that. This is why I brought it." She lifted the device to make sure that the tiny light indicating that it was working was green. "How about I read to her today?" Jasmine patted the book she was holding on her lap.

The cover depicted a couple in a passionate embrace, but their clothing looked very different from what he had seen people wearing so far.

"What is it about?" he asked.

"It's a love story from about three centuries ago."

He glanced at the cover again. "Is that what people used to wear back then?"

The man's outfit was overly ornate, and the woman's dress had so much fabric that he wondered how she could do any work in it.

Jasmine chuckled. "The nobility dressed like that. I doubt that common people did."

"That explains it. The clothing doesn't seem practical."

"It's not," she agreed. "This is a fantasy, so even though the story reflects the way of life of the period, it takes many liberties, and I also choose to suspend disbelief and not think of all the practicalities, like not having proper indoor plumbing."

As she opened the book and began to read, Ell-rom reached out and took Morelle's hand in his.

With his free hand, he reached up and removed his earpieces, setting them on the small table beside the bed. He let out a soft chuckle. "It's like we're back to a few days ago when you used the teardrop to talk to me. It's amazing how long it seems since I woke up and how little time has passed in reality."

Jasmine paused in her reading. "I was just thinking the same thing. I feel like I've woken up to a new reality as well. My old life seems like a distant past now."

Her old life was shrouded in mystery, and despite putting a brave face on it, he knew that it still haunted her. "Have you decided if you want Edgar to investigate what happened to your mother?"

As Jasmine's expression clouded, Ell-rom regretted bringing it up.

"I'm even afraid of what the hacker might find out. And I definitely don't want Edgar to thrall my father. If anyone is going to do that, it'll be me. That is after I transition and learn how to do that."

At the mention of transitioning, Ell-rom felt a spike of anxiety course through him. He didn't know when he would be capable of biting Jasmine, and the fear made him hesitant to engage in any sexual activity with her. But then another equally distressing thought hit him.

What if his reluctance pushed Jasmine away?

What if, frustrated by his inability to provide her with sexual fulfillment, she turned to someone who could and would?

Edgar might have his sights set on another female, but that didn't necessarily mean he was monogamous, and he and Jasmine had a history together. If she hinted her interest, maybe Edgar wouldn't deny her just because he was with someone else now.

The spiral of anxious thoughts must have shown on his face because Jasmine leaned forward with a concerned expression. "What's the matter? You look troubled."

Ell-rom glanced at Morelle's still form and shook his head. "I don't want to talk about it in front of her." He winced. "In case she can hear us, I don't want to upset her."

"That's easy to fix." Jasmine closed the book. "You could put your earpieces back in. I'll turn off the teardrop, and we can speak privately."

The offer was tempting, but Ell-rom shook his head again. "No, I don't want to discuss anything stressful here. We can talk once we get back to the penthouse."

"Now you're scaring me. Can you give me a hint?"

"It's nothing. My mind tends to wander into dark places."

Understanding shining in her warm golden eyes, Jasmine nodded. "I get it. My mind does the same." She opened the book. "But I'm also curious and anxious, so I will make it short. I'll only read two chapters, and when I'm done, we will go back to the penthouse and talk."

JASMINE

J asmine tried to immerse herself in the narration of the romance novel she had read so many times that she could recite it from memory, but her mind was churning the entire time and somehow managing two completely separate strings of narrative, one spoken and the other internal.

Had Ell-rom dreamt about more disturbing events from his past?

Or was it something else?

Was it about Edgar and her not telling him about their relationship?

When they entered the elevator, the tension that had been building ever since he'd refused to talk in front of Morelle intensified, hanging in the air between them like storm clouds. Any moment now, lightning would strike, and the thunder would shake the cabin.

She stole a glance at Ell-rom, noting the furrow in his brow and the thin line of his mouth. Whatever was troubling him was not something trivial.

This wasn't going to be a little tropical storm.

Jasmine braced for a hurricane.

As they stepped into the penthouse, she forced herself to remain patient but managed to keep her mouth shut only until they were alone in their bedroom.

"Talk to me, Ell-rom. What's bothering you?"

He took a deep breath. "I'm afraid."

That wasn't what she had expected. "Afraid of what? Afraid for Morelle?"

"I'm afraid that I can't be what you need. I can't induce your transition." He lowered his head. "I can't even give you the pleasure of a venom bite." The words left his mouth in a near whisper.

Her heart aching for him, she stepped closer and cupped his face in her hands. "Oh, sweetheart. You have nothing to worry about. It's just a matter of time until you are ready, and I have all the patience in the world. You are the one for me. I love you."

As the words hung in the air between them, Jasmine realized that it was the first time she'd said them out loud.

It was long overdue.

Her love for Ell-rom had manifested in a thousand different ways, and she had demonstrated her feelings with her actions, but until now, she had been too chicken to say those three words.

Ell-rom's eyes widened, wonder and joy spreading across his face. "Did you just say that you love me?"

She felt tears prick at the corners of her eyes. "I loved you even before I met you, and while getting to know you, I've been falling ever more in love with you."

"I feel the same," he breathed. "My Jasmine. My sweet angel. I love you so much."

Their lips met in a kiss that started tender and then turned passionate, a physical affirmation of the words they'd just exchanged, and when they pulled apart, Jasmine was breathless, and Ell-rom was smiling.

"I love you," she said again, reveling in the freedom to say the words.

"And I love you." Ell-rom's grin was bright like the sun.

They kissed again, and Jasmine felt a warmth spreading through her body. It was such an uplifting moment, and she didn't want to spoil it by pushing Ell-rom into intimacy. And yet, she had a feeling that he needed her to push, or he would never get over his aversion.

The trick was to do it gently.

"How about we take a bath together?" she suggested, keeping her voice light and inviting. "Just to relax and be close to each other. Nothing more."

To her dismay, Ell-rom's expression clouded, and a flicker of reluctance passed over his features. "I would love to, but I have to find out a few more things first to quiet the mind. Otherwise, I won't be able to concentrate on just being with you and enjoying myself."

Her stomach started churning again. "What do you want to know?"

Ell-rom hesitated for a moment. "I don't know anything about Earth's family structures, and I don't remember Kra-ell customs. Are immortals monogamous? Are humans? Do they mate for life or only until they produce offspring? Are there people who choose to remain celibate, and if so, why?"

Where had those questions come from, and why was it urgent for him to find out the answers now?

Was Ell-rom attracted to another woman and wanted to find out if he could have her in addition to Jasmine?

It sounded ludicrous even inside her head, especially after his declaration of love for her, and she really couldn't understand where it had come from.

"I don't know much about the Kra-ell." She took his hand, leading him to sit on the edge of the bed. "I've been told a few bits and pieces, and from what I understood, your people are not monogamous. They live in tribal units, usually comprised of one female and several males, but sometimes two females, each with their cadre of males. They don't form couple relationships the way we do. The females invite the ones they fancy to their beds, and the males consider it an honor to be chosen. They are grateful for the opportunity to father a child. Not all Kra-ell males get to be so lucky."

Ell-rom frowned. "I wouldn't have liked that kind of life. If I was forced to live in a Kra-ell society, I would have chosen to be a celibate priest."

Jasmine smiled. "I get it because I'm a one-man woman, too, or rather one man at a time, but there are many people who enjoy spreading the love, and there is nothing wrong with it as long as it is a free choice of consenting adults. Regrettably, that's not always the case, and in many parts of the world, women are treated like possessions and not like consenting adults. They don't have a say in the selection of a husband, and they don't have a say in their husband's decision to take more wives. There is more, but I'd rather not go there."

Ell-rom's eyes started glowing. "I wish you would tell me. I'm not a child to be coddled."

"You are definitely not a child." She squeezed his hand. "But I'm on a mission to put you in a positive mood, and I don't want to spoil things by telling you about savages."

She wanted him aroused, not angry.

"Will you tell me some other time?"

"Of course." She leaned over and kissed his cheek. "Now that I'm done with the Kra-ell and their strange mating customs, I can move to humans and immortals, which I'm more familiar with."

He frowned. "What strange mating customs? Are you referring to the invitation the females issue to the males they want to father their children?"

"Not just that." She debated whether telling him about the Kra-ell sexual fight for dominance would be a turn-on or a turn-off.

Maybe it was a good way to gauge his sexual preferences by his reaction.

"The female expects the male to subdue her. If he can't, he's not worthy to mate with her and father a child. Unlike humans and immortals, the Kra-ell males don't have a significant strength advantage over their females, so it's not easy, and the poor males emerge from the mating bed bloodied and sometimes humiliated."

Ell-rom grimaced. "That's savage. Where is the love? The care between mates?"

Well, that answered her question. "As I said before, with only two exceptions that I heard of, the Kra-ell don't form loving couple relationships. Gods, immortals, and humans, on the other hand, are supposed to have just one mate, but..." she paused, considering how to explain the complexities of human relationships. "Well, that's not always the case, and I'm not referring just to the primitives who think it's okay for a man to take several wives even though it goes against human nature." Seeing the confusion on his face, she realized that he needed a few more facts about humans. "There is no significant gender disparity in births like for the Kra-ell.

Human girls and boys are born in nearly equal numbers."

Ell-rom still looked confused. "I don't understand what you are trying to say."

"I'm sorry. I got carried away talking about an issue that is close to my heart." She pushed a strand of hair behind her ear. "Anyway, in an advanced, free society like ours, the ideal is a loving, exclusive relationship between two people, but not everyone is lucky enough to find their special someone right away. Sometimes, a girl has to kiss many frogs before she finds her prince."

Ell-rom's confusion only seemed to deepen at this, and Jasmine realized her mistake. "Oh, right. You can't understand the reference. It's taken from a children's story about a princess who kisses a frog, and it turns into a handsome prince."

"That's not possible. A frog is much smaller than a man. Even if transformation was possible, it would need to be of equal masses."

"True, but we are talking about magic. Are the Anumatian familiar with the concept?"

Ell-rom nodded. "The word magic in Kra-ell means creating something out of nothing, so I can see how it fits the story."

JASMINE

J asmine let out a relieved breath. At least she wouldn't have to explain what magic was. She wouldn't know where to begin.

As she settled more comfortably on the bed next to Ell-rom, she was reminded of another situation when she had spun a tale, which had also led to lovemaking.

That was how she and Edgar had started their relationship.

She'd always thought that it was her looks that attracted men to her, but evidently, it was her storytelling.

"Once upon a time, there was a beautiful princess who lived in a grand palace. She had everything she could ever want—beautiful dresses, delicious food, and all the luxuries a girl could ever dream of. But she was lonely."

Ell-rom smiled. "That sounds like my life, just without the dresses or the plentiful food."

Jasmine snorted. "Yeah, that kind of fits, but in our fairy tale, you are the prince, and I'm the frog, and instead of letting me eat from your plate and sleep on your pillow, you have to give me the kiss of a venom bite, and then I'll turn into something more. I'm sort of mixing two fairy tales together here in order to make my point."

He leaned and kissed her lips. "You are already the best there is. All I can give you is immortality."

"That's so sweet of you to say." She frowned as the rest of what he'd said registered. "Did you lack food in the temple?"

"I don't remember being hungry, but given the need to hide my and Morelle's identities, getting us food that wasn't blood must have been difficult."

"Right." Jasmine tucked one leg under her and turned to face Ell-rom. "I hope your mother made sure that you had enough to eat. She might not have been very affectionate with you two, but she went to great lengths to save you."

"That she did."

Ell-rom seemed to like what she'd said, and she understood why. He hadn't experienced much love as a child, and it was important for him to know that he had been loved despite the lack of attention and physical affection.

"Back to the fairy tale," she said. "One day, the princess was playing with her favorite golden ball in the palace garden and accidentally dropped it into a deep, murky pond. The princess was devastated and began to cry. Suddenly, she heard a voice: 'Why are you crying, beautiful princess?'

"She looked around and saw a small green frog sitting on a lily pad. The frog offered to retrieve her ball, but on the condition that the princess promised to be his friend. He wanted her to let him eat from her plate and sleep on her pillow."

Ell-rom smiled. "I love the way you tell a story. It's so animated." He leaned and kissed her again. "I love everything about you, my Jasmine."

It was so nice to hear him say he loved her, and it was also a reminder for her to do the same.

Jasmine had a moment of epiphany, realizing she'd had so little love in her life that the words felt foreign on her tongue. Her mother hadn't been around long enough for her to even remember what she looked like, let alone if she'd told Jaz that she loved her. Her father was a cold and bitter man, and those words had never left his mouth.

There had been a long list of boyfriends, but even though she'd believed she'd loved some of them at the time, she couldn't remember saying these words to any of them.

Evidently, she and Ell-rom had more in common than they realized.

"Jasmine?" Ell-rom's voice shook her out of her reveries. "Did you forget the rest of the story?"

"No." She smiled, not yet ready to talk with him about the lack of love in her life. "I was just taking a breather. The princess was grossed out by this idea," Jasmine chuckled, noting Ell-rom's amused expression. "I mean, who wants a slimy frog on their pillow, right? But she was so desperate to get her ball back that she agreed without thinking. True to his word, the frog dove into the pond and brought back her golden ball. But as soon as the princess had it, she ran back to the palace, completely forgetting her promise to the frog."

"That was dishonorable," Ell-rom said.

"The king thought so as well when he heard the story, and he admonished the princess, telling her to never make promises she did not intend to keep." Jasmine chuckled. "Someone should tell this fairy tale to all the politicians running for office. They all make big promises they have no intentions of keeping, just to get elected."

Ell-rom shook his head. "That's worse than dishonorable. That's criminal."

"I agree a hundred percent." Jasmine shifted to get into a more comfortable position. "That night, as the princess was having dinner, she heard a strange noise at the door. 'Let me in, princess,' called a familiar voice. 'It's me, the frog you promised to befriend!' The king, overhearing this, insisted that the princess keep her promise. Reluctantly she let the frog in, allowed him to eat from her plate, and even though she really didn't want to, let him sleep on her pillow."

Ell-rom nodded his approval of the king's decree.

"That happened each night for two more nights, and the morning after the third night, something incredible had happened. The princess woke up to find not a frog but a handsome prince in her room. He explained that he had been cursed by an evil witch and could only be freed if he could manage to persuade a beautiful princess to take him out of the spring and let him spend three nights in her home despite his unappealing appearance.

"The princess fell in love with the prince, they got married, and lived happily ever after," Jasmine finished with a smile. "So, you see, the moral of the story is that you shouldn't judge by appearances and that kindness and keeping your word can lead to unexpected rewards. Oh, and I guess it was also the origin of the saying that sometimes you have to kiss a few frogs to find your prince because you never know where he's hiding, right?"

As understanding illuminated his eyes, Ell-rom laughed. "I like this fairy tale." He leaned over and kissed her lips.

"I'm glad that my prince arrived fully formed with no magical transformation required, just in need of some nurturing." She took Ell-rom's hand. "In real life, it's more about getting to know different people, learning what you want in a partner, and not giving up hope that you'll find someone special. And sometimes, that someone special might come from a place you least expect, like, say, an alien escape pod buried inside a mountain in Tibet."

The smile that spread across Ell-rom's face at her words was breathtaking. "I'm glad I'm your prince, but I have no country and no riches to offer you."

"I don't need any. All I want is to be your princess."

"You are." A hint of playfulness shining in his eyes, he wrapped his arm around her. "So, about that bath..."

50

ELL-ROM

E ll-rom settled into the warm water of the bathtub with Jasmine's soft form pressed against him. The steam rose around them, carrying the subtle scent of lavender from the bath oils she had added.

Her words of love still echoed in his mind, soothing away the fears and doubts that had plagued him earlier, but the biggest boost to his confidence was the way she'd looked at him when he had removed his clothes.

She hadn't looked at him with worry or pity.

She looked at him with desire in her eyes.

"This is nice," he murmured, his voice low and content.

"Yes, it is, and just so we are clear, this is not about sex."

"It isn't?" he teased as if it was her putting up barriers and not him with his irrational fears.

"No, it's not." Jasmine's hands moved gently over his skin, spreading soap in slow, circular motions. "This is about closeness and trust."

Something inside of him eased at her words. He needed those even more than he needed to finally lose his virginity. Even without remembering much about his life, he knew that those two things had been missing from it. He and Morelle had only ever had each other, and they had trusted no one.

"I like that."

"Me too." Jasmine's fingers traced the contours of his shoulders. "I love being close to you like this."

He turned, cupping her face in his hand and bringing her in for a soft kiss. The passion that could sweep them away lurked just below the surface, but they both knew that letting it steal the moment would be a mistake.

Love, closeness, and trust had to take root first, and there was no reason to rush.

When they parted, Jasmine licked her lips. "I want to explain about the other night when I panicked for a moment."

Ell-rom tensed, remembering the fear he'd seen in her eyes. "You don't have to explain anything. It was my fault. I scared you, and I'm sorry for that."

She'd recoiled from him, and he'd hurt her by trying to prevent her from leaving. What had possessed him to do that? He had been lost to lust and hadn't been thinking at all. Instinct had taken over, and he'd reacted.

Perhaps he had been taught about the Kra-ell savage mating ritual and had subconsciously absorbed the message that he was supposed to overpower his mate.

Jasmine shook her head. "None of that was your fault, and you didn't scare me."

"You thought that I was about to bite you and wanted to get away from me, but I restrained you like some savage Kra-ell."

Jasmine sighed. "It's true that I thought you were about to bite me, and it's also true that I was trying to get away from you, but not for the reason you think. I was just afraid of blacking out in the bathtub, and we still don't know what your reaction to your first time will be like. Best to be away from the water for that. I was afraid of drowning in the bathtub, not of the bite. I know how pleasurable it is. " She smiled apologetically. "I had an immortal lover, remember? I was with Edgar throughout most of the trip to Tibet."

A twinge of jealousy shot through him at the mention of Edgar's name, but Ell-rom pushed it down. Jasmine had already assured him of her love and commitment, and Edgar was in her past. It didn't matter if the guy still had feelings for her and might jump at the first hint of acceptance she would send his way.

Ell-rom trusted Jasmine and believed in her love for him.

She placed a hand on his chest. "Don't be jealous. I had fun with Edgar, but he was just one more in a long list of lovers. As much as I enjoyed most of them physically,

I never loved any of them. Not the way I love you. Completely and irrevocably."

His heart skipped a beat at her words, and he covered her hand with his own. "Completely and irrevocably, that's how I love you too."

Her smile was brilliant. "You are my first love, and you'll be my last because I'm never leaving you. I'll never love any other male apart from you." A mischievous glint entered her eye. "Well, except for the son or sons we will have."

The casual mention of a future child sent a jolt through Ell-rom.

A son?

The idea of having a family with Jasmine was both thrilling and terrifying. He had nothing to offer her other than himself, and unless Annani found something for him to do, his prospects were not good. He had to find his place in this new world before he could father a child and raise it.

Jasmine must have noticed the panic rising in his eyes because she leaned in, pressing a reassuring kiss to his lips. "Relax, my love," she murmured against his mouth. "Life isn't a sprint, it's a long walk, and we'll take it one step at a time."

Ell-rom nodded. "In my case, I need to learn how to walk before I can run. I have no skills, no prospects, and no way to provide for a family."

Jasmine traced her fingers over his skin in a soothing, circular pattern. "Immortals and gods are not very fertile, so it might take centuries until we become parents."

That was a relief and a disappointment at the same time.

The idea of having a family was incredibly alluring to him, even though he knew nothing about what it entailed. To him, it seemed like a circle of love that expanded with each additional child, and he realized that he was a glutton for love. He wanted more of what he felt for Jasmine and what she felt for him.

He wanted to bask in love, to be cocooned in it.

51

ELL-ROM

"What are you thinking that makes you smile like that?" Jasmine traced the contour of Ell-rom's lips with her finger.

"Love and how it changes everything." He caught her hand and kissed her fingertips. "How does the venom bite feel?"

She chuckled softly. "I thought we were not going to talk about sex."

"We are not going to engage in it, at least not right now, but we can talk about it."

"Talking might lead to doing," she said playfully.

"We can do whatever we want as long as we are both comfortable with it."

"True." She looked at him from under lowered lashes. "Are you sure you want me to describe how being bitten by an immortal felt even when that immortal wasn't you?"

She had a point, but Ell-rom felt that hearing her describe how pleasurable it had been might help him get over his aversion. He wanted to give her pleasure, and he wanted to turn her immortal, and the stronger that desire was, the better chance he had of battling his revulsion for blood.

"I need to know what to expect."

Jasmine's eyes took on a dreamy quality. "The bite itself hurts, but not terribly so, especially if you lick the spot before striking. Your saliva has healing properties. The pain lasts only a split second, and then there is a rush of warmth and euphoria that spreads through the entire body. I climax, again and again, until I can climax no more, and then I black out and get catapulted into the clouds on a euphoric wave that takes me on a marvelous trip to a different reality. It's really indescribable how that feels, and sometimes, I don't want to come back." She cupped his cheek. "But I know that I will want to come back to you. You will be my tether to this reality."

Ell-rom felt a stirring of desire. The thought of giving Jasmine that kind of pleasure was intoxicating.

"I want to give you that so much."

Jasmine lifted her face to him and kissed him. "We'll work up to it slowly." There was a playful glint in her eyes. "We can start by exploring each other a bit. No pressure, no expectations. Just touch and be touched." She leaned in to kiss him again.

This time, the kiss was deeper and more passionate, and Ell-rom responded in kind, warming, and hardening.

"You're beautiful," he murmured against her skin, pressing soft kisses along her neck.

Jasmine hummed with pleasure, her fingers threading through his hair. "So are you. Inside and out."

Ell-rom liked the slow, exploratory pace and the absence of expectation.

He spent time marveling at the softness of Jasmine's skin, the subtle curves of her body, and the way she responded to his touch with soft sighs and quiet murmurs of encouragement.

As the water began to cool, Jasmine reluctantly pulled away. "We should probably get out before we turn into dried fruit."

Ell-rom chuckled. "Why would we turn into fruit?"

"It's just a saying. When you stay in the water too long, your skin gets all wrinkly, kind of like a dried fruit that was left in the sun for too long."

"Ah," Ell-rom said, understanding dawning. He looked at his fingers, noticing for the first time how the skin had indeed begun to wrinkle. "Fascinating."

As they climbed out of the tub, Ell-rom didn't miss the hungry look Jasmine directed at his erection, but she kept her word and didn't pursue more than he indicated he was ready for.

Careful to steady himself on the slippery floor, he took the towel that Jasmine handed him and dried himself off.

"How are you feeling?" she asked as they settled onto the bed, both wrapped in bathrobes.

"Good. Thank you for being so patient and understanding. I just hope that I'm not disappointing you."

She smiled, reaching out to take his hand. "Never. I love this slow pace. It allows us time to get to know each other better, something I have never bothered with before."

"Why not?"

She sighed. "It's hard to explain without sounding like I'm analyzing the twisted workings of my mind."

He lifted her hand to his lips and kissed her wrinkly fingertips. "I'm sure to be fascinated by those twisted workings."

Jasmine sighed again. "I didn't have much love in my life growing up. My mother died when I was very young, and my father was not affectionate with me. I did not even know what love was supposed to feel like, but I craved closeness. When I developed feminine curves and started to feel sexual urges, I didn't hold back. Sex provided the need for closeness and connection. I didn't need to work hard for it, it was pleasurable, and it filled some of the void in my heart."

As Ell-rom's heart flooded with sorrow for the lonely girl she'd been, he kissed her fingers again. "I vow to love you so much and so completely that your heart will be full to bursting with it."

JASMINE

"It already is," Jasmine whispered.

She'd never felt so…at peace?

Fulfilled?

Happy?

The right word eluded her, and perhaps it didn't even exist. The best analogy she could think of was arriving home, with home being a sanctuary of peace, love, and unconditional acceptance.

The soft glow of the bedside lamp cast a gentle light across Ell-rom's regal features, highlighting the curve of his cheekbone, the slope of his nose, and the fullness of his lips.

She was mesmerized by this male she'd fallen in love with.

Ell-rom's eyes were filled with adoration as he gazed at her face, and Jasmine reached out, tracing the line of his jaw with her fingertips.

"What are you thinking?" she asked softly.

Ell-rom caught her hand, pressing a gentle kiss to her palm. "I'm thinking about how lucky I am," he murmured. "To have found you in this strange new world."

"I'm the lucky one," she countered. "How many people can say they've fallen in love with a prince from another planet?"

A soft chuckle escaped Ell-rom. "One who wasn't a frog at any time before his arrival or after."

She wondered what animal name the translation had come up for 'a frog.' Did they have frogs on Anumati?

"It still feels like a fairy tale." Jasmine snuggled closer to her prince.

She reveled in the warmth of his body, the steady beat of his heart beneath her palm.

Ell-rom's arm wrapped around her, pulling her closer still. "Tell me what love feels like for you?"

That was a tough question because it was difficult to describe a feeling.

"A kind of a glow that starts in my chest and spreads throughout my entire body. It's the feeling that when I'm with you, I'm home. You are my sanctuary, my safe zone, my comfort."

She paused, gathering her thoughts. "I can be completely myself with you, flaws and all, and know that you'll accept me. It's wanting to share every moment, every thought, every dream with you."

Ell-rom leaned in, pressing a soft kiss to her lips. "That's beautiful. I feel the same way about you, but I wouldn't have been able to put it into words. Thank you for articulating it for me."

Jasmine felt her heart swell. She'd had relationships before, but nothing could have prepared her for what real love would feel like. "No offense, my love, but that's cheating. I don't want to hear my echo. I want to hear your thoughts and feelings even if you can't find the most precise words."

Ell-rom was quiet for a moment. His brow furrowed in concentration. "It's... overwhelming. It's like my heart is too full and might burst with everything I feel for you." His hand found hers, fingers intertwining. "It's also grounding. You anchor me. In this world that's still so new and strange to me, you're my constant. My home."

Tears pricked at Jasmine's eyes. "That was beautiful." She leaned in, capturing his lips in a kiss that was both tender and passionate.

He responded eagerly, his free hand coming up to cup the back of her head, fingers tangling in her hair.

When they parted, Jasmine smiled. "I love you," she whispered, the words still feeling new and thrilling on her tongue. "I love saying that to you. It seems like these three words were the key that opened the flood of emotions for both of us."

"It feels a little strange," Ell-rom admitted. "To say that I love you, I mean. I don't think I've used those words often or at all. The only one I loved was my sister, and I doubt we said that to each other more than once or twice in our lifetimes."

Jasmine nodded. "I wonder if I told my mother that I loved her when she was still around. I don't remember much of her, and sometimes I'm afraid that I didn't, and I feel guilty."

"Oh, Jasmine." Ell-rom tightened his arms around her, but Jasmine could sense that he was moderating his strength not to squash her.

He'd gotten much stronger over the past two days, which would have been impossible for a human but probably perfectly natural for an immortal.

A god.

Ell-rom was half god.

For a few moments, they lay in each other's arms, comfortable in their silence, as they exchanged soft caresses and gentle kisses.

"Can I ask you something?" Ell-rom said.

Jasmine lifted her face to look into his earnest eyes. "Of course. You can ask me anything."

Ell-rom hesitated for a moment. "Earlier, when you

mentioned children, was that something you've thought about before?"

"I have," she admitted. "Not in any concrete way, but I've thought about finding a nice guy and having a bunch of kids with him. I always thought that it would happen later in life after I got my big movie break, but now everything has changed. I have different dreams." She smiled. "I can picture a little boy with your eyes and my smile. Or a girl with your kindness and my stubbornness."

"You are very kind and not stubborn at all."

Jasmine laughed. "You still don't know me very well. I can be as stubborn as a mule."

"Give me one example when you were stubborn."

She thought about it for a moment. "I'm always stubborn. I'm not obnoxious, and I don't make demands, so it doesn't look like I am. I use a lot of charm and flattery to get what I want."

Ell-rom didn't look convinced. "I haven't noticed."

She leaned in, pressing a soft kiss to his forehead, then the tip of his nose, and finally his lips. "You are blinded by love."

"Is that a bad thing?" he asked.

"No. Not at all." She kissed him again.

Ell-rom responded eagerly, his arms pulling her closer.

As their kiss deepened, Jasmine felt a familiar heat building within her, but she'd promised not to press for more. Pulling away, she smiled and ran her fingers through his hair. "That's what love is, isn't it? Understanding each other's wants and aspirations, fears and hang-ups. Accepting each other's flaws and shortcomings. Supporting each other through anything and everything."

"Is it like this for everyone?" Ell-rom asked. "Love, I mean. Is it always this intense?"

"It is when it's real. When it's right." She met his gaze. "And this feels more right than anything I've ever dreamed of."

"For me, too. Even with my limited memories, I know that what I feel for you is special."

Jasmine snuggled closer to Ell-rom, her head resting on his chest. The steady beat of his heart was a comforting rhythm, lulling her towards slumber.

"Jasmine?" Her name on Ell-rom's lips sounded a little slurred.

"Hmm?" she murmured.

"I love you."

Jasmine pressed a soft kiss to his chest. "I love you too."

ELL-ROM

T he dim light of the bedside lamp cast a warm glow across Jasmine's features, enhancing her natural beauty.

Ell-rom was captivated by the smallest details—the curve of her lips, the flecks of gold in her eyes, the way her rich hair splayed across the pillow like a dark halo.

He wanted her, but he didn't know what his next move should be.

"What are you thinking about?" Jasmine's voice cut through the comfortable silence that had settled over them.

Ell-rom smiled, his hand moving to cup her cheek. "I'm thinking about how beautiful you are."

"You're not so bad yourself." Jasmine's fingers traced the line of his jaw.

He chuckled, leaning into her touch. "I'm glad." He cupped her cheeks and kissed her softly.

She melted into the kiss, kissing him back for all he was worth.

As their kiss grew more passionate, his hands roamed with increasing boldness. Ell-rom reveled in the quiet sounds of pleasure Jasmine made as he explored her body over the thin fabric of her nightdress.

Brushing his fingertips over the hardened tips of her nipples, he let go of her mouth and leaned away to look at her generous breasts, or rather their outline, which was clearly visible through the flimsy fabric.

Would she want him to kiss them? Suck on them?

The way her lips parted in breathless anticipation indicated that was precisely what she wanted him to do.

When he started peeling the first spaghetti strap off her shoulder, her breathing got heavier, and when he was done with the second one, he peeled the fabric down to expose his objects of desire.

When she pushed the garment off the rest of the way, he lowered his head and took one nipple into his mouth, sucking and licking on it until she cupped the back of his head and guided it to the other.

He was so hard that he considered reaching into his loose pants and gripping his erection, but she must have realized his predicament and did that for him.

Her hand was so warm and so confident, applying just the right amount of pressure, and as he marveled at her skill, he was forced to acknowledge that it was born of a lot of experience.

A wave of scorching jealousy surged through him.

Jasmine gasped, and her grip on his shaft loosened. "Was I hurting you?"

He realized with a start that it had been he who was hurting her, and he let go of her abused nipple. "I'm sorry." He gently licked the hurt away. "I didn't mean to suck so hard."

She chuckled. "It's okay. I don't mind a little pain with my pleasure. I just thought that I was hurting you."

"You weren't."

"In that case…" Her grip tightened around his length. "I like the way you feel. Velvet over steel."

"I like the way you feel, too." He reached with his finger to touch her over her panties. "You're so wet," he whispered. "Can I kiss you here too?"

Smiling with hooded eyes, she let go of his erection, turned on her back, and removed her panties. "Yes, please."

When he got to his knees between her legs and leaned forward, she moaned before his lips even made contact with her core, and when he kissed her, she arched her back.

The scent of her was intoxicating, and Ell-rom felt lightheaded.

"Take off your pants, Ell-rom," she commanded.

For a moment he was frozen, staring at the perfection of her tanned, smooth skin. It looked golden in the soft light of the bedside lamp.

"Your wish is my command, mistress," he slurred his words, his elongating fangs making speech difficult.

As soon as his addled brain made the connection between the state of his fangs and the purpose they served, though, his erection deflated, and his fangs retreated.

Jasmine frowned. "We don't have to do anything you are not ready for. I will be perfectly happy falling asleep in your arms."

He shook his head. "I might not be ready for some things, but I'm very ready for others."

A seductive smile bloomed on her face. "You are still wearing too many clothes for those other things you have in mind."

He was only wearing a pair of sleep pants with nothing underneath and no shirt, so it would be the work of a moment to get rid of them, but maybe there was an art of seduction to undressing, too?

Julian hadn't said anything about it, and the fact that Jasmine did everything in a sensuous way didn't mean that males were held to the same standards. Not that he cared if they were or not, but he didn't want to do something that would not be desirable to her.

Given that Jasmine was impatient, though, perhaps going fast was better.

"Wow, you're quick." Jasmine trailed her gaze over his naked body, stopping at his jutting erection. "Come here." She patted her chest. "I want to feel you skin to skin."

That was the sort of invitation he could never refuse.

As he covered her with his body, he was careful to brace his weight on his forearms even though he didn't have enough meat on his bones yet to be heavy.

"This is incredible." He looked into her warm, brown eyes. "The golden flakes swirling around your irises are hypnotic. I could spend eternity looking at your eyes."

"I could also gaze into your eyes for hours." Jasmine wrapped her arms around his neck and pulled his head down for a kiss. When she let go of him, his fangs were once again protruding over his lower lip. "But there are other things I would like to do with you as well." Shifting, she guided him to his side and put her hands on his chest. "You are so nicely made." She smoothed her hands in a downward sweep until reaching his erection. "Very nicely made, indeed."

He had trouble breathing, let alone moving.

"Touch me, Ell-rom," Jasmine breathed.

Still gazing into her eyes, he had followed her example and slowly smoothed his hand over the curve of her hip until he reached the juncture of her thighs. She was so wet for him.

"This is good," she encouraged.

As his finger sank inside her moist heat, Jasmine moaned. "That's very good, but I still need more."

He was going to climax from all the sensations bombarding him. The feel of her wet sheath tight around his finger, the intoxicating scent of her arousal, the sounds she was making.

"Add another finger, Ell-rom," Jasmine commanded.

He did, and she moaned even louder and arched up when he started slowly moving his fingers in and out of her.

"I want you inside of me," she whispered and shifted to her back, pulling him on top of her.

Gripping his shaft, Ell-room positioned it at Jasmine's entrance and pushed inside just the tip. Conflicting instincts warred within him, one urging him to surge into her and join them with one hard thrust, the other urging him to be careful with the woman he loved and follow her guidance.

When that resulted in a throaty groan, and she clutched his bottom, urging him on, he pushed a little more.

She arched up, taking more of his length inside of her.

"This is…" He didn't know what to say.

"Perfect," she finished for him. "Give me everything, Ell-rom."

He pushed all the way in and then stilled. The feeling was incomparable, the joining so complete that it was magical. If he moved, he was going to climax, and he refused to let it end so soon.

JASMINE

Ell-rom seemed in a daze as he thrust into Jasmine as deep as he could go, filling her with a surge of pleasure and then stilling. The connection between them was electric, and Jasmine's body sang with sensations.

There was something magical about true lovemaking, the kind that joined two ethereal souls in the physical realm.

Still, as extraordinary as it was, if Ell-rom didn't start moving soon, she was going to flip them around and ride him like a rodeo bull.

In her imagination, that is.

Ell-rom's first time needed to be about him. She wanted him to explore and discover his pleasure at his own pace.

"Ell-rom," she whispered. "Don't stop."

Her voice must have cleared the fog, and as his glowing eyes refocused on her face, he bared his fangs, pulled back, and slammed into her. The sudden movement took her breath away, pleasure sparking through her body like lightning.

"More," she encouraged, her hands gripping his shoulders tightly.

He obeyed, and as his thrusts became stronger and faster, sending waves of pleasure pulsing through her with every slam of his hips, the sounds that left her lips were definitely not ladylike. Each moan, each gasp, seemed to spur Ell-rom on, his movements becoming more urgent, even frantic.

Looking at him through the haze of her pleasure and satisfaction, she was amazed at the transformation he had gone through. When in the throes of passion, Ell-rom turned from a genteel prince into a lustful beast, his face a mask of concentration and pleasure and his body moving with a primal grace.

Sexy as hell.

Each thrust more merciless than the last, he pounded into her over and over. The bed creaked beneath them, the headboard thumping against the wall in a steady rhythm. Jasmine briefly wondered if anyone could hear them, but the thought was quickly swept away by another wave of pleasure.

He was about to erupt, and given his fully elongated fangs, there was a good chance he would get over his aversion and bite her.

Realizing that this might induce her transition, Jasmine had a moment of panic, but she pushed it aside. After all, this was what she wanted, and if her transition started a little earlier than she'd expected, it was all good.

Scary, but good.

Wrapping her legs around his waist, she arched her back to give him deeper access. The new angle sent sparks of pleasure shooting through her, and she cried out, her nails digging into Ell-rom's back.

He slammed into her even harder, the pleasure building up to the point of no return, and then she fell over the cliff, her body writhing as her climax squeezed around his shaft. The intensity of it took her by surprise, waves of ecstasy washing over her in relentless succession.

He jerked, spilling into her, and when he hissed, she closed her eyes and turned her head, exposing her neck, but despite the warning hiss, the bite never came.

When the waves of climax subsided and Jasmine opened her eyes, Ell-rom's head was turned away from her at an odd angle. The realization hit her slowly, breaking through the postorgasmic haze.

Had he bitten the pillow?

Jasmine tried hard not to feel disappointed. She'd told him to take his time. She'd told him that there was no pressure.

This was his first time.

He had just lost his virginity, and it was a cause for celebration. The fact that he hadn't bitten her didn't diminish the beauty of what they had just shared.

Tightening her arms around him, she kissed his neck, tasting the salt of his sweat on her lips. "I love you," she murmured against his skin.

"I love you, too," he murmured, his face still buried in the pillow. His voice was muffled, but the emotion in it was clear.

She caressed his back, drawing soothing circles on his skin, feeling the slight tremors that still ran through his body. "It was amazing, Ell-rom. You were amazing."

He finally lifted his head and looked at her with a skeptical expression on his face. His eyes were still glowing, and Jasmine thought he had never looked more beautiful. "Thank you, but I know that my performance left a lot to be desired."

There was room for improvement, but he had done great for a virgin. The problem was telling him that without crushing his confidence. Jasmine chose her words carefully, wanting to reassure him without seeming insincere.

"I climaxed so hard that I saw stars," she said, and it wasn't a lie. "The only thing better than that would have been another climax, but I'm not sure I had enough energy left for another one. It has been a long day."

His expression changed from skeptical to adoring, and Jasmine felt her heart swell with love for him. "You are so good to me, my Jasmine." He dipped his head and kissed her softly, his lips gentle against hers.

His fangs were almost fully retracted now, but he was still hard inside of her. If she wanted him again, he could easily bring her to another climax, but she hadn't lied about being tired. The events of the day, coupled with the intensity of their lovemaking, had left her pleasantly exhausted.

After all, there was no rush. They could make love again tomorrow morning, then after Ell-rom's afternoon nap, and again at night.

The thought of it made her smile.

"What are you smiling about?" he asked, his thumb tracing the curve of her lips.

"I'm planning our lovemaking sessions for tomorrow," she admitted with a playful grin. "Morning, afternoon, and night."

He chuckled, the sound rumbling through his chest and into hers. "Now I believe you that I didn't do so badly."

ELL-ROM

After they had cleaned up, Ell-rom lay in bed facing Jasmine and basking in the contented smile on her face and love in her eyes. She'd said she was tired, and yet she was awake, sharing with him the afterglow of their first lovemaking.

He had loved this female even before waking up from stasis. Her voice had brought him back to life. He just had to see who the angel was that was singing to him.

"When did you realize that you were in love with me?" he asked.

Jasmine furrowed her forehead in an exaggerated frown, pretending to think hard about his question. Then she smiled. "I think that I loved you even before I met you, but I was just in love with the idea of you. The tarot promised me a prince, and I couldn't wait to meet him. Still, I think I fell in love with the real you when we started to communicate, and I discovered how gentle and sweet you were and how much you cared about your sister. The more I get to know you, the more I love you." She paused, her fingers idly tracing patterns on his chest. "But if I had to pick a specific moment, that jolt to the heart that proclaimed you as the one for me, it was probably when you first woke up and looked at me. You were awake just for a couple of seconds, but the connection between us was undeniable."

Ell-rom sighed. "I wish I remembered that moment, but I don't." He leaned in, pressing a soft kiss to her lips. "I fell in love with your voice first," he whispered against her mouth. "I was confused, and I didn't realize what I was hearing, but I know for a fact that you helped me find my way out of the coma. I had to find out if the owner of the voice was as beautiful as her singing."

Jasmine wound her arms around his neck. "I promise to fill your life with songs." She pulled him closer and kissed him back.

Ell-rom lost himself in the sensation, marveling at how perfectly they fit together, how natural it felt to hold her, to kiss her.

He wanted to learn everything there was about Jasmine: every thought, every desire, every fear, and every aspiration. He'd wanted that before, but now it had turned into an insatiable hunger.

"Tell me something," he said.

"Hmm?" Jasmine murmured, her eyes half-closed.

"What's your favorite experience from before? I mean, from before you learned about the existence of gods and immortals."

Jasmine was quiet for a moment, considering. "That's a tough one," she said finally. "I have a memory that I'm not sure is real and not a dream or a fantasy I conjured as a child. It was a camping trip I took with my mom and dad before she passed away. We went up to this beautiful lake, surrounded by mountains. I remember sitting by the campfire, roasting marshmallows and looking up at the stars. My dad told me stories about the constellations, and everything felt perfect and magical."

Ell-rom's heart squeezed at the longing in her voice. "Perhaps we could go on a camping trip someday. I would love to see what Earth looks like outside the big city."

Jasmine reached out to cup his cheek. "We'll make great memories together."

Ell-rom nodded. "I was overwhelmed by what I saw when you showed me the view from the penthouse. I don't think that I ever lived in the city. Although given that Morelle and I grew up in the temple of the chief priestess, it must have been close to the royal palace, which should be in the capital. But maybe I'm wrong, or maybe the Kra-ell just don't build big cities."

"Would Aru and his teammates know that about the Kra-ell?"

"I don't think any of them has ever been to the Kra-ell capital, but Jade should know the answers to most of my questions. She served in my mother's guard, so she should be able to tell me more about my life."

"I'll see what I can do to get her to visit." Jasmine closed her eyes and put her head on his chest.

Ell-rom didn't want Jasmine to keep being the intermediary. She was almost as new to Annani's people as he was, and there was no reason for him to lean on her so heavily.

He'd just made love, so he couldn't be in too bad of a shape physically and mentally. He had been fine for many days now. The memory loss was a hardship, but at least he had retained all of his faculties.

Oh, Mother above, he just had sex for the first time in his life!

Jasmine's eyes popped open. "What happened? Why are you suddenly tense?"

"I'm not. It just dawned on me that I lost my virginity to the female I love. I should be soaring on a cloud of euphoria."

"You are not?" She pouted playfully. "I thought you were."

Was she really offended? She made it look like she was teasing, but he could detect a note of insecurity under the pretense.

"I will cherish the memory of tonight forever. I just don't think it's fully sunk in." He leaned to kiss her forehead. "Do you remember your first time?"

She groaned. "Not in a good way."

"What happened?"

"Nothing traumatic. It hurts the first time, especially if the guy is clueless, and mine was. It was better the second time."

Well, at least Jasmine was going to remember their first time together in a more positive way. Ell-rom was probably as clueless as her first lover, but since she had more experience, it hadn't been a complete disaster.

"Are you okay?" she asked. "No jealousy over not being my first lover?"

He chuckled. "I'm sorry that you didn't have a good experience, but I'm grateful that one of us knew what she was doing. Otherwise, it could have been as bad as what you've described."

"No way." Jasmine propped herself up on one elbow. "You're a natural, and you're doing amazingly well, considering everything you've been through."

It was on the tip of his tongue to ask how she would rank him compared to all of her other lovers, but he thought better of it. "Thank you," he said instead. "I just want to be worthy of you."

"You are." Jasmine leaned in to press a kiss to his lips. "Just by being you. I love everything about you. Even these flashes of insecurity. I'm so tired of guys who think that they are all that."

"All what?"

He wanted to make sure never to be one of those guys.

"Know-it-alls, conceited, full of themselves." Before Ell-rom could ask her to give him examples, Jasmine's lips were on his again, more insistent this time.

He responded eagerly, his hands sliding down her back to pull her closer. As their kisses deepened, Ell-rom felt heat building within him, a heady mixture of desire and nervous excitement.

Jasmine's hand slid down his chest, her touch leaving a trail of fire in its wake. When she reached the waistband of his sleep pants, she paused, looking up at him with a question in her eyes. "Are you up for another round?"

He arched a brow. "I'm always ready, but aren't you tired?"

"I've gotten a second wind."

56

KIAN

As Kian surveyed the familiar faces of his council members seated around the conference table, he once again debated the wisdom of his decision to add new ones. Perhaps it would have been wiser to keep the original group, which included a core of experts in different fields for most decisions, with the addition of the Head Guardians when the voting regarded issues involving clan security.

It had been an advisory council rather than a political one, and it had functioned perfectly. Now, with the addition of Kalugal, Jade, and Toven, it had turned more political, something he should have considered before inviting them to join.

Kian trusted all three and liked them as people, but he was uneasy about their vote potentially swaying decisions regarding the clan based on political agendas rather than the good of the community.

Politics was the bane of democratic societies and would eventually lead to their downfall. Their leaders were no longer public servants elected by the people for the people. They were turning more and more into tyrants, controlling the populace with fear and propaganda and silencing opposing voices so they could perpetuate their power and money grab.

The more things changed, the more they remained the same.

He should have separated the functions, included the newcomers only in informative meetings, and excluded them from decision-making. Thankfully, the clan representatives still outnumbered the others, but things might change soon enough. The Kra-ell birth rate was much higher than that of immortals, and in a century or two, they would outnumber the immortals in the village.

How long would he be able to maintain a majority of immortals in the council?

Even under the best of circumstances and the best intentions of each faction, the Kra-ell were very different people than the immortals and the gods. Other than mutual security concerns, their interests did not align with the clan's, and they might take his people for a ride none of them wanted to join.

He would have to come up with a solution for separating the two groups while still maintaining control over the Kra-ell, at least until he was sure that they wouldn't go back to their old ways of enslaving humans for free labor and breeding.

"Are we ready to start?" Shai asked.

Kian nodded, signaling to his assistant to begin the recording. "Would you like to start us off with your report about the bulletin board?"

Shai stood up. "As requested, we posted a bulletin asking for the perpetrator of the recent thefts and sabotages to come forward with a promise of leniency. Unfortunately, no one has confessed. However, the post has generated quite a colorful array of responses from the community." He paused, a hint of a smile lifting his lips. "Should I recite a few for the council's amusement?"

"Are any of them malicious?" Kian asked.

Shai shrugged. "Not explicitly, but discontent was implied. Someone suggested jokingly that the Kra-ell must have invisibility powers we don't know about and are doing those things to us out of spite. Another mentioned mischievous spirits and gremlins who love to cause trouble, which, in my opinion, is another thinly veiled reference to the Kra-ell."

As everyone cast glances at Jade, she shrugged. "People like to talk and complain. I wouldn't take it too seriously."

Nodding, Shai continued, "My personal favorite was: 'Wake up, sheeple! It's obviously a conspiracy to keep us distracted from the real issues, like the fact that the café ran out of pistachio ice cream and hasn't replenished it since last Tuesday.'"

Kian found the comment amusing despite the possible note of truth in it. He had considered that the small thefts and sabotages were meant as a distraction from a bigger plot.

Amanda chuckled. "Maybe it's a poltergeist. You know, one of those noisy, troublemaking ghosts from folklore. They're said to move objects around and cause general chaos to get people in trouble."

Kian shot his sister a mock stern look. "I think we'll stick to investigating the living for now, but thank you for the creative suggestion."

She dipped her head. "You are welcome."

Kian turned to Jade. "I'm sorry that so many are quick to blame the Kra-ell."

Jade shrugged again, her face a mask of indifference. "I share their opinion, so I can't be angry at them for thinking that. The problem is that I can't find the culprit despite my efforts, and that is after employing my most intimidating methods save for resorting to torture."

Kian winced. The Kra-ell were, in many ways, savages who appreciated strength above all else, and to hold their respect, Jade needed to be brutal, but he didn't want to know what her methods were. As the leader of the combined community, he should know that, but since he was contemplating separating their people at some point, in the interim he could let Jade govern them as she pleased.

57

JASMINE

J asmine sat at the vanity, brushing her hair as she watched Ell-rom getting dressed through the mirror.

The morning sunlight changed the color of his eyes, turning it into a shade of an incredible blue that on anyone else would have looked fake but fit her alien prince perfectly.

His beauty was ethereal.

Last night, following their first declarations of love for each other, had been their first joining, and she wanted to commit to memory every moment of it, save for the end when Ell-rom had turned away, biting the pillow instead of her neck.

Jasmine had experienced a moment of disappointment, but she'd quickly gotten over it. They'd made love twice, but he hadn't bitten her or the pillow the second time around.

She hadn't asked him about it, and she wasn't going to. She'd promised him that she was in no rush and that he shouldn't feel pressured to do anything he wasn't ready for.

Ell-rom approached her from behind and leaned over her shoulder to look at her in the mirror. "You look beautiful, my love."

"You look not so bad yourself." She turned her head and kissed the underside of his jaw. "I love you."

They had overslept this morning, so making love again would have to wait until after Ell-rom's nap. Right now, he was running late for his session with Julian.

"I'm sorry about last night," he murmured.

"Don't you dare." She turned fully and wrapped her arms around his neck. "Last night was perfect, and I don't want you to attach any negative feelings to this cherished memory."

Nodding, he kissed her lips. "You are right. It was perfect, but I need to get over my aversion to blood. I hope Julian's got the synthetic type for me to try."

Jasmine tensed, worried that he wouldn't be able to tolerate even the synthetic version, which would crush his hopes. "You can do it, and you will, but don't get discouraged if you can't the first time. Rome was not built in a day."

When he frowned, she waved a hand. "I keep forgetting that you are not from around here." She snorted. "Talk about an understatement. Anyway, Rome is a great city that was built over many centuries, and it is used as an example to remind people that great accomplishments take time, effort, and patience."

Ell-rom nodded. "I like that one. I hope I remember it." He kissed the tip of her nose and straightened. "I should be going. Will you be here when I return?"

"I will." She was a little uneasy about Ell-rom going alone, but he was not only adamant about going to the session with Julian by himself but also about not taking the walker. "Be careful. Don't try to show off."

"I'm going to be very careful." He headed for the door of their bedroom.

"Hold on." She rose to her feet. "Let me at least escort you to the elevator."

He cast her a reproachful look. "Your friends are waiting for you to join them for coffee."

Frankie and Margo could wait a few more minutes, but this wasn't about them. It was about Ell-rom being sick of her hovering over him and treating him like a child.

"Okay." She let out a breath. "I'll see you when you get back."

When the door closed behind him Jasmine felt a familiar urge to rush after him, to make sure he made it to the clinic safely, but she forced herself to remain in the room, acknowledging that her overprotective instincts, while well-intentioned, were becoming suffocating to him.

The helicopter mom routine would drive anyone crazy, Jasmine acknowledged, but the protective instinct was hard to resist. She needed to at least inform Julian that Ell-rom was on his way and without the walker, so if he didn't make it, the doctor would look for him.

Reaching for her phone, she dialed Julian's number.

He answered right away. "Good morning, Jasmine. What's up?"

"Good morning, Julian. Ell-rom's on his way to you, but he insisted on going without me or his walker. I just want you to be aware that he is coming, so if he doesn't make it, you will know to go look for him or let me know, so I'll do that."

"No problem. I'll text you when he arrives, and if he takes too long, I'll look for him."

"Thank you, Julian. I really appreciate it. Just don't tell him I called. He thinks that I'm mothering him."

Julian laughed. "What's wrong with that? Most men love to be mothered."

Perhaps those who had good mothers who hadn't smothered or neglected them.

"Well, Ell-rom doesn't like it, but I was too worried not to call."

"That's okay. Your secret is safe with me."

"Thank you."

KIAN

K ian rapped his fingers on the conference table. "After much deliberation, I have decided that we have no choice but to compel the truth from the Kra-ell. Since we don't want to appear as if we are discriminating against them and assuming they are to blame without having proof, we will need to question everyone. Toven will use his ability to compel the Kra-ell, my mother will question clan members, Kalugal will handle his men, and Arwel will deal with the humans. Any objections?"

Jade shook her head, which was a relief. If anyone had reason to oppose his plan, it would have been her, but then refusing to subject her people to Toven's compulsion would have cast suspicion on her as well.

Kalugal leaned back, a smirk playing on his lips. "Are you sure that you trust me to conduct an internal investigation?"

Kian met his gaze. "To be frank, I don't suspect your men or our clan members. As I said, the Kra-ell remain our primary suspects, but in the interest of fairness and to avoid any accusations of discrimination, we will question everyone. You are a compeller, so you can compel the truth from your people."

Edna lifted her hand to get his attention. "When do you propose to begin this questioning?"

Kian considered for a moment. "Wednesday. That gives us time to summon the big assembly on Tuesday and inform everyone of what's about to happen and why. We want to be transparent about this process to avoid any further rumors or speculation."

Jade turned to Toven. "We need to talk logistics. Where do you want to do this, and is there any particular order in which you want me to bring the people to you?"

After they had agreed on a system and a few more questions had been floated around, the issue was concluded, and Kian was ready to wrap up the meeting.

He swept his gaze over the assembled company. "Any other items you want to bring up to the council's attention?"

Bridget raised her hand. "I have some potentially exciting news to share."

Curious, Kian gestured for her to continue.

The doctor's eyes sparkled with enthusiasm. "I've started a new experiment that could have far-reaching implications for our community. Two young human women—Marina and Lusha—have agreed to be test subjects in a study to determine whether prolonged exposure to immortal venom can significantly prolong a human's life."

A ripple of excitement passed through the room, but Kian didn't share their enthusiasm. "Can you elaborate, please?"

"Of course. We've long known that immortal venom has healing properties and that it has a positive, short-lived effect on humans. We've never conducted a long-term study of the effects. The hypothesis is that regular exposure to venom might slow down the aging process in humans, potentially extending their lifespans by a significant margin."

Amanda's eyes widened. "That could be a game-changer for those seeking a mate but are impatient for their one and only to show up."

Kian shook his head. "That still doesn't solve the problem of children born to human mothers who will not have the godly genes. No parents want to outlive their children." He grimaced. "Except for the Eternal King and other degenerates, that is."

"It could be very helpful to the clan females," Amanda said. "They could finally have partners to raise their children with, but those men would have to engage in frequent wrestling matches with immortal males to keep a steady supply of venom. It will be difficult, but it would help to keep our birthrate from plummeting even further. Have you given any thought to what would happen if, by some miracle, all clan members find immortal mates? Our birth rate would become even more dismal."

"I did, but if the clan males all found Dormants to turn immortal, and they could finally father immortal children, that would have compensated for the reduction in conceptions."

"That's a good point." Amanda leaned back in her chair. "We also have Merlin's potions, but the jury is still out on that. I was hoping for many more pregnancies."

So was Kian, but he hadn't lost hope yet. If the potions had helped him and Syssi to conceive, they would help others.

"How long do you expect it will take to see results?" he asked Bridget.

"I will be monitoring cellular aging markers, telomere length, and other biological indicators of aging. I should have preliminary results within a few months, but to truly understand the long-term effects, we'll need to continue the study for years."

Toven shook his head. "I hate to disappoint everyone, but Orion was married to a human woman who knew he was immortal. I don't think his frequent venom bites prolonged her life, but you should talk with him. I might be wrong about that."

Bridget regarded him with a look that said she was aware of his son's history. "Orion's wife died at the age of fifty-three, which was a good lifespan for that time.

Still, I suspect that there were underlying genetic issues that the venom couldn't solve on its own. I will know more after I conduct my experiment in a controlled environment, where I know the test subject's health markers before I start and can monitor them along the way."

Onegus shifted to face Kian. "If the test results are positive, this could have long-term security implications. These humans will have to be restricted to the village and not allowed to visit their friends and relatives in Safe Haven. We don't want anyone noticing that they are aging much more slowly than normal."

Kian nodded. "Let's wait for the initial results of Bridget's tests before changing our policy on human partners and making plans for the future."

Brandon cleared his throat, drawing Kian's attention. "If I may, I think we should also consider the ethical implications. Provided that it works, who gets access to this life-extending treatment? Just the partners of clan members? What about their family members? Or the family of recently transitioned Dormants who do not share their godly genes or are too old to transition?"

It was a thorny question, and Kian could see the council members shifting uncomfortably as they contemplated it.

Even if they restricted the venom treatments to love partners, the males would have to participate in frequent fights to get regular injections, and that would not go well with the male immortals. Who wanted to spend their days in the ring fighting defenseless humans?

"These are excellent points, Brandon," he said. "We'll need to address them if, and it's still a big if, this experiment proves successful. For now, let's focus on the study itself and cross those bridges when we come to them."

59

JASMINE

The aroma of freshly brewed coffee drifting from the living room reminded Jasmine that her friends were waiting for her to join them.

When she entered the living room, Margo and Frankie were seated on the leather sofa with mugs of steaming coffee in their hands and a tray of cheese slices and crackers in front of them on the coffee table.

"Is everything okay?" Frankie said with a worried look on her face.

Jasmine sank into an armchair. "Everything is great. Why do you ask?"

Frankie and Margo exchanged looks, and then Frankie shrugged. "Ell-rom left without you, and we wondered if the two of you had a fight."

Jasmine chuckled. "We didn't. Ell-rom just wants to be

more independent, and he doesn't like me hovering over him."

"He didn't have his walker, either," Margo said. "But he looked pretty steady to me. That's good progress, right?"

"It is." Jasmine reached for the mug of coffee Frankie offered her. "It's nerve-wracking, but I'm trying to honor his wishes and not to hover."

As she took a sip, the warmth spread through her body, helping to ease some of her tension, but then she caught Margo and Frankie exchanging meaningful glances.

She narrowed her eyes at them. "What?"

Margo shook her head, a small smile playing on her lips. "Nothing. It's just so nice to watch love bloom and the bond solidifying." She sighed. "It's so sad to see the opposite happening, but I have good news about Rob."

Jasmine felt bad for forgetting to inquire about him. The guy had looked destroyed the day before, and she hoped he'd left feeling at least a little better.

"How is he doing?" she asked.

"Much better," Margo said. "Toven and Mia came over, and Toven told him about him being a Dormant and everything that entailed. Naturally, Rob thought that he was tripping, but he ended up convinced and ready to embark on a new life. He didn't even want to go home to collect his stuff. He left with Mia and Toven to go to the village."

Jasmine's eyebrows shot up in surprise. "That was fast."

Margo shrugged, her fingers tracing the rim of her coffee mug. "He didn't want to have to go back to face Lynda. I think learning about his potential immortality gave him the escape route he desperately needed."

Jasmine nodded. "It must have been overwhelming but also freeing. To have a whole new world open up just when his old one was crumbling."

"Exactly," Margo said. "It has given him hope."

A thought occurred to Jasmine. "What about your parents? Did Rob tell them what happened?"

Margo shook her head. "He was in no shape to do that, so I did. Surprisingly, they were relieved."

"Really?" Jasmine asked. "They weren't mad about all the money they spent on the wedding that wasn't going to happen and the embarrassment of having to tell all their friends and relatives?"

"Nope." Margo took a sip of her coffee. "Turns out Rob paid for everything, so the only hardship they will have to face is the embarrassment of calling all their guests to cancel, but then our mother came up with the idea of using the venue to renew her and our dad's vows instead of canceling. I told her that they should go for it, even though Rob probably wouldn't be able to attend because he went away to a spiritual retreat to calm down." She smiled sheepishly. "I couldn't use the excuse of a witness protection program again, and I didn't know when Rob would be allowed to leave the village, so I used Safe Haven as an inspiration for the story I told them."

Frankie put her mug down and reached for a cracker. "I'm surprised that your mom didn't freak out. She is always so proper that I was sure she would rather Rob married a shrew than face the embarrassment of telling the guests that his wedding was off."

Margo shrugged. "I thought so, too, but as it turned out, I underestimated my parents. They were both relieved because they knew that Lynda was not good for him. They just didn't know how bad she really was."

"Neither did Rob," Frankie said. "I'm so glad that it's over, and I hope he finds a beautiful immortal lady in the village who will fall madly in love with him."

Jasmine pursed her lips. "I wish he could meet Gertrude."

Frankie arched a brow. "You think he will like the nurse? She looks nothing like Lynda. Is he even into brunettes?"

Jasmine hadn't missed the appreciative looks Rob directed her way, even in the midst of his breakdown. "He needs someone completely different from Lynda, and Gertrude is awesome." Jasmine thought back to all the little acts of kindness the nurse had shown her. "She is beautiful, funny, and kind."

Margo snorted. "That would be truly poetic. Negal and Gertrude had a thing before he came to my rescue, and I was so jealous of her, but then Negal dumped her, and I felt bad about it. Still, introducing her to my brother would be a little weird."

"Right." Jasmine took another sip of her coffee. "Maybe when Ell-rom and I move to the village, and Gertrude goes back to her home, I can introduce her to Rob and let them take it from there."

Margo grimaced. "I don't know if Rob should jump into a new relationship right after what happened. He's not in the best state of mind to engage with someone new. He will just want to get back at Lynda."

Jasmine wondered how Lynda was taking the breakup and whether she was upset about it all. Then, a sudden thought struck her. "What about the tiny spy drone? The one Negal sent to track Lynda? Is it still on her?"

"It doesn't have enough fuel to get back to Negal, but we have a plan. We're going to fly it to rest on a shelf in Rob and Lynda's house. When I go to get Rob's things, I'll retrieve the drone as well."

Jasmine nodded. "Smart. No loose ends."

Her phone buzzed, and she glanced down to see a text from Julian: *Ell-rom arrived safely.*

A smile spread across Jasmine's face as she read the message, and when she looked, she found Margo and Frankie watching her curiously.

"Good news?" Frankie asked.

"Julian texted me that Ell-rom made it to the clinic."

Margo raised her coffee mug in a mock toast. "To progress and new beginnings," she said.

"To progress and new beginnings," Jasmine and Frankie echoed, clinking their mugs together.

60

ELL-ROM

B y the time Ell-rom reached the clinic he was exhausted, but he forced himself to stand tall and push through the protesting muscles and the fatigue.

The important thing was that he'd made it without leaning on anyone or anything, and he hadn't stumbled or stopped to rest even once.

Julian looked up from his desk with a knowing smile. "Look at you," the doctor said, his tone warm with approval. "Making the trek all on your own. How are you feeling?"

Ell-rom grinned. "Tired, but I made it, and that's all that counts."

"True." Julian gestured for him to take a seat. "Are you ready to combat your phobia?"

"Yes," Ell-rom said resolutely, even though he was not sure at all. "Did you manage to get the synthetic blood?"

"I did." Julian reached into a drawer and pulled out a small opaque bag. "This stuff is revolutionizing medicine. It does not even require refrigeration. What's more, it was developed entirely by humans."

"Fascinating." Ell-rom tried to keep his gaze unfocused so seeing the thing wouldn't trigger his gag reflex. "Is the synthetic blood new?"

"This type is."

Despite his determination, Ell-rom felt his stomach churn.

Julian had been so focused on what a positive impact this was going to have on the medical community that he hadn't noticed Ell-rom's reaction when he first brought it out. Now, he sensed his discomfort and immediately pushed the bag aside. "Maybe looking at it briefly is enough for today."

But Ell-rom shook his head. "No. I need to overcome this aversion."

He needed to do this for Jasmine and for himself, but he didn't need to explain it to the medic. Julian knew what was at stake.

The medic studied him for a long moment. "There is no rush, Ell-rom. It's better to take small steps in the right direction than to try to leap forward but fall down and break something. Imagine that you tried to run all the way to the clinic this morning. Would that have been prudent?"

"No," Ell-rom admitted. "But that's not a good analogy. Running when I have just learned to walk would have been foolish, but using the walker when I could do without it would have been caving in to fear."

Julian considered this, then put the bag back in the drawer. "I have an idea," he said, standing up. "How about we go for a walk first? When we come back, you can try something more daring. But let's build up your confidence a bit more before we tackle that challenge."

That was an odd suggestion. He was still tired from walking from the elevator to the clinic, which was not a big distance at all. Maybe Julian wanted to show him something?

"Where do you want to go?"

A smile spread across the medic's face. "Outside. I think it's time we got you out onto the street."

Ell-rom felt his heart skip a beat. He had seen the world from the terrace of the penthouse and had watched the bustling life of the city from above, but to actually be down there, in the midst of it all, was far more exciting.

"I would love that."

"Great. It'll be good for you to experience life on Earth as its citizen and not a patient. A change in perspective can do wonders for the psyche." He rose to his feet. "We don't have another walker, but you can lean on me if you feel tired, and we can take frequent rest stops on the way. There are benches every fifty feet or so."

Julian opened another cabinet and pulled out a strange-looking hat. "Put it on." He handed it to Ell-rom. "You need to shield your eyes from the glare of the sun, and I don't have another pair of sunglasses to give you."

Ell-rom examined the hat for a moment before figuring out which side was the front and which was the back. "Like that?" he asked.

"Perfect." Julian led him out of the clinic toward the elevator. "First stop is the lobby. If anyone gapes at you, just smile and keep walking as if you own the place."

"Why would they gape at me?"

Julian snorted. "They just do. Humans love beauty as much as the gods do, and you and I are better looking than most of their males, so they stare. I don't want you to get scared or offended by it. That's why I'm warning you."

Thankfully, there weren't many people in the lobby, and the guards didn't gawk at them or even pay them much attention after Julian waved at them and said a few words of greeting.

The lobby was massive, with soaring ceilings and huge floor-to-ceiling glass windows. When they neared the doors, they slid open automatically, and then they were outside, on the sidewalk.

Ell-rom was immediately assaulted by a cacophony of sensations. The sounds hit him first: vehicle engines, a distant siren, and the chatter of passersby who indeed gawked a little at him and Julian.

Then came the smells.

The air was thick with a mixture of fumes, the enticing aroma of the grass and trees in front of the building, and the artificial flowery and woodsy scents that the passerby left behind.

Ell-rom blinked, his eyes adjusting to the bright morning sunlight reflecting off glass and metal surfaces. The sidewalk beneath his feet vibrated slightly with the passing of a big vehicle, and he instinctively reached out to steady himself against a lamppost.

An elderly human couple ambled along arm in arm, walking into the building they had just left, and the female smiled at him before disappearing behind the self-closing doors.

As they began to walk, Ell-rom found himself marveling at the sheer diversity of the people around him. He hadn't known that humans came in so many shapes, sizes, and colors, and watching them was fascinating to him. It struck him how limited his world had been until now, even with all he had learned since awakening from stasis.

In a way, humans were lucky to be imperfect. Their imperfections were what made each of them unique.

They paused at a crosswalk, waiting for the light to change, and Ell-rom watched in fascination as vehicles whizzed by, marveling at their speed and variety. He had seen vehicles from the penthouse of course, but being this close to them, feeling the rush of air as they passed, was exhilarating.

"Watch this," Julian said, gesturing to the crossing signal. As the light changed, a chorus of beeps accompanied the visual signal. "The auditory signal is to help visually impaired people know when it's safe to cross."

Ell-rom nodded, impressed by this considerate design.

Jasmine had explained that humans were much more vulnerable than Kra-ell and immortals. They suffered from all kinds of ailments and disabilities, but they were making great strides in curing them. She was optimistic about the future of their medicine and believed that in a few decades, everything would be easily curable.

"You can lean on me," Julian offered as they crossed the road. "You can put your hand on my shoulder, or I can wrap my arm around you."

"I'm fine," Ell-rom said, and it wasn't a lie.

He felt energized by being outside. He felt alive.

"Let's sit on that bench over there." Julian pointed to a little green corner where bushes and trees surrounded a lone bench. "We can engage in people-watching while you rest."

That sounded lovely.

61

ROB

Mia opened the door and stepped outside, holding it open for Rob. "The best way to get to know everyone is to hang out in the café." She smiled apologetically. "I don't feel like cooking when Toven is not home. Usually, I go to my grandparents, who live right over there," she pointed at the next house over, "But they are not back from their weekend in the city, so that leaves the café."

"I don't expect you to cook for me, Mia. I feel bad enough about staying with you and Toven." He frowned as the rest of what she'd said registered. "Your grandparents moved with you into the immortals' village?"

"Of course." She closed the door behind him. "After all they have done for me, I couldn't just leave them. They like to spend time with their friends, though, so on the weekends, they usually go to their old house."

Following her down the winding path, he shook his
head. "If your grandparents can get to know about
immortals and join you in the village, why didn't Margo
tell me about what had really happened to her instead of
making up a story about witnessing a mafia crime and
being in the witness protection program?"

Mia smiled another apologetic smile. "It wasn't a story.
Not all of it anyway, and she couldn't tell you anything
as long as you were with Lynda. Also, Margo's transition was very recent, and mine happened more than a
year ago. I've had much more time to process everything and make arrangements for my grandparents to
move into the village. But my biggest advantage over
Margo is Toven. Aside from being a powerful
compeller, he's also the Clan Mother's cousin, and he
took responsibility for my grandparents."

There were still so many pieces of the story Rob was
missing, but his head was already spinning from the
whirlwind of revelations and changes that had swept
through his life in the past twenty-four hours, and he
wasn't ready for more.

Walking beside Mia through the winding paths of the
village, he tried to make sense of the surreal situation he
found himself in.

Yesterday, he had been about to be married. His life had
been mapped out in comfortable if somewhat stifling
certainty, and today, he was walking through a secret
community of immortals, contemplating his own
potential for eternal life.

The village was beautiful, with small to medium-sized homes that varied only a little in style and had been very obviously designed by the same architect and built about the same time. There were no streets or roads, just meandering paths steeped in lush greenery.

It was serene, and the few occupants they had passed on the way impressed him with the otherworldly quality of their grace and beauty, which made him acutely aware of his own mortality.

"That's the famous café." Mia gestured to an area located in the sprawling village square that was sectioned off with low shrubs. "That's the best place to meet people and get a feel for the community."

As they headed toward the small building in the center, where two dark-haired women were serving cappuccinos and pastries to a long line of patrons, the rich aroma of coffee and freshly baked goods enveloped Rob.

"Is it always this busy?" he asked.

Mia laughed. "This is considered a slow time. You should see what goes on here at lunchtime."

Several of the patrons looked at him, their curious gazes lingering. He felt a flush creep up his neck, suddenly very aware of his outsider status.

"Let's get a table," Mia said.

That was easier said than done since there were none available.

"Mia." A dark-haired woman sitting at a table with another blue-haired lady waved them over. "Come join us."

They were both lovely but not nearly as striking as most of the other patrons. Were they human?

"Rob, I'd like you to meet Lusha," Mia said, indicating the dark-haired woman, "and Marina," she added, gesturing to the blue-haired one. "Ladies, this is Rob, Margo's brother and the newest addition to the clan."

Marina offered a warm smile. "Welcome to the village, Rob."

There was a spark of interest in Lusha's eyes as she looked Rob over. "It's nice to meet you."

As they settled into their seats, he found his gaze drawn to Lusha. There was something about her that intrigued him. She wasn't as beautiful as the other immortal ladies, and she wasn't as well put together as Lynda, but there was a keen intelligence in her penetrating dark eyes and a quiet confidence that seemed to radiate from her.

"How is Margo doing?" Marina asked. "I haven't seen her since the cruise."

He frowned. "So that part was true? She really was on a cruise?"

"Why wouldn't it be true?"

Mia chuckled. "Margo told her family that she was in

the witness protection program because she had seen a crime committed and her life was in danger."

Lusha nodded her understanding, but Marina seemed lost.

"I don't understand," she said.

Lusha patted her hand. "I'll explain it to you later."

Marina frowned at her friend. "You weren't on the cruise. How would you know?"

"I know what a witness protection program is, so I deduced the rest."

When she launched into an explanation, Rob wondered why Marina hadn't known about it. Had she grown up in some cultish community where movies and television were not allowed?

"Now, I get it," Marina said when Lusha was done. "But Margo did not need to testify against the Modanas. It's not like the immortals reported them to the authorities for kidnapping her."

"What?" Rob lifted a hand to stop them. "Margo was kidnapped? I thought she had just seen a crime committed and had been whisked into the witness protection program until the trial."

Mia winced. "There is more to the story, but I think you should ask Margo about it."

"I can't." He threw his hands in the air. "Your fiancé took my phone and my laptop, which I need to do work. I have to put at least several hours in."

"Toven will bring them back after our tech guys secure them. He's in a council meeting right now, but he will do that as soon as it is over."

"Yeah, you told me so." He sighed. "I'm sorry for unloading my frustration on you. It's not your fault that my sister lied to me, my fiancé lied and cheated on me, and I was too dumb and naive to doubt their stories even though deep down I knew I should have."

62

SYSSI

S yssi sat on the floor next to Allegra, watching her daughter playing with a shape sorter but not engaging as she usually did. Her mind was preoccupied with thoughts about the upcoming lunch with her mother-in-law.

What was she going to tell Annani? That she had seen someone who looked like Jasmine standing on top of a sand dune and some ruins?

Shai hadn't found any record of ruins matching what she had seen in the vision, so she was not even sure that it had been the Arabian desert. For all she knew, it could have been the Gobi or Sahara Desert.

Doubt crept in, as it had been doing all morning. What if her wish not to see Khiann dead had influenced the vision?

What if she had seen what she'd wanted to see rather than a hint of the truth?

Syssi shook her head. That was not how visions worked, and she knew that. Whatever she'd been shown was real. The problem was interpreting it.

"Mimi?" Allegra asked.

"We are meeting Auntie Amanda later in the play-ground. She is at work with Daddy now, and when they are done, we are going to see Nana. After that, we can go to the playground."

Since Amanda was attending the council meeting, she had suggested that they both take the day off. Under normal circumstances, it would have been a welcome treat. Today, however, it just gave Syssi more time to stew in her uncertainty.

The change in schedule had Allegra a little off-kilter, but the visit to her grandmother's would get her in a good mood.

"Nana!" Allegra's eyes sparkled with excitement, and she pushed up to her feet.

Syssi laughed. "Not yet, sweetie. We need to wait for Daddy to get home."

The sparkle in Allegra's eyes dimmed, and she sat back down, choosing to pass the time with one of her many board books. She liked to pretend that she was reading out loud and making out sounds along with the facial expressions appropriate to the story she was narrating in her own way.

Usually, it was hilarious to watch, but today Syssi was

having a hard time thinking about anything other than the vision she'd summoned the previous day.

The vast desert landscape, the mysterious woman with the golden-flecked eyes, the ruins half-buried in the sand—it all swirled in her thoughts, a kaleidoscope of images that refused to settle into a clear message.

Allegra babbled on with a string of nonsensical sounds that brought a smile to Syssi's face.

"What do you think, sweetheart?" she asked. "Is your granddaddy out there somewhere?"

Allegra looked at her with a puzzled look in her eyes. "Gaga?"

That was what she called Syssi's father.

"The other granddaddy, sweetie."

Khiann wasn't Kian's father, but he was Annani's husband, and Syssi had no problem referring to him as Allegra's granddaddy.

Besides, Annani believed that all her children were fathered by Khiann's spirit and that the human men she had used had merely been the physical vessels for his spirit to occupy.

The problem was that, at the time, the goddess believed that her husband was dead, and she'd been searching for his reincarnation. If he had indeed survived and was in stasis, his soul was still trapped inside his inert body, so it couldn't have entered the bodies of the men who had fathered Kian and his sisters.

Then again, what did she know about the metaphysical world of spirits?

Before meeting David and hearing evidence that reincarnation was real, Syssi had been undecided about the existence of a spirit that survived the body's death.

But now, she not only believed in the soul's survival but was more inclined to also believe related stories, like the one about the soul leaving the body every time a person fell asleep and returning upon waking.

Maybe Khiann's soul had left his sleeping body from time to time to wander the world during the past five thousand years. Perhaps Annani was right, and his spirit had possessed the bodies of the men who had fathered her children.

Closing her eyes, Syssi wondered whether Jacob had been reincarnated already. Thinking of her brother always brought tears to her eyes and stupid, irrational guilt.

What if he was still wandering the spirit world and waiting for her or Andrew to have a boy so he could reincarnate in the family?

Did the soul care about keeping the same gender in its next incarnation?

Was it given a choice?

According to David, it depended on what the soul needed to accomplish in its current incarnation and what faults it needed to fix.

Jacob's only fault had been his impulsivity, and in the end, that was what had killed him.

Fates, how she hated motorcycles. Even as an immortal, Syssi couldn't look at one without thinking it was a death trap.

Opening her eyes, she glanced at the clock on the wall and sighed. It was still early, and as much as Kian wanted to keep council meetings short, they had a tendency to drag on, especially now that Kalugal, Toven, and Jade were also members. Jade wasn't a problem because she was even more curt than Kian, but Kalugal and Toven had big egos and liked to talk.

Nevertheless, Kian would make sure to be home on time so they wouldn't be late to his mother's.

Annani did not appreciate tardiness, even if it was justified.

Syssi wasn't looking forward to the visit. Her vision hadn't definitively shown that Khiann was alive, and it hadn't shown him dead either, so basically, it hadn't provided them with a definitive answer.

Annani would be disappointed.

63

ROB

Rob stewed quietly while Marina went to get them coffee and pastries. He was angry, hurt, and didn't know how to make himself feel better so he could at least be cordial to Mia, who was a sweetheart and didn't deserve his temper.

It wasn't fair to her.

"So, Rob," Lusha said, leaning forward, "what's your story? How did you end up in our little corner of the world?"

Rob hesitated, unsure how much he wanted to reveal about the tumultuous events that had led him here. "It's a long story. The short version is that my life took an unexpected turn, and then my sister and her friends made me an offer I couldn't refuse and brought me here." He gestured vaguely, encompassing the café and the village beyond.

Lusha nodded, a knowing look in her eyes. "Life-changing revelations seem to be a specialty around here. I remember when I first learned about the existence of gods and immortals. It was quite the adjustment."

Rob's curiosity piqued. "You're not originally from the village?"

Lusha shook her head. "No, I was born and raised in Karelia. Do you know where that is?"

"I think I do. Russia, right?" Lusha and Marina both had slight Russian accents, which now made sense.

"Very good, Rob. Not many people have heard of Karelia. It is a region that is mostly Russian territory, but a portion of it is under Finnish control."

"How did you end up here?" he asked, but what he really wanted to ask was if she was human or immortal.

"That's a really long story," she threw his words back at him.

"We have time." He leaned back in his chair and crossed his arms over his chest. "Right, Mia?"

Mia shrugged. "I don't know how long the council meeting will last. Toven said that he would come over here when he was done."

As Marina returned with a tray of coffees and a bag of pastries, she put them on the table but didn't sit down. "I wish I could stay and chat with you, but I need to get back to work." She smiled at Rob. "It was nice to meet you. If you ever feel lonely and need to talk with a fellow human, you can find me here Monday through Friday, from eight in the morning until six in the evening."

"Thank you. I might take you up on your offer."

Now that he knew Marina was human, he was pretty sure that Lusha was, too.

When she left, he turned to Lusha. "So, Marina works at the café. What do you do?"

"I'm an attorney, and I work for the clan's judge. Right now, she is also in the council meeting with Toven, so I have some time off."

"An attorney. That's interesting. Where did you study?"

"The same place most of us from the compound studied. The University of Helsinki."

"Your English is very good."

"Thank you." She smiled. "I'm working on it." She leaned closer to him as if to tell him a secret. "I'm trying to get rid of my Russian accent."

"You're doing a good job of it. It's barely there. Did you pass the bar in California?"

"Not yet. I'm studying for it and working for the judge in the meantime. But even without a local license, I got to defend a group of accused murderers and got their sentencing reduced from beheading to community service."

For a moment he thought she was joking, but the expression on her face spoke of pride, not teasing.

"I have to hear that one again. Did you say beheading?"

She nodded emphatically. "That's the Kra-ell way. They are not merciful people, but I got them to acknowledge that those males had no choice."

Rob listened as she launched into a fantastic tale about the Kra-ell settlers, the purebloods and the hybrids, and the powerful compeller who held all of their lives in his hands until the clan rescued them. Rob was captivated by her intelligence, spunk, and humor.

Lusha possessed a spark that outshone all the beautiful immortals in the café, and she had more charisma than most people he knew.

More importantly, though, Rob didn't feel the need to carefully measure his words or dumb himself down as he often had with Lynda. Lusha's quick wit and sharp intellect were refreshing, inviting him to engage in a way he hadn't in a long time.

"That's incredibly impressive," Rob said when Lusha finished speaking. "It must have taken a lot of courage to take on their case."

Lusha shrugged, but there was a pleased glint in her eye at his praise. "It was challenging, but it was the right thing to do. Everyone deserves a fair trial, and they had no one to speak for them. For me, it started as a challenge to see how well I could do, but it ended up as much more than that.

Those males were truly innocent of the crimes they'd committed, and I had to do everything in my power to save their lives. They were sentenced to a very long community service, which is good for them and also for the people who lost loved ones to them. It's a healing process."

Rob nodded. "I agree."

She beamed with satisfaction. "What do you do, Rob?"

"Guess," he challenged.

She narrowed her eyes. "Something scientific or math related."

"Very good. I'm a data scientist. I research and collect data for building software programs and creating algorithms."

As their conversation continued, Rob found himself relaxing for the first time since his world had been turned upside down. Lusha had a way of making him feel at ease. Her teasing and interest in his thoughts were like a balm to his battered self-esteem.

He caught himself laughing at her witty remarks and teasing her back, but instead of getting offended by every word that didn't perfectly align with her world-view, Lusha laughed and teased him in return.

It was a stark contrast to the walking-on-eggshells feeling that had characterized so many of his interactions with Lynda.

Before he realized what he was doing, Rob heard himself asking, "So, are you seeing anyone?"

As soon as the words left his mouth, he felt a flush of embarrassment. It was too soon, too forward, and probably entirely inappropriate given his current situation.

Lusha, however, didn't seem offended. "Yes, actually. I'm seeing one of the Guardians," she said with a note of pride in her tone.

Rob nodded, trying to hide his disappointment. He wasn't entirely sure what a Guardian was, but from the tone of Lusha's voice, it was clearly an important position. "He's a lucky guy," Rob said, aiming for a neutral tone.

"Thank you. What about you? Are you seeing anyone?"

"I... well, I was supposed to get married this week," he said, the words feeling heavy on his tongue. "But it turns out my fiancée had other plans. With someone else."

"Ouch." Sympathy flickered across Lusha's face. "I'm so sorry. That must be incredibly painful."

Rob nodded, surprised to find that while the hurt was still there, it didn't feel quite as raw as it had just the day before.

Experiencing this new world, meeting Mia's fiancé, who turned out to be a god, coming to this hidden oasis, and talking with Lusha had provided a distraction and a glimpse of a much better future than the one he had envisioned before.

Rob had a moment of clarity. Yes, he was attracted to Lusha, and talking to her made him feel good in a way he hadn't in a long time. But he also recognized that he wasn't ready for anything more than friendship right now.

He needed time to cool down and to process the hurt and grief of his broken engagement. Jumping into something new, no matter how appealing, wouldn't be fair to anyone involved.

"It's been difficult," he admitted. "But being here and talking with you is helping. It's giving me a new perspective on life."

Lusha leaned over and put her hand on top of his. "Sometimes a change of scenery is exactly what we need to heal and grow. And you've certainly come to the right place for new experiences."

64

SYSSI

At the sound of the front door opening, Allegra let out an excited squeal. "Dada!"

She never failed to recognize the sound of her father coming home, even when she couldn't see the front door.

It was a sixth sense.

"Hello, my lovelies," Kian said.

At the sound of his voice, the tension in Syssi's chest eased. "How was the meeting?" She pushed to her feet and greeted him with a kiss.

Kian wrapped an arm around her waist, pulling her close. "Productive and entertaining."

Syssi raised an eyebrow. "Entertaining? That's not a word I usually associate with council meetings."

Kian chuckled, sat on the floor, and pulled Allegra onto his lap. "Hello, sweetie." He kissed her cheek. "Are you having fun at home with Mommy?"

"Nana," she said in that resolute tone of hers.

"Yes, sweetheart. We are going to Nana's in a bit."

He turned to Syssi with a smile. "People left humorous comments on the clan's bulletin board in response to the request for the perpetrator to come forward. One person suggested it might be mischievous spirits upset about the lack of ghost-friendly amenities in the village and demanded we immediately install more rattling chains and creaky floorboards."

Syssi laughed. "That's funny. Did you check with Anandur to see if it was him? That sounds like something he would say."

"It could be, even though he denied it. He suggested we form a task force to investigate spectral activity, and he did it with a straight face."

Syssi shook her head. "That was him for sure."

"I think so, too." Kian studied her face for a moment, his expression softening. "Are you okay?"

"I am. I needed a good laugh." She leaned in, pressing a soft kiss to his lips.

Kian cupped her cheek and deepened the kiss, but their daughter wasn't about to be left out of the fun and grabbed his chin with her little hand. "Lala." She pouted.

Lala was how Allegra referred to herself and what she wanted was clear enough. Kian obeyed the command, peppering her face with kisses.

Allegra's pout melted into giggles as she basked in her father's attention.

As Allegra's giggles subsided, Kian glanced at his watch. "We should head out."

"I just need to put my shoes on." She pushed to her feet and walked over to the couch where she'd left them.

After gathering Allegra's things, they headed out the door with their daughter riding on Kian's shoulders and Syssi carrying a small bag with a few toys and a diaper change.

As they walked toward Annani's home in the village, Syssi ran through the vision again in her mind, organizing the details and strategizing the delivery. She didn't want to disappoint Annani, but she didn't want to oversell her vision either.

"It'll be alright." Kian seemed to sense her unease. "My mother is the strongest person I know, and she will not fall apart because you don't have a definitive answer for her."

As they approached Annani's door, Kian shifted his grip on Allegra's legs to one hand and rang the bell with the other.

After a moment, the door swung open to reveal Oridu, his face impassive as always. "Welcome, Master Kian, Mistress Syssi, and Mistress Allegra," he said in his melodious voice. "The Clan Mother is expecting you. Please, come in."

The Odu led them through the living area and into the dining room, where a table was already set for lunch, and a highchair was ready for Allegra. The only one missing was Annani.

The Odu pulled out a chair for Syssi and then for Kian. "The Clan Mother will join you momentarily," he announced before gliding silently out of the room.

As Kian settled Allegra into the highchair, Syssi took in the spread before them. The table was laden with an array of dishes, some of them Kian's favorites and some hers.

Annani always made a point of treating Syssi as a beloved daughter, and Syssi never failed to appreciate it.

Kian leaned over and took her hand. "Trust in your gift, my love. It will not steer us wrong."

Syssi wanted to say that her gift might decide that it was better for them not to know what had happened to Khiann, but she kept it to herself. There was no need to repeat what Kian already knew, especially not with Annani within earshot.

65

ANNANI

"Apologies, Clan Mother." Oridu bowed from the open door to her room. "Master Kian, Mistress Syssi, and Mistress Allegra are here."

Annani turned and smiled. "Tell them that I will be there in a moment."

As he bowed again and turned on his heel, she let out a long breath.

The call from Kian earlier that morning had set her nerves on edge. He had mentioned good news, but the fact that he and Syssi had Allegra could suggest otherwise. In Annani's experience, children were often brought along to soften the blow of difficult news.

It also could mean that they wanted to please her.

Annani loved spending time with her grandchildren, especially when they were still so young. There was nothing like holding a baby in her arms, kissing their soft cheeks, hearing their babbling, and watching their shenanigans.

Life did not make much sense without those experiences.

Without love, everything seemed pointless.

Annani sighed. She was not in a great mood today, and some of it had to do with her conversation of the previous night with her own grandmother and her friend the Supreme Oracle.

Their words of caution about visions and the unpredictable nature of precognition echoed in her mind. If the Supreme Oracle herself warned her against putting too much faith in foresight, she should heed that advice.

"Visions can be confusing," the queen had said.

"They can be misleading and are rarely helpful," the Oracle had added.

Annani had countered with Syssi's previous vision that had led to finding the pod, but the Oracle had not been impressed. "On rare occasions, foresight can be useful, which is why I have a role and receive lavish accommodations and privileges for performing it, but I know from experience that the instances of visions providing a clear path are few and far between."

The entire conversation had left Annani unsettled. If even the Supreme Oracle of Anumati could not provide clear guidance on interpreting visions, what hope did they have of finding Khiann through Syssi's foresight?

Then again, the discovery of the pod had not been Syssi's first or only successful vision. She had found David's mother and stepfather as well. It had been too late for the poor man, but David's mother had been rescued and was now living in the village, happily mated to Merlin.

Refusing to succumb to negativity, Annani put the hairbrush down, pushed to her feet, and exited her room.

"My dears," she said as she entered the dining room. "How wonderful it is to share a midweek meal with my family."

Kian rose to his feet and embraced her. "Hello, Mother," he said, his voice warm but with an undercurrent of tension that Annani immediately picked up on.

Syssi's hug was equally warm, but Annani could feel the strain in her shoulders. Whatever news they had brought, it was clearly weighing heavily on both of them.

Allegra, though, seemed oblivious to the undercurrents of adult tension and let out a happy squeal at the sight of her grandmother. Given that the baby had her own foresight, that was an encouraging sign.

Annani smiled, reached for her granddaughter, and pulled her out of the highchair, the simple joy of the child momentarily pushing aside her worries.

"How is my little princess today?" she cooed, planting a soft kiss on Allegra's cheek.

"Nana." Allegra cupped both her cheeks with her chubby hands and kissed her back with lips full of baby slobber.

"She's been excited all morning about seeing her Nana," Syssi said.

Annani walked over to the head of the table and sat down with Allegra in her lap.

"Let me put her back in her highchair." Kian reached for his daughter.

Annani was hesitant to let go of her shield, the bundle of joy that would keep her warm no matter how cold the news Syssi delivered, but she let her son take the child away because she was not a coward. Whatever news they brought, she could handle it.

When Allegra was securely fastened in her highchair, Annani rearranged the folds of her gown and lifted her chin. "You said you had news."

"I summoned a vision last night," Syssi said, her voice stronger than Annani had expected. "I thought about Khiann and hoped to see something that could lead us to him, and I think that the universe answered, but as is usually the case with my visions, what it showed me was just a hint that leaves more questions than answers."

Annani nearly sagged in relief. A hint was good. A hint meant that there was a reason to search, and hopefully, not just to bring Khiann to a proper burial.

"Tell me everything," she commanded.

"Of course." Syssi launched into a detailed description of her vision.

Annani listened intently, absorbing every word. The vast desert landscape, the mysterious woman with golden-flecked eyes, the ancient ruins half-buried in the sand—each detail painted a vivid picture in Annani's mind.

"The vision didn't show Khiann directly," Syssi said. "But I have a strong feeling that he's out there, buried somewhere in that desert, in stasis. And I think that Jasmine is supposed to help us find him."

Despite the warnings from her grandmother and the Oracle, Annani felt a spark of hope ignite in her chest. "You said that the face was partially covered with a scarf and that you could only see the eyes. The person was dressed in what is customary for men in that region. Are you making the assumption that it was Jasmine just because of the golden-flecked eyes?"

Syssi nodded. "It makes sense since she was able to scry for the pod. Otherwise, it wouldn't have occurred to me that it might be her."

Annani nodded. "Then we must act on this hint. What is the next step? Are we going to talk to Jasmine? Perhaps she could be given a map of the area and use her scrying abilities."

Kian looked hesitant. "I am planning to talk to her, but we probably need more clues to narrow the search. I don't want you to get your hopes up only to be disappointed."

Annani felt a flash of irritation. "My hopes are already up, Kian. I choose to believe that this vision suggests Khiann is alive." She took a deep breath, calming herself. "I want to visit Ell-rom today. We can go together, and I can talk to Jasmine directly."

Kian and Syssi exchanged another look, one that Annani could not quite decipher.

"Alright," Kian agreed. "We can go visit him after lunch."

That was easy. Usually, Kian required more prodding to fulfill her wishes. He probably felt bad for her and wished to please her.

"I need to change my plans with Amanda," Syssi said. "We were supposed to meet in the playground later."

Kian cast her a sidelong glance. "Allegra shouldn't miss her playdate. I'm sure Amanda will be happy to babysit her while we visit Ell-rom and Jasmine." He leaned toward his wife and smiled. "We haven't had an adults-only dinner in a while."

"True." She pulled out her phone. "I'll text Amanda."

As they began to eat, the conversation flowed more easily, but Annani's mind was still in turmoil over Syssi's vision despite Kian's entertaining stories about the humorous comments left on the clan's bulletin board.

"Mother?" Kian's voice broke through her thoughts. "Have you heard anything I said?"

"Yes, some. I am sorry for not paying attention. My mind is still on Syssi's vision." She looked at her daughter-in-law. "When we go to see Jasmine, we should bring a map of the region. And perhaps some photographs of ancient ruins in the area. It might help jog her intuition."

Syssi winced. "Shai searched the internet for ruins and artifacts matching my vision and didn't find any."

Annani smiled. "Contrary to popular belief, not everything can be found on the internet. Those ruins might have been discovered many years ago before anyone even dreamt about the internet. The archeologists could have recorded the finding in some obscure research paper or book, and they were later forgotten."

Kian nodded slowly. "That's true. I will have to hire someone to do some research. Maybe David can recommend one of his professor buddies from Stanford." He frowned. "Do they even have a history or archeology department at that university?"

Syssi shrugged. "I don't know, but that's something that can be found on the internet."

As Syssi pulled out her phone to do the search, Annani felt a sense of purpose settling over her. For the first time in years, they had a tangible lead, however tenuous, on Khiann's whereabouts. It might come to nothing, but the mere act of searching, of doing something, filled her with renewed energy.

Allegra's happy babbling drew Annani's attention, and as she turned to her granddaughter, her mood was immediately lifted by the child's smiling face, which was smeared with the remains of her lunch.

To someone who did not know Allegra well, she would have appeared blissfully unaware of the weighty matters being discussed around her. But Allegra was not a regular child, and Annani took her smile as an encouraging sign.

JASMINE

After Margo and Frankie left, Jasmine glanced at her watch and frowned.

It had been over two hours since Ell-rom had left for his appointment with Julian, and he should have been done by now.

Not that anything could happen to Ell-rom with Julian watching over him, right? But what if something had happened to both of them?

Jasmine did not want to hover, but worry had a way of creeping in despite her best efforts.

She tried to distract herself with a book, but her mind kept circling back to Ell-rom and wondering what could be keeping him so long.

Pulling out her phone, Jasmine held her hand over the screen. She wanted to call Julian, but she didn't want to

upset Ell-rom with her hovering and interrupt the rehabilitation session.

It would be better if she just went in person.

Ell-rom wouldn't mind that. He liked it when she was
near.

With the decision made, she strode out of the penthouse
and summoned the elevator. The ride down to the clinic
level seemed longer than usual, but she knew it was
only her perception of time and not a problem with the
elevator's mechanics.

To her surprise, the clinic seemed deserted when she
got there, which was odd. Ell-rom hadn't worn his
swimming trunks, so Julian couldn't have taken him to
the pool. Maybe he took him for a walk?

But then, who was watching over Morelle?

"Hello?" she called out, her voice sounding unnaturally
loud in the stillness. "Is anyone here?"

A moment later, Gertrude emerged from a back room.
"Oh, hi, Jasmine. Are you looking for Julian and Ell-
rom?"

"Yes." Jasmine nodded, relief washing over her at the
nurse's calm demeanor. If something was wrong,
Gertrude wouldn't look so relaxed.

"Julian decided to take Ell-rom for a walk outside. Said
it would do him good to get some fresh air and see
more of the world he's woken up in. They must be
enjoying their walk because they've been gone for a

long time."

Anxiety gripped Jasmine again. "What if something happened to them?"

The nurse smiled reassuringly. "Julian can handle random thugs, and his reflexes are so quick that the chance of them being hit by a car is negligible. They are fine. My guess is that Ell-rom got tired, so they found a bench, sat down, and forgot about time while chatting."

That sounded like something Ell-rom would do. He had so many questions about the world of immortals that she couldn't answer.

"Would you like to visit Morelle while you wait?" Gertrude asked.

"That's a good idea. I can sing to her."

Gertrude smiled. "In that case, leave the door open so I can enjoy your singing."

Something in Jasmine's chest eased at the implied compliment. "No problem."

Since Ell-rom's awakening, she had been thrust into the role of a caretaker, a cheerleader, and an educator, and along the way, she had lost her sense of self. She had to remind herself that she did not exist just to be Ell-rom's mate. She was a performer, and it was a big part of her identity. It was unwise to let that slip away.

It dawned on her then that the hovering was the result of her forgetting that she had wants and needs that did not involve Ell-rom. He had become her entire world, and she was terrified of anything happening to him. Ostensibly, that wasn't a bad thing and could be interpreted as an expression of her love for him, but it could also be suffocating.

Damn. Relationships should come with an operating manual. Love and respect were the foundation, but a house needed much more than that to become a home, and all those intricate details were so damn nuanced.

How much care was too much, and how much was too little?

How many displays of affection were reaffirming, and how many were overwhelming?

How did people navigate those nuances to build a successful relationship?

No wonder so few couples were genuinely happy with each other. Those were the lucky ones who found their perfect match by chance, and their language of love and care fit well together.

As she opened the door to Morelle's room, the sight of Ell-rom's sister, still and silent on the bed, tugged at Jasmine's heart. Today, however, something was different. Morelle lay on her side, propped up by pillows at her back.

Jasmine looked over her shoulder at Gertrude. "Why is she on her side? Did she get bedsores?"

Even though Morelle was still in a coma, her immortal body should have been able to fix small things like that.

"It's not good for her to lie on her back all the time," Gertrude said. "We turn her onto her side periodically to prevent complications."

Jasmine didn't want to know what those complications might be. She wanted an honest answer to the question that the medical staff might not answer truthfully with Ell-rom within earshot.

"Is she going to wake up? Tell me the truth. If the prognosis isn't good, I won't tell Ell-rom, but I'll start preparing him for the possibility."

The nurse's expression softened. "The doctors are being honest with Ell-rom. We are doing everything we can for her. Her immortal physiology is working while she sleeps, fixing whatever went wrong when she was in stasis. Her inner organs need rebuilding."

That was a piece of information the doctors had not shared with Ell-rom, and Jasmine wondered if it was an oversight or if they had just decided not to disclose that to him.

Jasmine sighed, gently squeezing Morelle's hand. "Ell-rom tries to hide it, but I know how much he worries about his sister. She needs to wake up soon."

A playful glint appeared in Gertrude's eye. "Maybe she's just waiting for her prince to wake her with a kiss. That's how it works in the fairy tales, isn't it?"

Jasmine chuckled. "And where am I supposed to find a prince for Morelle?"

Gertrude shrugged, her smile widening. "You're a witch. Why don't you scry for one?"

The laughter that bubbled up from Jasmine's chest felt cleansing, releasing some of the tension she'd been carrying. "As witches go, I don't even have the skill of an apprentice, but I'll get right on it. I'm sure that in no time handsome princes from all over the world will be lining up to kiss the comatose alien princess."

MARINA

arina smiled as Amanda breezed in, her presence immediately filling the café with excitement. The woman certainly knew how to make an entrance.

"Hello, darling!" Amanda settled onto a stool at the counter. "I'm dying for a cappuccino. I didn't have time to grab one before rushing into the council meeting, and I'm parched." She sighed dramatically. "I wanted to prove to Kian that I could be on time, and I regretted that decision the entire meeting. Kian didn't even think to get water bottles for the council members."

Marina looked at Wonder. "We should supply the meetings. Does Kian have an assistant?"

"Shai," Wonder said. "I'll talk to him. How did the meeting go?" she asked Amanda. "Any news on the saboteur?"

"No one came forward, but some clowns left funny comments. Joking aside, the comments hinted at a lot of resentment toward newcomers."

When Marina winced, Amanda waved a hand. "Not you, darling. No one minds the few humans. They just don't like your former bosses, and some still think that Kalugal's men are dangerous." She lifted the cappuccino and took a grateful sip. "Oh, this is fabulous." She took another sip and put the cup down. "Let's talk about happier subjects. We have a wedding to plan!"

The word 'wedding' sent a thrill through Marina's body, but it was accompanied by a churn in her stomach. It still felt surreal that she was going to marry an immortal.

"I've been thinking," Amanda continued. "How would you feel about having the ceremony on the village's central lawn?"

The central lawn was a beautiful space, a wide-open green area that was surrounded by trees, shrubs, and flowerbeds. The problem was that Marina and Peter didn't have that many friends. Having a small ceremony in a large clearing would feel awkward.

"Isn't it too big for a small wedding?"

"Why small?" Amanda leaned over the counter. "We love weddings, as you saw on the cruise. The entire village will show up. I can mobilize the Odus and Peter's friends to help make it absolutely beautiful." She spread her arms. "Picture twinkling lights in the trees, tables with white tablecloths, a band playing—"

"What band?" Wonder asked. "We don't have a band."

"We do, but they haven't played together for a long time. We also have a great singer, but she is not here yet."

"Are you talking about Jasmine?" Marina asked.

"Yes."

"How is she doing?

Amanda smiled. "She's tending to her prince."

Marina wasn't sure what Amanda meant by that, but Wonder seemed to know and gestured to Amanda to keep quiet.

Amanda waved a dismissive hand. "Soon, everyone will know."

Marina looked at Wonder and then at Amanda. "What are you talking about?"

"Never mind." Amanda sighed. "You will find out shortly. Back to the wedding. Did you start looking at dresses?"

"Where? In the city?"

Peter was allowed to take her out whenever she wanted, but it felt wrong to shop for a wedding dress with her groom. In the romance books she had read, it was said that the groom wasn't supposed to see the bride in her wedding dress before the ceremony. That it was bad luck.

"Can I get one online?"

"Fates forbid." A mischievous glint appeared in Amanda's eye. "That was done before when we were time-crunched, but that's not the case now, and you deserve a fabulous dress custom-designed for you. I have just the person in mind."

Amanda pulled out her phone and made a video call.

A stylish woman with sleek black hair and sharp, intelligent eyes appeared on the screen. "Amanda. It is so wonderful to hear from you. How did all those cruise weddings go?"

"Beautifully. I have another client for you, Vivienne darling. My dear friend Marina needs a wedding dress, and it has to be absolutely spectacular."

As Amanda turned the camera toward her, Marina smiled and waved. "Hi."

The woman peered through the screen, her gaze appraising as it swept over Marina. "Hmm, yes, I can work with this. Blue hair is an interesting choice. We'll need to consider the color palette accordingly."

Marina smoothed a hand over her hair. "I can change the color if it's a problem."

Vivienne's face broke into a warm smile. "No need. On the contrary. I love a challenge. Don't worry, darling. I will create something magnificent for you. I'll sketch out some ideas and call you back in half an hour." She ended the call.

Half an hour? She could come up with ideas and sketch them so quickly?

"Vivienne is fast," Amanda said. "That's what I like about her best. There are other talented designers, but they take months to come up with something, and I never plan so far in advance."

JASMINE

fter singing a few songs to Morelle, Jasmine glanced at her watch. Another half an hour had passed, and Ell-rom still wasn't back.

Any reasonable person would get worried by now, right? She wouldn't be perceived as a hovering girlfriend if she called to find out what was keeping them. Maybe they needed a lift?

What if Ell-rom was so totally exhausted that he couldn't walk?

Could Julian carry him?

Her car was somewhere in the clan's parking garage so she could go get them. Pulling out her phone, she dialed Julian's number. It rang several times before the doctor answered.

"Is everything alright, Jasmine?"

"Yes, here, everything's fine," she assured him quickly. "I just wanted to check on Ell-rom. Gertrude told me you took him for a walk outside, and I started to worry that you might have wandered too far away and needed a lift back here."

He chuckled. "If there was a need for a lift, I could have called a taxi. Ell-rom has enjoyed being outside, and we have taken frequent breaks to rest. The longer we have walked, the longer the breaks have gotten. The last one lasted nearly an hour. But he has been doing remark-ably well. The fresh air and change of scenery seem to be doing him good."

Jasmine took the first deep breath in what seemed like hours. "That's wonderful. When do you think you'll be heading back?"

"It might still take a while. We are on 4th Street, and we will need to take another break soon. Why don't you come to meet us?"

Jasmine was on her feet before Julian had finished speaking. "I'm coming," she said, ending the call while heading for the door.

She paused with her hand on the handle and turned to look at the nurse over her shoulder. "I'm going to meet them on 4th Street, and we will return together."

"I'll be here," Gertrude said.

The elevator ride up to the lobby seemed to take forever, with Jasmine's foot tapping an impatient rhythm on the floor. When the doors finally opened, she strode out, waved at the guards at the reception desk, and walked out through the sliding doors.

The bright sunlight momentarily blinded her as she stepped outside, the sounds and smells of the city assaulting her senses.

It must have been overwhelming for Ell-rom to experience all of this for the first time.

Shading her eyes with her hand, Jasmine oriented herself and headed toward the intersection.

Hopefully, she was going in the right direction.

The truth was that without her scrying stick, she was really bad at navigating anywhere, even the city streets she knew pretty well.

When she reached the crosswalk, she spotted two familiar figures approaching. Ell-rom was leaning heavily on Julian, his steps slow, and he had a baseball cap on, so she couldn't see his face, but she knew him so well that she could imagine his look of determination.

As she hurried towards them, she could see the toll the excursion had taken on Ell-rom. His face was pale, and his legs seemed to tremble, but his eyes were alight with excitement.

He smiled. "Missed me?"

"Tremendously." She leaned to kiss his cheek. "How are you feeling?"

"Tired," Ell-rom admitted, "but also exhilarated. A few

days ago, I wouldn't have lasted even one-tenth of the way."

Julian nodded. "He's done remarkably well, but he's stubborn as a mule. When he heard you were coming, he refused to sit on the bench and wait."

"I can make it to the clinic," Ell-rom said. "With your help, of course."

Ell-rom was leaning heavily on Julian, with his excitement seemingly the only thing keeping him on his feet.

"We could stop at the lobby café," she suggested. "That's another experience that you can add to your collection."

Julian shook his head. "We have to get back to the clinic and try the synthetic blood while Ell-rom is still riding this wave of accomplishment."

She shifted her gaze to Ell-rom, who didn't wince and didn't grimace. "Wish me luck. Maybe I can overcome my aversion today."

Jasmine's eyes widened in surprise.

Ell-rom looked exhausted but also determined. Perhaps getting him to this state had been Julian's plan all along.

There was something to be said for riding the wave of achievement.

Sometimes, when she hit a note she couldn't hit before, she became euphoric and sang better than ever before.

"You can do it." She fell into step beside him and took his hand.

To passersby and those sitting in the cars whizzing past, they must have looked like an odd trio, with Ell-rom leaning on Julian, who had his arm wrapped around Ell-rom's middle, and Jasmine walking beside them and holding his hand.

They probably thought that Ell-rom had too much to drink and his friends were helping him get home.

ELL-ROM

E ll-rom's muscles protested as he settled into the chair in Julian's office, but he couldn't keep the proud smile from his face. The walk through the city streets, while exhausting, had filled him with a sense of accomplishment he hadn't felt since awakening from stasis. Every step, even those that required him to lean on Julian for support, felt like a victory over his weakened body.

The sights, sounds, and smells of the city still swirled in his mind, a bagful of new experiences that exhilarated and overwhelmed him. He had seen towering buildings, heard a cacophony of sounds, and smelled a dizzying array of scents.

Everything was more vibrant, more alive than what he had seen from the penthouse. He felt like a part of things rather than an outside observer.

If he could conquer the streets of Los Angeles, he could face his aversion to blood. The thought still made his stomach clench, but the feeling was less intense than before. Perhaps it was because his stomach was now empty, its contents consumed by the energy expended during the walk, and he was so tired he could barely hold himself sitting in a chair.

In fact, he was slumped.

Jasmine's warm hand slipped into his, giving it a gentle squeeze. "Pretend that it is something else," she suggested. "Vegetable juice or wine."

Ell-rom smiled. "The smell will make it impossible to imagine anything other than what it is, but I appreciate your effort nonetheless."

A look of curiosity crossed Jasmine's face. "Does synthetic blood smell the same as regular blood?" she asked.

Ell-rom shrugged, a little embarrassed about his igno-rance. "I don't know what it smells like. Looking at it in a sealed bag was enough to make me gag."

The memory of his earlier reaction to the bag of synthetic blood made him wince internally. He hoped he could do better this time.

The sound of the office door opening drew their atten-tion. Julian entered, carrying a small glass rectangle. Ell-rom's enhanced vision could make out a tiny amount of red liquid smeared across its surface. The quantity was so small that the scent was barely noticeable, just a faint metallic tang in the air.

Julian settled behind his desk, placing the glass in front of Ell-rom. "That's more or less the amount of blood you can expect when biting a person either in aggression or desire," he explained. "Your fangs are built to deliver venom, not for sucking blood, so the moment they penetrate the vein, they release a healing compound to slow down the bleeding. If you can tolerate licking what's on this glass, you are good."

Ell-rom stared at it. The quantity was tiny, much less than he'd expected, just a small smear of red. Yet the thought of tasting it made his throat constrict. Nevertheless, he picked up the glass with a surprisingly steady hand.

"You can do it," Jasmine said softly.

Drawing a deep breath, Ell-rom brought the glass to his nose. The scent was stronger now, unmistakably blood. He felt his stomach churn in response.

"Lick it," Julian said, his tone resolute. "Just do it."

"Close your eyes," Jasmine suggested.

Ell-rom let his eyelids fall shut. In the darkness behind his closed eyes, he could almost pretend the glass held something else—vegetable juice. It was just red vegetable juice. He extended his tongue, fighting against every instinct that screamed at him to stop, and in one quick motion, he swiped his tongue across the glass.

The taste hit him immediately, coppery and thick, and his gag reflex kicked in instantly.

His stomach roiled in protest, but Jasmine's hand was still in his, her touch an anchor in the storm of his body's reaction. With a monumental effort, Ell-rom managed to swallow the bile that had risen in his throat instead of giving in to the urge to vomit.

"Here," Julian's voice cut through the haze of Ell-rom's discomfort.

He opened his eyes to see the doctor holding out a bottle of water. "That was an excellent first try."

Ell-rom had to release Jasmine's hand to open the bottle, immediately missing the comfort of her touch. He filled his mouth with water, swishing it around vigorously in an attempt to wash away the lingering taste of blood. It was only when he went to spit it out that he realized Julian hadn't provided a container for that purpose.

With a moment of clarity, Ell-rom understood the doctor's intention. He had no choice but to swallow the water and, with it, the trace amounts of blood that had been in his mouth. It was clever—a way to force him to consume blood without the psychological barrier of deliberately drinking it.

As he swallowed, Ell-rom was surprised to find that it wasn't as difficult as he had anticipated. The water had diluted the taste significantly, and while he could still detect a faint metallic flavor, it wasn't overwhelming.

"Congratulations," Jasmine said, leaning over to press a soft kiss to his lips. Ell-rom found himself wishing the kiss could last longer, eager to replace the taste of blood with the sweetness of Jasmine's mouth.

"By the way," Julian said. "The Clan Mother and Kian and his wife are coming over to the penthouse this evening, so you'd better get a good rest. Kian said that they would be bringing takeout from the Golden Dragon for everyone."

"Who is everyone?" Jasmine asked.

Julian shrugged. "I assume the other residents of the penthouses. The gods and their mates."

Ell-rom felt a familiar mixture of excitement and anxiety wash over him at the news of his sister's impending visit.

On the one hand, he was always eager to see Annani. On the other hand, her visits always carried a weight of expectation, a reminder of the memories he had lost and the uncertainty of what role he was meant to play in this new world.

It was good that the gods and their mates would be joining them. Having Annani's undivided attention was stressful, and he preferred to share it with others.

Jasmine's presence had been a constant source of strength and comfort throughout his recovery, and just having her beside him made the prospect of facing his formidable sister less daunting.

"Should Ell-rom eat lunch before getting into bed?" Jasmine asked.

"I don't see why not." Julian rose to his feet and collected the blood-stained glass.

Following the physician's example, Jasmine stood as well. "What if he gets sick?"

Julian smiled. "It's a risk worth taking."

She looked at Ell-rom. "Can you stay awake long enough to eat something?"

As he stood, Ell-rom felt a wave of dizziness wash over him. "I'm not sure."

Jasmine was immediately at his side, her arm slipping around his waist to support him. "Do you want me to run up and get the walker?"

He was tempted to say yes, but he had come this far, and he didn't want to finish on a weak note.

"I can make it back."

The way back to the penthouse seemed much longer than usual, each step requiring more effort than Ell-rom wanted to admit, and by the time they reached it, he wanted nothing more than to collapse on the bed.

Jasmine helped him get comfortable, adjusting the pillows and pulling up the blanket. "Do you want to eat in bed? I can bring in a tray."

He shook his head. "I need to sleep. I'll eat when I wake up."

"I'll wake you in time to get ready for Annani and Kian's visit."

"Thank you." He let his eyes drift closed.

Just before sleep claimed him, Ell-rom's mind replayed the events of the day. The exhilaration of walking through the city, the triumph of facing his blood aversion, the comforting presence of Jasmine by his side.

It had been a good day.

MARINA

As Amanda chattered on about the menu and the decorations, Marina's head was spinning with all the options and decisions that she had to make.

"How about I just leave it all up to you?" she finally said. "You are the expert, and I trust your opinion more than I trust mine."

The smile that bloomed over Amanda's perfect face seemed to indicate that was exactly the response she had been hoping for. "Are you sure? I can definitely do that, but usually, brides are more particular about what they want."

"Not me. I'll be happy to just choose the design for my wedding dress, and even that I'm not sure about. You will probably do a better job of choosing for me. I'm just worried about Peter not getting a say in his own wedding."

He had told her to do whatever she wished, but since he was so excited about the wedding, he must have some idea about what he wanted.

Amanda seemed surprised by the comment, but she recovered quickly. "Grooms are usually happy to leave everything to the brides, but I can ask him. If he wants to take part in the planning, he's more than welcome."

When Vivienne called back, Amanda handed Marina the phone so she could go over the sketches.

"Wow." Marina couldn't believe that the woman could sketch that fast, let alone come up with all those designs in a matter of moments. She must have had some on hand and only made slight adjustments, but still. "They're all so beautiful. I don't know how to choose."

Amanda clapped her hands together. "Well then, we'll have to put it to a vote. Vivienne, darling, can you email me these sketches? I want to pull them up on my tablet so we have a larger screen for our judges to look at."

"Of course. You'll have them in a few moments."

As Amanda pulled her tablet out of her fancy bag, she began calling over the other women in the café. "Wonder, Aliya, Sharon, Denise." She waved her hand in invitation. "Come over here. We need your expert opinions!"

The women gathered around, their curiosity piqued by Amanda's excitement. Marina felt a warmth spread through her chest as she looked at the group of women.

Two of them had become close friends and the other two she knew as well.

In such a short period of time, these immortals felt like family.

"Alright, ladies." Amanda pulled up the sketches on her tablet. "We need to choose the perfect wedding dress for Marina. Let's vote!"

A lively debate followed. Wonder favored a sleek, modern design that she claimed would complement Marina's figure perfectly. Aliya argued for a more traditional gown with a long train, insisting it would make Marina feel like a true princess. Sharon pointed out the merits of a design that would allow for easy movement during the reception, and Denise said that all of them were equally beautiful and she couldn't decide.

In the end a consensus was reached, mainly because Marina added her vote to Wonder's, and the others agreed that it was the best one for her. It wasn't too constrictive or elaborate, would allow Marina to dance the night away, and it was unique and unconventional like Marina herself.

She could already imagine herself walking down the aisle in it, Peter's eyes lighting up as he saw her. Then again, his eyes lit up when he saw her no matter what she was wearing.

Mother of All Life, she loved him so much.

Amanda seemed happy with the choice as well. "Let me call Vivienne and tell her what you have selected."

"Wait." Marina stopped her. "Do you know how much she charges?"

Amanda put a hand on her arm. "Don't worry about it. Vivienne will give me a special discounted price, and Peter will happily pay her."

She hoped that Amanda was right about Peter being happy to pay.

"Vivienne, you've outdone yourself," Amanda declared when her friend answered the call. "The contemporary design won the popular vote and that of the bride-to-be. I'll get you Marina's measurements so you can get your team to work on it right away. Now, what about bridesmaids' dresses? They need to match the contemporary design…"

As Amanda hammered out the details with Vivienne, Marina's mind wandered to all the people she wanted to invite to her wedding. There were so many from her old life that she wished could share her special moment. A pang of sadness hit her as she thought of her friends from Safe Haven.

She waited for Amanda to end the call with Vivienne. "I have a question, and I'm not sure that you can give me an answer, but I don't know who else to ask."

Amanda tilted her head. "What's the question?"

"Would it be possible... I mean, I know it's probably not, but... could I invite all my friends from Safe Haven to the wedding? I mean, all my old friends who came from the Kra-ell compound and who are compelled to keep the existence of aliens a secret?"

It would be so satisfying to know that her ex was watching her marry a Guardian.

Amanda's expression softened. "Oh, sweetheart. I wish it was possible for all of them to come, but it probably is not. As far as I know, Safe Haven is booked for retreats for the next six months, and they need everyone to maintain the lodge, not to mention the security concerns, but you can invite a select group of close family and friends. Are your parents still around?"

"Yes, and I would also like to invite Larissa and a couple of other friends."

Not including her ex. He wasn't worth the trouble.

Besides, why would she want someone who did not wish her well at her wedding?

"That shouldn't be a problem," Amanda said. "Write down the names, and I'll send them to Onegus for approval."

71

KIAN

As Anandur and Brundar arranged the takeout containers from the Golden Dragon on the dining table, Kian glanced at his mother.

Annani wore an imperial expression as she regarded the boxes.

His mother did not eat from cardboard containers or cardboard plates. She ate from fine china and used cloth napkins.

"Perhaps we should transfer the items into serving dishes," Syssi suggested, either reading his mind or realizing the same thing at the same time.

"Is that how you always eat dishes from a restaurant?" Annani asked.

"When it's takeout, yes. If we dined at the establishment, the dishes would have been served on platters, and we would have been given proper plates, but I doubt you would have approved of the ones they use in the Golden Dragon. It's not a fancy place, but the food is excellent, and they have a large selection of vegan dishes."

Annani sighed. "I might be perceived as particular for choosing to dine on fine china, but I believe in savoring and appreciating well-thought-out presentations, especially considering the length of our lives."

Kian had to admit that there was something to that, but it was much more expedient to just put out the boxes. "Would you like us to transfer the dishes to platters?"

She hesitated for a split second. "I do not wish to create unnecessary work for anyone. I shall join in dining from boxes."

"Then let's dig in." Kian reached for the box closest to him.

There was a communal sigh of relief as everyone around the table followed his example.

He had invited the gods and their mates to join them for dinner because he needed to pick their brains about tasking Jasmine with locating Khiann, but now that they were all gathered around the table, he was rethinking that decision.

For some reason, discussing Syssi's vision with them made him uneasy, but it was probably just another manifestation of his paranoia. His motto was to keep things on a need-to-know basis, and the fewer who needed to know, the better.

"I've heard so much about the Golden Dragon," his mother said. "I am eager to sample it even if it comes from a box."

"Let me help you select the tastiest dishes," Kian offered. "We've been ordering from there for many years."

Anandur snorted. "We are their best customers. You should see the welcome I get when I pick up takeout. I am treated like a member of the family."

"Is it family-owned?" Annani asked.

"It is." Kian reached for one of the boxes containing a chicken dish and tried not to show his aversion as he scooped a small portion onto his mother's plate.

On her other side, Ell-rom seemed as uncomfortable as he was, but he wasn't on the verge of gagging like he had been the other time.

Somehow, their shared veganism made Kian feel a rush of affinity with his uncle, and he wondered in what other ways they were similar.

Ell-rom seemed much more soft-spoken and mellow, but then he was still recovering and adjusting to a new world. He might grow more assertive as he gained confidence.

"Have you never tried Chinese cuisine, Clan Mother?" Gabi asked.

His mother put down the chopsticks she was struggling to use. "I do not dine in restaurants. My Odus cook for me, and when I travel, I use room service." She sighed. "I have not done much traveling lately, though. My eldest daughter and companion found her fated mate, and I have not felt like traveling by myself." She glanced at Ell-rom. "Perhaps when Morelle wakes up, she would like to take the position of my companion."

Ell-rom looked lost for words. "I cannot speak on behalf of my sister. I cannot even guess if this is something she would like to do. When she wakes up, I will have to get to know her as if we didn't grow up together."

Annani smiled. "Of course. We are all waiting with bated breath for her to wake up. I am also waiting for you to get better so I can take you to my sanctuary in Alaska and show you this marvelous place."

"I wish I could see it," Aru said.

"I wish so, too." Annani cast him a warm smile. "But you will have to get those trackers out of you before I can take you there."

"About that." Aru shifted so he was facing Kian. "Jasmine had an interesting idea about taking them out without faking our deaths."

Kian remembered then that Aru had mentioned something he wanted to talk to him about when he'd called on the weekend. "Is that the issue you wanted to discuss with me?"

"Correct." Aru leaned forward. "Jasmine suggested that we take out our trackers and implant them inside humans, who we would pay to traverse through Tibet, China, and Russia, so it would look as if Negal, Dagor, and I were still looking for the missing pods. The problem is that I don't know whether the trackers transmit biometric information in addition to location, so we will need to test it first. We will remove the tracker from one of us and implant it in a human."

Kian gave Jasmine an appreciative nod. "Good job. You keep coming up with unconventional solutions to things. I'm starting to think that I should hire you as my assistant."

Her eyes widened. "Thank you for the compliment, but I'm not good with business. I would be a horrible assistant."

Kian chuckled. "I was only joking. But I might give you a call here and there when I have a difficult problem. You think outside the box."

"She's also brave," Negal said. "Jasmine volunteered to be the test subject but, of course, we're not going to risk her life like that."

Jasmine rolled her eyes. "Is risking the life of some random unaware human better? At least I'd go into it knowing the potential risks."

Kian noticed the slight movement of Ell-rom's arm as he took Jasmine's hand under the table. He certainly didn't want his mate to endanger herself, and Kian was of the same opinion.

"Testing this on Jasmine is out of the question," he said. "I have a much better solution. We can use one of the human scum that we usually leave for the police to deal with. The traffickers don't deserve to live anyway, so I don't care if the tracker explodes in their body or poisons them."

As a heavy silence fell over the table, Kian glanced around, gauging reactions. To his surprise, even his mother and Syssi were nodding in agreement.

The one exception seemed to be Gabi, who had a wry smile on her face. "What about due process? Your Guardians are already skirting the law with their vigilante missions. The authorities might turn a blind eye to your activity because you do good work, and you leave the scumbags for them to pick up. But if you exterminate the vermin, they might start to worry and go after your people."

Kian turned to her, his eyes hard. "The police don't even arrest people who commit crimes on camera, so I'm not worried about them coming after us. They seem to go after only those they do not fear. And as to the morality of killing one of those rats, anyone who sells children to pedophiles doesn't deserve to live, let alone the protection of a legal system that's already subverted."

Unfazed by his vehemence, Gabi held his gaze for a long moment, and then her smile turned into a grin. "I was just playing devil's advocate. Sometimes, it helps to voice the opposing view to crystallize opinions."

As tension in the room eased and people started discussing the practicalities involved, Kian reflected on Gabi's ruse of devil's advocate. The idea of using human traffickers as test subjects for the tracker removal was pragmatic, even poetic in its justice, but she was right about it representing an ethical line to cross. It was a slippery slope.

Once they started playing judge, jury, and executioner, where did they draw the line?

72

ELL-ROM

Ell-rom did his best to follow the conversation around the table, and most of the time, the earpieces did a good job of translating for him. The problem was when people talked simultaneously. The earpieces jumbled what they were picking up and provided him with a salad of words. If the clan's tech was there, he would have told him that the earpieces needed modification.

Still, he'd had no trouble understanding the exchange about Jasmine volunteering to take the tracker into her body, and he was grateful to Kian for suggesting an alternative. But then Kian had added that the scumbags he wanted to use to test the trackers were selling children, and Ell-rom's rage reached critical boiling point.

As his hand tightened around Jasmine's, she turned to him with alarm in her eyes. "You need to relax, love. Getting so upset is not good for you."

Of course it wasn't good. Was she worried about his supposed ability to kill with a thought?

He didn't know who to direct his thoughts at, so they were safe, but if they were with him in this room and he knew who they were, they would be dead now, no thought-killing ability needed.

His bare hands and fangs would have sufficed.

"I'm okay," he whispered. "I just need to know who is selling children and why." He paused, brow furrowing as he tried to make sense of what he'd heard. "There was that word that the translator must have misunderstood." He turned to Kian. "Why are childish people buying children? And how is it possible to buy and sell people?"

A heavy silence fell over the table. Ell-rom looked around, noting the grim expressions on everyone's faces. Kian's eyes blazed with inner light, and his fangs, which had been slightly elongated since he had started talking about the sellers of people, were getting longer.

Ell-rom had a feeling that his fangs were similarly extended, and he lifted the hand that wasn't holding Jasmine's to his mouth to check. They weren't protruding over his lower lip yet, which happened when they were fully elongated, but they were definitely and noticeably long.

"The word your earpieces translated erroneously did not mean people who act like children. It meant deviants who are attracted to children. Some of them manage to suppress their depraved urges, but others buy children and abuse them, sexually and otherwise."

It took him a moment to process what Kian had said, and as understanding dawned, Ell-rom felt a surge of disgust and burning anger that seemed to rise from the very core of his being.

He was dimly aware of his physical reaction, the bile rising up his throat and the further elongation of his fangs, but these sensations were secondary to the storm of emotions raging within him.

"What is this depravity?" he demanded, his voice a low growl. "How can this be allowed?"

Kian's expression hardened. "It's not, but there is not enough law enforcement dedicated to protecting children and women. Not here in the US and even less so in other parts of the world." He paused, running a hand through his hair in frustration. "Lately, it feels like it's open season on the defenseless everywhere. I don't know what has happened to all the good people in the world. Have they all been cowed into submission? Into accepting a reality where depravity is more and more accepted, even celebrated, and everything that's morally right is turned on its head and called wrong?"

Ell-rom struggled to process Kian's words. In his limited exposure to this world, he had met people who all seemed decent and kind. Jasmine had filled his head with Earth's diverse cultures and natural habitats, but no one had mentioned that this planet also harbored demonic monsters.

He couldn't reconcile that kind of darkness with the future he imagined for himself and Jasmine.

For Morelle.

"I cannot believe that such evil exists."

Ell-rom looked around the table, taking in the faces of those gathered. The gods, Aru, Negal, and Dagor, wore expressions of sorrow, but he could see that the state of affairs on Earth didn't cut them as deeply as it cut Kian and Annani. The three newly arrived gods cared, but they didn't consider humans their people, they didn't feel responsible for them, and they probably deemed them an inferior species.

It was also possible that they had seen much worse on other worlds, so Earth's evils didn't faze them.

Annani, on the other hand, had tears in her eyes, and so had Kian's wife, and the gods' mates just looked like they were barely holding them in.

He turned to Jasmine, expecting the same sadness, but found fury.

Strangely, her anger seemed to cool his down. It was as if he had to get ahold of his emotions so he could help her get ahold of hers.

"Are you okay?"

She shook her head. "I need a moment to calm down."

Suddenly, he wondered how close to home this issue hit for her. Had she seen the effects of this evil? Had she, perhaps, been touched by it personally?

The thought burned through his momentary calm and made his blood boil. His vision was tinged with a red haze of fury, and he felt a surge of power building within him. There was pressure behind his eyes that he hadn't felt before, and he feared that his deadly ability was trying to manifest.

Panic seized him, but the rage refused to recede.

"Ell-rom," Jasmine's voice cut through the haze. She cupped his cheek and turned his face toward her. "Take a deep breath. Just breathe with me, okay?"

"Inhale and exhale, slow and steady, in and out…"

He focused on her face, on the sound of her voice, using it as an anchor to pull himself back from the brink. Slowly, he felt the pressure recede, his fangs retract, and the burning fade from behind his eyes.

"I'm sorry," he murmured, suddenly aware of the concerned looks from around the table. "I lost control for a moment."

"Your reaction is natural," Kian said.

He had mistaken what had just happened as the normal anger of a good male in the face of cruelty perpetrated against the defenseless.

Ell-rom wished it was just that, but he knew it wasn't. He'd felt the surge of power, and there had been nothing normal about it.

"What kind of society allows its young to be abused?" he asked.

"A collapsing society." Kian's tone was grim. "The clan is

doing all that we can to hold back the tsunami of evil, but there aren't enough of us to put even a dent in it."

73

KIAN

Ell-rom looked at Kian questioningly. "What do you do? How do you fight this evil?"

Kian sighed. "We have a limited number of fighters, but we have special abilities that are useful for raiding those dens of depravity. We rescue the victims and bring them to a sanctuary where our clan therapist is doing all she can to help them heal and to rehabilitate them until they are ready to re-enter society and be on their own. Julian, our esteemed physician, runs a halfway house for the rehabilitated former victims of trafficking, so they have a soft landing and can do things gradually and without pressure."

"Now I feel guilty." Ell-rom rubbed at his jaw. "Morelle and I are keeping Julian from doing his job."

"'Don't worry about it," Kian said. "Julian is the director, but there are many capable humans working in the halfway house, paid employees and volunteers. He can

do most of what he does there from the office here."
Kian smiled. "It's not like you and Morelle keep him
busy all day long."

"What do you do with the monsters?" Ell-rom asked.

"We make them wait for the human authorities to
collect, ready to confess their crimes."

Ell-rom lifted a brow. "With compulsion?"

Kian shook his head. "Compulsion is a rare ability. We
use thralling, which most immortals can do, and on
humans it's just as effective if not more so than compulsion. Thralling makes them believe that they want to do
what we tell them. Compulsion only forces them to do
that even if they try to fight it with all their might."

From the other side of the table, Aru groaned. "We did
not continue your shrouding and thralling lessons. We
should resume them."

Ell-rom nodded. "I've been working hard on my physical rehabilitation, and I forgot all about practicing my
mind-manipulating abilities. But I guess I will need to
master both if I want to join your efforts. I want to be
part of this fight."

Kian approved of the sentiment, but Ell-rom was in no
condition to fight anyone. "It takes many years to
become a fully-fledged Guardian, and I'm sure that
taking part in the missions is not the only thing you can
do. You need to discover all of your abilities, learn
English, and get a better understanding of this world
before you decide what you want to do with your life."

"Wise advice," Jasmine said. "You should heed it."

"I know, but I can't just do nothing." Ell-rom kept his eyes trained on Kian. "Even if I can't fight, there must be something I can learn to do to put a dent in the fight."

"Oh, Ell-rom," Annani spoke up. "Your compassion does you credit. It is a quality that will serve you well in our community. But Kian is right. You need time to heal and learn." She smiled. "Only fools rush in."

"You are right, my sister." Ell-rom dipped his head. "I shall follow your advice."

As the evening wore on, the conversation drifted to lighter topics, and Kian found himself relaxing and enjoying the meal. Still, part of his mind remained focused on the real reason for their visit.

They needed to talk about Syssi's vision.

He waited until everyone was done eating, the boxes with leftovers were stored in the fridge, and the empty ones were discarded.

Glancing at his mother on one side and his wife on the other, he wasn't sure whose hand he should hold and finally decided that he should hold Syssi's. His mother never showed weakness, which holding her hand might imply.

"Syssi had a vision." He clasped her hand. "That's the main reason for our visit today." He scanned his audience. "I didn't come here expecting to solve all the evils of this world, but I hope you can help us solve one mystery that is very important to my mother."

A hush fell over the table once more, and as all eyes turned to Syssi, she straightened in her chair. "I asked the universe to show me whether Annani's husband still lived and was buried under the sands of the Arabian desert. What I was shown wasn't exactly what I asked for, though. I saw a vast desert, some ruins that looked ancient, half-buried in sand, and a woman with eyes flecked with gold, who was dressed in men's clothing appropriate for the region." She turned her gaze to Jasmine. "I believe the vision was showing us where we should start looking for Khiann and who can help us find him."

Aru leaned forward. "A desert with ancient ruins narrows it down somewhat, but not by much."

He must have missed the part about the woman with golden flakes in her eyes, but Jasmine hadn't. She looked stunned and said nothing, probably not wanting to assume that Syssi meant that the woman was her.

"Do you think that the woman with gold-flecked eyes is Jasmine?" Ell-rom asked.

Kian nodded. "We do. Her scrying abilities helped find your escape pod and might also be the key to pinpointing Khiann's location."

74

ANNANI

The sight of Ell-rom and Jasmine exchanging loving glances and their hands intertwining beneath the table brought a bittersweet pang to Annani's heart. While she was overjoyed that her brother had found love and a chance at happiness so soon after waking up in this new world, it only served to highlight the absence of her beloved Khiann.

For millennia, Annani had believed Khiann was murdered by Mortdh, her former intended. The pain of that loss had never truly faded, even after she had moved on, even after she had named her son Kian in honor of Khiann's memory. But now, the doubt gnawing at her was growing stronger with every passing day. She was now convinced that the witnesses who had attested to the murder and incriminated Mortdh had been compelled by her father to do so.

It had served Ahn's interests perfectly. It was his way to get rid of an opponent who was gaining power and sowing division among the gods. The only thing that did not fit the new narrative she had created was what had happened to Khiann. Whether truly dead or in stasis, he had disappeared that fateful day. He could have been another victim of the massive earthquake that had buried Wonder, but then how had her father known about it?

Ahn would've had to be sure that Khiann was dead to come up with the scheme of incriminating Mortdh.

It was possible that he had gotten to the witnesses before they had testified in front of the big assembly and compelled them to change their story, but what was the real story that they had come to report?

Had it been to inform the council that Khiann's caravan had been swallowed by the desert?

If so, how had they escaped the same fate?

Things did not add up, and as hard as she tried, Annani could not complete the puzzle in a way that made sense because she was missing pieces. As for her gut, she could not trust it because it wanted Khiann to be alive so much that it could send her the wrong signals.

As the conversation hit a natural lull, Annani straightened in her chair. "Jasmine," her voice cut through the ambient chatter. "Once again, it seems that the fate of a lost prince is in your hands."

The room fell silent, all eyes turning to Annani and then to Jasmine, who looked nervous under the weight of expectation. "I don't know if I can."

Annani gave her a reassuring smile. "We can all just do our best and hope it is enough. I am forever grateful to you for saving my brother and sister in the nick of time, and I need your help again. My beloved Khiann, whom I thought I lost five thousand years ago, might be resting in stasis underneath the desert sands, and once again, Syssi's vision points to you as the one who can find him. Will you help me?"

Jasmine's eyes widened. "I will do whatever I can, but only after Ell-rom is fully recovered. I cannot leave him before that."

Her determined expression dared Annani to challenge her statement, but Annani had no intention of doing that. In fact, when the time came, she was sure that Ell-rom would insist on going with Jasmine.

The two were bonded mates or about to be bonded soon, and there was no way they could be separated for more than a day so early in their relationship.

"Naturally, I do not expect you to do this alone. You decide who you want on your team, and I will make sure that you are provided with all the support you need. I have been told about your methods, but I have to admit to possessing only a superficial knowledge of the Wicca traditions."

As Jasmine glanced around the table, seeming to gather her thoughts before speaking, Annani noticed the slight tremor in her hands and the way she unconsciously leaned closer to Ell-rom for support. But beneath the obvious anxiety, Annani could sense the core of steel that she had come to admire in Jasmine.

Her brother's mate might not see herself as brave or heroic, but Annani knew better. This unassuming young woman had faced dangers and challenges with uncommon courage and determination.

"I used the tarot cards to foretell my future," Jasmine said. "For many years, they always showed me a prince awaiting me. I didn't really believe that I would one day find a prince, marry him, and live happily ever after." She turned, casting a fond smile at Ell-rom. "I thought the tarot was showing me a prince to say that my man would be spectacular, a true prince of a man, but they were showing me both. Ell-rom is a real prince and an outstanding male."

Their love was so palpable that Annani felt a renewed surge of hope. If the Fates had brought these two together against all odds, surely, they could work their magic once more.

"So, the tarot prompted you to search for your prince?"

Jasmine chuckled. "Yeah, but I searched in all the wrong places. I thought Alberto was my promised prince. Boy, was I wrong."

"But the tarot cards were right," Annani pointed out. "It was your interpretation that was wrong. Not that it is your fault in any way. You did not have enough information."

The more they talked, the more Jasmine seemed to relax, which was Annani's intention. She wanted the girl to be at ease.

"Well, I'm not sure about that. If I hadn't gone with Alberto to Cabo, I wouldn't be here today, right? So maybe I was right after all, just not in the way I thought." She took a sip of water. "The scrying stick idea came to me in a moment of inspiration. I've never used one before. I'm still not sure how that worked, but it did. It's like I'm using the Wiccan tools of the trade as conduits for a power that is flowing through me."

Kian leaned forward. "We could try a similar approach this time. You could use the tarot cards to confirm Syssi's vision and perhaps even narrow down the location. Naturally, we will try to find where these ruins that Syssi saw are located because they seem to be a location marker. Then, if we can get close enough, you might be able to use your scrying abilities to pinpoint Khiann's exact location."

"The desert is vast," Aru interjected. "Even if we narrow it down to a specific region, we're still talking about an enormous area to search."

Annani felt a flicker of frustration with how doubtful everyone seemed to be. "We have to try. If there is even the slightest chance that Khiann is out there alive, we have to find him. It is our duty."

The thought of Khiann trapped in stasis for so long, waiting to be found, was almost too much to bear. Hopefully he was as unaware as Wonder had been, and when they found him and revived him, he would think that the earthquake had happened only days before, not thousands of years earlier.

Syssi reached out, placing a comforting hand on her arm. "My vision showed us the way once before. It will do so again."

"What do we need to do first?" Annani asked. "I want us to start planning." She cast a fond look at Ell-rom. "You are getting better by the day, and given the rate you are going, you will be ready for travel in a few weeks. You should start working on your English."

ELL-ROM

"I will do my best to master it," Ell-rom promised, even though he didn't know how he was going to accomplish that.

The earpieces were too convenient to take out, but if he wanted to learn to speak the local language, he would have no choice but to do so, and then he wouldn't be able to communicate with Jasmine and Julian and everyone else.

"You can use an online program to learn," Kian said. "I'll have my assistant send Jasmine the link, and I'll also get you a laptop. It's time you started learning how to use the device. It will help you learn everything faster."

"What about a phone?" Jasmine asked. "Now that we're not spending every minute of the day together, it would be nice to be able to call Ell-rom when I worry about him."

Ell-rom shook his head. "You worry too much. What can possibly happen to me in the underground of the keep that no one other than the clan knows exists?"

"You might fall down and break something, and you can't even call for help. That's why you need a phone."

As the topic of conversation shifted to all the conveniences and inconveniences of modern life on Earth, Ell-rom's mind drifted back to what he had learned at the start of tonight's dinner. The world he had awakened to was far more complex and darker than he had been led to believe.

The coddling hadn't been ill-intentioned. It was done out of concern for his fragile state. In a way, Ell-rom was grateful to Kian for letting slip those dark topics. It meant that he thought he was well enough to learn about the evils of this world and no longer regarded him as a patient who needed to be shielded.

What he wondered now was how much of this world was filled with evil and how much was filled by good people like the immortals, gods, and humans he'd met so far, who were fighting that darkness.

Kian seemed to think that evil was on the rise, but perhaps it wasn't as bad as he had made it sound, because he didn't seem alarmed—just angry and frustrated.

Then again, evil was evil, and unless faced with strong resistance, it spread like wildfire.

How did he know that? Perhaps it had been part of the education he had received in the temple that he remembered viscerally but not consciously and intellectually.

Returning his focus to his dinner companions, Ell-rom considered asking about the prevalence of evil on Earth but then thought better of it. He had been enraged when the topic of abusing children came up, and he'd almost lost control. He shouldn't go back to talking about things that brought him to the brink of detonating.

It was a serious handicap that might impede his ability to help the cause. Perhaps Jasmine was right, and his personality was more suited to the gentler occupations of spirituality and counseling.

Maybe his destiny wasn't to become a fighter.

He was dangerous because he didn't know how his power worked and how to direct it, and he also didn't know how to learn to harness it. Unless the Head Priestess had trained him and he just couldn't remember it, his so-called alleged talent was better kept dormant.

Later, as they prepared to leave, Ell-rom pulled Kian aside. "I meant what I said. I want to help, but perhaps I should focus on non-combat activities until I know what my hidden talents are."

Kian regarded him with suspicion in his eyes. "Are you starting to manifest compulsion ability?"

Ell-rom was glad Kian suspected compulsion and not the much worse talent he might command.

"Not as far as I know, but since everyone keeps telling me about how powerful my father and mother were, I'm worried about some hidden talent manifesting at the worst time."

Kian seemed to relax. "That's a valid concern. When you get strong enough to start training in the gym, we will push you to see what you are capable of."

"Push me how?"

"Wrestling, fencing, all the things you might have been taught and don't remember. Muscle memory is better than conscious memory, and you might discover that you are a formidable fighter."

Ell-rom chuckled. "I doubt it, but I'm curious to find out."

He planned to do as little as possible in those mock fights in case his fighting abilities were dangerous to his trainers. In fact, he might just claim an aversion to violence.

Given his blood phobia, that would be entirely believable.

76

JASMINE

J asmine's heart ached with empathy for Annani long after the dinner had ended. She couldn't fathom the pain of losing the love of her life only to have hope rekindled after five thousand years.

She wanted to help the goddess, but doubt niggled in her mind. Syssi's vision hadn't actually confirmed that Khiann was alive. It had only shown her a desert landscape and a woman who might be Jasmine.

It could have been someone else.

The golden flakes in her eyes were uncommon, true, but were they really proof that the woman in Syssi's vision was her?

How much of foresight was influenced by the seer's own experiences and painted with colors familiar to her?

Syssi had said that the woman in the vision had been dressed in desert garb, her face wrapped in a scarf to pass as a man. What if it had been a man who was a little padded?

Desert clothes were usually loose, so a lot could be hidden under them, including breasts and wide hips, but also a big belly.

Still, even as the thought formed, Jasmine knew it was unlikely that Syssi was mistaken, which was bad news for Jasmine.

She really didn't want to travel to the desert. She hated heat, she hated dry air, and she hated places where women had to wear a disguise to move around freely.

The oppression of women depressed her, and she despised all places that perpetuated it. How long would it take for them to join the twenty-first century and start thinking of women as people and not as possessions?

Didn't they care for their mothers, their sisters, their daughters?

Still, she couldn't refuse the goddess, and not just because she was the Clan Mother. Annani was Ell-rom's sister and her future sister-in-law.

She felt like cackling madly at the absurdity of the thought, but life was stranger than fiction, and this was going to be her reality.

Well, there was no guarantee that she was a Dormant, and she still had to transition to become part of Ell-rom's life. Not that she worried too much about that. Deep down, she knew that she belonged in this world, which meant that she had godly genes.

But what if Syssi's vision had not been about Annani's lost mate but a snippet from some different, unrelated future?

It could have been a scene from a Perfect Match adventure, or it could have been a different desert and a different search. Some of the missing pods might have landed in the Gobi Desert, and what Jasmine had been wearing in the vision could have been a Chinese desert outfit.

The truth was that she would have preferred to look for the other missing pods because she was afraid of failing to find Khiann or, worse, finding something they all dreaded, like a beheaded skeleton.

A shiver ran through her at the thought.

"Are you cold?" Ell-rom asked.

"No, I'm just scared of finding that Khiann has been dead all along. Annani will be devastated." Jasmine sat down on the couch in their room. "I don't think I could bear it if she blamed me for it."

He sat down beside her and took her hand. "Annani is tough. She will not blame you for his death or even for failure to find him. All she expects from you is that you do your best."

She nodded. "I'll do a spread first thing tomorrow morning. See what the tarot tells me. Maybe they'll offer us some clarity." She glanced at Ell-rom, noting that he still carried tension in his shoulders that hadn't quite relaxed since the earlier discussion about child traffickers and pedophiles.

Given the glow in his eyes and the fully elongated fangs, it had been hard to miss the spike of anger he'd experienced.

"How are you feeling?" she asked. "Are you still upset?"

He arched a brow. "About what?"

"Are you still worried about earlier when we were discussing the traffickers?"

Ell-rom's expression tightened, confirming her suspicion. "I'm scared," he admitted. "I'm terrified of my mind lashing out at some random stranger and killing him. I don't know how this power works. Do I need to know the person to send a killing thought his way? What if I just project these killing waves, and random people die because of me?"

She shifted closer to him, her free hand coming up to cup his cheek. "That's highly unlikely," she said, trying to infuse her voice with a confidence she didn't entirely feel.

The truth was that they were in uncharted territory when it came to Ell-rom's abilities.

"I can't be sure of that." Ell-rom sounded miserable.

"Well, no one close around you has dropped dead," Jasmine pointed out, attempting to inject a note of levity into the conversation. "But if you want, I can check the news for any unexplained deaths in the area."

She'd meant it as a joke, a way to lighten the mood, but Ell-rom's expression remained serious. "Would it be reported so soon?"

"Unless your killing thoughts cause visible wounds, the death would look like it was from natural causes, and those don't get reported."

"Can you check just in case there is something? What if my thoughts can kill a bunch of people? Humans are much more fragile than Kra-ell. What killed one Kra-ell guard could kill several humans."

Jasmine blinked, taken aback by the urgency in his tone. It seemed like he had given his death brainwave a lot of thought.

"Of course." She reached for her phone. "If it'll help put your mind at ease, I can check right now."

As she began to scroll through local news sites, Jasmine was torn between contradicting emotions. On the one hand, she was touched by Ell-rom's concern for others and his determination not to cause harm. It was one of the many qualities that had drawn her to him. On the other hand, though, she worried about the toll this fear was taking on him, the way it seemed to be consuming his thoughts.

"Nothing unusual happened recently," she reported after a few moments of searching. "Just the regular news cycle. No mysterious death-ray deaths."

"Good." Ell-rom didn't find her wording amusing, but he looked relieved.

She set her phone aside and took both of his hands in hers. "I know that this power scares you. It's a huge responsibility, and there's still so much we don't understand about it, but you are one of the kindest, most compassionate people I've ever met. Your first instinct is always to protect, to help, and I don't believe for a second that you could accidentally harm innocent people."

"That guard didn't deserve to die for taunting Morelle and me."

"He was planning to expose your sister, which would have resulted in both your deaths. I'm glad that you killed him."

"But what if—"

Jasmine cut him off. "No what-ifs. You can't let fear rule your life."

A smile tugged at the corners of Ell-rom's mouth. "I like it when you get like that. I find it very attractive."

"Oh, yeah?" She looked at him from under lowered lashes. "You like it when I boss you around?"

He shrugged. "Given what you've told me about my Kra-ell heritage, it shouldn't be all that surprising."

77

ELL-ROM

I t was a gamble, in case Jasmine did not enjoy being the dominant partner, but Ell-rom was desperate. Perhaps if she took the lead and got more aggressive with him, he would get carried away and bite her before his mind made the connection between biting and blood, between fangs and pain.

According to Jasmine, the venom bite was highly pleasurable, but at the moment of incision it was very painful, and he dreaded the thought of causing that.

She hadn't made a big deal out of it, but he suspected that she had downplayed the unpleasant part and overplayed the euphoric effect of the bite.

The desire to fully bond with her was all-consuming, but he feared that his aversion would kick in again and make him bite the cursed pillow.

It had been the low point of their previous lovemaking, and he still felt shamed by it, even though Jasmine had reassured him that everything had been perfect. She had also climaxed, but he wasn't sure if it was indicative of his skill as a lover or just an automatic response to the joining.

He studied her face, trying to gauge her emotions.

She looked tired, the weight of Annani's expectations evident in the slight slump of her shoulders, but her lips were curled in a seductive smile, and her eyes sparkled with mischief and desire.

"Are you tired?" He reached out to tuck a stray strand of hair behind her ear.

Jasmine leaned into his touch. "A little, but not enough to fall asleep yet." She sounded breathy.

He captured her lips in what he'd intended to be a tender kiss, but she responded with such hunger that his plan was forgotten.

Her arms came up to wrap around his neck, pulling him closer as she deepened the kiss, igniting passion between them. But despite the heat, the almost desperate need, there was also a gentleness, a reverence in the way they touched each other.

There was love.

When they parted, Ell-rom rested his forehead against Jasmine's. "I love you."

"I love you too," she whispered. "Sometimes, the intensity of my emotions scares me. You've become my whole world, and I feel like I'm forgetting who I am."

"I don't want that," he said.

"I know." She lifted her head and looked into his eyes. "It's not your fault. It's mine, and I need to work on it." She smiled, but it looked forced. "When you are fully recovered and we move into the village, I'm going to start working for Syssi's company—the Perfect Match Virtual Studios. I hope to become their spokesperson, but I'll settle for a lesser position."

"I hope I will find something to do as well. Maybe I can also work for Perfect Match? You said that trying out their travel adventures will allow me to learn about your world much faster, and since I am a blank page, I can provide them with unbiased feedback."

Jasmine nodded. "That would be lovely because I can't bear to be apart from you for more than a few hours. I start to get restless and anxious."

"I do, too," he admitted. "It's the bond, although we didn't fulfill all the requirements for it to form yet."

"There is no rush, my love." She leaned her head on his chest. "Sometimes I can't believe how much my life has changed since I met you."

"For the better, I hope."

"Of course." She looked up at him and smiled, but this time, the smile wasn't forced. "I'm a trained actress, and I'm supposed to know the whole spectrum of emotions, but I've never felt so alive as I do with you. It's almost as if I was sleepwalking through my life before, which doesn't make sense since I've done a lot and experienced a lot. All the productions I was a part of, the people I've met, the Wicca, and yet everything seems meaningless to me now. It's scary."

Her words resonated with him, but in his case, he actually had been sleeping for seven thousand years, and he had awakened to a new world and a new life, and at the center of it all was Jasmine.

Ell-rom leaned down and kissed her forehead. "You make me want to be better, to be worthy of your love."

"You are already worthy, my love, just the way you are. You are kind, brave, and determined, and you have a big heart full of love. You don't need to change anything for me."

That wasn't true, but the moment was too sweet to spoil with reality, like the fact that both of them were enjoying the clan's hospitality and that, at some point, they would be required to contribute to the community and not just take. Jasmine had skills she could offer the clan, but Ell-rom had none.

Well, that wasn't true either.

If they needed an undetectable assassin, he was their guy.

Except, he didn't want to be a killer for hire. He would rather mop floors or do any other menial work, just not do that.

Jasmine chuckled softly. "Stop thinking so hard and kiss me."

He leaned in, kissing her again and trying to pour all the emotions he couldn't quite articulate into the kiss. His hands roaming Jasmine's back, he pulled her closer and reveled in the soft warmth of her body against his.

With a soft moan escaping her lips, she melted into him.

For a moment, Ell-rom lost himself in the sensations, the taste, and the feel of Jasmine, but as his arousal intensified, so did his awareness of his fangs and the urge to bite that always accompanied his passion.

Anxiety began to creep in, tempering his desire with fear.

Jasmine must have sensed his hesitation because she pulled back, her eyes searching his face. "What's wrong?"

"Nothing." He cupped the back of her head, but she resisted his pull.

"It's not nothing. You are tense."

There was no hiding from this female of his. "The aversion to blood. It's still there."

Her eyes softened. "It's okay. We had fun last night without the bite, right? It was amazing."

Their joining had been spectacular despite his inability to bite her, but Ell-rom had feared that she'd been disappointed.

It was good to hear her say that she'd enjoyed it as much as he had.

"It was," he murmured. "I wonder if that was how I imagined it would be, but I doubt it."

She chuckled. "If your and Morelle's sex education in the temple was based on the Kra-ell customs, I wouldn't be surprised if it was your choice to become a celibate priest."

"It wasn't my choice, but if I was given one, perhaps I would have chosen celibacy over being mauled by a ferocious she-beast."

Jasmine laughed. "I wonder what Jade would have to say about being called that."

He pretended horror. "I would never dare say that to her face."

Jasmine shrugged. "Maybe she would find it funny."

"Jade doesn't seem to have a sense of humor. She's a warrior."

A playful smile lifted Jasmine's well-kissed lips. "You are her prince, and she said something about being duty-bound to protect you. I think you could say anything you want to her, and she would bow her head respectfully."

He hadn't known that. "I need to speak with her to learn more about my past, but once again, I forgot to ask Kian to arrange a meeting."

"No worries. You are getting a phone and a laptop, so you can call her yourself anytime you want. I'll show you how to do that. I'll also show you how to use a laptop, but I don't think either device will come programmed with Kra-ell, so you might have to learn English first. I'll help you with that, too."

Ell-rom felt his heart swell with emotion. He pulled Jasmine close again, burying his face in her hair, breathing in her familiar scent. "I don't know what I did to deserve you," he murmured.

Jasmine's arms tightened around him. "You're you. That's more than enough." She kissed him lightly and then untangled herself from his embrace. "Come on." She pushed to her feet. "Let's get into bed and just lie down together. It's too early to go to sleep, but I know that you are exhausted."

He was, but he didn't want to sleep.

They settled onto the bed, Jasmine curling into his side, her head resting on his chest. He wrapped his arm around her, enjoying how perfectly they fit together.

JASMINE

J asmine rested her head on Ell-rom's chest and listened to the steady rhythm of his heartbeat. The warmth of his body and the gentle rise and fall were soothing, but the current of awareness that still hummed through her veins kept sleep at bay.

She had known that he wasn't ready, but a small part of her had hoped for a miracle and that tonight Ell-rom would finally bite her.

She'd sensed his hesitation and had no problem with waiting however long it took him to get over his aversion, but in the meantime, they could make love as many times as they could manage on any given day.

The problem was that Ell-rom was not on board with that, and it wasn't because he suffered from low libido and didn't find her sexy enough.

He was just scared.

"Can't sleep?" Ell-rom's hand began to move, tracing lazy patterns on her back.

The simple touch sent shivers down Jasmine's spine, the good kind that translated into tingles in all the right places, and as she tilted her head, Ell-rom's gaze met hers in the dim light of their bedroom.

Love and need took on a ferocious gleam in his eyes, the hunger in them matching her own. Without a word, Jasmine shifted, bringing her lips to his.

He cupped the back of her head, taking over the kiss.

Jasmine liked the unexpected dominance and confidence he was suddenly displaying, and she had a feeling that this was the true Ell-rom, the one that she'd caught fleeting glimpses of before but who had hesitated to come out because he feared hurting her.

Her hands began to explore. Tracing the contours of Ell-rom's chest, she marveled at the play of lean muscles beneath her fingers. He was still very slim, and his ribs were still too prominent, but he was starting to fill out.

She loved his long, lean body, and she loved the way he responded to her touch, his breath hitching and his body leaning into every caress.

Ell-rom's hands were not idle either. They roamed over her back and her sides, leaving trails of fire in their wake. When his fingers brushed the sensitive skin at her waist, just under the hem of her shirt, Jasmine moaned in anticipation.

Ell-rom grew bolder and slipped his hand under her shirt, palm flattening against the small of her back, pulling her closer.

Jasmine arched into him and nipped gently at his lower lip, reveling in the low growl that rumbled in his chest in response. She could feel his arousal pressing against her thigh, matching the ache building in her core.

Ell-rom rolled them over, pinning her beneath him, and pulled back to look at her. "You're so beautiful." His voice was husky with desire. "Sometimes, I still can't believe you're real and not a dream."

Jasmine reached up, cupping his face in her hands. "I'm real, and I love you."

Her words seemed to break something loose in him, and he captured her lips again in a searing kiss. His hands roamed her body, mapping every curve and plane as if discovering it for the first time.

Would it always be like that between them?

Would every lovemaking feel like a gift?

"Take off your clothes," Jasmine murmured against his lips as she tugged at the hem of his shirt, desperate to feel his skin against hers.

He sat back and quickly divested himself of the garment before helping Jasmine out of hers.

As skin met skin, both of them let out a gasp of plea-sure. Jasmine ran her hands over Ell-rom's back while he trailed kisses along her jaw, down the column of her throat, and when he reached the sensitive spot where her neck met her shoulder, he paused, his breath hot against her skin.

As she felt his body tense, Jasmine knew he was thinking about biting her. Edgar had never bitten her unless he was climaxing or on the verge, so Ell-rom couldn't be ready to bite her now, but since he was new to this, he might do things differently.

When his lips met her skin, Jasmine felt the sharp points of his fangs, and a shiver of anticipation ran through her, but Ell-rom didn't bite. Instead, he scraped his fangs gently along her skin, the sensation sending jolts of pleasure straight to her core.

She arched into him, a breathy moan escaping her lips. Her hands roamed his back, nails scraping lightly, urging him on.

Ell-rom's responses were becoming more primal, his touches more urgent. He lavished attention on her breasts, his clever mouth and hands drawing gasps and sighs of pleasure from her.

"We are still wearing too many clothes," she murmured between moans.

ELL-ROM

I n a blink of an eye, Ell-rom discarded what was left of his clothing and then helped Jasmine remove hers until there was nothing between them but skin and shared breath.

She gazed up at him with desire in her eyes, her hands roaming over his back. "I love feeling your weight on me."

"I'm not too heavy?"

"No, you are perfect. I need you inside of me." She arched up, rubbing her mound against his shaft.

Ell-rom kissed her tenderly, pouring his soul into that kiss, communicating his love for her with his lips and his tongue. He'd planned on going slow, but when he pushed the tip in, he found her so wet and hot and ready for him there was no way he could hold back.

Surging all the way in, he wrested a gasp from her throat.

Their fit was perfect, as if their bodies were created to complete each other.

"Mother of All Life," he groaned. "I must have died and made it to the fields of the brave."

She chuckled and urged him to move by arching up and digging her fingers into the muscles of his butt, and when he did, she met each hard thrust with an upward motion.

As Jasmine closed her eyes, her head dropping back on the pillow, she exposed the column of her neck, and instinct took over. He latched on to her skin, sucking gently, careful not to nick her with his fangs, but not because of the aversion to blood.

It just wasn't time yet.

Ell-rom didn't have much experience, or any for that matter, but some things were instinctual, like knowing that swiveling his hips with every thrust would intensify Jasmine's pleasure.

He wasn't wrong.

As her sheath tightened around him in a spasming grip, and she shuddered and gasped, he held her tight, and as her orgasm exploded through her, it wrested the last of his control away from him, and his fangs started dripping with venom.

With a roar, he jetted into her, and this time, his fangs sank into her neck instead of the pillow.

She gasped again, but she didn't cry out.

As the taste of her blood registered on his tongue, it was completely unexpected.

It was exquisite.

If he were a Kra-ell male, he would have drunk more, but only from her neck, fresh and vital and warm.

Jasmine orgasmed again and again, and he kept pumping her full of his seed and his venom, prolonging her climax until he was spent and her tremors subsided.

Slowly, gently, Ell-rom withdrew his fangs and lapped at the small wounds, savoring every last drop and smear.

Jasmine had told him that his saliva contained a healing agent that would help heal her wounds in minutes and erase any evidence of his bite. She'd also warned him that she would black out and that it was a normal reaction to the venom, so he shouldn't panic.

Ell-rom was so glad that she had prepared him. If not, he would be rushing to the clinic right now and yelling for Julian to come save her.

Holding himself on his forearms, he watched her peaceful face, her beauty made even more spectacular by her euphoric expression.

The weight of what they had just shared pressed upon

him, a mix of awe, love, and lingering concern swirling inside of him.

He had done it.

He had overcome his aversion, and if they were lucky, Jasmine might soon transition—which was what they both wanted, but it was terrifying nonetheless.

Had the medics been truthful with him when they had assured him that the chances of anything going wrong with her transition were slim to none?

Gently, he rolled to the side, gathering Jasmine against him. Her body was warm and pliant, fitting perfectly against his. Her skin was so soft, so smooth, and its slight golden sheen gave her an ethereal appearance.

As she breathed deeply in her venom-induced sleep, the gentle rise and fall of her chest was hypnotic, and the intensity of what they had shared began to fade.

Ell-rom was still shocked that he had done it. He had bitten Jasmine, tasted her blood, and shared the most profoundly intimate connection possible between mates. The fear and anxiety that had plagued him for so long seemed almost laughable now.

The taste of Jasmine's blood lingered on his tongue, the flavor exquisite, but it was probably not the taste itself that had overwhelmed him, but the sense of completion that had come with it. In that moment, he had felt as if their very essences had merged.

Ell-rom lifted his hand, gently tracing the curve of Jasmine's neck with his fingers, lingering over the spot where he had bitten her. The small wounds were already gone, the slightest of remaining traces fading before his eyes.

His saliva was working its magic to erase any physical evidence of their encounter, but the memory of it, the feeling of his fangs sinking into Jasmine's soft flesh, the sound of her gasp, and the trust she had shown in allowing him to do so would stay with him forever.

A wave of gratitude washed over him.

This remarkable woman had given him so much—a reason to embrace his new life, the strength to face his fears, a love so deep and all-encompassing that he felt cocooned by it.

Looking at her, he was hyperaware of every little detail about her.

The way her eyelashes fluttered slightly as she dreamed, the small sigh that escaped her lips, the warmth of her breath against his chest. Each little thing was a treasure, a reminder of the incredible bond they now shared.

He tightened his arms around her sleeping form as if he could somehow convey the depth of his love through the gesture.

As Jasmine stirred in her sleep, nestling closer to him, he pressed a soft kiss to her forehead, inhaling the sweet scent of her hair. The euphoria of their lovemaking and the intensity of the venom bite had morphed into a sense of belonging, of rightness, that went beyond the physical.

Unbidden, Ell-rom's mind drifted to Annani's quest to find Khiann and Jasmine's role in that search. He thought about his own journey of recovery and discovery and the challenges he still faced. But mostly, he thought about the woman in his arms and their future together.

He would become the male Jasmine deserved, the partner she could rely on through whatever challenges she faced.

For now, though, he was content just to hold her, to feel the steady beat of her heart against his chest and bask in the warmth of her love. Tomorrow would bring new challenges, but tonight, at this moment, Ell-rom felt at peace.

"I love you." He pressed a gentle kiss to the top of Jasmine's head.

Love, he realized, was more powerful than any fear and any doubt.

It was the truest form of magic.

COMING UP NEXT
The Children of the Gods Book 88
DARK AWAKENING ECHOES OF DESTINY

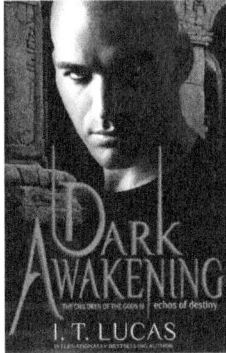

Secrets unravel and loyalties are tested in the gripping
finale of the Dark Awakening trilogy. As Ell-rom and
Jasmine face their most daunting challenges yet, a
young prodigy's awakening abilities threaten to upset
the immortal community's delicate balance.
As echoes of the past resurface, who will rise, who will
fall, and who will ultimately answer destiny's call?

DON'T FORGET TO CHECK OUT
ADINA AND THE MAGIC LAMP

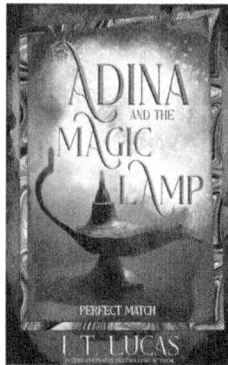

In this post-apocalyptic virtual reimagining of Aladdin, James, the enigmatic prince, and Adina, the fearless thief, navigate the treacherous streets of Londabad, a city that echoes London and Ahmedabad and fuses magic and technology. In the face of danger, the chemistry between them ignites, and the lines between prince and thief, royalty and commoner blur.

Also by I. T. Lucas

THE CHILDREN OF THE GODS ORIGINS
1: GODDESS'S CHOICE
2: GODDESS'S HOPE

THE CHILDREN OF THE GODS
DARK STRANGER
1: DARK STRANGER THE DREAM
2: DARK STRANGER REVEALED
3: DARK STRANGER IMMORTAL

DARK ENEMY
4: DARK ENEMY TAKEN
5: DARK ENEMY CAPTIVE
6: DARK ENEMY REDEEMED

KRI & MICHAEL'S STORY
6.5: MY DARK AMAZON

DARK WARRIOR
7: DARK WARRIOR MINE
8: DARK WARRIOR'S PROMISE
9: DARK WARRIOR'S DESTINY
10: DARK WARRIOR'S LEGACY

DARK GUARDIAN
11: DARK GUARDIAN FOUND
12: DARK GUARDIAN CRAVED
13: DARK GUARDIAN'S MATE

PERFECT MATCH

TRANSLATIONS

DIE ERBEN DER GÖTTER
DARK STRANGER

DARK ENEMY

DARK WARRIOR

LOS HIJOS DE LOS DIOSES

EL OSCURO DESCONOCIDO
1: EL OSCURO DESCONOCIDO EL
SUEÑO
2: EL OSCURO DESCONOCIDO
REVELADO
3: EL OSCURO DESCONOCIDO
INMORTAL
EL OSCURO ENEMIGO
4- EL OSCURO ENEMIGO CAPTURADO
5 - EL OSCURO ENEMIGO CAUTIVO
6- EL OSCURO ENEMIGO REDIMIDO

LES ENFANTS DES DIEUX
DARK STRANGER
1- DARK STRANGER LE RÊVE
2- DARK STRANGER LA RÉVÉLATION
3- DARK STRANGER L'IMMORTELLE

THE CHILDREN OF THE GODS SERIES SETS

BOOKS 1-3: DARK STRANGER TRILOGY—INCLUDES A
BONUS SHORT STORY: **THE FATES TAKE A VACATION**

BOOKS 4-6: DARK ENEMY TRILOGY —INCLUDES A BONUS
SHORT STORY—**THE FATES' POST-WEDDING CELEBRATION**

Books 7-10: Dark Warrior Tetralogy

Books 11-13: Dark Guardian Trilogy

Books 14-16: Dark Angel Trilogy

Books 17-19: Dark Operative Trilogy

Books 20-22: Dark Survivor Trilogy

Books 23-25: Dark Widow Trilogy

Books 26-28: Dark Dream Trilogy

Books 29-31: Dark Prince Trilogy

Books 32-34: Dark Queen Trilogy

Books 35-37: Dark Spy Trilogy

Books 38-40: Dark Overlord Trilogy

Books 41-43: Dark Choices Trilogy

Books 44-46: Dark Secrets Trilogy

Books 47-49: Dark Haven Trilogy

Books 50-52: Dark Power Trilogy

Books 53-55: Dark Memories Trilogy

Books 56-58: Dark Hunter Trilogy

Books 59-61: Dark God Trilogy

Books 62-64: Dark Whispers Trilogy

Books 65-67: Dark Gambit Trilogy

Books 68-70: Dark Alliance Trilogy

Books 71-73: Dark Healing Trilogy

Books 74-76: Dark Encounters Trilogy

Books 77-79: Dark Voyage Trilogy

Books 80-81: Dark Horizon Trilogy

MEGA SETS

The Children of the Gods: Books 1-6

INCLUDES CHARACTER LISTS

The Children of the Gods: Books 6.5-10

Perfect Match Bundle 1

CHECK OUT THE SPECIALS ON
ITLUCAS.COM
(https://itlucas.com/specials)

FOR EXCLUSIVE PEEKS AT UPCOMING RELEASES &
A FREE I. T. LUCAS COMPANION BOOK

JOIN MY *VIP CLUB* AND GAIN ACCESS TO THE VIP PORTAL AT ITLUCAS.COM

TO JOIN, GO TO:
http://eepurl.com/blMTpD

Find out more details about what's included with your free membership on the book's last page.

TRY THE CHILDREN OF THE GODS SERIES ON
<u>AUDIBLE</u>
2 FREE audiobooks with your new Audible subscription!

FOR EXCLUSIVE PEEKS AT UPCOMING RELEASES & A FREE I. T. LUCAS COMPANION BOOK

Join my *VIP Club* and gain access to the VIP portal at ITLUCAS.COM
To Join, go to:
http://eepurl.com/blMTpD

INCLUDED IN YOUR FREE MEMBERSHIP:

YOUR VIP PORTAL

- Read preview chapters of upcoming releases.
- Listen to Goddess's Choice narration by Charles Lawrence
- Exclusive content offered only to my VIPs.

FREE I.T. LUCAS COMPANION INCLUDES:

- Goddess's Choice Part 1
- Perfect Match: Vampire's Consort (A standalone Novella)
- Interview Q & A
- Character Charts

If you're already a subscriber and you are not getting my emails, your provider is sending them to your junk folder, and you are missing out on important updates. To fix that, add isabell@itlu

cas.com TO YOUR EMAIL CONTACTS OR YOUR EMAIL VIP
LIST.

Check out the specials at
https://www.itlucas.com/specials

Printed in Great Britain
by Amazon

47821879R00264